MOON FEVER

By the Author

MOON FEVER

by

Ileandra Young

2020

MOON FEVER

ISBN 13: 978-1-63555-603-2

THIS TRADE PAPERBACK ORIGINAL IS PUBLISHED BY
BOLD STROKES BOOKS, INC.
P.O. BOX 249
VALLEY FALLS, NY 12185

FIRST EDITION: AUGUST 2020

CREDITS
EDITOR: CINDY CRESAP
PRODUCTION DESIGN: SUSAN RAMUNDO
COVER DESIGN BY JEANINE HENNING

Dedication

To Mum and Dad, for always believing.

Chapter One

"Wakey, wakey, eggs and bacey."

The soft voice draws me out of sleep, a nudge on the edge of my senses I'd prefer to ignore. With it comes a hand on my forehead, fingers soft and gentle, brushing hair off my face.

I groan and turn toward the wall. "Five more minutes."

"You said that half an hour ago."

"I did?"

"And half an hour before that."

I claw for the duvet, struggling to bring it back toward my face. "Then come back in thirty minutes."

"Danika Karson, you get up right this second."

My eyes pop open.

Above me, expression stern, eyes bright, is the cheekiest, fun loving face I've ever seen.

"Morning, sleepyhead." Pip plops her butt on the edge of my bed, dumps a stack of papers in my lap, and shoves a mug of coffee at my face. "Oof, that's some intense morning breath, sis."

"Wow." I sit up, rub my eyes, and reach for the mug. "Okay, first of all—rude. And second, don't get jealous because *you* have no choice but to get up with your alarm clock."

"Ooo, grumpy." She ruffles her hair a little. "And I just wanted to ask if you needed a lift today? I can drop you off if you're quick."

"No, I'll manage. I won't be going in until about six thirty anyway."

She pouts. "After bedtime then."

"Sorry."

Pippa waves her hand in airy dismissal. "It's fine. Just thought I'd offer." Pause, and then, "You read all those reports yet?"

"The werewolf ones? No. There's pages and pages of it, and I really don't see how my time is best spent reading those when—hold on." I sit straight. "How do you know about those?"

She gives a sheepish little grin. "Rayne asked me to pass them back to you, and we got talking. Plus, y'know…" She shuffles the dropped papers into a neater pile in my lap. "I can read pretty quickly now."

"Show-off. I skim-read them yesterday and it all seems pretty weird. Increased sightings and infection activity? Why? There's no super moon due, it's not mating or battle season."

"There have been increased sightings of wolves in their hybrid and changed forms too. Even outside pack territory."

My chest tightens a little. "That's not good."

Pippa frowns. "Rayne told me that some of these witness accounts even talk of a new power."

"Pack power?"

A nod.

"Impossible. How can there be a new pack outside of battle season? Besides, I've not heard anything about that."

Shrug. "Read the notes. It's all in there. I'll let you know when breakfast is ready. By the way, you know Rayne is out there cooking you a three-course breakfast, right?"

I press my thighs together. "Really?"

"If I could still eat solids, I'd be all over it, but I guess all that bacon's just for you. All ten rashers of it."

My stomach flutters.

Rayne is so adorable and domestic. She always has something good ready for me if she's up first and always makes sure I have a good meal when she goes down before I'm back. Gestures like this, small though they may be, remind me of my mother and the way she would treat my father.

Just like Rayne, Mum would have food ready for Dad to enjoy before or after work. Sometimes, she'd even go as far as packing a lunch for him, so he wouldn't have to worry about what to eat during his workday.

A moment later, I realize that my fingers have come to rest on the face of the fat, black watch on my left wrist.

Eagle-eyed as ever, Pippa gives a little sigh. "I tried calling again a couple of days ago. She still won't answer."

"Stubborn bitch."

"At least we know where you get it from."

"Ha-bloody-ha, Pip."

She plays with a corner of my briefing notes. "*You* could try, maybe? You were always her favourite."

I snort halfway through the last gulps of my coffee. "Me? Oh, no. No, no, no, *you* were always the golden child. Me? I got into fights, ruined my best clothes, and watched kung fu movies instead of dating all the cute, wholesome church boys."

"Will you try, at least? Please?"

Ugh, that look. Just like when we were younger. I can barely count the amount of trouble she managed to land me in by looking at me that way.

"Fine, I'll try. But no promises, okay? Like you said, we both know where I got my stubborn streak. Mum has ignored us for weeks now, why should today be any different?"

"We have to keep trying."

She's right. But I don't have to like it.

"After work, okay? When I'm done with the meeting and everything else."

Pippa smiles. The gesture is so bright and sunny that I can almost forget my irritation at her little manipulation. Almost.

"Thanks." She bounds up from the bed and back toward the door.

Still strange to see her move so fast, the smooth, slick glide of an extra mundane creature.

She stops in the doorway. "I'm working here for the rest of the night. I'll be in my lab if you need anything."

"Stop bringing work home with you."

"Like you?"

"That's different."

Another laugh, this one brighter still, with a hidden edge of excitement. "I had to bring this one home. The experiment is time sensitive and won't last until tomorrow. I have some data to correlate and samples to mark off before the human team arrives for their shift, and—"

"Okay, I get it. You're working on something big. Like usual."

"But this is *really* big. I'm not allowed to tell you about it now, but I haven't been this excited for months."

"So I see."

Pippa rolls her eyes. "Just because your job is boring. And please, please open a window."

"It's not boring. I just don't like paperwork." The last of my rebuttal falls on an empty door frame as Pippa swans away, giggling as she goes.

I stare at the scattered papers and pick one up to read.

"Ugh." I attempt another sip of coffee and frown when I remember the mug is empty. "I'm going to need a hell of a lot more of this."

My eyes hurt. My back hurts. My arse hurts.

In fact everything hurts.

I lower the papers and stretch beneath my duvet, tallying the various clicks, creaks, and groans my body gives as I move. How can I sound like an old, decrepit grandma when I'm not even thirty?

You won't be this young and fit forever...

Ugh. Now, more than ever, it's frustrating that my mother was right.

Yes, perhaps, my body is a little sore and tired these days, but not like this. I'm not enjoying the sensations at all, but without stopping to see a doctor I have no idea what's going on. I briefly consider visiting Clear Blood for a check-up, but another glance at the pile of paperwork convinces me not to.

Again I sit. Again I pull the notes to reading height and again I begin to read.

Item Twenty-four: multiple reports of increased lupine activity. Location: Misona and lower West Side. Action: investigate and survey. No direct intervention at this time.

Weird. Very weird.

While Misona is known for being home to huge chunks of Angbec's werewolf population, the West Side is not. If anything, the West Side is a soft, human-heavy, tourist trap. Especially recently. Why would wolves be hanging out there?

I pull out a few more sheets of item twenty-four.

"Twelve pages? Are you kidding me?"

Pages and pages of it. All filled with werewolf descriptions, witness accounts, and more reports from SPEAR agents in the field.

Why? What on earth is happening?

Current suspects' wolf form: large, black shaggy fur, yellow eyes, white left front paw. Small, white and tan, yellow eyes. Small, brown, green eyes, tufted tail. Extremely large, pure white, red eyes.

My door creaks open. "Hey. How are you getting on?"

I smile, an automatic reaction to the sight of Rayne no matter where I am or what I'm doing. "Good morning, sexy butt."

She always looks so good first thing in the morning, even if morning is more like the middle of the night. Today is no exception.

"Calling names again, are you?" She cocks her head at me, gaze sweeping me up and down. I can feel it, a warm prickle that starts at my head and washes right down to my toes before traveling up again. "Did you sleep okay?"

"Yeah, pretty good." My fingers, wrists, and ankles creak and click when I stretch my body beneath the duvet again. Then cool air rushes in as I lift one corner, a silent invitation for Rayne to join me.

Despite being fully clothed, she does so at once, frown giving way to a grin.

Her body is soft against mine—warm, strong, and firm. Both arms curl around me, drawing me in, a strength I couldn't fight, even if I wanted to. When her lips touch mine, the prickle in my body intensifies, flaring from gentle warmth to crackling fire.

"I missed you last night," Rayne whispers against my mouth as if afraid to break lip contact.

I speak right back, straight into her mouth with a groaning purr. "Sorry. But you could stay in once in a while y'know."

"I have…extra work. You know that."

"Blow it off, then. One night won't hurt. Then we could be here."

"Mmm. Maybe I will." She kisses me again. Then again. And again. Her grip tightens on my sides while her mouth opens, allowing the firm press of her tongue to brush against my teeth.

Of course I let her in, and just like that, the kiss is deep and needy.

She feels so good against me. Smells so good. Tastes so, so good.

Rayne seems to have similar thoughts, because one of her hands snakes up to the back of my head, holding me in place. The other drifts down, sliding beneath the fabric of my nightshirt to touch my breasts.

Wow. This is forward.

Before I can assess the thought, she's moved on. Down my stomach, pausing at my belly button before diving beneath the waistband of my shorts. My breathing hitches, but still she has my mouth, her lips hot and moist against mine, trapping my words. Not that I have any sensible ones to say right now. I can't see straight. Can't think. Can barely move.

When her fingertips touch the first curls of my pubic hair, a long moan slides out of me.

"What are you doing, Rayne?"

Her fingers continue their achingly slow path along the top of my pubic bone. "Hmm?"

"I thought…don't we have work?"

"It can wait."

Sure it can. Of course it can. Hell, on any other day I might have dragged the duvet over my head and slept another half hour, but there's that stupid cross-team meeting today. I need to prepare.

"I don't think it can."

Another soft growl against my lips. "You work too hard. I didn't see you all of yesterday and I won't see you most of tonight. And you just encouraged me to blow off Clear Blood work. Can't you give me this time, now?"

"I—"

Rayne plugs my answer with another kiss, and this time my tongue catches the points of her fangs.

My body stiffens as if doused in starch.

Her hand stops dead.

❖

Silence.

In it, I catch the rasp of my breathing, the only sound in the sudden still.

Rayne is so quiet, so unmoving that without her skin against mine I'd never know she was there. No breathing. No discernible heartbeat. Not even the rustle of clothing.

I lick my lips. "Rayne?"

She yanks her hands away so fast that my hips try to travel with her. As my head flops back against the pillow she's already standing, facing the far wall, arms folded.

Shit.

"I'm sorry—"

She lifts a hand, a sharp, angry gesture. "Don't be. I understand. You're still nervous of me."

"What? No."

"Then why do you flinch whenever I touch you?"

"That's crazy, of course I don't."

Her left eyebrow arches into a smooth, delicate curve.

I shove the duvet off the bed. It pools on the floor. The fabric is soft beneath my feet as I walk over it and curl my arms around Rayne's waist. She links her arms around the back of my neck.

She's so small. So dainty.

I have half a foot over her, but I know, better than anyone, that she could haul me into her arms and sprint the minute-mile with no effort.

Fuck it.

I kiss her. I kiss her hard and shove my body against hers, driving her into the edge of my bed.

She yelps, momentarily taken aback. Her hands flutter impotently for brief seconds before she fists them in my nightshirt, yanking me closer with a long, deep growl.

"I want you." Rayne shoves me onto the bed, hard enough that I bounce twice before settling. Then she's on me, hands roaming, lips searching, breath hot against my cheeks.

Fuck.

I know she's worked up now. To be breathing like this, to be showing signs of her old human nature, she must be on the verge of losing control.

A silver rim hems her eyes then swells to encompass that autumnal brown as a low, heated growl slides through her lips. "Danika?"

"Y-yeah?" Surely it's not *my* voice trembling like that. "Yeah?" I try again, stronger this time, with less of the deer-in-headlights edge to it.

Rayne grins. "I'm going to strip you now."

When I shift to grab my nightshirt, she grabs my wrists in an iron-like grip, and shoves both hands above my head.

"I said, *I'm* going to strip you now."

I nod, not trusting myself to speak.

When Rayne releases my wrists, they stay in place. I'm not even sure that I *can* move them.

She trails her hands down my arms and across my shoulders. They linger briefly at my breasts before continuing the journey down, down, down to the hem of my T-shirt. She grips it.

My breath hitches.

The fabric tears easily as she pulls her hands in opposite directions, and the rush of cold air that follows makes me gasp and writhe.

Rayne's grin widens. "Remember the last time I did this?"

I can't remember anything right now. My brain is mush.

"Outside Club Starshine?"

"Starshine?"

"Mm-hmm." She shreds the last scraps of cotton away from my neck and arms. The pieces flutter to the floor. "I told you then that I wanted to strip you properly. And, after all this time…I'm going to make good on that promise." Her index finger circles then flicks my right nipple.

Fuck. Oh, fuck.

Lips next, so soft and warm. Her tongue performs a sweet little dance around the small nub of flesh, and I can't help but moan and arch my back.

She presses me down, one hand on my stomach, the other sweeping lower, lower, lower like before.

"I like the little sounds you make." A growl lives in her voice, a hint of the dangerous creature lurking beneath such a sweet exterior.

Again my body bucks. "Rayne—"

"Shh." Her fingers work the button on my jeans. "It's okay."

Is it though? Is it?

Again her lips fasten on my nipple, and again my brain checks out.

My hips are circling, thrusting up, my own lips parted to allow hot puffs of desperate breath to rush over my lips.

Her fingers snap the elastic of my shorts. Find my panties.

This time, when she touches me, there's no other thought in the world. Everything slides away as her fingers finally reach the hot spot inside my panties.

She's slow at first, gentle and exploratory, teasing out new territory a piece at a time. But as my moans intensify and my hips continue to jerk up and down, Rayne finds what she has clearly been searching for and begins to stroke with soft, even motions.

"Fuck…" It's the most I can manage. Not that it matters, because I don't think she even heard me.

Long, agonizing moments, Rayne continues her ministrations on my clit, teasing, caressing, flicking, and massaging before easing her hand away.

This time, my moan is disappointment and frustration, answered by a small chuckle from Rayne as she lifts that same hand to her lips.

She licks my slickness away with long, languid laps of her tongue, and my entire body gives an answering throb.

"You taste incredible," she whispers. "And you smell…even better."

I have no words for that. My mouth opens, but nothing comes out, so instead I focus on her fingers and the way they slide in and out of her perfect mouth.

I frown. Stiffen.

With a cry, I shove Rayne back from my body, crab-scrambling up the bed until my back slams into the wall.

She tumbles forward, caught off guard by my sudden motion. "What? What's wrong? What happened?"

My heart is pounding, my chest heaving.

Instead of answering, I fumble to get the shorts off my body, kicking frantically when they catch on my knees. They hit the floor on the far side of the room when I finally manage to get them off, and next I'm staring into my panties.

"I'm bleeding." The voice doesn't sound like mine. Not heavy with pleasure like before, but frightened and childlike. I hate it. But I can't stop.

"There's blood, I'm bleeding, there's blood on your hand. Why am I bleeding? What did you do?"

CHAPTER TWO

Rayne gasps and stares again at her fingers. I recognize the exact moment she sees what I did because her eyes widen and her jaw drops. "Oh, no." Her voice quivers. "No, Danika, I'm so sorry—how could I? I thought my nails were trimmed, and I—" The confused expression gives way to thoughtful consideration. She sniffs, then seems to relax. "Oh, thank goodness."

"Huh?" My mind stutters.

She lifts her hand for me to see. "Menstrual blood. It's your period."

The hammering in my chest eases a tiny amount. "Period?" Why do I sound like a child? "But..."

Rayne nods and continues to lick at her fingers.

My stomach knots. "What the fuck are you doing?"

"Don't worry. I don't mind a little mess."

"Mess?" My chest feels tight and thick. Even my throat seems to narrow. "You're licking my blood off your fingers, Rayne, what the actual fuck? And how do you know it's my period? I haven't had one in almost six years."

She pauses, mid-lick. "What?"

"SPEAR drugs screw up your cycle. It's something Mum always got pissed about because it meant I couldn't have kids. So why would I suddenly have one now?"

"I don't know, I—" Her eyes narrow. "Wait. Are you asking if I cut you?"

"I—no. Of course not."

"You think I did it. You think I scratched you on purpose." Rayne shoves off from the bed and stands, arms crossed, in the centre of the room. "How can you think that of me?" Her voice is high and shrill. Shock fills her eyes.

"Come on, Rayne—"

"No. What kind of monster do you think I am?"

"I think you're a fucking vampire." As soon as I say them, I want the words back.

Rayne turns her head aside. "The truth at last. So is this why you won't let me touch you? Even after so long? Do you truly believe I could bring myself to harm you?"

"No."

The fullness of her lips compresses into a tight, thin line. "I don't believe you."

"Rayne—"

"Just stop." She drags her hands back through her hair, mussing up her pixie cut the way I've always enjoyed doing. "Danika, I want you so much. I want the feel of your body beneath mine, my skin against yours. I want to hear those moans you make when I bring you pleasure. But that's *all* I want. I get my blood supplies from Clear Blood just like everybody else. I even drank before you woke just to be sure I was safe. All I want is time for us." Her gaze lowers. "I've hardly seen you in days. You barely let me touch you. You say you want me, but—"

"I do."

A sad shake of her head. "I'm not so sure. And I don't think you are either."

"I freaked out, that's all. I'm sorry, I just—it was unexpected. Even you have to admit it's weird for me to drop a period out of the blue, right?"

Silence.

"I-I know you won't hurt me. I *know* that. And I'm sorry. Please? I want you, too. Come on. We have time before I have to go…why not pick up where you left off?"

"Danika—"

"I'm half naked, Rayne. You tore my clothes off, remember? Just like you promised you would."

She looks at me. I dare to step forward and wriggle my lopsided panties off the rest of the way. They drop to the ground and I watch as Rayne's gaze follows them.

The tightness in my chest intensifies.

"Give me your panties."

It takes longer than it should for me to process the order. But I do, hooking them on the edge of my toe and flicking them upward.

Rayne snatches the flimsy cotton out of the air and spreads it across her fingers. I cringe at her intense scrutiny, hoping the last household wash cycle did its job well enough.

She stares for the longest time, and a flurry of emotions pass through her eyes. Most of them are gone too fast for me to read, but I know she sees more in my panties than I ever have.

"I have no interest in this blood, Danika." At last, Rayne finishes her inspection of my underwear and flings them over her shoulder. "I don't want your blood. I want *you*."

"Okay."

"Okay, what?"

"Then have me. Please, Rayne."

Her next step forward is the slow, graceful glide of a predator. I see the instinct in her eyes, the power in her motions. With two long steps she is in front of me again, staring hard into my eyes before slowly sinking to her knees.

My legs are shaking. I can't stop them. I can't control my breathing. I can't do anything except watch as she gently parts my thighs with a commanding tap of her fingertips.

I feel her breath on me, that cool gust against my most private and intimate of body parts.

I freeze.

She growls and whirls away. An instant later, she's across the room and riffling in my drawers to yank out a T-shirt.

I'm too slow to duck her overhand throw at my face, and the bra, when it comes, hits me too.

"Get dressed, Danika." Rayne's voice is hard, clipped, and heavy as thunder. "You'll be late for work." She stalks toward the door.

"Wait. Please?"

She does, but only for an instant. Long enough to look back and pin me with a cold, withering glare. "Why? Clearly I'm not safe to be around." With that, she's gone, the door clicking softly behind her.

I'm still standing there two minutes later, naked, cold, and confused.

No. Not confused. Not confused at all.

As my body begins to shake and my hands curl into fists, I realize that I'm angry.

Once I recognize the feeling, it begins to grow, a hot, prickling tension across my back and shoulders. I shove my legs into a pair of jeans and drag that thrown T-shirt over my head.

Then I'm after her

The door to Rayne's room is closed when I reach it. The number pad outside it glows with a faint green light, one I know will switch to red when the sun rises.

As if in reminder, my watch starts beeping, a subtle two-tone warning of the impending dawn.

I stop it, breathe deep, and raise my hand.

No. Actually, I'm too angry to knock. Instead I throw my whole weight against the heavy door, nodding at the satisfying crash as it flies inward and hits the adjoining wall.

Rayne stands in the centre of her room, part-way into sliding her blouse onto a wire hanger. She offers me the smallest of glances before buttoning the blouse and hanging it up. Then starting on her jeans.

"What the hell, Rayne?"

Hmm. Not the way I intended to start this conversation, but maybe anger has the better of me. Maybe.

"You'll be late for work," she says, now hanging her jeans over the back of her desk chair.

"I don't care. We need to talk."

She rests her hands on her hips, standing there defiant and beautiful in a light vest and panties. Both white.

Fuck.

"I don't think there's much to discuss. You made your feelings abundantly clear."

"Stop it. You caught me off guard, what did you want me to do?"

"I want you to trust me." A silver flare lights her eyes. "I want you to look at me and know you're safe. I want you to *know* that you never have anything to fear from me."

"I do—"

"You don't. You're holding back. Like you always do. You're afraid to let me in and it's not just because I'm a vampire. This is so like you, you always do this." Rayne's words trail off into a growl of frustration. "Why? Why won't you give me a chance to show you I'm trustworthy?"

"We live together."

"We share a house. That's not the same. I'm relegated to this cell, day after day, trapped and alone. You can hardly bear to let me lie beside you at night unless we're clothed."

I wince. "Th-that's not true. Besides, you know it's safer for you in here."

She lifts her hands skyward. "This entire house is vampire-safe. I'm the one who planned and supervised the modifications."

"But—"

"But nothing. After everything we've been through, the matter should be simple." She keeps folding, now balling her socks and underhanding them into the wash basket. Then the vest. Bra. Panties.

My breathing hitches.

"Rayne—"

"Perhaps if I were a werewolf it would be different." Rayne pulls back the covers on her bed and slips between them. She sits against the headboard with the sheet up to her shoulders, voice soft, expression neutral as she looks my way. "I always thought it was interesting how well you and Wendy enjoy each other's company, and of course there's Link and Norma. Even the rest of Kappa. Perhaps I'm simply not the right *edane* for you, even if you do have a taste for us."

"What the fu—"

Rayne gasps, back bowing, eyes rolling, body stiffening like a sheet of plyboard. A second later, with a heavy gush of expelled breath, her body slumps bonelessly across the sheets.

Sunrise.

❖

At least showers are quick and uncomplicated. I stand in ours, head lowered, allowing the hot spray to hammer my neck and back. It feels good, and here, alone, I can allow myself to think.

Not that it does much good. My mind chases thoughts in impotent circles while I clench and unclench my fingers against the clean white tile.

Once again I allow my memory to pull back the conversation with Rayne, that last parting shot she knew I'd be unable to respond to.

The wrong type of *edane*?

Did she really mean that?

Bad enough my mother won't speak to me over the gender identity of my dating choices, but now my girlfriend is questioning my species preference too?

"Dan? Dan-dan-dan-son. Kar-Karson?"

My eyes pop open.

Outside the shower, a scaly face presses up to the glass, curved beak above small black eyes like glittering beads. It's attached to a scaly, cat-sized body with fine, gossamer wings and a barbed tail.

"How did you get in here?"

"Kar-ka-Karson," my little pet tells me.

I smile and push open the door. "Come on, then. You may as well join me."

The chittarik, playfully named Norma, flies awkwardly through the small gap and lands on my head. She curls there with a deep purring sound rumbling at the back of her tiny throat. The tail, barbs and all, curls down and gently strokes my left cheek.

The water seems not to bother her, but I lessen the pressure anyway. The last thing I want is to wash her away.

My body continues to hum, confusion and thoughtfulness mingled with arousal.

And of course I'm aroused; Rayne is sexy and beautiful and perfect and not ten minutes ago had her hand inside my pyjama shorts. A rush of pleasure gushes through me at the memory, forcing me to bring my legs together, just for a moment.

Why, then? Why? Why can I not simply fall into the moment and let it take me?

I bite my lip, no closer to the answer now than I had been the last time we began to be intimate. Or the time before that. Or before that.

"Ugh. Fuck my life and everything in it."

"Nika? Dan son." Norma clings to my hair and leans down. She keeps going until we're literally eye to eye, her head turned to give me the full weight of her black, beady gaze. "Karson."

"Sorry. I'm sorry. You're right. I need to calm down."

Norma stares a moment longer before nipping the tip of my nose. The pocket flap beneath her chin flares open while her scales ruffle then settle. She seems satisfied with the apology, and after one more long glare, returns to her usual perch on my head.

But the more I think, the more I understand why Rayne may be verging on desperate. It's been three months, almost four, and we've not once touched each other more than the gentle and sometimes not-so-gentle kissing. In fact, earlier, when her fingers brushed up against my clit, that was the first time. Ever.

I've never waited so long with any other woman. Hell, during my early years at SPEAR one-night stands were pretty common when I used my rank and badge as a tool to lure pretty women into my bed on an almost daily basis.

So what the hell is wrong with me now?

It doesn't take long to clean up. Norma sweeps off my head as I shut off the water and flies out to land on the heat rack holding my towel. She pauses long enough to shake water off her body, then grips the fluffy material with her claws before launching forward to carry it to me.

She looks ridiculous.

"Thank you, baby."

Norma drops the towel right in the bottom of the shower and shoots off with a flutter of her wings, and that strange cackle I equate to laughter.

Bloody pest.

Still, the towel is just dry enough to get the worst of the water off me, and I return to thinking as I scrub my face, moisturize, and brush my teeth.

The cross-team meeting today is a big one. With a slew of new cases to work through, teams need to be assigned their roles for the upcoming weeks. Not only that, but the newest addition to Alpha needs to assert their place as team leader.

I spit a glob of toothpaste down the sink and swirl it away.

No matter what happens with this new guy, he can't possibly be worse than the woman he's replacing.

Francine Quinn was a cruel, cold-hearted bitch of a team leader, and I can't be the only one happy to see her go. Sure, very likely no one has the same history as she and I, but there's no way I'm the only person she hurt.

My mind flashes back to a SPEAR holding cell, white, bright, and stark. Quinn stands above a restraining table, a length of consecrated steel wire stretched between her hands, hanging above Rayne's naked, vulnerable throat.

My gut contracts, pain, panic, and anger rekindling at the memory.

No. I can't be the only one.

A dull throb of pain accompanies the thought, deep and centred low on my back.

I rub the offending area before snatching a blister pack of paracetamol from the cupboard above the sink.

This is not the time to be distracted by pain.

No, today is a big, important day and I need to be ready for it.

The two pills go down easy with a big glug of water, and then, with my damp towel no doubt leaving a wet trail on the tiles, I leave the bathroom and head back to my room, ready to start my day.

CHAPTER THREE

In the car I try to turn my mind to business and not think about the potential shit show I've made of my relationship with Rayne.

In the passenger seat, Norma sits tall and regal, more like a cat in this pose than at any other time. Her two front legs are planted firmly before her, backside resting on her longer back feet. Her barbed tail points straight up along with her wings, twitching left and right like sparkly antennae. She cocks her head at me, clicking softly at the back of her throat as I work the car into third gear.

The radio shifts from inane morning chatter to music. Something light and peppy, some nonsense written for teenagers too young to understand why faerie tale crushes on vampires and werewolves don't work.

I'd laugh if not for the sudden uncertainty in my own love life. Then again, at least these days all those fantasy stories about forbidden love make more sense. Who could have known they were all based in truth?

I find myself singing with the catchy tune, tapping my fingers on the steering wheel, shrieking the chorus when it comes.

Norma puts her head back and croons with me, loud and enthusiastic, though of course with her own version of the lyrics.

Damn. Actually, she sounds better than I do.

At this time of morning the roads are empty, and I turn left toward Misona only half aware of my decision to do so.

After reading through all those case notes and mission briefings, it seems my instincts have a plan of action, even if my waking mind is still distracted by the memory of Rayne slumping into her bedsheets.

I grit my teeth.

The steering wheel creaks beneath my grip.

"It's not my fault. Damn it, she would have freaked out too. I know she would have. Six years and then shark week, out of nowhere? Come on."

Norma belts out the last chorus with another resounding shriek of my name, then trails off with another soft cackle.

Another song begins, but I turn it right down, occasionally glancing at Norma as I continue.

"I mean at least I know why my body feels like crap now. No wonder I didn't recognize the feelings. It's been so long."

"Karson."

"Exactly. Back pain, stiffness, fatigue? I won't lie, I didn't miss all of that stuff."

"Son son."

The traffic lights ahead of me shift in my favour, and I ease the car forward again, aiming deeper into Misona.

The streets are fuller now, but shabbier and darker despite the growing natural light. Wandering figures clog the pavement in varied shapes and sizes.

"I'll have to ask Pippa when she wakes up. I bet she'll know what's going on. Or at least have a test to figure out why my body is being so weird."

"Nika?"

"Yep. Though not if she keeps telling me I smell. Rude."

Two hunched figures in tattered clothing start hobbling across the road several yards ahead, and I slow to let them go safely.

They still have that graceful *edane* glide, but it seems off balance somehow. Awkward in a way I rarely see.

They aren't the only ones either. Others huddled in doorways or leaning against burnt out cars, they all seem to be moving in a slow, unsteady way.

"Though I bet that would get Mum's attention, right? I could open a conversation with that…if she ever picked up the phone. 'Hey, Mum, guess what, my periods are back. Oh, still no grandkids though. I remain as gay as they come and my girlfriend is a vampire.'"

Norma lowers her tail, her cackles fading off to the soft chittering her species is named for.

My car rumbles.

I take a left turn. Cross a roundabout.

"What am I going to do, Norma? Why is everything so bloody difficult?"

"Dan dan-dan? Dan…dan…dan…kar…dan…ka…ka…"

"What?"

I chance a look at my pet.

Slam the brakes.

Norma has curled herself into a tight, scaly ball. Her wings are down and pressed tight to her back, the barbed tail almost vanished beneath her body which is shaking all over.

"Norma? Baby?"

She turns to me, head barely lifting, both eyes wide and bright.

"Norma—"

A stunning impact rocks my car.

My seat belt tightens, saving me from hitting the steering column, but the top of my head cracks hard against the ceiling.

"What the hell?"

Thud. Thud. Creak.

Norma curls tighter still into her ball, even the chittering sound vanished and replaced by a groaning moan.

Creak. Crunch.

Something hard pokes the top of my head, followed by a squealing shriek of twisting metal.

I look up.

"Oh, hell."

The ceiling is dented by a good three inches, and a ring-shaped set of punctures dents the scuzzy fabric lining off to the left.

Thud. Thud. Thud. Crunch.

A face appears beyond my windscreen, upside down and misshapen with fur bristling from features all mixed up and stretched.

There's a werewolf on my car. A werewolf in hybrid form gazing hungrily through my creaking windscreen.

"Oi. Get off my fucking car."

One huge, furry fist pulls back. Massive fangs glisten with sticky saliva.

The car roars as I floor the accelerator. Gears grind and cha-chunk through their sequence as I force the vehicle into reverse.

Tyres squeal.

The wolf yips.

Again my seat belt tightens, this time against abrupt backward momentum as the car slaloms along the street.

The werewolf clinging to my roof howls, a mix of surprise and fury, then clings for dear life as I increase the speed.

Brakes.

Another yelp and the werewolf shoots back out of view.

It tumbles thud-thud-smack across the roof, then slides down the rear glass out of sight.

I suck a hard breath through my nose.

What the hell is going on?

Howling. Lots of it. From every direction.

A glance through my side window shows humanoid figures stepping out from shadows between buildings. Humanoid figures with overlong arms and huge, thick legs.

"Dan...dan...dan...dan...dan...dan...dan..."

I grab Norma by the scruff and stuff her into my T-shirt. It's like trying to cuddle an unwilling iguana, but at least she's safe in there.

Her trembles continue against my stomach.

More gear grinding and the car rockets forward, this time with control and purpose. I heave on the handbrake for a Tarmac-scorching turn then continue, back the way I came.

Werewolves. Everywhere. Some changed, some not, all of them glaring at my car like a packed lunch box.

One darts at my window, forcing me to swing wide to escape. The off side clips a set of tall black bins and sends them careening down the once-abandoned pavement.

I grip tighter.

"Dan...dan...dan...dan...dan..."

"It's okay, baby, I'm here."

Another daring leap from a werewolf sends me in the other direction, this time sheering along the side of a parked car. Sparks fountain like a spray of celebratory fireworks and the acrid scent of charred paint stings my nose.

Not far now.

The roundabout I used to enter this area marks the end of pack territory. They shouldn't follow me beyond that.

Shouldn't.

Thud-thud.

More roof action.

This time I've no choice but to ignore it. A glance in my mirror tells me that.

There are seven wolves back there, and that's only the ones I can see. Another trick with my brakes will make it far too easy for them to catch up, and I *know* I don't want that to happen.

The lump of trembling scales against my stomach mumbles something, the words mostly lost in my belly button.

I try weaving back and forth, anything to dislodge the beast clinging to my roof. More thudding tells me this one has a better grip than the first.

Almost to the roundabout.

Just another seventy feet.

Cold air screams through my back window, chasing a scatter of glittering glass pellets. Some hit my cheeks, more shower down the back of my collar, and again I wrench at the wheel.

"Will you all piss off!"

An angry roar answers my plea.

Something pulls my hair.

I send the car the other way.

The pulling eases.

Fifty feet.

A figure steps out in front. Seven feet tall, at least, with heavy grey fur and arms like tree trunks. Tight, taut breasts are just visible beneath all that fur, and the huge bush of a thick tail shows between the wide spread legs.

It points, such a normal gesture, made terrifying and grotesque by the body behind it.

"Not welcome," it yells. "Leave."

"I'm bloody trying."

Thirty feet.

At the last possible moment, the hybrid wolf steps back and out of range of my car, though not without raking massive black claws down the side of my paintwork.

More sparks fly and I find myself wondering how I'm going to explain this mess to Pippa.

Ten feet.

The wolf on my roof makes one more snatch at my hair then leaps away with a graceful bound.

The shift in weight makes my entire car bounce, and the suspension groans in protest.

I pass the roundabout by simply driving over the painted white circle, taking myself out of pack territory and back into relative safety.

It's a mile on before I can convince myself to stop. I do so against the side of the road, a haphazard parking fail that would no doubt earn me a ticket, if anybody cared.

One by one, I peel my fingers off the steering wheel, then allow myself to sit back.

Relieved breath leaves my mouth in a long, shuddering sigh.

Norma's head pops out through the neck of my T-shirt. She eyes me haughtily before climbing all the way through and sitting on my lap with her wings flared.

"Karson," she snaps. I get the feeling she's yelling at me.

She's right to be angry of course. I should have been paying better attention to my surroundings. Guess I'm more distracted than I thought.

"I'm sorry."

"Nika. Ka, ka dan."

"What? They didn't get us, did they? We're fine."

She looks pointedly past me to the shattered back window. She may not be able to talk or even understand me fully, but I know full well what that look means.

Ugh.

"Okay, fine, I dropped the ball. Happy?"

"Dan-dan."

"Yeah, yeah, yeah. Come on, now we're definitely late."

After one last reproachful look, Norma returns to her seat on the passenger side and her previous upright position. Her tail jabs at the volume dial on the radio.

I obey the silent order and increase the volume, but this time, when the latest teen angst track begins in earnest, I can't bring myself to sing.

Chapter Four

"A uthorised. Agent Karson, Danika. Agent ID A2024001904K06."
I roll my eyes and step through the large hydraulic doors without comment.

SPEAR HQ opens up before me, a loud, bustling open space filled with desks, chairs, and the other administrative decor that belies the true nature of the place.

I wipe the holy water from the scanners off my chin and let Norma enjoy a little shake to do the same. Strictly speaking, she shouldn't come through the security portal with me and the system knows that full well.

Then again, strictly speaking, I shouldn't have her at all.

She takes off with a flutter of her wings, bobbing across the open space toward my new desk near one of the far walls. Several other chittarik come down to greet her, and the sparrow-like flock fly on together, yelling and chittering as they go.

I pull my ID lanyard from the pocket of my jeans and thread it through the loops on my waistband. Yeah, sure, it should be on my neck, but I still dislike the idea of carrying my own potential garrotte wire, thank you very much.

It's still strange to hear and see the changes in my identification, as if anybody would be crazy enough to put an entire sub-team of agents under my command. But there it is. Kappa team, otherwise known as Special Ops. Otherwise known as "Keep Karson out of our hair for a couple of hours."

I'm not stupid.

Now the initial excitement has worn off, it's plain to anyone who cares to pay attention that the new Kappa team is a dumping ground for troublesome agents. I mean, with me at the head, what else could it be?

As I fight off the daily grump about internal SPEAR politics, I spy a tall, grinning figure with a set of five kunai in his left hand. He hurls one in my direction with a wordless yell and runs across the open space.

Again? Really?

The mini throwing knife goes wide, but it's only a distraction against the other two already in motion.

I drop to a crouch and spin out to the right, grunting at the little twinge of pain from my back.

The second and third kunai hit the wall above my head, but I'm already gone, swinging back left to avoid the fourth which strikes the ground where my hand had been split seconds previous.

He's almost on me now, his long ponytail flapping on his own slipstream as he bears down with the fifth blade.

Another swing of my legs, like a breakdancer with my weight on my hands. My momentum gives me speed and I lash out with my heels one after the after, each striking his wrist to send the final kunai flying out of reach.

When he stumbles, I'm ready, back upright and driving my shoulder up on the way to shove him off his feet.

He hits the floor, panting.

I sigh. "You're not even trying anymore."

Noel González grunts and rubs at a spot low on his spine. "And where did you learn to do that? Swinging and kicking? Gymnast moves? That is new, sí?"

"Rayne showed me a thing or two."

He shakes his head. "Not fair. You have a pretty vampire personal trainer. Soon you will be unstoppable. More so. But who will teach me fancy new moves?"

"Link?" I lower my hand for him.

"Bah." Noel grasps my wrist and uses it to haul himself up. "He has too much fun teaching *edanes* now. He has no time for little me."

"Then stop being so squishy."

He mutters something in Spanish. Probably rude. And then, "You're late."

"And you're ugly."

"So grumpy today, Dee-Dee. Did you wake up on the far side of the bed?" He squeezes my hand a moment longer, a motion that pauses my initial instinct to jerk away. "Everything okay?"

"I—" Deep breath. "Yes. I'm fine."

A snort, then Noel drops my hand and moves to retrieve his weapons. "Did we not agree, no more lies? Say I should mind my own business, but don't lie."

Am I going to piss off everyone today?

"Sorry—"

"Nay. No sorry. Don't ever tell me sorry. Just be you, sí?"

One, two, three, and four knives. Noel counts them out into his hands, and I stoop to gather up the last one.

"I...it's Rayne."

His eyes brighten. "Girl trouble? Oh, then you come to the right man. I can heal all your problems with your lady friend, Dee-Dee. You tell me."

Can't help but laugh at that. "You've been single for as long as I've known you. I hardly think you're qualified."

"How little you know." Noel twirls the last kunai out of my grip and performs a set of flashy little spins with the circular hole on the end. "I am as qualified as I need to be." He begins to walk away, throwing a cheeky grin over his shoulder.

I follow, like he knew I would. "Okay, spill. Right now. Have you actually found a woman willing to put up with your bullshit? Who is she? Do I know her? What's her name? What does she look like? Is she an agent? Is she a body pillow?"

Noel laughs at my questions, and the sound is infectious. He taps a finger to the side of his nose, but I keep going now, too intrigued to stop. And the questions get more ridiculous too.

"Come on. Talk to me? Did you find her online? Like a dating site? Oh. Is she a mail order bride? Like from Korea or something? Did she come in a box? What are her special features, Noel? Realistic skin and heated orifices?"

He stops at the side of my desk. "You are disgusting."

"And impatient. Tell me."

After holding my gaze for several seconds, Noel dumps the kunai on my desk and puts his arm around my shoulder. "Look, no one else knows, sí? I don't want to jinx it, so I keep quiet. But if I tell you, you must promise silence."

I draw my fingertip across my chest in a broad X shape. "Cross my heart."

"No, no, like you tell your sister."

Wow. He's really serious then.

I shift beneath his arm enough to allow our eyes to meet. "On my locs and hope to trim, Noel. Okay? I won't talk about this to anybody else. What's going on? Why are you being so shifty?"

He grins. "Not shifty, just cautious. I have girlfriend now. I must protect her."

"So she's not an agent?"

"No. And she's private about her affairs."

"Ha, yeah, that sounds shifty, Noel. So do I know her at all?"

He shakes his head. "But you may know her boyfriend. He is from the Omega team."

"A medic, eh? Interesting." My brain takes a moment to catch up. "Wait, did you say her boyfriend? Isn't that you?"

Noel's grin grows ever more smug. "It is also me. She has lots of love to share and so more than one partner. In fact, I am the third."

My mouth drops open.

"See. That is why I don't tell. I tell you because I trust you. I trust you with everything from my life to my secrets. But you must understand before you judge."

"I don't think I do understand."

He hooks my chair from beneath my desk with a skilful jerk of his right leg. The hint is obvious, so I sit without complaint after wiping a handful of chittarik droppings off the fabric.

"She favours open relationships. Many."

"Poly?"

"That. That is the word. I forgot it."

"But are you okay with that? I thought monogamy was the end game for you."

Noel gazes at me for long, thoughtful moments. "This is why I trust you. You're curious, but not disgusted."

"Why would I be disgusted? I get it. Sometimes one relationship doesn't fulfil all those needs, but I never thought you'd be interested in a set-up like that. It might be okay for her, but is it okay for you?"

"I don't know. But this is the only way to find out, sí?"

He has a point.

"Well…I wish you all the best. I hope you get what you want out of it all."

His smile is so bright and relieved that I know I've said the right thing.

"Thank you, Dee-Dee. I will. And thank you for—"

I cut him off with a raised hand. "Don't thank me for not being a narrow-minded idiot. It's none of my business who you date. I just want you to be happy."

"That means much to me."

I arch an eyebrow at him. "Though, you should let her know, if she hurts you, I will hunt her down and break her legs with my fair bare hands."

"You will try." He laughs. In fact, he's still laughing as he walks away from my desk, holding his stomach and roaring like a crazy man.

Idiot.

And yet his laughter is catching, and I find myself chuckling as I open my laptop.

❖

So many emails. So many messages and questions from all sources.

The computer stuff wouldn't have taken so long except now that I'm in, every agent and his dog has some sort of question for me.

I can barely start typing before the next person comes along with a question or problem.

Most are from my own sub-team, other Special Ops agents clarifying one point or another. I remind them that we have a cross-team meeting in the next half hour and that we should all focus on that.

The responses I receive in return are varied in their phrasing and politeness.

More than anything else so far, their answers prove that my team is composed of agents who think a lot like me. One, a werewolf named Duo, tells me that if not for my insistence that we all take part, he would be in the field already. Another, a stubby goblin by the name of Erkyan, mocks the sheer level of paperwork that will no doubt come of such a meeting, telling me that she never joined SPEAR to be a secretary.

Neither did I.

But I handle it, message by message, query by query, complaint by complaint, until a loud voice draws my attention.

"Karson. Are you coming or what?" It's the new guy, Quinn's replacement and my direct supervisor, Maurice Cruush. "You're going to be late and we will *not* wait for you."

"Yeah, I'll be there—"

"Two minutes and we start. Be there."

"I said yes, damn it, give me a sec."

Wow. Maybe this guy isn't going to be that much better than Quinn after all.

I stand, and look for Norma, searching the high roosts and pillars dotted all over the space.

No sign of her. Weird. Maybe she's still sulking after the earlier werewolf incident.

"Karson." He's still looking at me, deep frown creasing the wide expanse of forehead visible beneath the receding hairline. "The briefing room is this way."

"I heard you, Maury."

Guess I've no choice but to leave her.

I head for the briefing room, but halfway toward the stairs, I hear my name again.

"I'm coming as fast as I can—"

But it's not Maury. This time it's a runner from the Delta team, huffing and blowing, one hand pressed to her side as if to ease a cramp. She puffs a lock of bone-straight, pink hair from her eyes and flags me down with her spare hand.

"There's someone," wheeze, "to see you," cough, "downstairs," gasp.

"You okay, there?"

"Downstairs." She gulps in a few more unsteady breaths. "With a troll."

That stops me dead.

There's only one person I can think of who would show up here with a troll on their tail. Can this day get any weirder? It's barely nine a.m.

"I don't suppose this person is tall, toothy, and very well dressed?"

"It's the mayor."

Yay.

"I'm busy. Tell him I'll ring him—"

"He says it's urgent."

Eye roll.

It's always urgent where Jack's concerned. I can't remember the last time he insisted on seeing me that wasn't some sort of emergency blown far out of proportion.

"I have a meeting."

The woman finally catches her breath and straightens to her full height. Not that it's much. "But he's the mayor."

"I still have a meeting. Put him in one of the suites. He'll be fine until I'm done."

"But—"

"Seriously, he won't mind."

She looks unsure. "You want me to make him wait downstairs?"

"Yep."

"With civilians?"

I open my mouth to affirm, but at the last moment snap it shut.

This early in the morning there won't be many people around, but that also makes me question why Jack is here. He never shows his face before noon unless he truly has to, and even then it's under duress.

"Did you run all the way up here from reception?"

The runner nods.

"That's three floors."

She shrugs. "Gotta get my steps in. Cardio, y'know?"

"Fine. I'll come. Tell him I'll only be a second. I need to let the others know I'll be late."

Relief washes across the woman's face. She nods once then takes off again, a full sprint back across the office space and down the stairs.

Great. Now what do I tell Maury?

I'm saved from thinking about it too deeply by a familiar cackling from my left.

Norma glides through the air toward me, trilling as she comes. She lands lightly in my outstretched hands and nuzzles her beak against my cheek.

"Where the hell did you go, huh?"

She's shaking again. Not like before, but something has clearly rattled her.

"What's up, baby?"

"Dan ka ka-kar dan."

"I wish you could talk. But your timing is good, so listen, okay?"

"Son son." Norma stills herself and relaxes in my arms. She even turns her head to better look at me, for all the world as if she understands every word.

"I'm going to talk to Jack. You go to the briefing room so Maury knows I'm on the way."

"Nika'?"

"Briefing room." I turn and point, up the stairs where another of my colleagues slips through the door and out of sight. "Maury."

Norma growls, low and soft at the back of her throat.

"I know, but better than Quinn. I hope."

"Nika, nika, nika, nika, nika, nika, nik—"

"All right." I hold her beak closed with my thumb and forefinger. "Just go do it, will you? I'll be there in a few minutes."

"Dan dan. Danika Karson."

"Good." I toss the little chittarik into the air and, after one little trill, Norma flies off toward the stairs.

Great. Now to see what the hell Jack wants.

The troll is the first thing I see when I make it downstairs. A huge, broad-shouldered lumbering beast of a thing, with a tiny head and arms as long as half my entire body. It turns as I approach, stepping heavily into my path with narrowed eyes and a brief baring of fat, blunt teeth.

I wait.

It stares.

Great.

"Jack? Jack, come on, I have shit to do."

Another figure steps out from behind the troll. This one is taller than me, though not by much, with deep brown skin with the texture of tree bark. A nest of green hair halos the head, though closer inspection reveals this to be cluster upon cluster of oak leaves, rather than true hair.

A sprite, then.

Last to leave the shadow of the troll are two human men, one in a blue suit with dark sunglasses—really?—and another in a pale blue suit and a smart, matching waistcoat.

Jackson Cobé, mayor of Angbec, former fang junkie and current pain in my backside.

He smiles, showing off his perfect white teeth. "Good to see you, Agent Karson."

"Oh, stop it. I'm not a potential donor."

The smile wilts. "I'm trying to be nice."

"Try not wasting my time."

The rest of the smile fades off, replaced by a grimace. "What's eating you? Aside from Rayne, of course."

"Goodbye." I turn back to the stairs.

"Wait, wait, wait. Sorry, Danika. Really, it was a joke."

"I'm not in the mood."

"So I see." He ducks the rest of the way around the troll and grabs my arm.

I would have thought by now he'd know better than that, but I let it go with nothing more than a stern glare.

He coughs but doesn't release my arm. "I'm sorry. But I really need to speak to you and I'm glad I caught you before the meeting. Come on." He tugs on my elbow drawing me toward the far wall, on the opposite side of the colourful SPEAR insignia picked out on the floor tiles.

The troll looks down as if searching and, after a long, ponderous second, spots that Jack is no longer behind him. It grumbles, a loud sound like rocks falling, and starts to walk toward us.

Jack stops it with a raised hand. "Stand down, Honey, I'm okay."

Laughter erupts from me. "Honey? You called it Honey?"

"That's the only thing we can get it to eat. We didn't know what else to try."

I shake my head. "Okay, privacy, fine, but if you form the majority of your bodyguard team from *edanes* you'll have to do better than this. I guarantee that all of them, except your black and white penguin wannabe can hear every word we're saying."

"Fine. Is there a room we can go in? Just something out of the way. This is important and it can't wait."

I glance about the reception area.

Like upstairs, the space is large and airy, but that's where all similarities end. This civilian-facing portion of SPEAR HQ is colourful, bright, and packed with agents in suits, carrying briefcases.

Carefully pruned potted plants fill every naked corner, and the walls tell the story of various agents, awards, thanks, and accolades the organization has received in the past.

Among all of that are stat sheets, infographics, and maps, all designed to direct the innocent public through the building without them nearing the working areas dedicated to field agents.

In the centre, a huge desk unit makes a broken square with Delta team reception staff in the middle to answer calls, field questions, and direct visitors toward various meeting rooms on the right, made private by blinds on the inside and soundproofed walls.

It's to one of these private rooms that I pull Jack, now using his grip on my arm to tow him across the space.

Jack calls over his shoulder to his trio of mismatched bodyguards. "I'll be with Agent Karson from here, please stand by. You know the protocol."

The troll nods, and a long stream of dirt flows to the ground from behind its ears, causing the human to sidestep to save his shoes. The sprite shrugs and turns to lean against the wall, arms folded, eyes closed.

"Hmm. These ones are better trained than the last ones."

Jack snorts. "Yep. And it only took three weeks to find them."

I push open the door to the office and gesture Jack through. As he helps himself to one of the bigger, softer chairs in the place, I shut the door, flick on the light, and activate the soundproofing via another switch on the wall.

"Now then, what the hell is so important?"

"No." I say it again, louder this time. Maybe if I say it enough times, he'll leave me alone.

Jack sighs and shoves off from the table. "But why?"

"You really have to ask? Or have you forgotten the last time I agreed to investigate something on SPEAR time without going through the proper channels?"

I've been pacing. Maybe that's why my feet hurt, from stomping across the carpet like an angry elephant. But I can't help it.

Jack, of all people, should know better than to ask me to investigate anything on a private basis.

Agreeing to do so for the last mayor almost cost me my job. And my life.

"But that's what I'm trying to tell you. This isn't private investigative work." Jack falls in step beside me, but his relaxed stride isn't enough to keep him level. When he drops back, he scurries to keep up, almost colliding with me as I turn at the wall and stalk back the way I came.

"What else is it, if not private hire, Jack? Your news about the werewolves isn't new, we already know. That's where I'm supposed to be right now, upstairs with the rest of the team talking about how we're going to deal with it. Why are you coming to me with this rather than reporting it through the proper channels?"

Jack grins. "And where do you think SPEAR got the intel in the first place? Do you really think I'm that stupid?"

"Stupid? No. Arrogant? Maybe."

"Come on, Danika." He cuts across my route, forcing me to stop pacing or mow him down. "Danika? It's me."

I sigh. "I know. It's just…things are crazy right now, you know that. Every team leader on Alpha is watching me, waiting for me to screw up. They clearly regret giving me Kappa—I don't want to risk it over something stupid."

"This isn't stupid."

"Look, the werewolves are under control. We can handle it."

Jack sidesteps to stay in my way as I begin another step. "That's the point. I want *you* to handle it."

"But why me?"

"Because you're the only agent the wolves trust. They listen to you. They like you. I don't know why, but they do. We have to use every advantage we have if we're going to figure out why all these turnings are happening."

I take a step.

He doesn't move.

Ugh.

Rather than forcing him out of my path, I pull out a chair from beneath the huge conference style desk and dump myself into it.

He joins me in a far more graceful manner.

"Danika, there are three new wolves at Clear Blood right now. Each of them changed in the last week. None of them wanted it. None of them had a choice and they want answers. There are two more wolves—not sure which pack—but they've been attacked too. They have huge wounds on their backs and chest that just refuse to heal. We need help."

"What?"

He grins. "Oh, so there *is* something you don't know after all?"

"Jack…"

"Okay, calm down. I'm only saying I've never seen anything like this before. None of us have. The three new ones are odd enough given it happened without consent, but the other two? Their wounds are clearly bite or scratch marks, but rather than healing like a werewolf should, they're still bleeding. And the wolves themselves have been unconscious since they arrived. Well, it's more like a deep sleep than true unconsciousness. Some of them are muttering or crying out but we can't wake them up. Nothing we try has worked and they're still in hybrid forms."

My heart thuds a little harder against my ribs. "I don't remember reading that. How is that even possible? Werewolves heal similarly to vampires. That doesn't make sense."

"We think it's related to a new pack power."

"But new packs can't rise outside battle season."

Jack nods. His face is grim. "Don't preach to the choir. We know. And yet, here we are."

I swivel the chair left, right, then back again. It creaks with every half rotation. "So what do you want me to do about it?"

"Nothing that you wouldn't already be doing. My point is I want *you* to do it. No one else."

"Jack—"

"Danika." He grabs the arm of my chair to stop it from spinning. "You know as well as I do that you and Kappa are best suited to getting to the bottom of this. I don't doubt the other units, of course not, but you have the edge. You *know* you do."

I do know.

Putting aside this morning's odd mishap, I'm one of the few agents even permitted in various packs' territory without an escort.

I break away from my thoughts to find I've been chewing on my bottom lip. It's sore, but the pain is a welcome distraction from the unease beginning to creep through me.

"I don't know about this."

He pulls at my chair. It rolls on the casters until it bumps his. Both hands now, Jack turns me to face him fully.

"I wouldn't ask unless I needed this. You know I wouldn't. But I'm worried. I've been mayor for such a short time, so many of my plans aren't off the ground yet. If something like this spirals out of control I won't be able to help anyone. You know Clear Blood is working on the artificial blood synthesis. Imagine what the world would be like if we could find an artificial blood source for vampires. Or inhibitors for the werewolf virus."

Damn him.

He would pull the "helping the *edane* population" card.

Another long, weary sigh. "I hate you sometimes."

Jack grins. "Thank you, Danika. Thank you so much."

"Yeah, yeah, yeah. Just…just make sure they all know you put me up to this, okay?"

"Who?"

"The team leaders. They already hate me, this isn't exactly going to help my popularity around here."

He cocks his head at me. "You could try being less difficult. Y'know, follow the rules every now and then?"

"And *you* could try being less of a dick."

He smirks. "Really, what's *wrong* with you? You're not normally this ratty."

"Time of the month."

"Ha. Yeah, right. You don't have to tell me if you don't want."

I consider correcting him, but at the last moment decide against it. Of all the people I might want in my business when it comes to my menstrual cycle and other body issues, Jackson Cobé isn't one of them.

The chair creaks one last time as I stand and shove it back under the table.

"Are we done then? Can I go back upstairs, Mr. Mayor?"

"Ouch." He shakes his hand around in mock pain. "That burns, Danika." He laughs.

He's still laughing as I stomp out of the room and back up the stairs toward my meeting.

CHAPTER FIVE

Halfway back to the field agent portion of SPEAR HQ, I slow my brisk pace. Eventually, I stop in a corner on a bend of the stairs and plant my hands on my hips.

My back is starting to ache again, but that's not what's bothering me. No, it's Jack and his irritating request. Oh, and the near-confirmation of a new pack.

How did this happen? How *could* this happen? And when? And what kind of power would allow werewolves to cause wounds *to other wolves* that refuse to heal?

The unease bubbling through me since sitting at my desk rises and crests like a wave. It makes my stomach writhe and my shoulders tense.

Maybe...maybe if I can get back into Misona—without being chased off this time—I can check in with Wendy and the rest of the Dire Wolves. If anybody would know about what's happening among Angbec's packs it should be them and, as I'm a pack-friend, they're more likely to confide in me. Perhaps if I could just—

A bellowing shout from above draws my attention upstairs. It's followed by thudding, like overturned furniture and the pounding of heavy feet.

What now?

I take the rest of the stairs at a sprint, hugging the inside banister for extra speed.

One flight. Two.

The shouts are getting louder.

I burst onto the main floor expecting to see a riot, but the sounds are still above me.

The briefing room?

Another set of stairs, feeling the burn in my thighs now as I race toward the yelling.

The door to the briefing room is open. Several agents are visible through the gap, some standing on tables, others pointing, all of them shouting or calling over each other.

I peer through the door. Laugh.

Two agents turn to glare at me, but I can't help it.

Four of my fellow agents, superbly trained and highly-skilled professionals, are standing on the tables, leaping about like clowns trying to catch a cackling, fluttering Norma.

She glides above them just out of reach, making as much noise as everybody else, perhaps more, all with that throaty clicking I know equates to amusement. In her claws, she holds a hand gun which is clearly too heavy for her to carry comfortably because she fumbles a little over the trigger loop and guard.

One of the agents on the table is Maury, the round bellied, wide-foreheaded leader of this supposed cluster of mighty individuals. His belt holster is empty.

Uh oh.

Maury gathers himself with a shake of his shoulders then leaps from one table to the other, making a snatching grab at Norma on the way. She ducks out of reach with another cackle and a hearty round of "dan dan dans" for good measure.

Okay. Amusing as this is, it has to end.

I place my thumb and forefinger in my mouth and whistle hard, a single shrill note that cuts through the bedlam.

Norma shrieks, drops the gun on the table, nosedives straight into my arms, and nuzzles against my chest with a crooning sigh. The other agents, caught mid-action, pull themselves back to more casual stances. All except Maury.

His leap, while unsuccessful in catching Norma, did manage to take him over the edge of the next table and into a crumpled heap on the floor. He stands, rubbing at a spot on his shoulder and limping to favour his right leg.

I organize my features into what I hope is a suitably contrite expression.

"Where the hell have you been?" he snarls.

Clearly not contrite enough. "Downstairs. Jack had a message he wanted to pass on."

Maury narrows his eyes at me. "A message more important than your job? This meeting started twenty minutes ago. I *told* you on the way in."

"I know, I'm sorry, I—"

"I'd heard you were a bit of a loose one, but this is going too far. And you have control of that thing?"

My contrite expression slips. I feel it happen when a muscle in my cheek starts to twitch. "This is *Norma*, if that's who you mean."

"Dan? Dan dan dan, kar-dan nika—"

I grab her beak to hold it shut. Now is probably not the time.

"Norma?" Maury spits the name as though it tastes bad. "Like a pet?"

"Um—"

"Will someone get that bloody thing out of my meeting so we can continue?"

No one moves.

I push Norma's struggling form gently into my T-shirt. "I asked her to let you know I was on the way. Like I said, I got sidetracked by Jack when a runner came from downstairs and I—"

"Jack? Jack who? And what makes this 'Jack' more important than official SPEAR business?" Maury finally retrieves his gun and slams it back into the belt holster. He also takes great care to press the security pop stud into place over it.

A couple of uncomfortable coughs. Some shuffling.

Interesting. Seems my fellow agents have decided to watch the show rather than intervene. I spy Noel from the corner of my eye, leaning against the far wall, well removed from the scene. He hadn't been leaping around trying to catch Norma and even now seems to be biding his time.

He does catch me looking though and offers me the smallest, near-invisible shake of the head.

I take a deep breath. He's right of course. But I still want to punch Maury in the throat.

Instead I keep my voice soft, low, and hopefully non-aggressive. "Sorry, maybe you know him as Jackson Cobé. He had some intel to pass on."

More coughing. A sneeze.

"The mayor?"

I nod.

"Mayor Cobé came to see *you*."

It doesn't sound like a question, but I nod anyway.

Norma wriggles and I tighten my grip on her beak.

"Does he do that often?"

I hesitate.

Noel leans off the wall, his headshaking more obvious now.

"Ye—I mean no. No, he doesn't. So I didn't think I should keep him waiting. He clearly thought it was important enough to come in himself."

Less headshaking from the corner. Instead, a hand, held palm flat in a sort of "steady now" gesture.

Maury holds my gaze for long tense seconds.

I wait.

Norma grunts.

"And why would *the mayor* come to *you*, a troublesome and undisciplined agent, when there are long-standing and experienced team leaders available to speak to?"

Oh, now I really want to punch him. Maybe a kick too, for good measure.

"Maybe because he knows I'm damn good at my job. Perhaps better than most."

Noel groans and lowers his face to his hands.

The uncomfortable shuffles and throat clearings drop away to leave a flat, dead silence.

I don't care. This has gone on long enough.

Maury's dark eyes narrow even further. He walks—no limps—around the tables to reach me and stops within six inches of mowing me down.

"You. Are. Late. No excuses. See me later when we're done."

"Sure. Glad to." I smile, but I know the gesture is more a savage bearing of teeth than anything as friendly as a true smile.

"And get rid of that thing so we can get on with this."

"No need for that." I open up the T-shirt. Norma crawls out of the neckline, across my shoulder, and up my neck to take her usual roost on top of my head. I pat her once, choose a chair at the edge of the table, and sit with my hands clasped in my lap. "She'll behave now."

Silence. It's thick enough to taste, heavy enough to cut.

Between the pair of us, Maury and I have the attention of every other agent gathered in that room.

Noel watches us both through a gap in his fingers.

"Shall we continue?"

Maury's lips open and close a few times. I can see the war in his face, the struggle in his eyes. Eventually he grunts and limps back toward the front of the room. "Everybody sit. We're running behind."

I let go of the breath I'd been holding and scoot my chair left to make space.

Everyone sits, and after much scraping and dragging of chairs, Maury begins to speak.

Yeah…this seems to be going as well as expected.

"So with everybody now up to date we'll assign the tasks. Myself and the other G7s have decided that the best way to do so is through a unit by unit breakdown. That way deputies can then form their units based on the manpower required. Any questions?"

I sit straight.

This is the part I've been waiting for, though at this point, having sat through thirty minutes of Maury's circular and ego-stroking "brief," I've come to think of it as reward for getting through this meeting in one piece. And without punching someone in the nose.

"Actually, I have a point to raise."

Maury glares at me. "What?"

Pause. Deep breath. "Given the nature of the werewolf issue and that we're as yet unsure about the full implications of the changes, I move that you assign them and all associated tasks to Kappa."

"Really. Posh words, Karson, did you plan that on your way up?"

"Actually, yes. I figured I'd better have myself ready because you'd no doubt forget about a core portion of the teams available for dispatch. And sure enough, not you, nor any other of the G7s have once mentioned Kappa."

He leans over the table. "Unless called upon, Kappa members revert back to their original units. At present there *is* no Kappa."

My fingers curl into tight little fists.

I force myself to count to ten before speaking.

"Kappa is Special Ops and—"

"I know what Kappa is," he snaps. "I also know that werewolves are well within the capabilities of any Alpha-level agent. Besides, it isn't your job to decide or assign roles. This is outside your remit."

He's right. I know he's right, but I can't get Jack's desperate expression out of my mind. If I don't do this now, if I don't get a handle on the assignment of these cases, I'll never be able to help him.

I glance about the room.

A sea of indifferent faces stares back at me, all but one. Noel again, right across the table from me, but angled to fall outside Maury's direct eyeline.

He's staring at me, gesturing something with his hands, a loop with a stick on the end, over and over.

Lollipop? Traffic sign? Tennis racket?

I widen my eyes at him and he begins afresh, this time with new gestures. A line. A curved line with a straight bottom. A double curve, one on top of the other. An L-shape with a strike down the centre—

"Numbers?" I mouth at him.

He nods frantically, signing again, the line, which I now recognize as a one, then two, three, four, five, six…

I understand.

"Karson." Maury is staring as though I've lost my mind, but this time when I face him, I'm able to do so with a smile. "Did you hear me?"

"I did. And in ordinary circumstances you'd be right. But Kappa is a new team and—"

"You said it. The general is still working out how you fit, and to be honest if you're even required at all. If it were up to me, you'd be back with us and the rest of your Alpha teammates and there'd be no more trouble, but unfortunately I don't have the final say."

"No. The Kappa team leader does. The highest ranking member of the Kappa team is the agent authorized to mobilize the team and take control over any task they decide requires special treatment."

His grin in reply is almost feral. "There is no Kappa team leader."

"No, there isn't. But there is a deputy."

A soft hush ripples through the room.

Noel grins broadly at me, then hides his face behind his hand again.

I wait.

"What?" Maury looks lost.

I lean forward over the table. "Kappa has a G6 agent and, like with any team, in the absence of a G7, that deputy steps in to fill the role. So…" I stand and move around the long conference table to join Maury and the other G7s at the front of the room. "Maybe we need to reopen the discussion about how our current tasks are assigned. Y'know, since previous decisions took place without the valuable input of one of your team leaders."

"You can't."

"No?" I scoop up the lanyard hanging from my hip and turn the ID to show off my agent number. "Are you sure?"

This time, when I glance across the tables, I can see Noel's shoulders bucking with poorly controlled, silent laughter.

Well. At least someone is having fun today.

CHAPTER SIX

It's quieter now.

The briefing room is mostly empty after Maury decided to send the other agents away. Probably for the best, but I can't decide whose pride he's trying to save by doing so.

Not that it matters.

Only the G7s remain, a handful of agents from other teams I know to look at but not to hold a decent conversation with.

Alpha, as the smallest and most elite team within this branch of SPEAR, has only one leader. Maury.

The others watch him as he stands in the centre of the small space, commanding attention simply by standing. I have to give him credit for that; he certainly knows how to draw and hold the attention he requires to get the job done. He always has an air about him that demands obedience or at least respect, something that Quinn always lacked.

It's a shame that I need to go against him now because I've no intention of losing.

He faces me, one hand fisted against his hip, the other pointed my way. "What you just pulled is grounds for disciplinary, Karson. What the hell do you think you're doing?"

"My job."

He bristles.

I talk right over him.

"I've no idea what your problem with me is, but we can't let it get in the way of our jobs. Jack—Mr. Cobé—asked to see me this morning to specifically request that I lead any units investigating this werewolf issue. I agreed and now I want to make sure it happens."

"You can't simply waltz in and claim a task like that. SPEAR is about protecting the people, not glory-hogging and ego-stroking."

"Is that what you think this is?"

He snorts. "I've read your files, Karson. My predecessor left some pretty full and damning reports about you."

"Wait, Quinn? Are you talking about notes from Quinn?"

"You're still an agent through luck alone, and it's only a matter of time before that runs out. How many times can you get City Hall to yank your arse out of the fire? Hmm? Especially when you were the one to put it there."

Norma shifts on my head. She had been sleeping, lulled to rest by monotones and monotonous conversation. But mention of Quinn brings her back to full waking and sets the barbs of her tail quivering.

I pat her back and whisper soothing nonsense to her until the scales on her body lie flat once more.

"I don't know what Quinn wrote about me, but you must know that there's a certain level of bias where she and I are concerned. Besides, this is nothing to do with glory-hogging. Hell, if I could, I'd leave this to you and go back to the pixies we found in the sewer system last week. They need to be removed and rehomed before they start damaging the pipes. And let's not forget the naga living in the spire of that abandoned church near Harmony Rise. Someone has to get that thing before it snacks on any more unsuspecting bachelor types stumbling back from the pub."

"Then why not do that?"

"Because like it or not—and for me, some days it really is 'not'—*I* am best qualified to deal with werewolves right now."

There are a couple of angry mutters from the other G7s. One of them, a short Asian woman with her hair caught in a thick braid down her back, lifts her hand. "What makes you better qualified than any of us?"

More mutters, these ones of agreement.

"I'm not talking about skill. We're *all* skilled agents here. We have to be or else we wouldn't be here. I'm talking about relationships with the *edanes* in question."

Another woman, this one taller, paler with freckles and frizzy red hair, moves forward from her seat at the far end of the table. "Shacking up with a vampire doesn't make you any more qualified than us, Danika."

Ugh.

While I knew that would eventually come up, the fact that it did still hurts. And irritates.

"Oh, come on. Rita, is it? You know that's not what I'm talking about."

She cocks an eyebrow. "Then what *do* you mean?"

"The wolves trust me. They named me a pack-friend. They're more likely to talk to me and mine than any other agent in the place."

"You can't—"

"It's true." I cut straight across her, impatience finally getting the better of me. "For whatever reason, I have a working relationship with the *edanes* of the city, which makes it easier for me to talk to them and work with them. It's been that way for years. If there really is a new pack rising, doesn't it make sense to send someone who is already trusted by other wolves of the city? Someone who can go in peacefully and without appearing as a threat? Someone just wanting to find out what's going on?"

The first woman speaks again. "But why can you do that better than us?"

"Because I don't need to carry weapons when I travel into pack territory."

Silence.

Seems I've got them there.

"It sucks—believe me, I *know* it sucks. I originally told Jack to stick it up his arse." Several surprised gasps follow that comment but I press on regardless. "But he made the same point I'm making to you now. As a pack-friend, I'm protected when I travel into their territory. They can't attack me without starting some sort of riot. Which means I can go in more easily and more peacefully than you. It just makes sense."

They're thinking it over. I can see them. One or two even begin to nod slowly, and the knot in my chest begins to unfurl.

"Karson, what happened to your car?"

Ah. Shit.

The unfurling stops and flows in reverse.

Slowly, I turn my attention to Maury. "There was an *incident* this morning and—"

"We analysed some of the damage to your vehicle. Given your current claims about pack-friendship and non-violence, the findings are pretty interesting."

"I didn't ask anyone to check my car."

He shrugs. "No, but when you bring in a vehicle so obviously damaged by *edanes* it's our duty to check it out. For your safety."

Bull. Shit.

"You had no right to touch my car."

"It was only an external examination. No one opened it or disturbed it in any way except to investigate the potential causes of such extensive cosmetic damage. We have a few ideas, but it would be interesting to hear, in your own words of course, what you believe could leave six-inch claw gouges in the side panels of your vehicle. Oh, and what could be heavy and powerful enough to dent your roof in so many places."

They're all looking at me now, and just like that, I'm losing the battle.

Damn it, where's Noel now that I really need the backup?

The door to the conference room flies open with a crash. Through it tumbles an agent I vaguely recognize as a G3 from the Beta team. Blood pumps lazily from a gash in his forehead and several tatters of cotton show where his right sleeve once was.

"I'm looking for Danika Karson."

Oh, for crying out loud.

❖

Maury shoots me a furious glance. "I'm Maurice Cruush, Alpha team leader. What seems to be the problem?"

With the door open, I can hear yelling and thumping coming from below.

I stand but a warning grunt from Maury stops me dead in my tracks.

The agent looks to me, then Maury. "We have a werewolf here for questioning and—"

"What the hell is it doing here?" Maury's voice rises several octaves. "You should know better than that. We have containment units for that sort of thing."

Again the agent looks at me. This time when he speaks, the words are certainly directed my way. "We had to. It—I mean *he* refused to go to a holding unit. He insisted that he knew Agent Karson and that he be allowed to speak to her."

This time I ignore the looks shot my way and step around the tables to meet the agent. "I'm Danika. What's happening?"

"The werewolf. We were told to bring him in on suspicion of unlawful lupine infection, but he resisted."

Eye roll. "Of course he did. No wolf wants to be accused of that. But why bring him *here*?"

"He said he knew you. He said he was set up and that he'd only come without a fuss if we brought him straight to you."

I can all but feel Maury's death glare boring into my back.

A quick whistle through my teeth sets Norma airborne again. "Go check it out, baby, tell them I'm on my way."

"Ka-ka-karson." She flies off at once, through the open door and out of sight in a flash.

The agent, I point in the opposite direction. "You go see Omega, right now."

"But—"

"If that's a werewolf wound then you need to be checked for infection. Do it now. Just tell me who this wolf is before you go."

"Um." The bemused agent fingers his forehead, seemingly surprised at the blood on his hands. "We don't have a name, only a description. But he's kinda old with this crazy big beard, all bushy and wiry. Dark hair, lots of clothes, like in layers—"

Well, shit.

I don't wait to hear the rest.

Instead I'm shoving past him and dashing down the stairs, with furious yells from Maury still ringing in my ears.

It's chaos downstairs. As to be expected. With most agents out or still in morning briefings, there are few left on the main floor to deal with this mess. Those that are have clearly already been out in the field, kitted out with guns, knives, utility straps, and belts.

Most have their guns free and aimed at the scene in the centre, but none of them are willing to take a shot. Halfway down the stairs I realize why.

Noel stands toe to toe with a huge, shaggy werewolf in hybrid form, his arms spread wide as if to form a shield. He's talking softly, but urgently and, for the time being, holds the complete attention of the furry beast. On the other side, Norma darts in daring circles, yelling at the top of her tiny lungs with several other chittarik joining her in a deafening chorus.

It's enough to save that wolf in the centre, but not for long.

Instead of taking the last few steps, I vault over the banister and hurry toward them.

The wolf notices me before anybody else does and immediately thrusts his hands into the air.

"All right. Don't shoot me, you piss-poor human reprobates." His voice is gruff and feral, almost lost beneath the growl that rumbles deep in his furry chest.

But I know it well.

I stop in front of him, pausing to give Noel a brief, but grateful pat on the shoulder.

He sighs. "Gao, Dee-Dee. What have you done this time?"

"Would you believe I actually have no idea?"

"No."

Yeah. Can't say I blame him.

I face the hybrid wolf towering a full two feet above my eyeline. "What's going on, you filthy mongrel?"

The misshapen mouth, caught halfway between human jaw and lupine muzzle, forms a poor approximation of a grin. "Hi, little meat sack. You took your time."

Chapter Seven

I hate having so many guns pointed at me. Makes me nervous. Perhaps not as nervous as the agents facing down a wolf in hybrid form, but that's part of the problem. Nervous fingers are twitchy fingers.

I lift my hands. "This is Wendy Gordan—"

He snarls.

The little flock of chittarik cry out and screech.

Confused looks and snickering issue from the surrounding crowd.

Try again. "This is Wensleydale Gordan. He's the alpha of the Dire Wolf pack and a friend. He's not a threat to anybody."

An agent with a rifle looks up over the sight. "He's a menace. We brought him in for unlawful infection charges."

"Lies." Wendy's furious roar rattles my ribs. "I would never do that. I'm not an idiot. Do you know who you're talking to, boy?"

I put my hand on his shoulder. It's a stretch to reach that far, and when I do the fur is matted and damp beneath my fingers. I hold on anyway. "Stop it."

"But they—"

"I said, stop. I mean it."

He grumbles. "Bloody humans."

"They're scared. Do me a favour and shift back, will you?"

"No."

"What the hell is a werewolf doing in my headquarters?" Maury hurries down the stairs with his own gun aimed toward us. Several of the other G7s follow in the same manner and fan out to join the circle of other agents.

"It's under control—" I begin.

"The hell it is. Move away from that thing right now."

"But—"

"You're in our sight-line, Karson, move. You too, Agent Gonzales."

I glance at Noel. "You can if you want. Thanks, but you don't have to risk yourself for me or this idiot."

A soft growl. "Hey—"

"Shut up, Wendy."

Noel shrugs. "I am here now, sí? Might as well stay. Over there I'll miss all the fun."

"You're so bloody weird."

"I think you mean 'thank you,' Dee-Dee."

Yeah. I do. But he already knows that.

"Maury, we're fine." I look past my friends to meet my superior as he begins to move closer. "Please trust me."

He snorts. "The agent you failed to debrief told me what this beast has done. There are three others with Omega right now and you ask me to trust you? You're insane."

Wendy flexes his claws. "We didn't hurt anybody. Those injured are the result of self-defence, nothing more. No one is fatally—"

"Shut up, wolf—"

"For goodness sake, guys, put your fucking dicks away." I know I shouldn't. I know I'm letting frustration get the best of me, but this morning and the whole day so far has been one stress after another. I've had enough.

Maury continues to watch Wendy over the sight of his gun. "He shouldn't be here."

"No, he shouldn't. Should he?" I offer Wendy a savage glare. "But he is, so now we have to deal with it and I'm telling you now—I can handle it. And we're going to start, Wendy, with you shifting back to your human form."

"I said no, Agent."

I tighten my grip on his shoulder. Lower my voice. "Come on. They're *looking* for a reason to shoot you. Don't give it to them."

"They already have. I didn't enjoy it."

For the first time, I realize that the dampness beneath my fingers is blood. I give him a startled glance and he answers with a grim nod. Yellow eyes gleam in the midst of dark, shaggy fur.

Just the same. Something needs to give and it has to be him. It *has* to be.

"Wendy...please. Trust me. Shift back."

The tension is so thick I imagine I could lean back into it. Any moment now, if something doesn't change, someone is going to snap. I don't want it to be an agent's spine.

Noel stands close to me, his arms still outstretched. A tiny bead of sweat collects on his forehead.

"Wendy. Shift. Back."

A sigh. Then the huge, muscled shoulder ripples beneath my hand. Subtle, then visible, and Wendy drops his hybrid form with a full body shake like a wet dog. A neat, clotted bullet hole on his right shoulder swells then ejects a bullet like a pursed set of lips spitting a watermelon seed. It hits the floor with a clatter and rolls away beneath the desks.

At last he stands before me in his human form, layer upon layer of tatty, but clean clothing, riddled with bullet holes and claw marks. His thick beard is as wiry and bushy as ever, while his eyes, no longer yellow, are stern and confident.

"Happy?" he mutters.

"It's a start. Now put your hands on your head for me."

The furious expression remains, but for a wonder, Wendy does as asked. He even goes so far as to lower himself to his knees, though not without loud complaints about the state of his back and knee joints.

Norma and her flock of chittarik pals finally stop guarding his back and settle to roost. One or two of them alight on his legs while Norma lands on his shoulder, rubbing her face against his cheek.

Wendy chuckles and croons nonsense to the small creature who coos back with little, broken whispers of my name.

Most of the guns aimed in our direction lower to keep Wendy within sight. A couple of others waver, then drop point-down to the ground.

It'll have to do.

"Okay." I make my voice calm, but firm. Loud, but steady. "Now we can all talk like civilized adults."

A couple of the agents move forward, reaching for handcuffs and chains.

I step straight into their paths. "Don't you bloody dare."

"But—"

"I said don't."

Maury stalks up beside me, his gun still aimed at Wendy's head. "We have protocol and a procedure for a reason, Karson."

"And sometimes it's bullshit. The situation is calm now, why would you do something to heat it up again?"

"To protect the agents of this cell."

"That's my job too. And I'm telling you now, cuffs are not how to do it."

"Cuff that werewolf."

I hesitate.

How far can I really push this? I've been lucky this morning, but the tic beneath Maury's left eye suggests he might snap any second. How close to the edge can I dance before tumbling into the disciplinary abyss?

"Now, Karson."

Wendy clears his throat. "I am Wensleydale Gordan, alpha of the Dire Wolf pack, unchallenged and undefeated." His voice deepens, swelling with power, pride, and authority. "I place myself under the dominion of

Agent Danika Karson until such time as she releases me from my pledge. My words, my actions, my body, and life are hers to command. With all persons here gathered in witness, this I vow upon my blood. Upon my life."

Oh. Well, shit.

Maury's mouth falls open. He stares first at me, then Wendy as though his jaw has dropped and locked in place. "What?"

"You heard me, meat sack. I'm under the girl's command now. I'll do as I'm told. So long as *she* says it."

"Wendy." I shake my head. "Why? I didn't want this."

He pulls a crooked smile. "Neither did I, girl. But here we are."

More agents lower their guns.

Noel backs off completely, leaning against one of the nearby desks with a sigh and a trembling hand pressed to his chest.

Still Maury looks lost. "What does that mean?"

Wow. Someone really needs to buff up on their werewolf societal rules.

I offer him a wry glance. "It means, Maury, that I can do this: Wendy, get up."

Despite his creaking knees and aching back, Wendy obeys, scattering all the chittarik but Norma who simply shifts to rest on his head instead.

"Sit down."

And again.

"Bark like a dog."

Wendy frowns. "Girl, I'm not—"

"Just do it."

Though clearly embarrassed, Wendy obeys the ridiculous instruction. Even in his human voice the sound is clearly canine and still more of the agents stare at me in open bewilderment.

"Great. Now tell me that I'm the most beautiful woman you've ever seen."

Wendy laughs, but repeats the phrase word for word, complete with fluttering eyelashes, longing looks, and clasped hands.

"Finally...put those cuffs on your wrists."

Sighing, Wendy steps away from me to the agent on his left.

The poor man looks about ready to bolt and offers no resistance as Wendy plucks the cuffs from his grip. He unfastens the loops one by one, then feeds his own wrists into them. A few clicks later and the cuffs are fully closed.

"Happy now?" This he directs at Maury.

"I...uh...well...I guess so." Finally, Maury lowers the gun. "How long does this go on for?"

I shrug. "Like he said, until I release him."

"Oh. Then…then I guess it's okay." He continues to stare, only now his expression has changed. No longer is it one of anger and vague distrust, but consideration and, dare I say it, respect.

Makes a nice change.

"Wendy?"

"What, meat sack?"

"Get rid of those cuffs and come with me. We need to talk."

The skin on Wendy's arms and hands immediately ripples with a sudden growth of fur and claws. With it comes a flex of abruptly thicker muscle, and the cuffs break apart like loops of paper. After brushing away the shattered pieces of steel, Wendy allows the change to stop and flow in reverse while strolling to meet me.

He positions himself slightly behind me, on my right side, close enough that his chest occasionally touches my arm.

I shift my elbow to maintain the physical contact between us.

Maury grunts. "Who the hell went into the field for a werewolf pickup with *steel* cuffs? Don't you people know anything? Did you at least have silver bullets?"

There are sheepish looks and lowered gazes from the agents around us.

I leave them to it, guiding Wendy up the stairs and toward the conference room.

We need to talk. At length.

I was hoping I'd seen the last of the conference room for the day, but at least the atmosphere is more relaxed. Enough so that Norma, now no longer on guard duty, has fallen asleep on my shoulder. Her soft breath is warm against my neck through my T-shirt, while her claws occasionally dig into my shoulder.

Do chittarik dream? Until recently I hadn't known that vampires could dream, so it's not an unreasonable question. I absently wonder about what a small cat-dragon-bird-creature with barbs and tail could possibly have to dream about.

Wendy paces back and forth in front of the desks, grumbling and muttering into his thick salt-and-pepper beard.

I sit with my boots up on the table, watching him go, waiting for the right time to ask. Because I have to ask.

"How's Rayne?" he mutters.

I flinch. "Fine."

That stops him. Wendy looks me up and down, shrugs, then returns to his circuit in front of me. "And Pips?"

"Great, actually. Sure there were problems at first, but she's adjusting really well."

"And they're both okay?"

"I assume so." I chance a glance at my watch. "At this time of day they're both out cold. Why? What's wrong?"

He sniffs. "Just wondered. What with you smelling like a walking buffet."

"Excuse me?"

"Blood, girl. The blood. Did the Foundation change your shots?"

Ah. Of course he can smell it.

Strange, but unlike Jack, I know Wendy will be unconcerned and frank about such personal talk.

"No. It just happened. This morning."

"I've never smelled the lunar blood on you before."

"Is that what you guys call it?"

He shrugs. "If we call it anything. Anyway, I don't like it. Do something about it. It makes me...feel things."

I gape at him. Can't help it. "Wait, are you saying—"

"I'm not saying anything except that if *I* can smell you, your sister and girlfriend must be half-mad with wanting. Do something about it."

Wow.

Wait...how had I not thought about that? It makes so much sense now.

Suddenly this morning's whole episode appears in a completely different light and the weight I'd hardly been aware of seems to lift off my chest.

So if that's what caused Rayne to come on so strong, if it's really as simple as that, then at least we can talk. I can explain. I can do something about it.

I can apologize.

Even Pippa's comments about the smell of my room make more sense now.

I smile my first real smile in hours.

"I will, Wendy. Thanks. But we're not here to talk about me. What about you? What's going on?"

More pacing. More growling. More muttering.

"I didn't infect anybody," he whispers.

"Was it the one-armed wolf?"

"This isn't a joke, girl. Do you have any idea what's going on out there? I'm not the first wolf pulled in on piss-poor charges like this. I'm just the only one who knew to ask for you."

"Yeah, and knew how to con a rookie team into bringing you here instead of taking you to Shakka."

Wendy spits on the floor. "I have no problem with the warty little goblin, but this is serious and my pack is in trouble. I'd rather speak to you. You get things done."

Well, at least someone appreciates me.

He reaches the end of one line then spins round to begin again, each step heavy and angry against the carpet tiles.

"This is ridiculous. It's stupid. We're being framed."

"Oh, come on, Wendy. For real?"

"Yes." His anger is palpable. "You know me, girl. I'm not prone to fancy and make-believe. I trust what I see, what I hear, and what I smell, and I'm telling you, someone is out to get me. Could even be someone within the pack."

"Proof?"

He snarls at me. "Unlawful infection? Come on, girl."

He's right. I know he is. But that's not enough for SPEAR. We're going to need more proof than that. The worst part is that both he and I know it.

The conference room door opens gently. Through it steps Maury, calmer and without weapons, though still wary. He pauses at the sight of us so casually arranged, then treats me to a long, steady look.

Sigh. "I'm working on it."

"Very well." He gestures that I should continue, then sits on one of the tables nearest the door. Not close enough to block it exactly, but certainly near enough that any attempt to leave would have to go through him.

Great.

On my shoulder, Norma shifts but doesn't wake, now folding her wings down across her back. Her breath hitches in tiny snoring sounds.

Wendy snarls again and shifts his weight to the balls of his feet. "I've nothing more to say with him here."

"Wendy—"

"I said, I have nothing more to say."

I glance at Maury.

My supervisor shrugs and pulls a pair of handcuffs off a loop on his belt. These ones are duller and thicker, with additional loops to hold onto the captive's thumbs. These are cuffs designed with werewolves in mind. No fancy partial-shift will break these. In fact, even the contact against the bare skin around the thumbs will be enough to weaken Wendy considerably. It doesn't take much.

"There's only so much freedom I can give you, Danika."

Wow. "Danika" not "Karson." Maury really has changed his opinion of me over the last half hour. His attitude is almost friendly.

This, it seems, is as far as I can push.

Wendy glares at Maury then returns his attention to me. He's outwardly calm and docile, but I can see his fingernails darkening.

"Don't make me pull rank," I whisper.

"You wouldn't."

"You spoke the words. If I have to, I will. Please, don't make this harder than it has to be. We're on your side."

"*You* are."

"We all are."

Another snort.

I sigh. So be it.

"Wensleydale Gordan, sit down."

His eyes widen. The dark colour abruptly vanishes from his fingernails. Still gaping, Wendy pulls at a chair from beneath the desk and lowers himself into it.

I hate seeing him like this. He's a werewolf—hell, he's a pack alpha. No human should be able to give him orders. If any members of his pack came to know about this, the negative effect on his position within the pack would be immeasurable.

Alphas and their betas lead through strength, respect, and sometimes fear. They lead because they have a proven track record of acting in the best interest of their pack and being strong enough to make those decisions. To my knowledge, no pack alpha has ever willingly put themselves, and so their pack, in the hands of a human. Likely because if one ever did, the pack killed them long before any trace of the tale made it into the open.

"I need to know what you know. And you will tell me."

"And the knock-kneed human?"

I try not to laugh. "He's fine. Please don't tell me I have to vouch for him like I did for Rayne."

At last some of the tension eases out of Wendy's shoulders. He laughs and allows his hands to rest on top of the table. "I'm not cruel, girl. Having you responsible for this piss-poor specimen would see you dead within the week."

From the corner of my eye I spy Maury open his mouth, as if to speak, then quickly think better of it.

He's learning.

"So, Wendy. Why do you think you've been set up?"

"Buckle in, girl. This is a crazy one."

Great. Because I need something else weird and stressful to fill my day.

❖

Wendy's story is brief and to the point. Unsurprisingly.

Once convinced Maury won't be going anywhere, he proceeds to explain as much as he knows about what has been happening among Angbec's werewolf packs.

A lot of it I've already inferred based on the notes from SPEAR, but to have the presence of a new pack confirmed by someone in the know sends an icy cold chill down my spine.

How? Just how? Outside battle season, the magic or whatever it is that controls pack powers simply doesn't work. Sure, packs can splinter and form new spin-offs, but there are no new powers, and the new alphas don't have the ability to pass those powers down within the new groups.

Wendy's brow furrows as he talks about the injuries he's seen on other wolves—bites that refuse to stop bleeding, gashes and slashes that remain even after a wolf has shifted through various forms and back to human. Inky black sores and pus more reminiscent of dying vampires than anything to do with werewolves.

Oh, and the smell.

"I can't explain it, but any wolf out there right now knows this smell and fears it. Like death, decay, and pain all rolled into one. It's disgusting, and worse than that, even humans can smell it. Well…good ones. Not your traditional civilian or base level agent."

I ignore the haughty look at Maury over that comment and hope that he has the sense to do the same.

"But is it an organic smell or mechanical? What is it coming from?"

"No one knows." Wendy shrugs. "The wounds we've seen have traces of it around them, but mostly it seems to be coming from the countryside beyond Loup Garou territory."

I glance at my watch. Considering how much has already happened, I'm surprised to realize that it's not quite eleven a.m., yet. But that's a good thing. It means I can go out now, *with* Wendy, and start investigating.

Nothing like positive action to chase away the rotten mood.

"Okay, come on then. We may as well have a look."

I stand, Wendy follows, and we both make our way to the door. Norma wakes with a flutter of her wings and a bleary "Dan-dan-dan." She turns expectantly to the door and lays her tail across the back of my neck.

Maury greets us there, arms folded, a wry smile on his face. "Karson, really? Come on."

Back to "Karson" are we?

"What?" I give him my sweetest smile.

"You can't honestly expect me to let you walk out of here."

"We could run out?"

He frowns. "This isn't a joke. Whatever special *relationship* you have with this werewolf, he was brought in under serious charges. He needs to go to holding."

"But—"

"But nothing. Unlawful infection? Attacking and injuring SPEAR agents?"

Behind me, Wendy opens his mouth. I stop him with a raised hand.

"He's already said that was self-defence."

"So?" Maury actually looks frustrated now. He touches my arm, not a grab like before, but a gentle, almost pleading touch. "Try to see this from where I stand. This wolf has been charged. He was brought in, and yes, you've questioned him, but what you've actually done is have a little chat about bad smells and impossible new packs. Nothing is concrete. There's no proof. We have to act in accordance with our protocol and hold him while we investigate."

"But he didn't do anything."

"So he says."

I clench my fist.

Again Wendy stands close on my right side, his chest brushing against my arm. It's a subtle gesture with no apparent equivalent to how true wolves act in the wild. Though if he were in his wolf form, Wendy might have his tail held low, not quite between his legs, but certainly not tall and erect. He might even try to lick the skin around my mouth and neck.

The touch is request for solidarity and comfort, for him and for me. My choosing to maintain that physical contact tells Wendy that I, his current dominant figure, support him.

"Just say the word, meat stick. I'll bite his shiny bald head off."

I step away from his chest.

Wendy grunts and snaps his mouth shut.

Whether Maury understands the quick, silent exchange or not, he does have the sense to understand a threat when he hears one. He lifts his hands, palm out. "I'm just stating facts. And if I let the pair of you walk out of here now, I'll be facing down a riot within an hour."

"Fine." Wendy returns to his previous chair. "I'll stay."

I shove a finger in my ear and twist it. "I'm sorry, what?"

"I said I'll stay. On one condition."

Maury chuckles. "You're not in a position to make demands, Wendy. You're under arrest."

A loud snarl ripples from Wendy's lips. "Call me that again, human, and I'll pull your spine out through your backside. Once I've remove the thick stick you clearly already have wedged there."

Maury pales. A neat trick considering his skin tone.

I lean close to offer a faux whisper. "I wouldn't call him that again if I were you. Go with Wensleydale if you want to call him anything. Mr. Gordan might actually be better."

"But you call him—"

"He likes me, Maury. Can't say the same for you."

Silence.

Awkward shuffling. A cleared throat.

"Wensleydale—"

Another snarl.

"Mr. Gordan…you're under arrest. This is not the time for demands."

"Eat shit, human." Wendy laces his fingers in his lap. "Now…I'll stay and act nice-nice with you SPEAR idiots if I have to. There's too much at stake to let pride get in the way. But I'll stay on the condition that you let Agent Karson get out there to do her job. Do that, and I'm all yours."

Maury considers. Once again I can all but see the cogs of his mind working. At last he sighs. "This isn't going to work any other way, is it?"

"No."

"I doubt it."

Both Wendy and I speak in the same moment and offer each other a small, knowing smile before looking back at Maury.

He sighs. "I guess that ticks one item off the team meeting agenda."

It takes every scrap of willpower I have to keep from victory punching the air. Instead, I smile and reach out to pat my boss lightly on the shoulder. Even Norma croons a comforting string of "Nika, nika ka-ka dans" before hoping off her roost to wait patiently and expectantly near the door.

"It's like I said before, I can handle this. Kappa will round this up and wrap it up before the end of the week, you'll see."

"Let's hope so."

I grin. "Come on, you mongrel. I'll take you over to Shakka and get myself started."

"Mmm." Wendy stands, patting his stomach through layers of clothing. "Been a while since I tasted goblin."

"He's joking." This I offer Maury who has turned a queer shade of green. "I promise you, he's joking. Right, Wendy?"

He shrugs. "Mostly."

With a grunt, I grab Wendy by the hand and haul him out of the room with me before we manage to upset Maury any further.

Chapter Eight

I don't like this car. It's a SPEAR vehicle, built rather like a police street car, but with further reinforcements to the back seat.

After pushing Maury to allow Wendy to travel without restraints, I knew it would be impossible to ride in my own car. I've definitely reached the limit of how far I can feasibly push. In light of that, I also leave Norma behind, despite her clear agitation.

I tell her to go home, but there's no way of knowing for sure if she understands. The tilt of her head and slow blinks might signal obedience, or at least understanding, but I don't get my hopes up.

Wendy sits in the back on the passenger side, backbone straight and stiff, his hands clasped neatly in his lap. The hot rush of his breath occasionally billows against my neck, not enough to be distracting, but enough to know he is still with me. Otherwise he's silent and still, almost invisible the same way Rayne was earlier that morning.

Rayne.

Just thinking her name makes my insides grow warm. I think back to her rough lips on mine, the eager hands pulling up my clothes, her tongue against my—

"Stop it, girl."

I pause the car at a red light and let the engine idle. "Stop what?"

"Thinking sexy thoughts or whatever the hell it is you're doing. It makes you smell like…like…just stop it."

"Fine. Why don't you tell me what you were holding out on back at HQ?"

He chuckles. "You *are* good at your job, girl."

"No—well, yes, I guess, but I *know* you. The second we got company I knew you'd clam up. And you did. So spill. What didn't you want Maury to hear?"

"It's not just me." Wendy leans forward and hooks his fingers through the small holes in the reinforced grate separating the front seats from the back ones. "My wolf form is on a list or something. People know to look for me. And they're also looking for my most loyal followers."

"Your beta?"

"And more. You know I rarely go full wolf anymore, but your SPEAR buddies knew my exact markings, size, and colour. How could they know that unless someone described me specifically?"

Large, black shaggy fur, yellow eyes, white left front paw.

At long last, my discomfort about those descriptions becomes clear.

"You're in our report," I mutter. "You're right. From your markings, to your eye colour, it was you exactly. No one describes wolves that way, not even other wolves. These descriptions came from someone who knew exactly who they wanted to get rid of."

A last car rumbles across the junction in front of me and I coax our own vehicle to continue the route to the SPEAR holding facility.

Wendy goes on. "So now you see. Someone doesn't want me investigating, or they didn't want me coming to you. Or both. I don't know. But whatever it is, this stranger is causing trouble for me and mine and I won't have it. The other thing I kept back is…uh."

I watch him through my rearview mirror. "Well?"

He scratches his nose. "I know these new wolves."

"From the new pack?"

"Yes. Not properly, but I've seen them and I recognize a few. Seems this new pack is building numbers from loners and banished wolves inside and out of the city. At least one of the ones I saw was from Fire Fang."

"Does that happen often?"

"It's not unheard of, but to have wolves join an unestablished pack is strange. And they're fast. Strong. Like nothing I've ever seen. And violent. When they fight, they fight hard."

"You've seen battles?"

"Heard a story or two. They're savage, Agent, you need to understand that. They fight to the death. No mercy, no prisoners. It's brutal."

"Have you ever seen another pack act this way?"

"Not in all my years."

Right turn. Narrow street. Right turn.

My thoughts gallop off ahead of me, leaving the rest to catch up. But I'm having trouble. The more I hear about this case, the more I wish I could leave it with another team. But of course, the more I hear about it, the more I understand that Kappa is best suited to handle it.

Excluding myself, my new team is entirely *edane* and powerful ones at that, including a couple of werewolves. If this new pack truly is as strong as Wendy claims, then a team with less squishy members can only be a plus.

"And why didn't you want Maury to know?"

"You heard him—all that talk about proof and concrete evidence. I haven't seen these fights. I've only heard of them. Speculation isn't enough, is it? Agent?"

He's right of course, but now I'm sitting on not second- but third-hand testimony that I can't use. I *need* to see these packs in action myself, or get hold of someone else who has.

"Where did you hear about all this?"

"I got reports just under a week ago, all from another wolf with descriptions clearly passed around, by the way. Then again, it's not hard to recognize Chalks."

"Chalks?"

"Pete Dunn."

I'm still lost. "Dunn...Dunn...Dunn...wait. You mean the whispering midget with the bird's nest hair?"

Wendy chuckles. "You'll be sorry you said that."

"I've never met him, just repeating what I heard. Anyway, why 'Chalks'?"

"Pure white hybrid and wolf forms. Some voted for 'Snowy,' but others decided that wasn't very...PC."

Again my mind drifts back to the descriptions in the report that morning. Pure white. That was definitely in there.

"And he's loyal to you?"

"My second."

The car stalls as my foot slips. It takes longer than it should to get back in gear, but I do so while gaping into my rearview mirror.

"Dunn is your second? I thought he was a teenager. Why would you do that?"

"I don't have to explain my pack to you."

"Of course not, but the beta should be the buffer between dissenters and you. From what I hear, a stiff wind would knock him flat on his arse."

A quick shake of his head. "In human form, perhaps. But when changed...that wolf is bigger even than I am. Strong."

"As strong as you?"

"Stronger."

I find that hard to believe. Size and strength aside, there's a reason Wendy, despite his age, leads the Dire Wolves. He's wise, powerful, and commanding, traits every alpha needs. By all accounts, Chalks has none of that.

I round the last corner of my route and guide the car down a sloped slip road that leads to a gated entryway barely seven feet high.

A series of blinking lights flickers to life overhead, five large dots coloured red. They wink in and out while the car is assessed and switch to green one by one.

When the last of the five becomes green, the gate clicks free of its lock and grinds upward into a recess hidden above.

A crackling voice issues from the speaker beyond my side window.

"Enter and be ready to present credentials."

I make sure the SPEAR lanyard on my hip sits firmly in my lap and guide the car into the darkness beyond.

Four agents greet us when I park the car. All hold rifles and wear protective gear with reinforced fabric to protect their vitals.

None appear to be expecting me and show surprise when I step from the vehicle.

Probably should have called ahead.

When I move round the car to open the rear door, the rifles aim toward the gap. I even hear the sharp click of two safety catches being released.

"Steady, guys, it's just one guy and he's a friend."

One of the four lifts the visor on his helmet. I don't know this guy, but I do recognize the grim boredom and latent anger of a Gamma team grunt.

"Why isn't he restrained?"

"He is. By his word."

Snorts and incredulous grunts issue from the gathered agents.

I hate this.

"Fine. Wendy, lace your hands behind your head, please. Take a knee."

He does so without complaint, though I can see the anger burning in his eyes. Makes me wonder if such rage is on my behalf or his.

The agents exchange bemused glances.

I cut across the lot of them. "I need to get to holding. This werewolf will be staying here while I and my team investigate a case."

"Credentials?"

I lift the lanyard off my hip and hold it up.

A second of the four agents pulls a little handheld scanner from his pocket and runs the red light it emits over the face of my ID.

"Karson, Danika," says a mechanical voice. "A20240119K06."

"Hmm," mutters the agent. "So you're Karson. Thought you'd be taller."

At five-eleven I'm not sure what he wants from me, but I let the comment slide and point to the security door leading deeper into the holding complex.

"Can we get on with this? I have things to do."

"Sure, whatever. Remember to sign out when you leave." The four agents step outward to allow me and Wendy through.

Chapter Nine

So many cells.

After going through more security, more checkpoints, and multiple scans of my ID, we've finally reached the cell area.

It's a high ceilinged space with recessed lights, dozens upon dozens of outlets for fire safety, and a double line of open and private cells.

Many are already occupied, a couple of vampires, a werewolf or two, three brownies, one gargoyle, a gaggle of pixies, and a troll.

None pay especial attention to us, but the figure in front of the large panel of buttons and switches hops down from his stool as we approach.

"Karson," he snaps.

"Shakka. How are you liking the new placement?"

"Just fine until you showed up. I thought coming out here would be enough to get me away from you."

"Is that any way to speak to an old friend?"

"Stick your head in a dung heap, Karson."

Behind me, Wendy hides a chuckle behind his hand. "Do you have that effect on everyone you know?"

"Most of them."

Shakka's beady little eyes narrow even further. Despite his diminutive height, he can glare as well as anyone else. And somehow, with his warty skin, scarred crooked nose, and mangled ears, the sight is more gruesome than usual.

"Wensleydale?"

"Shakka."

The pair of them study each other for long seconds. Not tense or aggressive. Curious.

Shakka breaks first. "So…are you a set-up too?"

I arch an eyebrow.

He shrugs. "I got two wolves in there, one from Dire and the other from Grey Tail. Both insist they were set up. Seems to be going around."

Wendy fixes me with a steady, meaningful stare.

"Okay, okay, I get it. Someone is after you. Let's get you inside, turn down your linen, and fluff your pillows so I can get on with it, huh?"

It's true, I do need to do this quickly, but I know full well that's not what Wendy was trying to say with such an intense look.

With one of his own pack held down here, we're both going to have to be careful about how we speak to each other from now on. Especially me. If I give away that Wendy has pledged himself to me, he'll be in still worse trouble than he is right now. And that won't be the sort of trouble I can help him with.

Shakka climbs back onto his stool to reach the panel of buttons that operates the doors and other cell features. He twists a dial, flips a switch, and the doors to the cell beside one of the wolves silently swings open.

I guide Wendy through the last checkpoint—a reinforced steel door with bars as thick as my wrists—and into the holding area.

Like Shakka's last holding position, this area is designed for all manner of *edane* creatures. Some cells have manacles and chains, others have comfortable beds and sinks. There are even some with bars set into the walls and ceiling so smaller creatures can roost off the ground if they wish.

The cell containing all the pixies has exactly that set-up, with many of the small creatures sleeping with their heads lolling and their wings tucked close to their backs. One or two are awake and dart at the main bars as we approach, but the electric current running through them sends them to the rear of the cell in a hurry.

The cells holding vampires aren't barred like the others, but enclosed with four walls and a proper door. A viewing slot affords the curious a glance inside, but the main difference is on the inside. Sound- and light-proofed but for an emergency hatch in the upper right corner of each. Though shut off right now, the hatches are light traps which, in extreme situations, will allow sunlight to filter down and fill the room.

We've never had to use them. Yet.

The werewolf cells are opposite, back to bars, though as well as the electric current, these are also constructed with silver in the make-up of the metal. Harmless to humans but uncomfortable to werewolves. Just another way to keep them calm and docile. Well…that and the drugs they often get filled with.

Wendy stops in front of the first of the two locked cells.

The wolf inside leaps up on spotting him, rushing as close to the bars as safety allows before dropping to his knees. He lowers his head far enough to fully expose the back of his dirty, skinny neck and rests both hands, palm flat on the floor.

"I'm sorry," he begins, "I tried to be careful, I tried—"

"Okay, cub, calm down." A soft growl from Wendy. "What happened? What are the charges? How long have you been here?"

"Unlawful lupine infection. Endangering humans. They brought me in two days ago and I haven't been able to call out."

My stomach knots, a mix of anger and confusion. "You should have been allowed a phone call."

The werewolf shrugs. "I didn't get one. I asked, but got nowhere."

A low chuckle comes from the neighbouring cell. This belongs to a woman with floppy blue hair, shaved bald on one side. In place of the hair there, she sports a huge tribal tattoo in shades of black and grey. "Neither of us did. We ain't got nothing like that. You SPEARs disgust me."

"I'm sorry. You should have been allowed to make a call."

Though she doesn't move, the wolf turns her nose toward me and inhales long and deep. "Hmm. Interesting."

"I won't lie to you. What's the point?"

"Nothing, but it doesn't stop the rest of you from lying." Yes, this wolf is definitely from the lie-detecting Grey Tail pack. She continues. "But at least you ain't. Counts for something, I suppose."

The first man lifts his head a tiny amount. "Wensleydale, please, get me out of here. I'm going crazy. I know it's only been two days, but my blood—my head—I can feel the moon."

Wendy extends his hand as if to reach through the bars.

"Stop."

I don't mean to make it an order. I certainly don't mean to yell, but both of the captured werewolves now watch me, sharing their gaze between me and Wendy's hand, frozen on its way to the bars.

Wendy clears his throat. "You dare—"

"Sorry." I lift my own hands, playing the part of startled human as best I can. "I just meant that the bars would shock you. Even from this side. You don't want that, right?"

"I can look after myself."

I open my mouth. Close it. How do I do this? How can I get him to just step into the cell and shut up until I leave?

I'm saved from figuring it out by the sound of the cell block doors opening. Through them limps Maury, breathing heavily, but otherwise just as I left him not long before.

"What are you doing here?"

He gives a wry smile. "Backup is always good, Agent. Even for the simplest of missions."

Great. Now I have to watch his mouth as well as mine.

"Well, our detainee was just about to get into his cell and I was about to leave. Right, Wendy?"

He gives me a level look. It lasts almost long enough to be uncomfortable before he sighs and faces the open door to the next empty cell.

"You fix this," he mutters. "I mean it."

"Of course."

"You'd better, meat sack." He steps into the space beyond.

I step in to shut the door behind him.

Maury clears his throat. "Aren't you forgetting something? It's pre-moon. This wolf and all the others need a sedation shot."

Oh. Balls.

"Maury—"

He holds up a small jet injector, already loaded with clear fluid. "This close to the full moon we need these guys dosed up."

The woman in her cell yawns and returns to the drop-down shelf that serves as a bed. She flops onto it with her hands folded across her stomach and glares at the ceiling. "Sedation shot. Like a fucking animal. Bloody humans…"

The Dire Wolf prisoner looks at Wendy. "Do I have to?"

Wendy hesitates.

Maury doesn't. "It's that or we move you to a more secure location. I don't mind, but given the amount of paperwork required to move you out of the city, it's not easy to get back once we ship you out."

"It's okay, cub." Wendy once again reaches toward the cell bars, but stops short of touching them. "I'll protect you."

Such simple words, but the effect is immediate. The man in his cell beams, bright and sunny, and leaps back to his feet. Where before he had been bowed, drawn in, and unsure, now he stands tall and firm, bright eyed, and confident. He even rolls up his sleeve and holds his arm out.

"Do it," he murmurs.

I find my fingers twitching into fists.

I know this is protocol. Of course I know, but…it still makes me uneasy.

Wendy is the alpha. He *needs* to be *compos mentis* and in full charge of his faculties, physical and mental. The sedation shot does exactly what it says and slows all that stuff down. If anything were to happen to him… plus he's shackled by his pledge to me.

This all stinks. And there's nothing I can do.

Maury waves a hand toward Shakka behind the protective glass. The goblin flicks a couple of switches on his panel, and the low, latent hum of electricity in the air fades by a fraction. The vague charge in the air eases, and the doors to the young Dire Wolf's cell clicks open.

"Agent, cover if you please." He gestures to the gun holstered on his hip. This is bullshit. All of it.

I spend enough time around testosterone to recognize a power play when I see one, but what can I do? Maury knows full well that Wendy will give his life for mine right now, meaning I have nothing to fear from either of the captured Dire Wolves. He also knows that in this space, surrounded by other agents, the likelihood of one of them making a successful getaway is slim to none.

So why? Why ask for cover?

I pull the gun from his holster with a savage glare.

Because it's another way to assert his control and dominance over the situation. To make clear to them, and me, that he is the one in charge.

Arsehole.

I steady the gun in the younger wolf's direction and wave Wendy into the line of fire.

"Go on then." I make my voice low and steady. "Get yourselves into position."

Wendy snarls, his upper lip curling back to expose slowly lengthening teeth.

I unlatch the safety mechanism on the gun. "Give it a rest, puppy."

A moment of silence. Then Wendy positions himself in my sight line, with his hands slightly raised.

Smirking, Maury saunters in with the jet injector and presses the nozzle to the first wolf's forearm. "Sweet dreams."

The wolf shudders as the sedative fluid enters his bloodstream, blinks, them stumbles toward the back of the cell. He slumps into the corner, not unconscious, but certainly useless for the next few hours.

That must have been a strong dose.

Another wave to Shakka to restore this door and then again to decharge those to the female's cell.

She doesn't bother getting up, simply thrusts her arm out for the shot. As she is dosed up, her body ripples with an almost liquid shudder before becoming limp and floppy. Her haughty look remains though, even as her jaw slightly slackens and her toes flop outward.

Maury, apparently enjoying himself, chuckles as he closes the door to her cell.

"And now, Mr. Gordan, your turn."

Wendy sniffs. He doesn't look at me exactly, but I know he's weighing his options. Unfortunately, this is the only viable one he has.

Calm and unhurried, he lowers the drop-down bed and sits on the end of it. One by one, he peels off layers of clothing including his longer outer coat, two thinner jackets, a jumper, and one tatty shirt. Still frowning, he folds each item and lays them out in a neat line at the back of his cell.

"This isn't the army, wolf, you aren't about to be inspected." Maury ejects the empty drug canister from the jet injector and inserts another. Something looks strange about it, but before I can question the sight, he's already inside the cell, aiming the nozzle at Wendy's exposed forearm.

"Let's get on with this, shall we? I have places to be."

Wendy sniffs again, his nose now directed at the jet injector pressed to his arm.

"Wait." I can't help it. I can't let him do this. Not with so much happening, not with new packs and odd powers running amok. Wendy *needs* to be at full strength.

I find myself crossing the small space and yanking the jet injector out of Maury's hand.

He lets me take it, but only to add, "This is pointless, Karson." His voice roughens. "Protocol dictates—"

"I know, I know, but…this isn't right. Doesn't it feel…*not right* to you?"

"No."

"Come on, Maury. Something weird is happening out there, we should be asking these guys for help, not locking them up and dialling their wits down to one."

He gives a lazy shrug. "I do what needs to be done. As should you. Now give him the shot."

"I…I can't."

My voice wobbles a little. Still worse is the knowing look of smug triumph as Maury extends his hand for the injector.

"Then I'll do it. Regardless, it must be done before either of us leave. This close to the full moon we take no chances. A fact you know full well."

"Girl?" Wendy looks up from his study of his bare forearm. It's possible that weeks have passed since he last saw his own naked skin beyond that on his hands. "Just get it over with, will you?"

"But—"

"No, meat sack. The longer you're in here arguing, the longer it takes for you to get out there and figure out what's happening. Give me the damn shot."

"Wendy…"

"Give me the shot, girl."

Again, infuriatingly, he's right. I know he's right. But I don't have to like it.

I press the nozzle of the injector flush to his skin and hit the trigger.

Wait…what's that?

With a yell, I pull up on the injector, but the dose has already gone, fired into Wendy's body on a geyser of fluid under high pressure. It vanishes into his skin with no trace and the empty jet injector clatters to the floor at my feet.

"That wasn't a sedation shot." I whirl on Maury with my hands clenched into fists. "That wasn't the same thing you gave the others. What was it?"

Maury nods approvingly. "I wasn't sure if you'd notice. Guess you do have a keen eye."

Wendy slumps in his seat. A line of drool dribbles from the side of his mouth.

"Damn it, Maury, what the hell did you put in that injector?"

Wendy drops further from a slouched, relaxed slump to full-on prone on his drop-down bed. He's not dead or injured—far from it—but the slack, relaxed smile on his face is unlike anything I've ever seen before.

This isn't a normal sedation shot.

Shit.

"Maury, what the hell? Talk to me."

His nodding gives way to a smug smile. "It *is* a sedation shot, like the others, just stronger. It contains a new silver compound the brains at Clear Blood have been working on. Test subjects were shown to be calm, docile, and infinitely more manageable for longer periods of time following a single shot."

"But if it was a test drug you need written permission from—"

"Not for this, Agent. I'm fully authorized to use this. And, I must say it seems to be working exceptionally well."

I could punch Maury. Right in the damn nose.

Instead I grit my teeth, flex my clench fingers, and stomp out of the cell. Seconds later, the low hum of electricity picks up again as all three wolves are trapped inside.

My fingers are itching. I want to grab something, squeeze it, punch it, kick it. Instead I stalk back up the steps that lead to the viewing room where Shakka waits with his buttons and dials.

He looks at me but says nothing, simply returning to his stool to watch.

A few moments later, Maury joins me.

"I had to," he murmurs.

"No, you didn't."

"Of course I did. I was reading up on him after you told me his name. Wensleydale Gordan. Do you have any idea of his record? His powers?"

I raise my hands skyward. "Of course I do."

"Then why would you question this? He's been leading that pack for almost twenty-five years. No one survives that long as an alpha. That must mean he's strong, cunning, and powerful."

"Yeah, so?"

"Then he *needs* sedation while here."

"I'm not disputing that, I'm just pissed that you decided to use some weird, experimental drug that will knock him on his arse for the next who knows how long."

"Not my problem."

I hope he's right, I really do, but the sinking feeling in my gut doesn't comfort me.

"How long will it keep him down for?"

Maury glances upward, visibly thinking. "Not sure. Could be three days. Could be a week. It seems different on every wolf."

I drag my itching fingers down to my sides. "You'd better hope we don't need him."

"And why would we need him?"

"The Dire Wolves are one of the strongest packs in Angbec. Not the biggest, but the strongest, and that's all down to him." I point a trembling finger down at Wendy. "It's his command, strategy, and skill that keeps them all alive, and without him they barely stand a chance. If this new pack and the powers they have are really as dangerous as you think then you've just incapacitated our strongest ally."

Maury sniffs. "You're overreacting."

"You'd better hope I am."

He studies the retrieved jet injector, then shoves it into his pocket. "Okay, fine. The wolf is powerful, but maybe there's another way."

"Like what?"

"Well, he pledged to you, right? So you control him now?"

My stomach drops right into my toes. I cast a glance at Shakka, but it's plain he's heard every word.

The goblin's eyes are as wide as I've ever seen them go, and his mouth is open to match. He slides off the step stool to give me his full attention. "What?"

"Nothing, I—"

"No, no, no, Karson, what did I just hear? Did that idiot wolf pledge himself to you? Did he say the words?"

Damn it. "Yes."

Shakka's eyes take on a sinister gleam. "So *you* control the Dire Wolves."

It irks me. It frightens me. It distresses and angers me, but there it is. That's the truth.

"If you breathe a word about this—"

"Me? Don't be silly." Shakka lifts his hands, palm up.

"I'm serious, Shakka. No one else knows and it *needs* to stay that way. Do you understand?"

He cocks his head. Rather like Maury, I can see him thinking it through, but his tell is the way his gnarled and knobbly hands abruptly start rubbing together.

"What's the problem?" Maury, as ever, has failed the see the larger picture. He cuts straight across Shakka to once more address me. "He pledged to you, which is perfect. Why don't you tell him to bring in all the Dire Wolves? That way they're safe from whatever is on the street and we also get a chance to question everybody about what they've seen and when. It's a win-win from what I can see."

How can one man be so painfully clueless?

"No alpha would ever order his entire pack into SPEAR custody. If I tell him to do that we'll have a war on our hands within the hour."

"But—"

"Don't be so blind, Maury. If I give that order, every member of his pack will know he's no longer in charge of them. They'll kill him immediately for being weak, then come after me to reclaim power. Once that's done, there will be dominance battles to decide who the new alpha is. And given the state of the packs right now, a new leader will have new ideas about how things should be run. This is more delicate than a string of wet lace and you want to set fire to everything."

Maury glances at Shakka, then me again. "I still say you're overreacting. We should be grasping every lead and advantage with both hands. There's no way I can allow you to sit on this perfect opportunity."

"Well, you're going to have to, because I'm not doing it. Shakka?"

The goblin stops dry washing his hands long enough to look up.

"If anybody finds out about this, I'll know it's you. I'll know and I'll come back to get you. Understand me?"

He tuts at me. "Threatening a fellow SPEAR employee? Whatever next."

Indeed.

I can't take any more. I need to leave.

It's that or else I'll be the one locked in a cell.

I walk away, from Maury, from Shakka, from Wendy and the other two wolves. All of it.

"Karson?" Maury's angry voice follows me toward the door. "Karson, where the hell do you think you're going?"

"Home." I wave an angry hand over my shoulder. "I'm clocking off before I end up doing something none of us enjoy. See you this evening."

CHAPTER TEN

A bath will make me feel better. It always does.

I keep the thought in mind as I sink into the tub, letting hot, soapy water slosh over my body.

Perhaps if I tell myself that, perhaps if I believe it in my heart of hearts, then the words will prove themselves true. Perhaps.

My mind wanders as I recline against the bath's sides, pacing back and forth over Rayne, Wendy, and Maury. How can it be so early in the day and yet so much of my temper has been pulled, twisted, stretched, and frayed?

I sink into the suds and hold my breath for a while under the water.

Somehow, down here it's easier to think. Yes, of course sound is muted and my sight is hindered by the fluffy underside of bubbles, but it also muffles my thoughts. Allows me to pick at them one by one and study each in turn.

Norma?

She hasn't come home, but I didn't really expect her to before sundown. No doubt she's huddled up with the rest of her clutch mates back at SPEAR HQ, causing mischief and havoc in my name. Atta girl.

Rayne?

Nothing I can do about her until she wakes. That will be one hell of a conversation, but at least I know what I need to apologize for. Sometimes that's the best place to start. And I know I was out of line this morning.

Wendy?

All I can do is my job. Whether he's being set up or not, I need to find out what's actually happening with the werewolf population of the city and bring it back under control.

Sounds simple on paper.

My air runs out before I can turn my thoughts to Maury, and I allow my body to bob upward in the tub. My hair breaks the surface and water streams down my face and ears in warm, thick streams.

Not enough to block the sound of my phone though.

I've no idea how long it's been ringing, but I lean out of the bath to tap the screen, thus bringing the call to life. Another tap transfers the call to my speaker function.

"Karson."

"Oh, good, you're awake. I needed to talk with you."

"Jack?" I peer at the phone again. The number is one I don't recognize, but that's certainly Jack's voice crackling down the semi suitable line.

"Yes, sorry, I had to call from—" He clears his throat. "This isn't my phone, but they wouldn't let me grab mine. Look, I need an update on these werewolves."

"I only saw you this morning."

"I know, I know, but...but you really need to figure this out. Sooner than you think."

I let the water slosh a little, just to cover the parts of me currently exposed to air. "It's in hand."

"You're sure?"

"Yes. Jeez, what's your problem today?"

There are strange sounds coming down the line. Unlike Jack's normal phone, this one seems to carry a lot of background sound. I catch the hum of low voices, the grunt of an engine, something large and heavy like a truck perhaps. Shouting.

"Where are you?" I ask.

"Away."

"What kind of answer is that?"

"The only one you're getting. Come on, Danika, I need you to focus. You've got to take this seriously."

All my moving in the tub has caused a tiny pink shadow to appear on the water between my legs. It reminds me that my period is something strange and unusual. Something that I need to get checked as soon as possible. Preferably by one of the Foundation doctors, since my usual GP won't have the slightest clue. A fact I've learned the hard way.

"—they will take over everything and I don't know how that works."

"What?" I snap away from my thoughts with a jolt. Hadn't realized Jack was still talking. "What did you say?"

He sighs. "You didn't hear a word of that, did you?"

"No, I—"

"I don't have time right now. They're listening, and I have another call coming through. Just..." His voice hitches, almost trembles. "Be careful. I can't help you if you're on the wrong side of all this. Please remember what you're supposed to be doing and do it quickly."

"What's that supposed to mean?"

"I can't—"

"Jack?"

Water splashes as I attempt to stamp my foot before remembering where I am.

"Fine, I...there's a protocol. It's new and untested, but it's a contingency for Angbec to be used if *edanes* get out of control. I think it's called Project Revival and—"

"But I've never heard of it." I splash away a few more threads of pink wriggling through the water.

"Good. No one is supposed to know. You need to trust me when I say you don't want this contingency enforced. You have to figure out what's going on with the werewolves before someone gets hurt."

"Like I said, I've got this. Why don't *you* trust *me?*"

"I'm trying to."

The background sound on the call abruptly becomes louder. The hum of voices evolves into a questioning mumble and the engines sound closer than ever.

"Jack, where are you?"

"I...I need to go," he murmurs.

"Wait, Jack—"

The line dies.

I sit back in the water again, nibbling my bottom lip, running over the conversation in my mind again.

Project Revival? What the hell is that?

And now that I think about it, who are "they"?

I know I should sleep, but I can't. Not only does my body seem to be rebelling against increasingly irregular work hours, but all I can think of is Rayne.

Tossing and turning against those sheets, I try to plan out all the things I want to say when the suns drops. I ponder the best ways to apologize and explain that my hormones have gotten the better of me. Just thinking such nonsense makes me cringe. After so many years, what has suddenly changed in my body to do this to me?

My rational mind calmly points out that Foundation drugs are a work in progress and may have side effects we don't yet know about. The rest of me is cruelly pleased that Mum will never know. At least not if she continues to give me the silent treatment.

"But it wasn't my fault."

I've said it at least once a day, every day since that night at Club Starshine. I did everything I could to save Pippa, truly I did. Hell, I beheaded a smooth-talking, vampire bitch-queen with an orc-made battleaxe. But despite everything I did, how many rules I broke and how hard I tried, the only way to save Pippa had been to make her a vampire. Something Rayne did *for* me, not in spite of me.

I remind myself of that fact too.

My watch beeps and the automatic shutters on the windows to our house begin to lift.

Sundown.

So much for the nap.

I turn in bed again, facing the door, wondering how I'm going to do this.

Thirty seconds later, someone raps at my door. Three guesses as to who.

"Hi, Rayne, come on in."

She tiptoes through the door like a timid little thief and shuts it softly behind her. Her gaze is pinned to the floor, where her bare feet scuff back and forth against my carpet.

So. Fucking. Beautiful.

Her hair always looks a little crazy, whether she's just woken or not, but I love it regardless. Soft strands sticking up every which way to frame the delicate features of her near doll-like face. That mouth, those eyes, her soft, smooth skin. She has her underwear on, but nothing else, clearly having come straight to my room on waking. It's a mismatched set of black panties and baby pink bra but she has never looked more perfect.

"Hi." Oh, boy, even her voice is gentle and fearful.

Deep breath. "I'm sorry."

Her shoulders twitch, but she doesn't leave the door. "Me too. That was a cheap shot and to fire it on the cusp of sunrise was…cruel."

She's right, but we're talking without yelling. I don't want to do anything to throw fuel on the embers.

"I know you didn't mean it. It's okay. I…I shouldn't have reacted the way I did."

"You were scared."

"But I shouldn't be scared of *you*. That's the point we're making here, isn't it? You're my girlfriend. At least I hope that's what you consider us to be. I should know that you'd never deliberately hurt me."

At last Rayne looks up. Her expression is one I've no idea how to read, but at least I can see her eyes now. They have a faint sheen of silver in them, and when she licks her lips, the tips of her fangs are visible.

"You're right. I'd never hurt you on purpose."

Why do I feel like she's saying something else?

I push the sheets away and climb from the bed. Slowly. When I pick my way through the mess of my room, I can feel her watching me, that calm, assessing gaze she reserves only for me.

Her hand, when I pick it up, is cold. "You need another blood bag."

She stiffens but doesn't pull away. "I had one yesterday, I should be fine."

"Rayne, I'm really sorry. I freaked out earlier and blamed you. That's not fair. And you're right. I *have* been holding back but, cliché as it is, it's not a you-thing, it's a me-thing. And I need to deal with it. PMS isn't helping, but at least I know that's happening. And..." I consider how to phrase this without sounding creepy. "Wendy said I need to be careful."

"What?" Rayne's eyes widen.

"No, no, not like that. No, no, I mean that I need to do something about the...smell." My own nose wrinkles. "Why can't I talk today? I mean that with my period in full flow—" I catch myself. "Ha, full flow. Get it?"

She rolls her eyes.

"With my period here there's obviously going to be blood, right? If Wendy could smell it, the scent must be double for you. So this morning wasn't your fault. It's not something you could control."

"I see."

"Well, it makes sense, doesn't it? I mean vampire, blood, blood, vampire? I can't believe it took me so long to connect those dots. Now that I know, if I do a better job of being clean, or something, then maybe it won't be so hard on you."

"Oh. Thank you."

"Why did that sound more like 'fuck you'?"

Rayne pulls her hand away. "You always smell like blood, Danika. It fills your entire body. There isn't a second between us that lacks that knowledge. I can *see* your pulse. If I focus I can hear your heart beat. If I'm close enough I can *feel* the blood moving beneath your skin. Every night of my life is full of that knowledge. And every night, I control the urges that leaves in me."

"But this morning—"

"I came to you this morning because I want you." The faintest of growls enters her voice. "I wanted to touch and pleasure my girlfriend. Yes, there's blood, but I didn't even notice until I found it."

"But you were so pushy and forward. I thought the blood might—"

"Everyone smells of blood." She reaches for my shoulders, then stops without touching. "Danika, I can't forget what I am. Not for a second. When Vixen turned me into this monster she made it impossible for me to forget. Every moment, every night, if I'm with humans, I'm thinking of blood. All the time. I smell it, I taste it, I want it, I—" she breaks off with a sigh. "I can control it. I have to control it. I have no choice."

"I know."

"Do you?"

I reach for her hand again, stunned when she pulls back out of reach. "Rayne?"

"Don't. You're right. I need a blood bag. I'm going to grab one from the emergency store. Then you can tell me about the meeting this morning."

The reminder wipes my mind of all this emotional, relationship trouble.

"Wendy's in trouble."

Rayne nods. "Let me get dressed. Ten minutes."

True to her word, Rayne moves at speed and, a mere five minutes later, we're in the kitchen sitting across from each other over the long, wide table.

Pippa darts back and forth behind us packing for her night, shoving supplies into her bag while she chatters on the phone.

Rayne sits with one leg tucked up beneath her on the straight-backed chair, both hands resting on the table. I've flipped my own chair around to straddle it, resting my chin on my overlapped wrists.

"Unlawful lupine infection?" I say again, grinding my fingernails into the soft wood of the chair. "Bullshit, right?"

"Of course. You know it, I know it, Wensleydale certainly does, but you have to remember, SPEAR doesn't. They have to follow protocol."

"So I shouldn't be pissed that he's in that cell, dosed up with who knows what?"

"That's not what I said. Phillipa?" She turns to my sister.

Pippa treats Rayne to a questioning look.

"Do you know anything about a new drug given to werewolves on a full moon?"

A slight frown followed by a sharp, "I'll call you back." She swipes the phone screen then shoves the whole thing into her pocket. "Yes." A pause. "There *is* something. One of the research teams in Scotland synthesized a sedative called Quilax."

I lift an eyebrow.

"That's not the actual name. It's Q174X or something like that, but Quilax stuck because it's catchy…and because we have some real old school nerds on the research team. Anyway, it contains traces of silver azide and is *supposed* to be in trial phase."

"Why do you say it like that?"

Her frown deepens. "I don't like it. Put aside the silver azide for a moment, we still don't know enough about the blood chemistry of werewolves to be experimenting like this. We don't have enough volunteers to keep up with sufficient research so we've no idea what this will do to them."

Rayne and I share a look. She opens her mouth, but I get there first.

"Is any of it in Angbec right now?"

"It shouldn't be. The Foundation authorized the initial synthesis and reproduction of the chemical on a small scale, but so far nothing from the Scotland team suggests it's ready for werewolf testing. It should still be in their lab. How do you even know about this?"

"I think Maury used it on Wendy."

Pippa's eyes widen.

"You're speculating, Danika."

"Then why was he so cagey with me?" I glare at Rayne. "He wouldn't tell me what it was when I noticed and tried to sneak it past me even before that point. Why?"

"Because you're a known loose cannon with reckless disregard for authority?"

"Hey—"

"It's true." She shrugs. "We need to give him the benefit of the doubt. Besides, it may not be this new drug from Scotland. What if it's something else?"

"And what if it isn't?"

Pippa joins us at the table. "Guys, calm down. The drug hasn't left Scotland. It can't have. Last I heard, they still needed to find a substitute for silver azide and so far there isn't one."

"And what's wrong with silver azide?"

"Aside from the fact that it's an explosive? Not much. It's pretty useful stuff, just incredibly volatile. A few milligrams of the stuff would make a significant bang."

I stand. "We have to get Wendy out of that cell."

"We will."

"No, we need to do it now."

"Danika—"

"It's my fault he's in there. He came to me for help and I let Maury bully me into putting him in holding. I should have fought harder to keep him out."

A sigh from Rayne. "From what you've told me, Maury can't bully you into anything, no matter how hard he tries. Besides, we can't *take* Wensleydale from holding. We need proof."

"But you didn't see him this morning. He was lying there like some limp spaghetti string. I've never seen him look so out of it. If someone really is out to get him, then—"

"Then we stop *them*. We have to work it that way round, Danika, we have no choice. Please. Don't do anything crazy."

I'm pacing now, hadn't even realized I'd started moving. At the end of the kitchen, I twirl and turn, following the line of the cupboards lining the kitchen.

She's right of course. But in my mind's eye I see Wendy's docile smile again and the limp slide onto his bed. This can't be good.

"Dani?"

I look down to my sister.

"I need to go, but…I don't think you need to worry. For one thing, Mr. Gordan is one of the strongest wolves I know. It's going to take a lot to hold him down and I don't know that anything could for any length of time. He's the pack alpha for a reason. For another, whatever it is that Maury used, it can't be the Q174X. That's still in a lab in Scotland, not ready to be used yet. He'll be fine. Okay?"

I'm nodding, but the spiky lump in my throat makes that hard to feel genuine.

She pats my shoulder and heads out.

Rayne looks up at me from her slouch in her seat. "We should talk to the rest of the pack."

"Yeah. Let's take the rest of Kappa though."

"You're sure?"

"Yeah. I think we're going to need them and…I need to tell you something about the car."

Rayne sits upright and stiff against her seat belt. Her nostrils flare as she scents the air, one hand tracing the gouge marks in the ceiling above the driver's seat. "This is a lot of damage. Why would they do this?"

I've asked myself the same question over and over since this morning. Still no answers. Aside from fear of SPEAR following Wendy's arrest, there are no reasons I can think of for the attack on me. Not from Wendy's pack, anyway.

Funny, I hadn't been nervous this morning, but now, even with Rayne at my side and other members of Kappa on the way, my stomach is looped into tight, rigid knots.

"Did they recognize you?"

"I hope not." I flex my fingers on the steering wheel. "I mean, I'm a pack-friend. Wendy himself vouched for me and placed me under pack protection. If they knew it was me, then we have yet another problem to add to the list."

Rayne nods and turns her attention to the road. Though it may not seem so to the casual observer, I know she's now on high alert, scanning every dark corner and shadow for signs of danger.

So nice having a vampire on side.

The neat, clean streets give way to muckier, grimmer ones as we near the edges of Misona. Traffic thins, then dies off altogether, most humans well aware of the fact that this land belongs to werewolves.

Those few pedestrians out on the pavement walk with the graceful glide of *edanes*. Not all werewolves, to be sure, but certainly less squishy than the average human.

We pass a couple of hollow, burned out cars and the shabby carcass of a children's play area wedged between two tall flats.

The road ahead is blocked, two skeletal cars shoved nose to nose with a stack of cardboard boxes, twisted shopping trolleys, and old furniture piled up behind.

Rayne wrinkles her nose. "That's new."

"Something to do with the new wolves?"

"Could be."

I stop the car well back from the blockage, actually taking time to turn and face back in the opposite direction. While I don't expect it to happen again, it would be nice to have a clean getaway path this time.

The moment I step from the car, I know something's wrong.

Chapter Eleven

The very air tastes of menace, unease, and fear.

At my side, Rayne clenches her fists and stands close enough to actually crowd my space.

I give her a wry look, but she shakes her head and juts her chin toward the rear of the blockage. It takes longer than I'd like to see what she's pointing out.

Eyes. Dozens upon dozens of gleaming eyes in creepy, shining pairs. Some yellow, some green, others amber, all of them fiery and fierce.

That knot in my stomach tightens significantly.

"My name is Danika Karson. I'm here on behalf of Wensleydale Gordan, alpha of the Dire Wolves."

"SPEAR." The hiss is soft but angry, from somewhere low and far behind me.

Rayne whirls and presses her back to mine, growling deep in the back of her throat.

The cry is repeated again and again, sibilant whispers on the dull breeze.

I fight every instinct that tells me to reach for my gun. "Yes, we're from SPEAR. My companion is Rayne, you know her too. We are pack-friends."

"Vampire."

Again the voice from behind.

I nudge Rayne in the ribs, indicating that she turn. Though she grumbles, she doesn't argue, instead sidestepping while keeping her back pressed close to mine.

Where the hell is the rest of our team?

Finally, I'm facing the opposite direction, toward our lonely-looking car out on the pavement edge. There are shadows around it, seemingly moving and swirling, but more pressing are further pairs of those eyes.

Why are these wolves in hybrid form?

"Where is your leader?"

"SPEAR," comes the cry again, this time chased by low growls of anger.

"This is unusual werewolf behaviour, Danika."

"You think?" I treat Rayne to another jab in the ribs. Then to the crawling night air, "I want to speak with Pete Dunn."

Some of the growls stop. Not enough, but a few. Several of the eyes wink and blink before dropping the eerie supernatural glow. Those in front, near my car, don't.

Instead a figure fully eight feet tall steps out from the shadows. I catch a glimpse of a long sleek muzzle and tail before it darts out of sight.

"Hey—"

Rayne snatches at my arm, halting my step forward.

"Don't you dare," she mutters.

I glare, but wait, taking the time to clasp my hands in front of me. Got to keep them away from the gun.

Several seconds pass before a man approaches from the darkness. He's taller than me, but most of that height likely comes from the twelve-inch Mohawk crowning his head. He's dressed wholly in black, with acne-scarred skin and a tasteful ring piercing in his left nostril. His large hands hang loose by his sides, a gesture I might have taken for relaxed interest if not for the glint of *edane* colour in his eyes.

Each step in our direction cracks on the air like snapping twigs. His steps are light and soft, but I find myself flinching with each one.

Who the hell is this guy? He seems familiar, but I can't place why.

He finally stops before us and smiles, hands resting lightly on the selection of slender, studded belts hanging stylishly on his hips. "I remember you being taller." His eyes meet mine directly.

Guess the height is mostly hair then.

"Who the hell are you?"

I can all but feel Rayne's eye roll, but I don't care. Enough is enough.

The man eyes me a moment longer before cocking his head. "I'm Aleksandar. You can call me Alek, though. If you'd like."

"I'm looking for Pete Dunn. Where is he?"

"He? Hmm. Not here. But you can speak with me."

I open my mouth again, but Rayne's hand is already on my shoulder. She squeezes hard enough to make me wince. "Danika." Her voice is low, but enough for me to hear. The warning is clear.

"Wendy—I mean, Wensleydale sent me here to help. I know what's been happening to your pack. I want to clear your names."

"SPEAR wants to help us? How…interesting."

"*I* want to help you."

"Then we'd better have a chat hadn't we, Agent Karson?"

I squeeze Rayne's hand, flexing my shoulder as her crushing grip slips away. "I don't know you. Pack law dictates that in the absence of an alpha, the second should step forward in their place and—"

"Don't you dare cite pack law to *me*, human." The calm, easy manner dissolves in an instant. Rage contorts Aleksandar's heavily made-up goth features into something ugly and feral. Even his hair seems to bristle. "As if a low, human servant would know anything about how the Dire Wolf pack conducts itself."

In an eyeblink, Rayne is no longer at my back, but beside me, bearing her fangs at the werewolf. She makes no move to attack, but the silver sheen in her eyes is hard to ignore.

"And a blood-sucking parasite to boot. The Dire Wolves were once the largest pack in this city. The strongest. Now we babysit SPEAR and allow oversized mosquitoes to walk our territory. Shameful."

Footsteps from the right.

This time I can't help it, the gun is in my hand and pointed before I can think it through.

What the hell is happening now?

Aleksandar snarls, but Rayne is in his path, still passive, but ready for action. Watching. Waiting. Taunting? Perhaps.

The person approaching from my right is running hard, leading a small gaggle of stragglers. Their paper-white skin seems almost to glow in the darkness, while their long, thin hair flaps behind them like a banner. They skid to a stop in front of me panting and gasping, clutching their skinny chest through a worn leather jacket.

"A-agent Karson?"

Short, pale skin. Wild, nest-like hair. Soft, whispering voice...wait, *very* pale skin. Colourless. Pale pink eyes. Ah, now I recognize them. Not what I expected though.

"Pete Dunn? I thought you were—sorry. Um, is it Petra?"

"Both." They pull a shaky smile. "S-sorry...I took...so long..."

"It's okay, get your breath back—"

"Y-you said there-there were new cubs hiding on the West Side." Pete looks straight past me to Aleksandar.

Anger melts from Aleksandar's face as though it had never been. His lips part into a small O of surprise. "They weren't there?"

"No."

"But there were several according to reports passed to me. And I just had to let you know, especially in the absence of our great and powerful leader."

Wow. The air seems to chill around me, enough that I have to fight the urge to rub my shoulders. Instead, I tuck the gun back into my holster and step back far enough to give Pete a clear view of Aleksandar. Rayne joins me.

The pair glare at each other for long, tense seconds.

The men and women behind Pete stare with poorly concealed hatred in their eyes. Some of them even sport the long black fingernails of their hybrid forms.

In the space around us, behind the blockade and on the nearby pavement, other werewolves glare right back, with the same barely contained fury.

Pete drags slim, daintily manicured fingers back through their hair. "Great, well, uh, next time, like, be more certain. There were gargoyles nesting in the building you described. We had to bust our way out."

Aleksandar presses both hands to his chest. "There were? I'm so, so sorry. Did everyone get back okay?"

"A few scrapes and bruises. But we're fine."

"Good. I'd hate if anything happened to you."

Now *there* is a "fuck you" if ever I heard one. Rayne seems to think the same, because her fists are clenching and unclenching gently, even if her facial features are smooth, bland and placid.

A long moment of silence stretches between us.

It breaks only when the low rumble of an approaching vehicle drifts in on the night air.

It's a SPEAR vehicle, a van laden down with the rest of my Kappa teammates.

About bloody time.

Aleksandar casts them a wary glance before turning. "Since you're back, Petra, I'll leave you to your meeting with these SPEAR agents. Maybe *you* will be able to find us some answers. Our safety depends on information." With that last jibe, he walks away, back into the shadows near my car.

With him go many of the other pairs of eyes watching from the background.

Soon, they're all gone, leaving just myself and Rayne with Pete and their little handful of companions.

Pete heaves a huge sigh. "Agent—"

"What the hell?" I yell.

"I know, I know, but—"

"Who is he and why is two-thirds of the pack hanging on his tail? Where even were you? What's happening?"

They lift a hand. "Please don't, okay? Like, enough shouting at me. One of you is enough. Can you just…will you come with me? Like, please? It's not safe out here."

Understatement of the year, anyone?

But instead of arguing, I follow, leaving Rayne to fill in the rest of our team.

We need to get to the bottom of this whole new pack mess, but apparently, there's one more mess we need to deal with first.

CHAPTER TWELVE

Pete leads me to the entrance of a squat apartment block a few yards on from my car. With a quick gesture for their companions to remain outside, they lead me inside and up two flights of steps to a landing of three closed doors.

One is twisted off its hinges and barely serving its purpose, the other two are wedged tightly shut. They rap on the second of this pair with the back of their knuckles, once, twice, three times.

It jerks open with a squeal of protesting hinges.

"Sir? You're safe? What happened?" The voice from inside is sharp and clipped, a vague hint of some northern accent in the vowels. It belongs to a woman with straight black hair down to her hips and three small spiral tattoos on her left cheek.

"He lied," mutters Pete and enters the apartment.

The woman rolls her eyes but doesn't add anything else, instead looking me up and down before holding the door wider. She waves me in, then slips past to keep guard outside on the landing.

Inside the apartment is bare, dark, and cold. This isn't a living space by any stretch of the imagination. No furniture or even light bulbs, just a few half rotted boxes and broken pallets.

The only reason I can see anything at all is because someone has left a dim, battery operated lamp on top of one of the boxes.

I squint. Sigh. "Pete—"

"Why are you here?" They don't look at me, instead watching the street outside through the filthy, cracked glass of the nearest outward facing window. "It's not safe."

"I'm here to help."

"You can't."

"Wendy asked me to."

Pete stiffens. Their skinny shoulders draw up toward their ears. "You can't help us. No one can. This is a wolf problem, like, we have to deal with it ourselves."

"How old are you?"

"Does it matter?"

"It does to me."

They draw the tip of one slender finger down the window glass. "Seventeen."

I could kick Wendy. I could kick him and punch him for doing this to what is essentially a child. "And you're second in command."

"Yes." Pete's voice takes on a little growl. "Is that a problem?"

"I—no. No, it's not a problem. We all have to trust that Wendy knows what he's doing and—"

"Don't call him that."

I squint.

"Don't call him 'Wendy.' It's, like, disrespectful. He's our alpha and leader. He deserves our respect."

"Your *alpha and leader* is in a SPEAR cell right now, trapped, sedated, and off his stupid, furry face. He asked me to come down here and figure out what's going on because he *knows* I can help."

Pete's fingertip stroke becomes a screeching claw scratch. "You think this is helping? I saw what happened to you this morning. You're not safe here. You're just getting in the way."

"I'm doing my job."

"And I'm trying to do mine."

I snort. "And how are you going to do that with Aleksandar digging the floor from under you? You know what he's doing, right?"

At last they look at me. "Of course I do, like, I'm not an idiot. But I can't...I'm not strong enough to stop him by force."

"You have to be."

Their pale pink eyes narrow. "No, I have to be *smarter* than him. Look, you think I'm weak, right? Like a child. But I know what I have to do, Agent. I'm not here for fun. I'm trying to hold us together. But Aleksandar was right in what he said before. You can't interfere with this, get it?"

I bite my lip. "Pete, please. I get it, really I do, but I need to—"

"No, you don't. Don't you understand? Wensleydale is mega out of touch, he's, like, losing the pack. If you butt in now, the fingertip grip I have on these wolves will slide and then poof, it's gone. If you want to help, stay out of it and get out of the Bowl. Like, now."

A light tap at the door breaks through the conversation.

The woman with the tattoos opens it to let Rayne through and the expression in her eyes twists my innards in knots.

"I left the rest of the team outside." She walks to my side and puts a hand on my arm. "They're watching the doors with the handful Mx. Dunn brought, but it's not enough. I overheard Aleksandar. He knows we have Mr. Gordon and claims we're here to take the rest of them."

Frustration boils within me. "But that's bullshit."

"I know that and you know that." Rayne frowns. "I'm quite certain even *he* knows that, but the rest of these people are afraid and without a strong leader."

"Uh, hello?" Pete clears their throat.

Rayne arches her eyebrow. "Yes?"

Silence.

She continues. "He was the one who ordered you driven off pack territory this morning. This is no longer a safe place for any of us."

"We're pack-friends—"

"Only so long as the alpha who ordered it remains in control of the pack." Her grip tightens on my arm. "Come on, Danika. We can't stay here. You have to know that."

"But Wendy…"

She shakes her head. "We'll find another way. Please. Before it's too late."

No. No way. There has to be a way I can fix this. There has to be something I can do to help Wendy and get him out of that cell. I can't leave him there.

I pull my arm away. "We're focusing on the wrong things here. We're supposed to be investigating this potential new pack and figuring out who framed Wendy. We need information."

Pete sighs. "All we know about the new wolves is that they're physically strong and, like, major powerful. And they're recruiting. As for Wensleydale, I can vouch for him whenever you want. I've known him, like, since I was a kid so I'm an awesome character reference. He would never hurt anybody the way they said. Like, for real."

"But who would?"

"You really have to ask?"

My mind darts back to the man outside. "Aleksandar. Are you sure?"

Another sigh from Pete. Part of me begins to wonder if they have some sort of lung capacity issue.

"Are you blind? Like, I don't know what's happening in SPEAR, but down here? We have our own problems to deal with. It's not all about you guys. Internal pack politics boils over all the time, but we'll handle it. Like always. Yeah, I'm seventeen, but I've been Wensleydale's second for three years. There's a reason for that."

I snort. "Yeah, that being no one wants to challenge a child to a death match."

"I'm not a child."

Loud howls break through our argument, long, high, and haunting. Damn it. What's happening now?

Rayne growls and shifts her weight to the balls of her feet. Pete dashes over to the window. I follow.

Down on the pavement, close to my car, a huge half-circle of pack members, almost three deep surrounds the tiny cluster of Pete's followers close to the door. Between the two groups stands Aleksandar, one hand on his hip.

"What's happening?"

Pete grunts. "Stay here." And they're gone, out the door and down the stairs with a clatter of heavy booted feet.

Stay? Ha, right.

I'm already moving, through the dim room toward the door. I'm aware of Rayne behind me, a silent, deadly presence at my back. She doesn't speak, but I can feel the tension on her like a prickly jacket.

On the landing to the three apartments, the woman with the tattoos cuts across our path with outstretched arms.

"What are you doing?"

"I need to see what's happening."

"You *need* to stay here."

I look her up and down. Yeah, tall and slender. I could probably take her. Then again, she is *edane.*

"I have to—"

"We want to put our support behind Mx. Dunn." Rayne speaks over me, softly but with urgency. "We know it's not our place to interfere, but our teammates are also outside. We should join them."

"Oh. Yeah, um. That makes sense."

"We've no intention of putting ourselves between Mx. Dunn and what must be done."

"Your word on it?"

Rayne touches her chest. "My word and my bond."

"Right. Um, then I guess that's all right."

"Great." Enough of the pleasantries, I have to get out there. "Move it, spirals." I shove past her and down the stairs, hurrying as much as possible without risking a twisted ankle. In moments, I'm at the bottom, through the door, and out onto the street…straight into the back of Pete who stands facing outward.

They right me as I stumble, but otherwise ignore me.

"Ah, and here she is." Aleksandar smiles my way, flashing unnaturally white teeth. He gestures to his companions. "Agent Karson. Your interference here belittles our pack and our power. Any leader in their right mind would ensure that you left as quickly as possible since you don't belong here."

Pete sighs, but gives the smallest of nods. "You need to leave, Agent. This isn't your fight and, like, we've not broken any laws. There's no reason to stay. I've got this."

"But—"

"Just stop, okay? You need to get out of here."

I eye the crowd. I know they're watching, both sides, following my every move with near hungry intensity. "Pete, please. Let me back you up. You know you need me. Wendy needs me."

Aleksandar's chuckles. His smile grows even wider. "Need you? We don't *need* you, Agent, none of us do. Or rather, only the weakest of us do. Do you *need* her, Petra? Do you *need* help from outside the pack to guide us while our leader is under SPEAR control?"

The silence and expectancy those words carry are thick enough to feel. I can taste it.

Pete shifts uncomfortably, mouth opening, closing, then opening again.

Shit.

"It's not SPEAR control." I step forward. "We all know Wendy was falsely accused. All we want to do is find evidence of that."

"So why come here? You think one of us framed him?" Aleksandar glances back at his followers before continuing. "You think one of us could be so dishonest and calculating as to conspire against our alpha? You dare insult us?"

Even the wolves siding with Pete begin to murmur at that one.

Still Aleksandar goes on. "Petra, will you allow this human to come onto *our* land and talk to us like this? Exercise your right as acting alpha and control her at once."

At last they turn to me. "You need to leave, Agent."

"No." I allow my voice to drop to a heated whisper. "Don't you see what's happening here? If I leave now, you'll have no one and—"

"I'll have the pack. You need to get out of here, while you still can. I'm serious."

"But—"

Aleksandar snarls, soft but menacing. "Pathetic. Do you see? This is what I've been talking about. Petra can't control a single human, let alone this pack. Since Wensleydale was taken this morning, two more of our number have been arrested. Before that, three went missing. Between you and our *alpha,* our pack is going to fade away into nothing."

"But—"

"Shut up, human." Aleksandar's eyes flash with fury. "I've known it from the start. I've known it since you marched down here and took half our number on some fanger-based death mission. Four brothers and sisters died in Club Starshine and now you're back to gather more fodder from our numbers. How dare you use us like that?"

Starshine? Oh, bloody hell.

At last I recall Aleksandar's face. This is the guy who spoke against Wendy the last time Angbec grew hot. This is the same wolf who refused to join the mission with me against Vixen and the rest of her nest. The one who refused to bow and show his neck when Wendy gave his pack the option to stay out of the fight.

A chill ripples through me.

Even back then I said that lad would be trouble. I warned Wendy. He brushed it off to help me, but we both knew what kind of trouble such open disrespect could cause.

How long has Aleksandar been playing this game? How much time has he spent planting the seeds of dissent, building up his own little offshoot of followers?

"Wait—"

But Aleksandar doesn't wait. He speaks faster and louder, now jabbing a stiff finger right at Pete's startled face.

"This is *your* fault, Petra and I won't stand by and let you kill us all one by one. Our alpha is gone and we need a strong leader to keep us together. But that leader isn't you."

I know what's coming. I can feel it on the air. "Wait, Aleksandar—"

"Without our alpha we're as good as sitting ducks waiting to be swept up by SPEAR or this new pack threatening us and everybody else."

"Will you just listen to me—"

"Face it, Petra, you can't guide us. You never could."

"Please—"

"From the start it was clear Wensleydale gave you his second position out of pity, nothing more. He knew as well as the rest of us that you would never challenge him because you're too weak. You're. No. Threat."

Pete seems to sink lower and lower with every word. Their gaze drops to the ground and stays there. "I'm doing my best—"

"Your best isn't good enough. It never was. And now, without Wensleydale here to protect you I think it's time I proved that to everyone else."

"Wait—" This time Rayne is the one to cut me off, snatching at my arm and yanking me back to the side. She shakes her head. I let out a whine of frustration and silently beg Pete to lift their head.

Pete flinches but keeps talking. "I don't need Wensleydale's protection."

"Good." A chuckle from Aleksandar. "Then at least this will be a fair fight. Petra Dunn of the Dire Wolves, chosen second in command…I challenge you."

Oh, shit.

Chapter Thirteen

The words are like a hammer on the fragile truce between both sides. The moment they leave Aleksandar's mouth, both sides of watching wolves break apart into clear, wholly uneven factions. Those around Aleksandar begin to shout and punch the air while those closest to Pete form a thick protective ring around them.

There are others, a mere handful that stand in the centre, avoiding both sides. They huddle together like children though their backs are together and their faces pointed outward. Their position is perhaps more dangerous than Pete's and it's clear they know it.

Rayne's grip tightens on my arm. "We need to get back to the team."

"No—"

"Yes. You know there's nothing we can do now. We need to get out of the way before this starts."

From the corner of my eye I see Aleksandar grinning, accepting praise and well-wishes from his huge cluster of followers. There is no hesitation or regret in his expression or actions, just excitement and eagerness.

When he spies me staring, he pauses long enough to thumb his nose and blow a lewd kiss in my direction.

I take a step.

Rayne yanks me back. "We need to get to the van."

"But—"

"Now, Danika."

And then we're running.

I can hear the wolves behind us preparing for the fight, the dominance battle that will decide who rules the pack in Wendy's absence.

This is so bad. We don't have time for this right now, there are more important things to be worrying about, and—

The first punch is loud enough that even I can hear it. The thick, meaty thud of bony fist against squishy face.

Pete skids toward on us on the ground, mouth and nose dribbling bright red blood. They snarl and flip onto their front, balanced lightly on hands and knees. A ripple across their back and arms shows the change beginning to take over.

"Move." Rayne hurries me ahead of her.

At the van the rest of my team stands at the open doors, beckoning me through. One gargoyle named Hawk, two werewolves playfully nicknamed Solo and Duo, a goblin we've named Erkyan, and a willow sprite who conveniently calls herself...Willow. Erkyan, Hawk, and Willow wear expressions of horror and fear, though the two werewolves, currently in their human form, peer past me toward the mayhem happening behind.

Rayne is first into the van and leans out to pull me in, but I stop just short of the doors. Turn.

"Danika."

I can't. I need to see.

Pete is already up, wiping blood smears from a face growing increasingly furry. Where once small and delicate, their body morphs into something huge, wide, and fierce. Muscles ripple beneath melting skin and their mouth yawns wide in a roar of rage. Their fur is sleek and white as snow, or chalk if the nickname is to be believed.

They bound upright and dive forward, sprinting across the short space between themselves and Aleksandar who has yet to shift.

The pair collide with a thud I feel on the air, and they immediately settle into a rhythm of biting, punching, and kicking.

My insides twist and writhe.

Pete can't win, not like this. They're too weak, they're—

Aleksandar's body spins through the air like a hurled ragdoll. He lands on top of my car with a sickening crunch and sinks deep into the metal which bows beneath his weight and impact. Pete follows with a bound, landing on the bonnet and scoring the paintwork with sharp, deadly claws.

Oh, well. I've been saying for a while that I need a new car.

The watching crowd shifts to accommodate the movement of the action, always keeping the fight to the centre. The motion blocks my view, leaving me with growls, yells, and snarls to interpret.

"Hey, Hawk, boost me."

The gargoyle frowns and sneaks a glance back at Rayne.

"I'm not going to do anything stupid. Just boost me up. I need to see. Come on, Hawk."

Again he hesitates.

"Fine." I dart round the front of the van and scramble up onto the bonnet. A quick two-step takes me up the windshield and another scramble gets me on the roof.

From this new vantage I can see Aleksandar prying himself free of groaning, twisted metal. He does it with a roar and a flex of freshly enlarged muscles. When he stands, the car groans even further under the increased weight.

Yeah, that pile of scrap metal won't be driving anywhere now.

"Fight me properly, Petra." His voice is a horrifying blend of animal and man. "You call that fighting? You're weak. You're pathetic. You don't have the power to lead us—"

A huge slab of white fur and muscle tackles him clear off the roof of the car.

Other wolves scatter and the pair resume their battle on the ground.

I've seen werewolf battles before. Even at Club Starshine with Rayne, we caught the tail end of a dominance battle spilling from the bathrooms onto the dance floor. But this is something else. This is deadly and terrifying in a way I've never seen.

Pete is huge, the largest creature I've ever seen that didn't have troll blood. Their huge red eyes are wide and angry, ringed by bloodied white fur. Their claws are pale, though long and sharp, with teeth sized to match. By comparison, Aleksandar is whippet slender, though muscled and lithe. His fur is a patchwork of grey and black, with small hints of white around his amber eyes.

Both roar at each other, furious bellows of defiance and rage.

And then they clash again.

Aleksandar slashes with huge, heavy claws, while Pete ducks out of reach. Then Pete snarls and aims a bite that goes wide as Aleksandar darts to the side. The fight is a dance, a graceful, powerful, deadly ballet that can only end one way.

None of the other wolves have shifted, just staying close to bear witness. I see one or two of them swapping money, while others point and stare, and a few of them even begin to laugh.

Soon Pete's fur is splotched pink and dozens of crimson droplets dot the ground.

I tell myself that the white fur makes it look worse, but the panting, yelling, and gasping doesn't help.

Then again…Aleksandar runs in from the left, feinting side to side before driving upward with a powerful punch. It grazes Pete's chin, then nothing but air as the huge white form bends like a sapling in a stiff breeze. Aleksandar stumbles, cursing and shaking his furry fist.

If Pete looks a little the worse for wear, then Aleksandar is truly struggling. His own breath comes in rasping little gasps and several long claw-slashes mark his once smooth fur.

I find myself punching at the air, grinning and stamping my feet. The van rocks beneath me, causing startled yelps from inside, but I don't care. Pete could actually win this.

My companions still watch with wary eyes, Rayne especially sharing her gaze between the action and myself. She frowns up at me.

I glare right back. "It's going to be okay."

"You sure about that?"

"Ye—"

Hawk gives a loud yell. I have just enough time to see him scoop Erkyan and Willow into his arms before he leaps into the air, barely avoiding Aleksandar as he slams into the side of the van.

The whole vehicle wobbles from side to side forcing me to duck low and cling or be thrown. From inside, Rayne gives a startled yelp while both Duo and Solo growl menacingly.

Aleksandar peels himself from the paintwork limping and shaking his head. For the first time, an expression of fear fills his eyes. He hauls himself upright and faces the crowd boiling around our van. His followers still call and shout and cheer, but his gaze is all for Pete.

The beastly white form stalks forward on powerful digitigrade legs, bushy tail swishing for balance. Huge muscled arms spread wide, pale claws gleaming like knives. "Stand down, Aleksandar." Even the voice is pure animal, low and rough and powerful.

How can the small, soft, and timid Pete shift to become this hybrid monstrosity?

I find myself glued to the spot, unable to move or even think about doing so. Maybe I misjudged them. Maybe they really do have this in hand and Aleksandar is about to experience a rude awakening.

Aleksandar turns to our van, amber eyes wide and frightened. He spies me, Rayne, then Duo and Solo. His wide nostrils flare with a loud exhale of rage. "You two should be ashamed. Which pack did you abandon to join SPEAR?"

Solo and Duo share a glance. As ever it's a little unsettling to see two identical faces and bodies right beside each other, but I've become used to the werewolf twins.

In perfect sync, both Duo and Solo arch their left eyebrows.

"Don't distract yourself," says Duo.

"You'll lose," adds Solo.

As if to compound the sentiment, Pete steps closer still, clawed toes grinding at the road. "Do you yield?"

The fear melts away as though never present at all. "Never. I yield to no one, certainly not the likes of you, too concerned with what's happening outside the pack to protect your own." Aleksandar begins to sidestep, always with his back to the van.

"It doesn't have to be this way."

I have to commend Pete for trying, even now, to use words. It won't work, I know that, but the effort causes me to pause long enough to admire their efforts. Though I struggle to admit it, I know Wendy would be proud.

Then Aleksandar leaps onto the roof of the van.

I've no idea what he's intending, but Rayne and Pete clearly make the same leap in logic because several things happen at once.

Rayne slithers out of the van like an eel, eyes burning the brightest, glittering silver. She claws at Aleksandar's legs even as Pete dives past her to grab his departing tail. They both pull, yanking Aleksandar away from me even as Hawk drops out of the sky beside me and tries to scoop me off the van.

I bat at his hands, still trying to see, still trying to watch Pete win this impossible fight.

But this interference seems just what Aleksandar is waiting for because instead of pursuing me, he releases his grip on the roof and slides down as both Rayne and Pete want. Then, on the ground, he flips onto his back, slips between Pete's legs, and shuts his powerful jaws on their tail.

Pete howls in fury and pain, scrambling back to escape. But the grip is too strong and without the tail to counterbalance the huge body, Pete tumbles over in a heap on the road.

Aleksandar wastes no time in pressing the advantage. Never once releasing his grip on the tail, he spins again and sinks both sets of claws into Pete's stomach.

Blood bubbles up through the horrendous wounds and another feral bellow cuts the night.

Rayne reaches the roof just as Hawk pins my wrists and the pair drag me down to the ground on the other side. Away from the fight.

"No. No, I need to see."

"Danika—"

"Get off me."

"Wait a second—"

"Let go."

A shrill, startled yelp cuts the air, followed by a thick, wet tearing sound.

Then silence.

Even the bellowing crowd of onlookers has stilled.

Trapped between Rayne and Hawk, I can hear the petrified hammering of my own racing heart.

"What happened?"

More silence.

"Pete?" My heart is in my throat. "Pete?"

More wet tearing. A sharp gasp from dozens of throats.

Then a bone rattling cheer.

Our van crunches beneath new weight as a furry figure bounds onto the roof. A tall, slender figure with sleek fur in patches of grey and black. A figure holding something long, white, and dripping bright red blood.

Hawk swallows audibly. "Is that...?"

"Mx. Dunn's tail," whispers Rayne.

Nausea bubbles within me. I choke it down as best I can, but my stomach still turns in tight, coiling knots. "Pete? Pete, say something."

The cheers intensify. I can hardly hear anything now, just the roar of many voices calling and shouting, cries that gradually morph into a low, chilling chant. "Aleksandar...Aleksandar...Aleksandar...Aleksandar..."

A small stream of red flows between the front wheels of the van, slow, sluggish, and choked with clots of fur and thicker lumps of gore.

"Pete."

"Aleksandar...Aleksandar...Aleksandar...Aleksandar..."

Stamping feet now, marking out the rhythm of that chant.

"Aleksandar...Aleksandar...Aleksandar..."

"Pete, please, say something—fuck's sake, will you two let go."

At last, both Hawk and Rayne release me.

I run around the van, but the crowd there is too thick and no amount of shoving will get me through. The wolves are a closed wall, blocking the scene from view.

"Pete. Please, Pete, speak to me."

"Aleksandar...Aleksandar...Aleksandar..."

Someone howls. The call is copied. Then again. And again. And again.

Within moments, all but a few of the wolves are howling and calling, some even beginning to shift as the excitement gets the better of them.

"Aleksandar...Dire Wolf...Dire Wolf...Aleksandar...Dire Wolf..."

"It's over." Aleksandar holds the torn tail high above his head, mindless of the blood dripping from the severed end. "Petra fought and lost and now...I lead you."

"Dire Wolf...Dire Wolf...Dire Wolf..."

"With our alpha gone, captured unlawfully by SPEAR, it's up to us to do what he couldn't. We'll rescue him. We'll do what that," he points downward, "pathetic screw-up couldn't or wouldn't do. But before we do that..." a long, drawn-out pause. "We'll clean our land."

Ice floods my body. Again I shove at the wall of bodies and this time someone moves. It's not much, but enough to allow me glimpses of Pete prone on the ground in a spreading pool of blood. One ear is mangled and torn, the other ripped almost wholly off. A gaping hole at the base of the spine pumps a steady flow of blood that first soaks into fur before joining the widening stream running off down the street.

Worse still, they're not moving.

"Get that pale furred mongrel out of my sight. We don't need weakness like that in our pack. It's about time we culled the weakest from our pack, from our blood. Pups like that have no place among us Dire Wolves."

"Dire Wolf...Dire Wolf...Dire Wolf...Dire Wolf..."

In snatches and half glances, I can see some of Pete's followers lift them from the ground. Body limp, arms dangling, they carry the maimed form to the inner edge of the circle of onlookers. But they can't get through either.

"I'm not without mercy," Aleksandar goes on, now speaking with a smug smile on his face. "Those of you who disobey will be punished or cast out. Maybe both. Those who show sense and follow me...well, you'll be able to tell Wensleydale that you were one of those who did everything in your power to protect our territory and our land. Make the choice quickly. We have work to do."

"Aleksandar." I have to bellow to be heard above the din, but his ears twitch in my direction as I speak. "Aleksandar, stop this. Please, you have to—"

"Have to? I *have* to?" The furry form slides off the roof of the van. The crowd scatters to make space immediately, giving him a clear path toward me. "I don't *have* to do anything you say, SPEAR agent. Unless we break a law, you have no power here."

Actually I do. The words are almost on my lips before I recognise how foolish that would be. Now, more than ever, it's imperative that Aleksandar never learn that Wendy pledged himself to me. I'd be dead in seconds and Wendy himself would soon follow.

"You killed Pete."

"I merely showed Petra what true strength and power is. But a young thing like that? I couldn't kill. No, no, never. Maim?" He shakes the tail, scattering blood everywhere. "Perhaps maim, yes, but I'd never kill."

"But—"

"Now you and your team have interfered quite enough. I'd thank you, but it might set a dangerous precedent. Instead, I'm giving you thirty seconds to clear off pack territory."

I bunch my hands into fists. "You can't do that."

"I just did. Twenty-nine."

"Aleksandar—"

"Twenty-eight."

Rayne grabs my arm. Her skin is a queer shade of green, but she still manages to yank me back against her and drive us both toward the open van. "Come on."

"But Pete—"

"Will be better off than us if we don't move."

"But—"

"Your fanger friend is right, Agent. Twenty-seven."

I don't know what to do.

How could this escalate so quickly? How could Pete lose? Why wasn't I able to help?

Duo and Solo are already in the front seat. The engine starts with a roar and Rayne bundles me in through the side door, following close behind to trap me there.

Hawk shuts it from the outside, then takes to the skies without looking back.

From in here, the yells, chanting, and howling are muted but not wholly gone. I sit on one of the edge seats, numbed and silent, obediently following a touch to my wrist and lifting my arm.

Rayne snaps a seat belt in place around me then double taps the front two seats.

Then we're moving, leaping forward with a squeal of grinding gears. Another crunch as Aleksandar leaps off the roof and a yelp of surprise from upfront as the remnants of Pete's tail slides down the windshield.

I lower my head to my hands and take a couple of deep breaths.

They don't help. Not even a little bit.

CHAPTER FOURTEEN

About half a mile away, Duo stops the van. He leans back over the top of his seat, peering at me and Rayne. Ugh, who am I kidding, he's looking at me.

Solo mirrors the gesture leaning over his own seat with the edge of his bottom lip pulled up between his teeth. "Are you okay?"

Redundant questions for all, please.

I shake my head. "What have I done?"

"Nothing—"

"Wendy trusted me." I cut across Rayne with a grunt. "He came to SPEAR specifically looking for me and look what happened."

"You couldn't have stopped that, Danika. None of us could."

"But—"

Rayne touches my arm. "You really think your actions kick-started that? Come on, Aleksandar was undermining Mx. Dunn before we ever arrived and look how many of the pack were behind him. This is *not* your doing."

"But—"

Solo clears his throat. "She's right, Danika. You're human, you can't see it, but I can."

"And me." Duo looks to his brother. "It was so strong."

"We could smell it—"

"—and so could every other wolf there."

"Aleksandar is a fighter—"

"—a born leader—"

"—and he never would have allowed Chalks to lead for as long as he did—"

"Except Wensleydale was always around."

"But not today."

"Okay, okay, you two." I lift my hand. "Can you stop that for a second. It freaks me out."

Both hang their heads in perfect unison. "Sorry." Their voices come out as one.

Bloody hell.

A thump outside our van signals Hawk returning. He arrives with both Erkyan and Willow, the first clinging to his back, the second cradled in his arms.

All three are clearly shaken, Hawk perhaps more than the others. Several dots of blood mark his pale green face. His clawed hands shake as he wipes the marks away, the long spines of his wings trembling to match.

He swears, something truly filthy and angry. I know most of the words, but Gargoyle isn't a language I know well. The gist is clear enough though.

I jerk the doors open and step out onto the street.

Wow. Even from so far away, I can hear the remnants of the fight. Howls, calls, and yells, carrying on the night air. My skin crawls.

"Okay, we need to calm down." Not sure who I'm telling, but I need the pep talk as much as anybody else. "If we stay calm and think this through, it will be fine. We just need to figure out the next steps."

Duo grunts. "There are no next steps."

"Aleksandar won. The fight is over." Solo climbs out of the van.

"But—"

"He. Won. It's over." There's quiet regret in Solo's voice, but he adds no more than that. Instead he walks back along the street, head bowed, hands clenched into fists.

I let him go. "Okay, fine. So he leads the pack now. What about Wendy?"

Rayne steps close to my side. Her body is still and silent, but her presence is a comfort even now. I'd give a lot for a brief moment alone with her, just to feel her arms around me.

As if sensing my thoughts, she reaches for my hand. Her fingers brush mine for the briefest moment before sliding away. "We still have a job to do," she says. "Remember? It's not just Mr. Gordan's pack. We need to figure out why werewolves as a whole are acting as they are. Perhaps we can visit another pack and get some answers."

Willow smiles at me. Her teeth are slightly green and pointed, her eyes wide around slitted pupils. Her hands move, a little flutter of signs and patterns with long, dexterous fingers.

"We will work together."

Or at least I think that's what she says. Sprite Sign is still new to me, but I have enough for basic conversation.

I flutter my own hands and fingers in response. *"Thank you."*

Her smile widens.

Back to Rayne. "Next stop is Grey Tail, then. They aren't as accommodating as the Dire Wolves, but that's still somewhere to start. You guys up for that?"

Hawk, Erkyan, and Willow all nod. I glance back to the van at Duo, but he doesn't seem to have heard me. He's still at the wheel, clutching it with both hands.

For the first time, I notice how pale his knuckles are and that his eyes are scrunched tightly shut. In fact, his entire body is tense, muscles coiled up like a spring.

"Duo?"

His eyes snap open. "Get in the van."

"Huh?"

"Right now, everyone in."

The urgency in his voice propels all of us into immediate action. Erkyan and Willow move first, diving through the open doors without a word. Hawk eyes the vehicle, then bounds upward, landing lightly on the outstretched arm of a nearby street lamp.

Rayne pulls at me.

"What's happening? And what about Solo?"

"The Dire Wolves are moving," Duo snaps. "He'll follow at a distance, but we need to get off the road."

"What?"

"Move."

Back into the van again, but not before I finally notice the sound previously on the edge of my hearing.

All that yelling and howling, it's closer now. Close enough in fact that I'm stunned I hadn't heard it clearly before. With it I catch a rumbling sound, like marching, but there are too many feet for it to be anything as human and mundane as marching.

No, this is something else.

Rayne slams the door just as Duo guns the engine.

The van leaps forward, ka-chunking swiftly through gears.

Duo's eyes are narrowed, his hands carefully positioned at two and ten. He speeds us away from the edge of pack territory and toward more populated and touristy areas outside the Bowl.

But the sound of howls is gaining on us.

"One of you get the radio," I call out while moving toward the back of the van, smearing condensation with my hand to better see through the glass.

Nothing. Just empty streets.

Why then do I feel so sick and tense? Why is my stomach knotted with deep, crawling fear?

Static crackles through the vehicle's speakers followed by Duo's stiff voice.

"Hawk, you got eyes up there? What's happening?"

More crackling and then, "Uh…do you want the good news or the bad news?"

Great.

"Tell us, Hawk." Still I watch our rear. "What's happening?"

"Good news is, I can see Solo and he's fine. He's wedged under a car on the outskirts of Dire Wolf territory. I think they know he's there, but no one seems to care."

Duo grunts from his position up front. "He's fine. What's the bad news?"

A pause.

"Hawk?"

"They're moving. The Dire Wolves I mean."

"What?" I crane my neck, but from within the vehicle there's no way I can see him. "What are you talking about?"

"Aleksandar is at the front, still in hybrid form. Dozens of others, maybe all of them, are with him. They're running."

"Where?"

"You don't want to know."

"I think I do, Hawk. What's happening?"

The others gather around me, now fighting to see out the back window. They needn't have bothered.

Around a corner at the end of the road strides a single werewolf in hybrid form. An instant later comes another. And another. And another.

Within seconds, the road at our rear is a boiling mass of sprinting monsters, a wave that swells and engulfs our vehicle in seconds.

Duo puts his foot down, but we're not fast enough.

The wolves overtake us en masse, flowing around us, over us, never once stopping, but buffeting us from every angle as they continue on their way.

Erkyan screams and waves her tiny fists, while Willow joins in. Her screams aren't cries so much as breathy, rasping gasps, like skeletal twigs brushing together in a high wind.

Only Rayne and I remain calm, our fingers entwined.

She stares at me. "You didn't do this."

"Rayne—"

"You *didn't* do this. You even said so yourself—Aleksandar has been undermining Mx. Dunn's position for a while."

And just like that, it all falls into place.

Fuck. How could I have been so stupid?

The attack this morning, the snide and snippy comments within earshot of other pack members. Even sending Pete on some wild goose chase to pick up supposed new werewolves. It has all been a set-up. Right from the start.

All those threads, all those little, seemingly innocent actions, all leading to this.

"He wanted this. He wanted an excuse to fight Pete, and I...I gave it to him."

"Danika..."

"Stop it. Can't you see? Aleksandar set me up. He set us all up. Giving wolf descriptions to SPEAR, getting Wendy out of the way. Once he'd done that all he needed to do was take down Pete."

"But why? If he wanted control of the pack why not just do it without all this fuss?"

I sigh. "Would *you* want to fight a wolf with Wensleydale's reputation? This way he doesn't have to."

At last the pack of hybrid wolves moving around us ebbs, then fades to nothing. The last wolf bounds off our roof with a joyful howl and speeds away into the night.

Duo stops the van, drawing a heavy breath through pursed lips.

The speakers crackle. "Guys?"

I sigh. "Yes, Hawk?"

"They're heading for the West Side."

Ice floods my veins.

At this time of night, even on a weekday, the West Side is a roaring hub of tourist activity. For humans, the West Side is the safest place to enjoy *edane* culture with shops, restaurants, clubs, and bars all open from dusk until dawn.

Willow stamps her foot. Once she has my gaze, she signs at me. *"We have to stop them."*

"I know, but—"

Another foot stamp. *"Civilians in the area. They must be protected from the cucumber."*

I frown. "Cucumber?"

Erkyan giggles.

Willows rolls her eyes and signs again. *"Danger."*

A rippling snarl from up front draws my attention to Duo.

He has his eyes closed again, though this time, his hands are pressed to his temples. His lips move, though no words come out. He seems to be arguing, though for the life of me I don't understand how.

A second later his eyes fly open and he pounds both fists against the steering wheel. "Chalks is hurt. Badly. He can't move."

"What? How do you—"

"Solo is there. He says he needs medical aid."

Ah. So these two must have been Fire Fangs before they joined SPEAR.

Well, shit. Can anything else possibly get fucked up tonight?

"Where's the rest of the pack?"

"With Aleksandar."

That makes me wince. "All of them? What about those who were with Pete? What happened to them?"

Duo stares at me. The expression in his eyes is enough.

Fuck.

"Solo can move Chalks, but it will be slow. Without help the blood loss will kill him."

"Can't he shift back?"

A brief pause. Duo seems to look inward for brief moments. "No. The injuries are too severe."

No need to ask how he knows. I've seen enough oddness and magic in my time to know he has some strange connection with his twin, either from simply being a twin or from starting his werewolf life as a Fire Fang. I don't have to understand it to make use of it.

"We need to go back."

Willow makes a horrid little rasping noise, like tree branches splintering. Her hands move quick and jerky. It's far too quick for me to catch the signs, but I know what she's saying.

"But we can't leave him there."

For the first time, Erkyan speaks. "You'd trade all the civilians of the West Side for one werewolf?"

Ouch.

"Of course not, but—"

"Then let us go do our job."

I cover my face with my hands. She's right, but can I really leave Chalks out there, alone and dying when it's my fault this happened?

And what would Wendy say?

For the first time in a while, I remember that Rayne is still holding my hand. I notice because she squeezes my fingers with hers. It seems an age since we've touched.

"The entire pack is mobile," her voice is soft and low, but I know we can all hear it. "Nothing like this has ever happened before. At least not in such a heavily populated city like this one. We have to call it in because we can't handle it alone anyway."

"Fine. Do that. I'll go back to the Bowl and help Chalks."

The grip on my fingers becomes crushing.

"Okay, okay, you come with me. Just calm down. That's my gun hand."

Duo looks ahead. "I won't have all werewolves smeared by Aleksandar's actions. I'm going out there to stop him."

"But—"

"But nothing. That one is rotten, Danika. He even smells bad. If he does something to hurt people, who do you think will get the blame? Not you, not SPEAR, not Wensleydale, but *all* wolves. I'm going after him. And I'm taking the van."

Our roof rumbles, then gives a little on one side. Moments later, Hawk drops to the ground outside the window. He yanks open the door. "I'll take you back. I can fly quicker than this heap of junk anyway."

I stare at him for long seconds. "Thank you."

He shrugs. "You're a good person, Danika. For a human. And a good leader. I want to help you."

"Good, then let's get out of here. Duo, you take the others on. All of you fit an earpiece and stay on comms. We'll be in touch once Chalks is safe."

Erkyan passes out the small communications earpieces while I clamber out the van. Rayne follows close behind, fitting hers on the way.

Her eyes glitter with traces of silver as she watches me scramble onto Hawk's back. "You're not going without me," she mutters.

Hawk grins. "Then keep up, fanger. We'll stay in contact." He taps his left ear where his own comms earpiece is already in place and bends his legs.

I have just enough time to grab my own device before Hawk bounds into the air with a spring like a goat.

Fuck.

My stomach threatens to drop out of my body, and I cling to his shoulders with my eyes scrunched shut. I tell myself this is worth it, that this is the best and quickest way to get back to the Bowl and save Chalks.

Just the same, as Hawk puts on a burst of speed with a powerful flap of his wings, my guts flip-flop and try to escape through my nose.

I would rather have walked.

Chapter Fifteen

I want to throw up. I'm going to throw up. I do throw up.

Right at the last moment, Hawk twirls in the air, a horrible manoeuvre that leaves me upside down but also allows the thin trail of vomit to hit the ground instead of his shoulder.

"What the fuck, Hawk?"

He chuckles. "You should get used to travel like this. It's so much faster."

"Never. Never-the-fuck-ever again. Put me down."

"But we're not—"

"Hawk, so help me, I will vomit in your ear."

That stops his chuckles flat. Within seconds, we're swooping down and I'm swinging my legs to the side to land neatly on the pavement. At least that's my plan. Instead the momentum carries me on too far and I stumble several paces before landing on my knees…and retching like an invalid.

Great.

Hawk lands in a crouch beside me, careful to sweep his tail away from the puddle. "I'm sorry. I had no idea you were such a bad flier. You've never done that before?"

"I don't have wings."

He shrugs and straightens to his full height. "Get up."

Still groaning and grumbling, I stand and take in my surroundings. Quiet. Eerily so.

We're back within Dire Wolf territory, but I can't see a single wolf. There are signs of their passing, more trampled cars, the occasional tuft of fur, but of a living soul? Nothing.

The air feels heavy but weary, as though put through great trials. A weird sensation, but I can't figure out how else to describe it. The area has seen great battle and now is winding down.

"Come on."

"What about Rayne?"

I offer Hawk a wry smile. "She'll catch up."

We continue the rest of the way on foot, me jogging, Hawk bounding along on hands and toes. He moves with the smooth, loping gait of a cat, tail hooked out for balance. So strange to see him move that way, switching so easily between two limbs and four.

A few yards on we find the first body. A woman, naked but for a few scraps of shredded denim, probably from where she tried to shift. Her body is a patchwork of deep gouges and teeth marks, her mouth spread wide in a silent scream. A little after that, two men—boys really—huddle close together with their fingers just touching. It's hard to tell through all the blood, but I suspect that these are some of those loyal to Pete.

The bodies increase in number now, some faces I recognize, others I don't. It looks as though not *every* member of the pack was willing to follow Aleksandar on his little mission. Those who objected clearly weren't given much of an alternative, but at least they went down fighting. Fighting for themselves, for Pete, for Wendy.

I slow as I walk through this section, making sure to look into every single face. I need to remember these people and what they went through because of—

"This is awful."

Though Rayne echoes my sentiment, I half leap out of my skin to find her right at my side. She offers me a wry look as I press a hand to my chest. "Damn it, Rayne."

"You need to be more aware."

"And *you* need to be less sneaky."

She shrugs. "I told you I'd follow."

Yeah, but never mind how fast she must have been moving to catch up with us. I remind myself that there is still so much about vampires that I don't know and that no matter how human she looks, there is still very much of the predator about Rayne.

I can see it now as she jogs through the carnage with me, from the tense set of her shoulders, to the silver gleam in her eyes. The points of her fangs show between slightly parted lips, and I catch the first hints of a growl at the back of her throat.

With three of us together, Hawk goes back to the skies, scouting out ahead and behind, watching us from a clear vantage point. He calls down directions as we move, giving us shortcuts through alleys and over fences.

❖

Halfway back to the site of the battle we find Solo. He has shifted to better accommodate Pete's immense body, but still struggles beneath the dead weight. He sighs when we approach and lowers the panting form to the ground.

Pete looks half dead already. The once brilliant white fur is matted with fresh and drying blood. One ear is wholly gone, leaving nothing but a choked-out hole of gore and sinew. The other looks about ready to follow. A similar red mess marks where their tail once was, and even I can see that without it, Pete can't walk in this form.

Rayne hisses through her teeth and snatches up her phone. She barks into it, giving precise location details and directions to Omega who, from the sounds of it are already en route. Good. The quicker the better.

Pete looks up at me, their red eyes damp and lidded with pain. "Danika?"

"Hey. We're here to help. Don't talk."

"But Aleksandar—"

"We'll deal with him. We need to get you to a medi-team as quickly as possible."

Solo grunts and stretches his back until all the bones click. "Aleksandar is going for the new pack. He wanted to hunt them down and exterminate them the moment they showed up, but Wensleydale wouldn't let him. Now there's no one to get in the way."

"He can't do that."

"Of course he can." A shrug. "The pack is his until Wensleydale returns. He can do exactly as he likes. You can already see what happened to those who went against him. I don't think there's much we can do."

But there is. There's something *I* can do. But will that make it worse?

With Wendy pledged to me right now I have control of the pack. Not in a literal sense, but since I can simply tell Wendy to give his followers any order…what if I told them? What if I made clear that this isn't what Wendy wants and that I can act under my own authority?

As quickly as the thought comes I squash it flat. Wendy needs to maintain his aura of power and control. Now, more than ever, he can't afford to appear weak before his pack.

Pete groans, shaking from head to toe. "I have to warn Wensleydale. He has to know I failed him."

"Don't worry about that now—"

"He has to know. If I don't make it, you have to tell him. Please. Tell him Aleksandar took the pack and that there's no one left to watch his back. Tell him, Agent. Please."

"I…okay."

Relief shows visibly as a ripple of calm through every muscle. Pete flops back against the ground and closes their eyes.

Solo eyes me up and down. "Why are you here?"

"For Pete."

"I have him, you should have stayed with the others."

"Now wait a minute—"

"No, *you* wait," he snarls. "I know what Duo told you, I heard him. You don't need to be here right now. With those idiots heading out into who knows what, every agent available needs to be out there to protect the people."

"And what about *this* person?"

"You can't be everywhere at once. You can't save everybody nor should you try. I. Have. Chalks. Go on and meet with the others." He chuckles. "In fact, if you want to protect someone, watch over my idiot brother. He still owes me money and isn't allowed to die just yet."

A pause, then just like Duo did earlier, Solo seems to glance into himself. His furry shoulders buck with mirth. "And while you're at it, tell him only the weakest pups dine on scraps."

"I get the feeling you just told him that yourself."

My phone rings, ending the gentle banter.

A glance at the screen confuses me, another number I don't know. Solo shrugs and Rayne is still on her own phone so there's no one to run it by.

"Agent Danika Karson, who's calling?"

"Danika? Danika, where are you?"

I blink. "Jack?"

"Where are you?" His voice is frantic, the sounds around him loud and garbled. Is that screaming?

"I'm in Misona with the Dire Wolves. Or what's left of them. Where are you? What's going on?"

Jack is panting, speaking quickly and barely audible above the din around him. "I'm on Chadwick Road with some…some contractors. There's some sort of riot outside. What's happening?"

That feeling of nausea begins to bubble afresh inside me. "Stay inside. Don't go out under any circumstances."

"But I have to. The new protocol—" A loud boom echoes down the line obliterating anything else he might have said. For long, horrible seconds I hear nothing but screams, shouts, and the crashes of breaking glass and furniture.

"Jack? Hello, Jack? Jack. Say something."

Eventually he returns to the line, voice cracked and groggy. "There's werewolves everywhere. It's a riot. They're wrecking the place."

Solo looks up from Pete's rasping form. He growls.

I tighten my grip on the phone. "Werewolves?"

"Dozens of them. And they're fighting. It's insane out there. I thought you said you had this under control."

"I'm trying, Jack."

He cries out, vanishes from the line for a moment or two, then returns even more out of breath than before. "Rescue your team. I have no choice now. Keep them out of it, but I have to call them in."

"What? Who?" I feel my fingers shaking, on the phone hand and the free one, but I need to grip something or else I'll lose my mind. "Jack? Jack!"

Interference begins to mess with his voice. "I need...when...for the next...but they...and the military...can't have you...with the wolves... revival..."

"Jack? You're breaking up. Jack?"

"...part of Project Revival and then they...martial law and...you can't have the...inside SPEAR..."

I pull the phone away from my ear, despairing at the shitty signal. Solo snatches it from my grip and tucks the speaker right up into his own furry ear, listening intently. After several seconds of waiting he tosses it back to me.

"He's gone. What's happening?"

"I have no idea, but we need to get to Chadwick Street." I tap the button on the side of my communications earpiece. "Erkyan? Duo? What's going on?"

A pause, then Erkyan's voice. "This horrible. Rapid response comes, but we are too few. More wolves from other packs join."

Solo nods. "Duo says Aleksandar's movement has the other packs mobilized. They see it as an act of aggression. Frankly, can't say I disagree."

"But what does that mean? To wolves I mean."

"That's there's more than one pack we need to deal with tonight. And that we're going to need all the help we can get." He shrugs. "Like I said, I've got Chalks. You three get going."

Rayne hurries over, tucking her phone back into her pocket as she comes. "The Omega team is on the way, but they're having to take side streets. Some sort of riot is happening in the West Side and no one can get through."

"*We* can get through."

"Well, I can get there, but what about you?" She looks me up and down. "You're good, but..."

I glance to Hawk watching us from above. My stomach turns in miserable anticipation. "I think I'll have a lift."

CHAPTER SIXTEEN

This time flying with Hawk is made easier by the low height and reduced speed. We're barely above street level, watching the roads boil with people as we follow the path of devastation left by Aleksandar's followers. An easy trail to identify, marked by trampled cars, claw-gouged pavements, and bent street lamps.

Also below, Rayne sets the pace at a running speed, following directions from us above.

Seeing her from this angle is so strange, and even though I know I should be watching the road, I find myself watching her. The easy back and forth sway of her arms, the cyclic motion of her feet. Her hair ruffles lightly on the breeze of her own momentum, and each time she moves into the darkness between street lamps, her eyes blaze with vampire silver.

We all spot the first retreating figures long before they see us.

Two men, sprinting away from two bisecting streets where a pair of smoking cars lie crumpled nose to nose. They move with the panicked jerkiness of blind terror and stop only when they see Rayne. The first points and yells something about vampire monsters while the second freezes dead in his tracks. Then they dart left and down another street, anything to get as far away from us as possible.

Two streets on and it's like walking into a war zone.

Panicked civilians are everywhere while smashed up cars line the streets alongside broken storefronts and shattered glass. A fire burns bright through the window of a souvenir shop, and werewolves in both changed and hybrid forms roam through the madness.

Rayne ducks into a shop doorway and drops to a tight crouch. "What happened out here?"

I don't know but I can hazard a guess.

A couple of the wolves in hybrid form are fighting, not the full-on mercilessness of a dominance battle, but dangerous nonetheless. Their fight carries them back and forth across the street, destroying vehicles and scattering those humans still unlucky enough to be within range.

"Hawk?"

He takes us down, a tight but slow circle rather than the swooping dive like before. It's better for my stomach, but in truth, I can't dwell on it overmuch.

My gun is in my hand before my feet touch the ground. Several more people are running my way, and I point the weapon upward.

"Hey. Hey, this way, come on."

It takes time, but at last my voice carries through the din and people begin to swarm my way.

"Keep going, clear the area. Come on, now, get a move on. Let's go, move, move."

Apparently, all these frightened people need is a guide because as soon as I offer them a route, the flow of startled humans begins to change. Further on, nearest to the flames, Rayne follows my lead and starts directing people away from the area.

Hawk's voice crackles in my ear. "I'm going to look ahead."

"Fine, but stay off the ground unless you really have to land. I don't know what the vibe is, but I don't want you caught in it."

"Sure." The breeze of his passing overhead catches my hair and ruffles it. Then he's gone too.

The wolves are still fighting, but traveling further and further up the street as they go. They pay no mind to the humans around them, focused wholly on tearing fur and skin off their opponent in strips.

Rayne wades her way toward me. The silver is gone from her eyes now, but her expression is grim, her muscles tense. "Aleksandar has caused a major riot. He's dangerous."

"You're telling me."

"Should we keep going?"

"We have to." I start off again, still directing the odd straggler back and away from the fight. Rayne is at my back, keeping pace easily, her hands free of weapons, her eyes narrowed and focused.

I want to stop the fight, but without the rest of my team it would be suicide to try. I know Rayne could probably at least dent those two, but I'm more concerned now by the sounds of more screaming up ahead.

Traffic has ground to a halt, the road choked by abandoned cars.

Here the wolves are fighting again, and this time I see signs that there is another pack involved.

The Dire Wolves are abnormally large, even for werewolves. Once fully transformed, their wolf bodies are easily big enough for a large human to ride, almost like horses. Other packs are smaller, and even though they often have different subtler gifts, they're easy to spot when compared to a Dire Wolf.

I see some now, facing off against a massive beast with patchy black fur. Three surround the one Dire Wolf who bays and claws at the air with thick, heavy paws. Beneath it, the car on which it stands slowly but steadily bows under the weight.

Rayne is first to locate the source of the screams. "There's someone in there."

It takes me a moment, but there, sure enough, a pair of petrified faces are visible through the cracked and twisted windscreen. They've ducked low to avoid the bowing roof, but the doors are crushed and clearly can't be opened from the inside any more

I hear them calling, screaming, begging for help, and cut Rayne a sidelong glance.

She nods.

I heave a deep breath and aim straight for the car.

The three smaller wolves surrounding the first don't notice us approaching. They're too focused on their target and barely flinch when I fire a warning shot. One of them pauses long enough to scent the air. I don't know what he's looking for, but the scents on the breeze clearly upset him, because he bays again and launches a daring tackle at the figure on the roof.

The move drives the bigger creature to the ground, and then all four start again, a rhythm of biting, clawing, scratching, nipping, and growling.

I tug on the car doors. Sure enough, they're jammed. Or locked. Or both.

Inside, the couple is still screaming, crying, begging, pleading. The driver of the pair begins to climb backward over the seats, perhaps to try poking through a window.

"Think you can get in, Rayne?"

She eyes the vehicle. "Sure."

A set of claws scrabble against the back of the vehicle. More screaming from within.

"Do it. I'll cover."

I put my left shoulder against Rayne's right and train my gun outward.

Still the wolves ignore us, but their fight repeatedly edges closer and closer to the car. One of the smaller wolves slips around the back of the fight and creeps in ducked low to the ground. It dives in for a sneak attack, but a swipe from the Dire Wolf sends it careening into the car.

The whole vehicle shunts back six feet forcing both Rayne and me to duck out.

The screams from inside become feral howls of terror.

"I need to pull the door off."

The wolf at my feet stands, shaking its head. For the first time, it seems to see me and snarls hard and loud. Long streams of drool hang from bared teeth.

I level the gun. "Don't."

It steps forward.

I steady my aim. "Don't do it."

It leaps. I fire.

The shot goes wide, missing by several inches as I throw myself to the ground. I roll, over and over and sweep up to one knee, ready to aim again. But now I can't fire.

Rayne is in my path, holding the wolf above her head with one hand around the throat, another braced around the hips. The usual brown of her eyes is drowned out by silver, and her own fangs gleam in the mucky street lights. She spins on her heel like a discus thrower and hurls the wolf back into the fray.

It yelps as it goes, smashing through the others like a bowling ball through unsuspecting pins. All four crash down into a heap, temporarily stunned and slow.

"Cover," she yells, then returns her attention to the car. Rayne digs her fingers into the scratched and twisted metal of the passenger door. It grinds and scrapes but holds its shape as Rayne sets her stance then yanks the entire thing off the hinges.

My heart gives a slight flutter. Shock? Fear? Arousal? Who knows?

The pair inside scream again, now wedging themselves into the cramped foot well.

I run over and flash my badge through the mangled doorframe. "Hey, Hey, calm down. We're with SPEAR, don't panic. Stop screaming, damn it, we're here to help."

The woman is the first to catch herself. She looks first at her companion, then Rayne. I hear her swallow the boiling fear and I silently applaud the obvious effort she makes. "Thank you. Oh, God, what's happening? What's happening?"

"The wolves are—"

I cut across Rayne with a cleared throat. "You two need to get out of there. Let's go. If you run that way you can get away from the worst of the fighting. My colleague will keep watch over you from the air."

"But why are they fighting? I thought this was a peaceful city."

The man glares at her. "Come off it, Doreen, it's just like I said: any city filled with monsters is a riot waiting to happen. Just look at this place." He grabs her hand. "Let's get out of here." For the first time, he looks at me. "Look, uh, Agent, I don't know what's happening here, but you better fix it."

I hear the wolves begin to move, shaking off the stupor of their abrupt fall and looking for new targets.

I point. "Get going."

The man clutches his companion close and finally begins to move.

"Hawk? Hawk, you got them?"

Silence, and then, "Yeah. I got them. They're moving the right way, but it's a real shit show up ahead. You *need* to get in there and join the other teams."

"Guns out or herding?"

He chuckles through my earpiece. "Bit of both, boss. Bit of both."

"Okay, come on, Rayne. Rayne?"

She's still holding the door, eyes downcast, shoulders slumped. The tiniest bead of blood gathers in the corner of her mouth, then vanishes as she licks it away. I don't think she realizes she's done it.

"Rayne?"

Her gaze flicks toward me, then back to the ground. "Nothing's changed, has it? Not really?"

I know what she's talking about, and though everything in me longs to reassure her, I'm not sure I can. "Let's just keep moving."

"Fine. You lead, I'll follow." She sighs, wedges the door back into the frame of the car, and follows me up the street.

❖

Chadwick Road.

It's like a bad horror film. The further we travel along the path Aleksandar took, the more obvious it has become that people, human and *edane* alike, are taking things...badly.

The Angbec police have responded quicker than I've ever seen. There are uniforms everywhere, most with their attention on getting civilians to safer locations. They don't get involved with any *edane* threats, rather they retreat and stand by as other SPEAR units sweep in.

More and more arrive as Rayne and I try to catch up with our team. Tactical units in riot gear, most in protective clothing, all of them armed.

I even spot Noel at one point, directing his own team toward a building with snarls and howls coming from the inside. It looks like a restaurant from the fragments of shattered tables joining the fluff from shredded seats and cushions.

Usually this area is busy, lively, and cheerful. Now the air stinks of burning and rings with the echoes of battle further away. It's empty, eerily still, and bare.

Clearly most of the carnage has moved on, leaving behind this awful, near-apocalyptic mess.

Police have formed a line, hopefully to stop any curious human trying to get through because I can't think what else they're planning to do. Several SPEAR vans have also fanned out along the street with their own teams spilling out to seek and disperse.

Hawk glides above us at roof level, occasionally calling out information to keep us in the loop. He isn't the only gargoyle in flight now; several others and a few sprites are also in the air, offering their bird's eye view to the ground teams.

"Can you see any sign of Jack?"

"The mayor?" Hawk swoops round to catch the air currents directly overhead. "No, why?"

"I have to know he's okay."

"I'm sure he's fine. He's not an idiot."

"Well, actually—"

Hawk shushes me and cuts his wings back to climb higher. Ten feet, twenty feet, thirty, forty. Soon he's high enough that I can barely see him in the gloom, just the smeared outline of his form against the grey clouds above.

"There are some really big trucks heading in from the south."

"Ours?"

"Nope. Too big. And too many. Twenty at least. No idea who they are."

"Guys? Solo? You all getting this?"

A brief pause and then Erkyan's voice. "Yes. I see them. We are by river, on main road to motorway slip. They come fast."

"Who are they?"

Duo this time. "They're not from the city. I can smell that much."

Rayne chips in. "Where's Aleksandar?"

I hear the shrug in Duo's voice. "We lost him." He continues over my sounds of disbelief. "Other packs stepped in, some to stop him, others to join him. That's what the disruption is. In the chaos he got away. You should see it, Danika. Even out here, way away from the city's centre, everyone is fighting or defending territory. I've never seen anything like it."

"Can we stop it?"

"Can you be in thirty places at once?"

I drag my hands through my hair. "Then what *can* we do? What about Aleksandar?"

Hawk drops to his hands and toes beside me. The hard planes of his face are angled into a deep frown. "There's something else coming from the air. I'd say they're birds, but they're following the trucks."

"Weird, but I can't think about that right now. Has there been any—"

A voice cuts through on my earpiece. From the startled expressions on Rayne's and Hawk's faces, I know they hear the same thing.

"All SPEAR units, stand down, repeat stand down. Evoking emergency protocol code 6991, Project Revival. All SPEAR units return to headquarters for debrief. Repeat, emergency protocol Project Revival is now in effect. All units return to headquarters."

From miles away, Solo snarls his disgust into our comms. "What's this bullshit?"

I can hear others murmuring, muttering, questioning.

Rayne looks my way with wide, frightened eyes and pushes her way over to my side. "Is that the general?"

I find myself nodding. Though the voice is mechanical and clearly a computer, the only person with authority to give an order like that is the general. But why?

An agent I recognize vaguely as a Beta Grade Six, speaks into her own comms unit. "That's it, guys. We need to go back."

But why? How? Why are we all going back when there is so clearly a threat to be contained?

"Hey." I jog toward the other agent. "Hey, what's going on?"

"You heard, right?" She tucks her gun into her holster. "We go back for debrief."

"But—"

She talks right over me, beckoning to a cluster of other agents gathered near the police line. "Let's go. If we hurry, maybe we'll learn what started this mess." She pauses long enough to tell me, "You should hurry on too," before moving on with the rest of her team.

Yet again my phone rings. The same number as before, but still unknown.

"Jack?"

A huge sigh of relief from the other end. "You're okay. Thank goodness."

"Of course. What about you?"

"I'm fine I...they got me out. Are you still in the city?"

"Yes, but—"

"You need to get away. Right now. There are wolves on your team, right?"

"Jack—"

Again he cuts across me. People are rude as hell today. "Get them inside. Below ground if you can and keep them there for at least two hours. It's the only way they'll avoid the drug."

"What drug?"

His voice drops to a whisper. "Didn't you hear anything I said before? Project Revival is in force now. The Army is coming to...lend support." The worry in his voice is obvious. "Get off the streets right now."

I open my mouth to ask more, but before I can, something large and dark flies overhead with a dull, mechanical whirring sound. A second follows, then another and another, until the air vibrates with the buzzing of dozens of black machines.

Drones?

One of them clicks, turns, then extends a narrow black pipe that expels a stream of ashy white gas. An instant later, the others perform the same motion. Within seconds the air beneath the street lamps is heavy with the strange white vapour that sinks and spreads like mist.

Rayne's hands are already on my shoulders, shoving me off the road toward the nearest building. "Move."

"What is that?"

"No idea, but I don't like it. The stuff smells weird. Don't inhale."

More and more, the little black drones are appearing now, all of them spinning to release the strange gas. Hawk smears himself almost flat against the ground and scuttles past us like a lizard. "Smells like an old elf mine. What is this?"

Shrieking explodes over my comms unit.

With a yelp, I wrestle the tiny receiver free, but the screams are loud enough that I can still hear them, tinny and weak.

"Duo? Duo?" Solo's voice joins the cacophony, panicked and shrill. "What's wrong? What's happening?"

Wheezing gasps fill the line.

My gut clenches like a vice. "Duo? Erkyan? Guys, come on, what's happening? Talk to me."

"The drones...the gas..."

Rayne increases her shoving on my shoulders. "Come on."

Too late.

In my shock my steps have slowed and already the misty white gas has collected above me and sunk around my head. It's falling faster now, seeming to solidify like flakes of dry snow. It's all over my hair, my arms, my hands, my face. I can feel it coating the insides of my nostrils with every breath, and fear shudders through me.

The wheezing around me turns to coughs, hacking, chest-shuddering splutters I can almost feel in my own lungs.

Still stumbling on, I brace for pain, for burning, itching, or hampered breathing, but nothing happens. Just a faint scent, rather like Hawk said, that reminds me of my mother's old jewellery box. All of her oldest trinkets were in there, from silver rings, to wide bracelets and long silver necklaces, grey and murky with tarnish marks.

Wait...silver?

The coughing and wheezing stops with startling abruptness. Silence.

Oh, shit.

❖

"Solo? Get inside, right now."

"I can't. Duo needs—"

"Get. Inside. And take Pete with you. These drones are throwing out some weird silver compound. It's a gas. Get inside."

Even over the busy line I can hear the terror in Solo's voice. "Duo?"

"He'll be fine."

"But I can't hear him. I can't feel him, he's...he's gone. Duo.!"

"Please, get inside, Solo. We'll find him when it's all cleared, but you have to get inside now."

Raync finally finishes pulling me toward the buildings. Some of the urgency is gone, but she still looks as though she wants to tuck me inside her clothing for safekeeping.

The solidifying gas has left ashy flakes of white and grey smeared on her hair, face, and clothing. She looks like the victim of a house fire.

A pause, and then grunts from Solo. I hear him both explaining and reassuring who I assume to be Pete.

Okay, next. "Erkyan?" Two-second wait, then again. "Erkyan, talk to me. What's happening?"

She sighs. "I have Willow. Safe, but can't hear Duo now. He is quiet."

"Can you guys get to him?"

"Yes..."

"What? I hear a 'but' coming."

She sniffs. "The trucks we see? They are military. Many men inside climb out with guns and tactical suits. More come. Never seen so many men with weapons outside the SPEAR headquarter. Is this the Revival?"

"It must be."

"Well, they block our path. And they gather all no-humans."

Rayne chips in. "All *edanes*, or just werewolves?"

Another pause. "Werewolves not moving. They lie on ground, like dead."

A heart-wrenching howl from Solo.

"*Like* dead, not true dead. The machine mist makes them sleep."

"Did it hurt you?"

"Just werewolves."

This is all happening so fast. I can barely think straight. Then, once more through the comms is the order to return to HQ.

More buzzing and mechanical whirring from above indicates the drones have moved on. The misty gas is clearing enough now for me to see the fallout. The humans, both police officers and SPEAR agents, are fine, if a little ashy and confused. The few *edane* SPEAR agents still out seem to be unfurling themselves from bent and cowed positions. A few crawl out from within cars or slip out of buildings. Some figures lie on the ground, silent and unmoving. It takes only a moment to realize these must be werewolves.

A closer look confirms the fact, one or two of them caught between shifts from their human forms to their hybrid ones. Their bodies are knotted and twisted in painful looking contortions, skin reddened and sore from contact with the gas. Not one of them is conscious.

Shit.

"Solo, please tell me you're inside."

Grumbles and then. "We're inside. Some of that stuff followed us in. Chalks got an eyeful and can't see shit. What the fuck is happening? Did SPEAR just gas us?"

"Not SPEAR," Rayne mutters. "The military. Didn't you hear? Project Revival is in force."

"And what does that even mean?"

I've no idea. But I know who does and I mean to find out.

"Erkyan, you stay out there with Willow and try to retrieve Duo. We need him back in one piece."

"Yes, of course. Ah, Willow says she maybe can wake him."

"If you can, great, if not, get him inside. Don't let anybody take him. Solo?"

He grunts.

"Stay inside with Pete."

"Not much choice. He still can't walk, Omega hasn't shown up yet and if we go out there now, we'll both get swamped by that stuff."

"Let me know when Omega arrive."

"*You* let me know when Duo is safe."

I want to ask why he can't check himself, the way the pair always seem to do for each other while we're out. But now doesn't seem like the right time for potentially antagonistic questions. Instead, I simply reassure him that I'll do exactly that, then turn my attention to Hawk and Rayne

Hawk is on his feet again, though his chest and belly are smeared with the ashy remnants of the Project Revival gas. When he brushes it away, it flakes free like dandruff and dots his green feet with white.

"What are we going to do?"

"We're going back to HQ. We need answers, and right now that's the only way to get them."

"Fine. Let's go." Hawk holds out his hands for me again, but I back up out of reach.

"No, no, no. No way. There's enough of us out here I'm sure I can catch a lift."

Hawk grins. "Wuss."

"Damn right. I'm not built for flying."

"You could be. All it takes is practice." Still chuckling, Hawk vaults into the air and sweeps a wide circle around us. "See you back at HQ. I'll save you a seat at the front, where the babies sit."

I show him the back of my middle finger.

He flies off.

Rayne touches my arm. "Are you okay?"

I shrug her off. "No. I've cocked up. I should have paid more attention to Jack earlier."

"What's going on?"

Sigh. "I'll fill you in on the way. Come on, let's hitch a ride back to base."

Chapter Seventeen

HQ is rammed; every agent field and otherwise packed into the atrium and lining the balcony looking down from the mezzanine. Dozens of faces I recognize, others I see only in passing when working admin or liaising with research teams. The confused chatter is loud enough to feel, a weight pressing down on my senses.

More concerning are the faces I don't recognize, strangers in black and green, with caps angled down over their eyes. They hold rifles and though not one is raised right now, just seeing them makes me nervous. These aren't SPEAR agents. They look more like soldiers.

Close to my side, Rayne eyes the crowd with a narrowed gaze. I don't know what she's looking for, but by the time she looks down to me, her forehead is wrinkled with a deep frown.

"There aren't many *edane* agents here," she whispers.

"Perhaps they're still coming in."

She nods but doesn't seem to believe it. "Did Jack tell you anything else? Anything at all?"

I sigh. Though I wish I could tell her more, the brief outline I gave on the journey back is all the information I have. Project Revival is an emergency protocol, designed to kick in when *edanes* get "out of control."

If anything is out of control, it's Aleksandar and what he's done with the Dire Wolf pack, but even I can tell this has moved far beyond that. I don't know where the military teams are based, but for any large force to reach Angbec when it did, they must have been mobilized more than an hour previous.

A hush ripples through the crowd. Heads begin to turn. I angle my gaze to follow and find myself looking at Maury, who stands on one of the tables in the centre of the open space. With him, head lowered and hands clasped, is Jack.

My stomach flip-flops.

Both of them are filthy and smeared with blood. Crusted rust-red stains form an arc across Jack's face and more of the same marks Maury's arm and shoulder. Both appear exhausted, but at least they're alive.

Maury extends a hand, and someone in the crowd passes him a microphone.

A burst of feedback crackles through speakers set in far corners of the open office, and then he begins to speak.

"Agents, thanks for coming in so quickly." Like usual, Maury's voice is calm and strong, authoritative and powerful. Now however, there's something else there too, a weariness I've only ever heard after extended periods talking to me. "You all know by now that the werewolf population of Angbec has mobilized and that some kind of turf war is taking place. At this moment in time, we don't know what caused such a violent turn so if any of you have any information in that regard, we'd really love to know it." He pauses long enough to scan the crowd. Can't help but think he's looking for me.

Apparently, Rayne shares the same thought because her hand closes around the back of my jacket and pulls. Just like that I'm bending, hunched enough to knock three inches off my height.

"Hey, you can't—"

"Shh."

Maury continues. "Mayor Jackson Cobé is here to explain more about what you heard over comms, the facts behind Project Revival. We don't have much time, but it's important you know what's happening going forward."

"You gonna tell us what that freaky weaponized gas was?" This voice comes from an agent I don't know, somewhere on the left of the huge crowd.

Murmurs of agreement follow the outburst, followed by a few more yells.

"Are you trying to kill us?"

"My team dropped like flies. What are you trying to do?"

And on and on.

Jack, now holding the microphone, clears his throat loudly. But that isn't enough to cut through the increasing barrage of questions hurled at those on the table.

"Are the wolves going to wake up?"

"Do you have weapons against other *edanes* or just wolves?"

"All right, agents, I need you all to calm down." Jack speaks, but his voice barely carries, half lost because the microphone is held away from his mouth. "Agents…agents."

"Why didn't you warn us what was going on?"

"How are we supposed to do our jobs when you gas us with drones?"

Rayne maintains her grip on my jacket but leans in toward my ear. "He's sweating."

"It's hot in here."

"Not that hot. And look at the way his eyes are darting. He's scared."

"Vampire vision versus human, Rayne. I'll take your word for it."

Again he waves his hands. "Please, agents, please. Please—"

Another man vaults onto the table beside Jack and Maury. He's a small, wisp of a man with tightly cropped grey hair, a neat little beard, and dozens upon dozens of stripes, colours, and pips on his epaulets. While Maury and Jack have clearly been out and caught in the mayhem, this man looks clean and collected, as though just stepping out of the house. He snatches the microphone from Jack, presses the thumb and forefinger of his spare hand to his lips, and whistles hard into the small device. The shrill sound pierces the complaining and questioning like a hot poker through plastic.

Silence. And then, "Right, you lot, I'm Colonel Benedict Addington, and it's about time you learned some bloody discipline. When I'm speaking, you don't. When I'm giving orders, you listen. When I'm done, you move out. Does everybody understand?"

More silence.

The looks on the faces of my fellow agents must mirror my own, but this Addington guy seems to take that as agreement because he nods once and continues.

"Your mayor, Jackson Cobé, initiated Project Revival at twenty-one-thirty-five this evening and—"

Jack darts in and leans over the microphone. "Under advisement from my team and from agents within SPEAR itself, I thought, given the purveyance of the werewolf problem and the sudden flux of activity from within Misona, that the best course of action was a preventative, pre-emptive strategy, and—"

Addington jerks the microphone to one side. "Are you quite finished, Mr. Mayor?"

Yikes. Even I can feel the bite in his tone.

Jack blanches and backs up super quick, returned to his lowered head and clasped hands position. He doesn't speak again.

For long seconds Addington glares at Jack, as if daring him to open his mouth. Eventually he nods, squares his shoulders, and begins anew. "Project Revival, as initiated under the authority of Mayor Jackson Cobé, hands complete tactical and operational control of all extra mundane relations to myself and the Extra Mundane Control unit of the British Army. As such I'll be leading and coordinating all operations for the foreseeable future. Any questions so far?"

"But who the hell are you? What about the general?" Despite having similar thoughts, I'm glad this voice isn't mine. It comes from someone on the far side of the room, near the wall and under the roosts where the chittarik often rest.

Addington snorts. "General? How cute. Fine, your *general* is no longer in control of SPEAR. While Revival is in force all control operations are passed up to a higher, more suitable power, i.e. the EMCU." His upper lips curls enough that even I can see it from way, way back. "You people have been allowed to run amok for long enough. It's time we regained a little control over this oversized house party with guns."

The murmurs begin afresh, only this time with an edge of anger.

"How long will you stay?" Another voice, this time one I recognize. It's Noel, on the right-hand side and close to the table now serving as a stage. He looks scuffed and dirty but largely unharmed, though he has one arm wrapped around a member of his team sporting a saggy, bloodied bandage around her head.

"Until such time that our services and organizational superiority is no longer required."

That's a nonsense answer. I open my mouth to chip in, but Addington whistles into the microphone again.

"I speak, you don't, remember? Now, the werewolf menace has been largely neutralized following the successful application of our drone based sedative. You agents will round up any werewolf stragglers and deliver them immediately into military custody. We have ample mobile units designed to detain and contain all manner of extra mundane threats including werewolves. Additional security in the form of military personnel will be situated around each containment unit now and until further notice. All other extra mundane agents are to report immediately to SPEAR holding facilities where you will be detained for debrief and further processing. You will disarm immediately and follow my units who will escort you under guard."

Uproar.

Rayne's own indignant response is lost beneath the abrupt swell of displeasure from almost every agent. Though there aren't many werewolves among those gathered right now, there are plenty of sprites, pixies, gargoyles, and even a couple of vampires. Certainly not enough to outnumber humans, but more than enough to make their voices heard.

I hear expletives, cries of shock and fear, and the more general babble of disbelief.

Rayne's grip slips away from the back of my jacket. "I don't understand."

"It's okay," I say at once. "He can't do that. He just can't. Even before SPEAR recruitment policies changed, no one has been able to segregate *edanes* like that since the Supernatural Creatures Act. It's illegal."

"I'm not sure those laws hold right now."

Another whistle, this one longer and more piercing than the last.

"Listen to you." Addington sneers down at us from the table. "Complaining like children. Shrieking like babies. Do you understand what's happening here? What's at stake? Your vows were to protect and serve, and I expect you to do exactly that. Those are my orders and you will obey them immediately. Anybody with a problem is more than welcome to speak with one of my soldiers." A dark chuckle. "They'll sort you out. Now…get on with it."

He shoves the microphone into Maury's startled hands, leaps off the table, and stalks away. As he moves, a small circle of uniformed soldiers closes in around him, a shield cutting off any attempt to reach or speak to him. The rest, posted all around the huge space, stand straighter and taller and shift their grips on their guns.

Fuck.

"Uh," Maury clears his throat into the microphone, "you heard our orders. Um. We have a lot to do, so—"

"This can't be right, Maury, no, no." Again Noel's voice. "All *edane* agents to be suspended?"

"That's not what he said—"

"That is the reality, sí?" Noel waves to encompass the other agents. "Our comrades are to be debriefed, but why? They know as much as we do. They can help."

More murmurs of assent.

Maury makes calming, soothing gestures with his hands. They don't work. "I know this is a bit of a shock, but we all need to calm down and take into account that this is the right thing to do. Remember we've never seen anything like this happen before, not here, not anywhere. We *need* help to contain all the werewolves who, apparently, have gone mad. Colonel Addington and his unit is here to help us all our job."

No. No way. Fuck that.

I grab Rayne's sleeve and begin to back through the crowd.

"What are you doing?"

"We're leaving. Before they lock this place down, come on. Let's go."

"But—"

"No. I'm not letting you go into SPEAR holding for debrief or whatever the hell that dick-stick said. Don't you get it? They're trying to clear all *edanes* off the streets. All of them, not just the wolves."

Rayne trots along with me, still protesting as she comes.

"You haven't done anything wrong and, fact is, we know exactly what's happening right now. And we know how to stop it."

Her fingers wriggle within my grip. "Then we need to tell Colonel Addington."

"No, we need to get Wendy. Come *on.*"

❖

Getting away from the atrium proves harder than anticipated. Sneaking around to avoid both armed soldiers and fellow agents means that by the time Rayne and I clear the area, the pair of us are tense as iron bars.

Right at my back, Rayne's presence is a thick, solid weight. She moves with the cat-like smoothness of a vampire on the prowl, and more than once I catch the edge of silver glinting in her eyes.

She pushes me into the meeting room from earlier that day and pulls at the door. It doesn't close, instead allowing a small slither of light to pour through from the corridor beyond.

Only now, away from prying ears, does she speak. "Get Wendy? What do you mean, 'get Wendy'?"

"We need to get him out of holding before everything locks down."

"You can't be serious."

"Of course I am. Can't you see? He's the only one that can stop this. He has incredible relations with other packs and he's alpha of the pack that started this in the first place. If we can get him back to the Dire Wolves, it yanks the power right out of Aleksandar's hands."

Rayne leans against the table nearest the door. "So you want to break him out? Does this sound at all familiar to you?"

"I—" I fiddle with the ID badge hanging off my hip. "That was different. I needed you for intel. You would have been killed."

"And now?"

"It's the same thing. We have no idea how long that Addington guy is going to keep everyone locked up, so we need to act before he cements anything. Hell, we might be able to—"

I must have blinked because before the next word can leave my mouth, Rayne is in front of me with her hand pressed against my lips. She has her head cocked, her eyes narrowed, clearly listening to something I've no hope of hearing myself.

"Jack," she whispers, "and Agent Cruush."

"Perfect. Maybe they can give us a hand with—"

Her hand presses harder against my lips. "They're arguing. Come on, back here." Rayne steps back and I'm inexorably drawn with her as the door abruptly flies open. We're behind it, not hiding exactly, but shielded from immediate view.

It's Maury I hear first.

"This is insane. Can they really do that? Can they really just walk in here and take over everything?"

"I suppose so." Jack sounds flatter and more defeated than I've ever heard him.

"And the general? What's happening up on high?"

"Come on, Maurice, you know as well as I do that the general isn't really a general. That's just the title you guys use. This protocol hands over all authority, and we have to accept that."

"And what am I supposed to tell my agents? You saw them out there. This is crazy. We can't just start pulling *edane* personnel in for debrief. Debrief for what? You have to do something about this, Mayor. You can't let them do this to us."

I glance down at Rayne. She shakes her head, indicating that we should listen a moment longer. Impatience burns in me, but with one of Rayne's hands on my shoulder and the other still hovering over my mouth, I have little choice.

I hear footsteps, quick ones with a short stride, as though someone is pacing back and forth across the room.

"I'm sorry. Really I am, but I tried to tell you. I warned you this protocol was no small thing and you pushed me anyway. This is what we have now."

Maury sighs. "You never told me the military would essentially turn us into foot soldiers for their miniature Genghis Khan."

I snort into Rayne's hand. Can't help it. Her fingers press tighter, but the two men are clearly too wrapped up in their own conversation to hear my sniggering.

"What do you want me to do, Maurice? It's done now. I have no say in what happens next."

More footsteps. It must be Maury pacing. Another sigh. "Just get low and stay out of the way. I've no idea what's going to happen, but I need to speak to the general. There has to be something we can do to fight this." One more circuit of the room and then the footsteps are gone.

In their place I hear low breathing, barely audible at all above the din from outside.

Rayne's hand slips from my mouth. I push the door shut.

As it swings away from the wall and where we were trapped behind it, I find Jack perched on the end of one of the tables. He has one hand over his eyes. The fingertips gently massaging his temples.

When he sees me and Rayne standing against the wall, he chuckles, soft and wholly without mirth. "Why am I not surprised?"

"Did you really hand over full control of SPEAR?"

He stares at me. "Once upon a time I would have given a lot to have you and I alone in the same room together. Now? Well now, all I want is you, out there on the streets, fixing all this."

"I *was* fixing it."

Rayne clears her throat.

"But I was. I told you I was handling it."

"According to Agent Cruush, your 'handling' of the wolves is probably what started this whole rampage in the first place."

My next words stutter a little over the sensation of guilt. "The unlawful turnings and attacks are confirmed to be from the new pack flaunting their new pack power. The Dire Wolves were trying to investigate, but without their alpha, the inter-pack politics got a little out of hand."

"Oh, Lord." Jack rubs harder at his temples. "So Agent Cruush is right?"

"Hell no, he isn't. If he had let me bring Wendy out of containment back when I asked we could have avoided all of this." The confused look on Jack's face reminds me that he doesn't have all the facts I do.

I fill him in quickly, explaining what happened between Aleksandar and Pete.

By the time I'm done, Jack is no longer massaging his temples, but staring at me intently. "So getting this Wendy character out would fix all of this?"

Rayne cuts in. "Not everything, Mr. Mayor, but it would at least allow Wensleydale to regain control of his pack which means that Aleksandar can't use them the way he is right now."

He frowns. "A few months back I'd ask what you were doing, hiding in here, but it's pretty clear that you're going to the holding units. You're going to break him out, aren't you?"

"Yup."

"Even though he's been sedated?"

"Yup."

"And even with the military on your back the whole time?"

"Yup."

Quick shake of the head. "Fine. I guess the least I can do is help out— when you get there, give the personnel on the door this code. Ready?"

I start patting down my pockets for a pen, but Rayne simply nods. Jack rattles off a long series of numbers and letters, and though I manage to hold on to half of them, the sequence is too long without more time to go over it.

Rayne grins and taps the side of her head. "Got it."

"Good. I don't know how long my authority will hold over there so you need to be fast. It's probably already been blocked off, but that's the most I can do for you right now. Get a move on."

"Hey, Jack." I wait for him to look my way. "Thanks for this."

"Just fix it," he mutters. "We were on a knife edge before, this is going to tip us one way or another."

"You're doing a good job, you know." My voice softens and I fight the urge to touch his shoulder. He's so slumped over and drawn in, all of that height means nothing with him so curled in on himself. "Hey...none of this is your fault."

"I'm supposed to protect the people," he murmurs. "*All* the people of this city. I haven't been able to do that. I might even have made it worse."

Rayne opens the door. "Well, this is a good step toward helping. Danika, if we're really going to do this, we need to do it now."

She's right. With one last comforting smile at Jack, I follow her out of the room.

Halfway along the corridor, Jack stops me with a hand at my elbow. He drops a set of keys into my hands. "My car is around the back of the building in the private spaces. Take it. If you're subtle about it, none of the soldiers will stop you and you'll be able to get there in good time."

"You sure? What about you?"

"Right now the safest place for me is inside this building. I'm not going anywhere. Just..." He squeezes my elbow. "Don't wreck it, okay?"

"The car? Um. No promises." I slip free and hurry after Rayne before he can respond.

CHAPTER EIGHTEEN

Hawk meets us outside the building. Perhaps wisely, after seeing all the armed soldiers gathered outside HQ, he elected to stay outside and watch from above. I fill him in as best I can, but he's almost hopping from foot to foot in his haste to share his own news.

"The Omega teams finally got to Solo and Chalks and will move them to a more secure location."

"Can Pete shift yet?"

A shrug. "Solo left when Omega arrived. He's looking for Duo."

"Anything from Erkyan or Willow?"

"They aren't on comms anymore."

I look out onto the street, eyeing the empty roads surrounding HQ. "Probably for the best. We don't know if EMCU have our frequency. I'd rather not have them listening in."

Even as I say it, a huge armoured tank rolls down the street. I've no idea what the Army expected when they set out, but the grinding caterpillar tracks and the heavy tank gun up top suggests the worst. A line of armed soldiers walk alongside, guns held in ready positions out in front.

My stomach knots uncomfortably. "We're going to the containment units, Hawk. Will you track down Erkyan and Willow? I know they're probably fine, but we need to find Duo."

"What about you?"

"I've got to do this. We'll check in later."

He nods and vaults upward with a little flex of his knees. Soon he's nothing but a slight smudge against the dark of the night.

Rayne leads the way to the underground car park.

More soldiers down here, standing in subtle but strategic positions near the exit and entrance barriers. Others guard the lifts leading into the building itself, and a few more walk in amongst the cars.

I prepare to drop to a crouch, but Rayne starts walking, straight across the open space without a care in the world.

I scurry after her. "What are you doing?"

She plucks the keys from my hands and opens the doors to Jack's Jaguar. "We aren't doing anything wrong as far as these guys know. No need for us to draw attention to ourselves by acting strangely."

Again, she's right. None of the soldiers disturb us as we guide the car through the parking structure, and even at the exit barrier, they pause only long enough to give us a cursory glance.

Rayne drives and I sit in the passenger seat with my hands performing nervous flutters and tricks in my lap. I find myself fiddling with my ID, my kit belt, my fingernails. I can't keep still and, even as we pass through the barrier and get onto the street, my anxiety only seems to increase.

"Calm down, Danika." Rayne never takes her eyes off the road, but I get the feeling that she's watching me intently.

"I can't. I just…I did this. I should have insisted with Maury. I should have been more help to Pete. This huge mess is only getting worse because I fucked up."

"You didn't mess up."

I chance a smile. "You're right. I said 'fucked up.'"

Rayne chuckles. "Just try to think about what we're going to say to Shakka when we get there, okay?"

Oh, yeah. That.

There are several ways I can handle the warty little goblin. Outright threats seem to work pretty well, but less so in recent weeks. Perhaps he's simply becoming used to my offers to string him up by his toes. Bribery is often a good one, especially for goblins, but SPEAR pays him well enough that all his needs are met. Information? Perhaps there is something I can give him, or a trade. Despite all his money, he still spends time complaining about this, that, and the other.

It's only when we reach the holding facility that I realize what has happened.

Rayne takes us through the security checkpoints by flashing her ID and my own, as well as typing the string of numbers from Jack into a keypad. At each checkpoint, the number, not our IDs is what gets us through, and I silently thank Jack for his help.

The car stops in a reserved parking slot near a pair of reinforced metal doors, and before Rayne can step out I clear my throat, short and sharp. "Hey…thanks."

She smiles. "Whatever for?"

"Distracting me. For helping me with that talk about Shakka. For being calm and constant when all I want to do is…bah. Just, thanks, okay?"

The smile broadens. "I didn't do anything, Danika." She's still smiling when she climbs out of the car and zips around to open my door.

I clamber out. "When this is all over…when I fix this, I'm going to take you back home and—"

Rayne clears her throat. Her expression hardens, enough to set me spinning on my heel, looking for who might be watching.

Two soldiers. Green and black. Rifles.

Suddenly, my hands are in fists.

"Who are you two?" The first of the pair lifts the visor on his helmet to reveal greasepaint-smeared features and a turned down mouth.

"I'm Agent Rayne, this is Agent Karson. We're leaders of SPEAR's Kappa unit."

"Kappa?" The two soldiers share a glance. "What's that?"

Rayne touches the back of my hand before she speaks again. "We're a new specialist unit designed for close contact *edane* encounters."

"And you're both human?"

"Well, I—"

"Enough." I step forward. "We're here under direct orders from Colonel Addington and Mayor Cobé. There's a prisoner inside in need of interrogation, and I'd like to get done before others start pouring in."

The second soldier lowers his gun. Slightly. "From the colonel?"

Rayne chips in. "We just came from HQ where he was giving a briefing. Feel free to check in, if you'd like."

More quick stares between the pair. The first reaches for a radio clipped to his shoulder.

I speak fast. "But hurry along, will you. We need to get back and report."

"To the colonel?"

I nod. "And we need to do it before anybody else interrupts him with pointless news. Remember how pissed he was at that call he got while we were talking?"

Rayne blinks, then breezes along, clearly catching my drift. "He doesn't seem to like interruptions, does he?"

"Nope. I thought he was going to discharge that poor guy."

The first soldier removes his hand from the shoulder radio. The knots in my stomach ease a tiny amount.

"Just get on with it, will you? We need to be on standby for when other *extra mundanes* start to come through."

I grin and flash my ID lanyard at the door panel before they can change their minds. "No worries, we got this. Come on, Rayne."

With that, we're both through the door and moving, before either of the pair can say more.

As the doors close, Rayne eyes me up and down. "When did lying become so easy for you?"

"It isn't. Except to those idiots. Besides, anybody who knows me can tell when I'm lying. I'd never stand a chance against you or even Noel."

Rayne doesn't answer that, but a smile rides her lips as we walk down the corridor.

Chapter Nineteen

More and more evidence of the Army's presence is visible as we walk toward the holding area. Usually there are checkpoints before reaching the cells, but not with armed personnel.

There are still SPEAR agents around, but none of them seem to be moving without some sort of Army escort.

"I'm beginning to dislike green."

Rayne nods and opens the last door before the cells. She tucks her lanyard back around her neck and ushers me through ahead of her.

Like before, the cells are visible through a huge screen of reinforced glass. On our side, the panel of buttons and switches, as manned by an agent, are covered with coloured dials and LEDs.

Shakka sits on his stool in front of it all, spooning small clots of something thick and red from a wide plastic tub. He studies each clump before dropping it into his mouth, chewing loudly and with gusto. He doesn't even flinch when we enter.

"You took your time, Karson." A small line of red drool pools in the corner of his mouth. "Something more important out there?"

"What do you know?"

He grins, showing off his needle-sharp teeth. That, combined with whatever he's eating, gives him the look of a deranged, flesh-eating clown.

Gross.

"Well, whatever this new Revival gargoyle shit is, I figured you'd be back lick-split-quick to pick up your…" he pauses long enough to widen the grin, "…pet."

"Shakka, I swear, I'll—"

"Oh, don't worry about me. I won't tell a soul. But you owe me for this."

My hands are still fists. I don't remember doing that. "Just open the doors."

"Say it, Karson. I want to hear the words out of your mouth."

I grunt.

Rayne sighs. "Don't."

"Well?" Shakka's long, knobbly finger hovers over the button that opens the main doors.

"I owe you, Shakka."

He laughs. It's that horrible, high-pitched cackle I've heard before. The shudder it sends across my shoulders reminds of me of fingernails grinding down a chalkboard.

"Yes, you do, Karson. Yes, you do."

"Open the doors."

A click, and the slow, hissing release of compressed air. At last.

Shakka waves at me as I make my way down the steps. He looks positively gleeful. "Have a good evening, *Agent*."

"Stick your head in a dungheap, Shakka."

He laughs at that. In fact, I can still hear his laughter as I lead Rayne down the centre of the double rows of cells, to where I left Wendy.

I don't really know what I expected to find in there. Perhaps not my old friend as I know him, alert, lively and eagle-eyed, but certainly not this.

Wendy is prone on his drop-down bed. In fact, to look at him, I'm not sure he's moved since I left him there yesterday.

His hands and neck bristle with short, coarse fur, as though he has tried to change and simply given up partway. One arm hangs limp off the side of the bed, while the other is half propped up against the wall, from elbow to shoulder. Elbow to fingertips, the rest of his arm kind of flops down like a sad flag without a proper shaft to hold it upright.

His eyes swivel as I open the door but not so much that I believe for a second he can see me clearly. Sure enough, a moment later, his nostrils flare.

"Aaaah. Meat sack." His voice is low, slurred, and slow, as though turned down with a tempo dial. He peers at me from his turtle-like sprawl and smiles awkwardly. "Why are you walking on the ceiling?"

At my side, Rayne puts her hands to her mouth. "This is really bad."

"You're telling me. I step fully into the cell and crouch beside him. "Wendy? Can you get up? Can you stand?"

He sniffs. "Maybe. But there's jelly in my legs. You ever had jelly, little meat sack? Like sucking the best, juicy bits from a bone."

Now there's an image.

"Wendy, you need to get up. Now. Can you do that for me? Please?"

"Yeah, yeah, yaaar," he mutters. "Just give me mo-moment, you impatient human...uh...thing."

Rayne joins me in the cell. "Mr. Gordan? Wensleydale?"

His eyes narrow, but he does, at last, manage to turn on the narrow lip of the bed he's made a home. "What do you want, fanger?"

"To help, I—"

"You're not helping. You're dangerous. My meat sack here, she's sitting in the lunar blood right now. I bet you can smell her, right?"

Rayne backs up fast, not a step, but a vampire-swift flash from one side of the cell to the other. She smears her back against the bars and waits there, eyes narrowed, lips slightly parted.

Wendy rattles on, as though he hasn't just dropped a verbal bomb on us. "You smell her just like I can. All juicy and sweet and tasty. I smell the hunter on you, just like I smell the moon on her. You got the fever."

I can't move. Or is it that I don't want to? Not sure which. I only know that my body is locked in place by my own mind and that every thought I have is racing through my head a mile a second.

"I'm sure you can smell just as well as I can, Mr. Gordan. But you've a keen eye. I'm sure you can see just as well that I'm fine."

On anybody else I might have missed it. Hell, I'm not entirely sure I heard it, but there's something in Rayne's voice, a faint hitch on the word "fine."

I swallow back the spiky lump of concern at the back of my throat. "Come on, Wendy. We're getting you out of here. Get up. Right now."

He sits. Sways. Slumps back down. "Oopsie."

That lump swells right back up into my throat. Never, in all my years, have I heard Wensleydale Gordan, werewolf and alpha, say something as childish or ridiculous as "oopsie."

I look helplessly to Rayne. "This is the sedative. It has to be. How are we going to get him out of here?"

"Are you sure you still want to?"

"Yes." I don't mean to shout, but I can hear the single syllable echo slightly off the surrounding walls. "He can't stay here. If any other pack sees him like this, Aleksandar will be the least of Dire Wolf problems. Come on, Rayne. You know I'm right."

She nods, but still doesn't move off the bars. "Then how do you want to do this?"

❖

I watch Wendy rolling back and forth on the bed. His smile is back, and the fur across the back of his hands fluffs up as he scratches the back of his neck. We need help. No two ways about it.

With a sigh, I step away from Wendy and out into the main open space between all the cells. I can see Shakka watching through the glass. "Open the two neighbouring cells." Silence. "Come on, Shakka, I know you can hear me."

More silence, then a faint crackle. Following that, a tinny version of Shakka's grumbling voice spills out the intercom system. "What the hell for? I thought you only wanted Wensleydale."

"I need backup."

A snort. "You'll not get backup from the female, Karson. You know Grey Tails don't care for Dire Wolves."

I do know that, of course I do, but as I turn to my right, I can see the woman with the shaved head watching me from her own bed at the back of the cell.

She tilts her head at me, face angled to expose her nostrils more widely.

I speak again, loud for Shakka's benefit, but with direct eye contact to the woman in her cell. "Times are changing. With Project Revival, we don't know how long wolves are going to be kept in here. I need to get Wendy out now. And I'm happy to make a deal with anybody who helps."

More grumbling over the intercom. "You already owe me, Karson."

I rub my temples with my fingertips. "I'm aware. Want to make it a sweet double?"

Silence.

Buzz. Electric currents die off. Click. Doors unlock. Two sets of doors swing open on silent hinges.

A dark blur streaks out of the left-most door. It's the younger Dire Wolf. He dives into Wendy's cell with a little cry, and I can hear him speaking softly to his alpha. Coaxing him to stand.

Slower, comes the woman on the right-hand side. In the brighter light outside the cells, her blue hair takes on a metallic sheen, and the tribal tattoos on the bald side of her head stand out in sharp relief on her skin.

She looks me up and down. "Either you're very good at lying, or you believe what you said."

"Or it's actually the truth? What's your name?"

She sniffs. Not to scent me exactly, but more an expression of irritation. "Jadzia. Call me Jadz if you must."

"I'm Danika Karson. Nice to meet you." I hold out my hand...and end up pulling it back again when she just stares at my fingers. "Okay then." I turn to head back into Wendy's cell, stopping only when a hand on my arm pulls me back.

Jadz looks up at me, so close that I can feel her hot breath on my neck and shoulder. She's a little taller than Rayne but not by much. "I know your name better than I know you. If you really are Danika, then I'll trust you."

"But? Because I can smell one coming."

She gives a wry smile. "But if you hurt me or anybody I care for, I'll break your legs with my fair bare hands."

Something about the way she says it seems to suggest more than a simple threat; it's oddly familiar too, but I don't have time to figure it out. The younger Dire Wolf finally has Wendy on his feet and he, with Rayne's help, is carefully leading the drugged up alpha out of the cell.

Wendy moves, but nothing like his usual self. He looks more drunk than anything, with added sluggishness and graceless lumbering. The younger wolf has his hand tucked under his arm to keep him moving, while Rayne holds Wendy's collection of coats.

"And what's your name, kid?"

"I'm not a kid, I—"

"He's called Spannah. At least that's what he said to me." Jadz shoves past me and up to Wendy. She eyes him up and down, shakes her head, then takes his other arm. "What a shit show," she mutters. "Where are we going?"

Spannah, Jadz, Rayne, and myself. I hope that's going to be enough, but until Wendy is in a fresher state, there's no point going back to the Dire Wolves.

Sensing my hesitation, Jadz gives a loud sigh and an obvious eye roll. "Didn't think this through, did you?"

"I didn't think he'd be this bad."

"You think this is bad? Last night he was singing and crawling around the cell like a pup on acid. Whatever they gave him, it's not the same as what they gave me and the kid."

An exasperated grunt from Spannah. "I'm not a kid."

I keep my focus on Jadz. "Then I need somewhere to take him. Somewhere safe until he can recover. Somewhere not affiliated with SPEAR or any other pack."

Jadz looks down at the ground. Her free hand swipes back through her glossy blue hair. "Damn it. Look, I have a place, but you need to agree to keep it secret, okay? You need to agree that..." She frowns.

The intercom crackles. "Humans and puppies, make your way to the nearest exit or don't. I don't care." Shakka sounds amused. "Just do it fast because I have several Army thugs out here wanting to bring in prisoners and I'm bored of stalling for you."

Rayne shrugs.

I look at Jadz. "Whatever you need, whatever oath or promise you want, you have it. But we *need* to get Wendy out of this building."

"Swear it. On your blood."

Wow. She really means it. I bend low enough to pull a tiny throwing dagger from inside my boot. A quick swipe of the point draws a line of blood across my palm. From the corner of my eye I see Rayne stiffen, and I quickly put my back to her. The bloodied hand, I hold out toward Jadz.

"On my blood and on my life, from Danika Karson to Jadzia—uh…"

Eye roll. She's worse than me. "Ramachandra."

"From Danika Karson to Jadzia Ramachandra, I vow to keep your confidences as well as I keep my own." I wait for the answering gesture.

The lap of Jadzia's tongue against my palm is both startling and unsettling. I half expect it to be soaking, but she's bizarrely dainty about it, licking nothing but the scratch. "And I, Jadzia Ramachandra, accept your vow and will hold you to it." She pulls a strange half smile. "Hmm. Okay, done. You really do taste as good as you look."

"Excuse me?"

"You're pretty hot for a human, that's all."

"Thanks. I guess?"

"Hmm." She continues to look me over. "I guess he's right about you."

"Wait, what? Who? Who was right?"

No answer. Instead, she steadies her grip on Wendy's arm. "Come on. I'll take you to a safe place." She starts walking, guiding Wendy toward the steps with a joint grip shared with Spannah.

I look back at Rayne. "Let's get out of here. And we should probably stop by the weapons store and stock up."

She stares at me, lips slightly parted. No...not at me, at my hand.

Fuck.

"Rayne? Rayne."

Her gaze finally snaps up to mine. "Yes, fine. Let's go. You first."

"But—"

"Please just go first."

I tuck my hand into my pocket and follow the trio of wolves toward the steps. As I walk, I wonder if the head start of a couple of steps would make any difference at all if Rayne abruptly decided she wanted the blood beading on the inside of my palm.

CHAPTER TWENTY

I knew the journey would be cramped, but cramming weapons, three werewolves, a vampire, and me into Jack's car has me on edge. My seat is comfortable, of course, as I'm driving, but it's not about physical space.

The sheer power roiling off and around the four *edanes* with me is enough to suffocate and smother.

In the back, Wendy sits between Jadz and Spannah. He seems calmer and more aware now that we're away from the cell, but he's clearly not himself. More than once he directs a comment at Rayne that he never might have otherwise and, while calm, it's clear to me that Rayne is struggling.

She sits as far into the opposite side of her seat as possible, half-reclined against the window to leave a sea of space between us. Even her legs are turned toward the passenger door. She refuses to look at me, instead watching the scenery slide past us through her window.

The radio doesn't work, nor does any of the other entertainment inside the car. We travel in stuffy silence, broken only by the occasional whisper from Jadz as she directs us through the eastern side of Angbec.

I've never spent much time on this side of the city, at least not in these largely suburban areas. Semi-detached houses with large drives or huge swathes of neatly cut grass forming their road-facing gardens. Most of the homes have two cars, sometimes three, and evidence of families is visible in the form of swing sets, or brightly coloured cartoon curtains hanging in upper windows.

"Left here, Agent, then to the end of the road and on the right. The house is there."

I follow Jadz's direction, perhaps faster than I should in a residential area. The car rumbles and stills as I kill the engine and the doors fly open to release my passengers.

Jadz immediately runs up to the house and lets herself in, a quick burst of *edane* speed that takes her out of sight.

I exit and walk round to meet Spannah as he supports Wendy once more with a grip on his arm.

"You okay, Wendy?"

He looks me up and down. A little of the old fire returns to his eyes, just a flicker but enough to give me hope. "I hope you know what you're doing. This shit show can't be allowed to get worse, hear me?"

"That's exactly why you're here instead of back in SPEAR holding."

He snorts. "And where is 'here'?"

"Uh…"

Jadz walks slowly out of the house. Her expression is hard to read, but I'm pretty confident in thinking she's not angry. Yet.

"You guys better get inside. Also, hide the car in the garage. Not much point coming here in secret then leaving a huge 'come get me' sign outside the building."

I point Spannah toward the house. "Go on. I'll be there in a second."

He and Wendy limp their way inside while I return to the car and climb back in.

Rayne still hasn't moved. In fact, the only move she makes is to lean still further away from me.

"S-sorry, I—"

"Don't be," she mutters. "It's not your fault."

I put both hands on the steering wheel. It's that or start wringing them. "Are we going to talk about this?"

"About what?"

"Rayne…"

Finally she looks at me. No, *glares* at me. "What do we have to talk about, Danika? That I'm a bloodthirsty monster? That every time I look at you, all I can see is the blood packaged by your skin?"

Ahead of us, the doors to the garage at the end of the drive start to slide up. I can just make out a pair of feet—they must belong to Jadz—walking along on the other side.

"But—"

"But what?" She slams her fist against the dashboard. The plastic creaks but holds. For now. "It's getting worse, Danika. The more time I spend in close quarters with you, the more you bleed. It's getting painful being able to smell you like this."

I lick my lips. They're dry and cracked, annoyingly so, but I'm not surprised. "Should I go?"

"I don't want you to."

"I know."

"But yes. Get out. I'll drive the car in."

I hesitate.

She hits the dashboard again. This time a crack wriggles out from beneath her fist. "Go. I'll be there in a minute and I'll bring all the weaponry. Please. At least with the others in here there were other smells to think about, but now all I have is you. And I want to devour you."

I try not to rush and make her feel worse, but those simple words chill me more than anything she has ever said to me. Devour…consume me until there's nothing left.

I scramble out of the car with little to no grace, slamming the door behind me. From the corner of my eye, I can see Rayne slide across the front seats and into the driver's side. The seat rumbles and clunk-chunks forward as she adjusts it to accommodate her shorter legs.

The front door of the house opens before I can reach it, swung wide to admit a figure I never expected to see here.

My mouth hangs open, I know it, but I don't care. "Noel?"

He smiles as I approach. "Ah, Dee-Dee, I'm glad to see you. I worried for you earlier. You said nothing to this new colonel about his ridiculous plans."

He grins wide and spreads his arms for me. He knows better than to try for a hug, but he does clap me heartily on the shoulder when I reach him.

"What are you doing here? How do you know Jadz?"

He winks at me. "I did tell you before. I wanted to keep my private affairs secret as long as possible. That way, no one questions."

My brain races to catch up. "So Jadz is your…"

His grin widens. "Come. I see you are confused. Maybe I can break it into bite-size pieces for you."

I allow Noel to lead me into the house without another word. Frankly, while it's good to see him, I don't know how many more surprises I can handle.

Noel, Jadz, Spannah, Wendy, Rayne, and me. The house is large, with an interior to match, but this living room is near bursting at the seams with tension and nerves.

Against one wall, Noel and Jadz stand side by side, fingers slightly intertwined while they watch the rest of us. They don't speak but have clearly decided to wait for more details.

Spannah sits on the sofa, as close to Wendy as he can get without sitting in his lap. Wendy is bowed forward, elbows resting on his thighs, hands dangling between them. His breathing is heavy but steady, though his gaze is pinned to the large but tasteful off-white swirls in the rug stretched across the laminate floor.

Rayne loiters near the door with our bag of supplies, not quite on the other side of it, but I get the impression that's where she wants to be. She doesn't look at me, or anyone else in fact, just waits with her eyes closed and her arms folded.

Great. So I'm in charge?

"Uh, thanks, Noel. I had no idea you lived out here."

"I don't." He shrugs. "Jadzia does, but I was looking for her. Now I know what happened. Thank you for releasing her."

I'm not sure what surprises me more, the fact that he and Jadz are already intimate enough that he can be in her house without her, or that this is *her* house.

"No problem, I guess." I clear my throat. Then again.

At last, Wendy saves me from myself. "On the way here," he murmurs, "the air was thick. Don't know what it was, but the smell was wrong. And it was quiet. Couldn't scent another wolf for miles. What's happening?"

I glance at Rayne, but she still hasn't moved or opened her eyes. Guess I really am on my own for this one.

"SPEAR is no longer in charge of *edane* relations. During the riots, Jack called in—"

"Riots?" Spannah's eyes grow wide. "What are you talking about?"

Guess I'd better start at the top.

I draw a deep breath. "You better stay sitting down, guys. This is going to be a rough one. You too, Noel."

He sighs. "When you say things like that, I worry. But at least I'll have answers now."

"Yeah. I guess."

He and Jadz sit together on a smaller sofa and look expectantly at me. Great. Here we go.

Half an hour later, if not for the slight wobble in his step, I might never have known that Wendy was anything less than himself. He paces the living room, tight, stiff steps back and forth across the rug which already has a faint trail of grime from his filthy shoes. Another, longer trail marks Spannah's retreat to the bathroom a few moments before when the lad removed himself with the excuse of a churning stomach.

Whether the product of true nausea or fear, it doesn't matter; I fully sympathize with Spannah and half wish I could do the same. Instead, I force myself to watch and wait.

Even Jadz and Noel have stepped away, their excuse being to give us privacy and to keep Dire Wolf matters from the ears of Grey Tails. I've no doubt that Jadz could listen in easily if she wants to, but the gesture is appreciated regardless.

Wendy growls under his breath, clenching and unclenching his fingers which are tipped with inky black claws. "That dog," he cries. "That mutt. That mongrel. That…that…" he snarls, that awful, throat-rippling, feral exhalation so foreign on a humanoid body. "I knew he had ideas, but that he'd go this far? Swine. I'll kill him. I'll tear his limbs off his body one at a time. How dare he do this? How dare he splinter my pack—*my pack*—like this."

More fur bristles on Wendy's hands and neck, ever more visible as his rage swells. When he next looks at me, his eyes glow with werewolf amber. His fury is palpable against my skin.

"Wendy, it's going to be okay—"

He whirls on me with a roar, huge fangs exposed between his thinly stretched lips. "Chalks is injured. That is *not* okay." His pacing becomes a wobbly but purposeful stride toward the door. "I'm going after them. Now. Aleksandar can't get away with this. He'll know what it means to cross me. He'll—" Wendy bares his teeth at Rayne, still standing in the doorway. "Move."

At last she looks up. Her gaze skips to me for the briefest second, but then she directs her attention to Wendy. "No."

"Get out of my way."

"No." Her voice is soft but firm. "Until we know the streets are safe and that you are in a fit state, you should stay here."

Wendy's shoulders rise visibly. More fur erupts across his face and neck. "You don't tell me what to do."

"You're too close to the situation to think clearly right now, Mr. Gordan. Your rationale is flawed."

"Don't make me say it again, fanger."

"Okay." I step forward, hands raised. "Maybe we all need to stop for a second and think clearly."

"I'm clearer than I've ever been. I let my pack down. I trusted you, but I should have followed my gut instinct and stayed with my pups. I'm their alpha, their leader. They need me and I wasn't there. I let that monster take them all on his mad little mission and now who knows where they are. I need to find them. And end him. I should have done it before, but I'm…I was too soft." A note of sadness drifts across his voice, gone as quickly as it arrived. "I won't make that mistake again."

Rayne moves to stand more firmly in the door. She even puts her hands to either side of the frame to block it fully. "We need information first. You don't know where Aleksandar is, you don't know where the rest of your pack are, you have no idea what the sedation shot has done to you long-term, and we have no idea how long the drug from those drones stays active in the atmosphere. We need a plan."

"I need to find my people. Last chance, fanger." Wendy's weight shifts to the balls of his feet. I can see him preparing to pounce.

In response, a silver sheen slides across Rayne's eyes, clouding the usual autumnal brown.

I wedge myself between them, extending both hands to make space. I may as well have shoved against a brick wall for the difference my efforts make against Rayne, but Wendy actually stumbles a step back. He regains the lost ground quickly, but not before we notice the difference.

I expect him to back down after that, or at least acknowledge that he is still weak, but if anything that ignites his stubborn streak to a more passionate flame. Wendy glares down at me from his increased height, frowning through features almost lost beneath the fur and angled jawline of his hybrid form.

"Don't make me hurt you, meat sack. I need to get out of this house."

"You're in no state to go outside tonight."

"I won't say it again."

"Neither will I. This is for your own good, Wendy, please. Don't make me pull rank."

"You wouldn't do that to me."

"Try me."

He growls.

I wait.

Rayne touches my shoulder. It's only an instant, but enough to grab my attention. "You need to get out of the way."

"But—"

"This is going to get ugly. Please move."

Frustration boils through my gut. Why can't I fix this? Why won't anybody listen to me? Fuck, why is there nothing I can do?

A glancing blow across the side of my face throws my head to the side. Brightly coloured stars spin across my vision, but I'm still standing. I right myself and find Wendy preparing a second punch. He's slow though, and I drop to my knees and out of reach even as his arm goes overhead. He topples, falling beside me in a heap of panting, angry wolf fur.

"Wendy, please. Come on. You must see that you're not right. That sedation shot, its effects are still in you."

"But my pack—"

"You can't even hit *me*. Please." I put my hand on his shoulder.

He flings it away with a roar of rage and scrambles to his feet. Or at least he tries to. Rayne stands over him in a heartbeat, one hand pressed down against the back of his neck. He pushes up against it, but her grip is strong and immobile.

"Let me go, fanger. You hear me? You won't stop me helping my pups, you won't stop me—"

"Wensleydale Gordan," I speak as loudly as I dare. "By your pledge and your word I order you to sit down and stop fighting."

Silence.

I can almost taste my pulse.

"You…you…"

"I'm sorry." The words are out before I can catch them. "I'm sorry, Wendy, but you *have* to stay here tonight. Don't make this worse."

"Worse? How can it get worse?" He sighs, the fight visibly flooding out of him. "My pups. I've failed them."

Slow and easy, I scoot away from him on my hands and arse. "You haven't failed them. We just need more time."

"Time." Wendy grunts but doesn't move. "The one thing we don't have. What now, meat sack? If I can't leave this house and you don't know where my pups are, what are we going to do?"

"We need help. And I think I know who to call."

"Voicemail again." I end the third call from my mobile and drop it in my lap.

In front of me, Wendy has returned to pacing, only this time Spannah is with him. He follows right on his alpha's heels, scurrying to avoid being trodden on each time Wendy turns. He doesn't speak, but his eyes dart constantly with worry and fear.

"If you can't get hold of her, why keep me here? We're wasting the time I could be using to find my pups."

Back in the door frame, Rayne readjusts her stance, but says nothing.

"You punched me and I barely felt it, Wendy. You *can't* go back out there until we check on you. We need to know that the sedative hasn't made you—"

My phone rings, a standard two-tone chime of a call from a number I don't have stored. I have it answered and against my ear before the round of rings end. "Karson. You need to get off the line I'm waiting for a call, and—"

"No, no, don't hang up, it's me."

A huge sigh of relief flees my lips. Hadn't quite realized I'd been holding my breath. "Pip?"

"Yes, what's wrong?" Her voice is low, almost a whisper, and muffled as if by her hand.

"I need your help. Can you get out here? I have an address for you and—"

"I can't."

My grip tightens on the phone. "Come on, Pip, I wouldn't ask for this if I didn't need it. Please don't be stubborn and weird about this."

"I'm not. Haven't you heard? SPEAR is on lockdown."

"I..." I lick my lips. "Of course I know, but what does that have to do with you?"

A pause, rustling, and then her voice is back, more muffled than ever. "Some guys showed up from the military and started ordering us around. They stopped all our research. They've locked down every experiment running through the Foundation and are collecting all the researchers."

"What? Are you okay? Where are you?"

"I'm fine, I'm fine. Honest, I'm hiding in a supply cupboard right now. I had to find somewhere I could use a phone without them trying to cart me off somewhere. What's happening?"

This time as I wrap my fingers harder around the phone, it's as if gripping a lifeline. "Jack kicked off some weird emergency fail-safe. It brought the military in."

Pippa gasps. "Project Revival?"

"And how do you know about that?"

"There's a lot of stuff I know about that I probably shouldn't. It's amazing what people let slip in the cafeteria queue. Anyway, if that's what this is I don't want to get caught hiding. They'll arrest me."

"But I need you. You're the only one I can trust right now, and Wendy is all messed up. Remember the sedative I told you about? The new one that Maury used? It's still in him and it's making him weak. It has to be the Q-whatever it was you said."

I can all but hear her nodding. From over the line come a few muffled bumps and half whispered conversation. It passes after a moment or two.

"Quilax?" She makes an annoyed clicking sound with her tongue. "No, I told you, it's still in Scotland. We're not allowed to use it here."

"Then I need you to confirm what they *did* use because Wendy is in big trouble right now. He can barely stand."

Wendy completes his latest circuit of the rug and snatches the phone from my hand. As I move to retrieve it, Spannah slides into my path with a slow shake of the head.

"Pips, you little she-wolf, it's me." Wendy speaks into the phone with the faintest of smiles on his furry lips. "Yeah, yeah, well you know the meat sack, mayhaps better than me. She's an idiot."

"Hey."

He ignores me. "An idiot, but I'm grateful for her. I was rotting in that cell." A pause. "No, I feel fine up top, but my body...I hate to say it, but I'm slow. Couldn't string up a cat right now."

Wendy continues talking to my sister while I impotently try to get close enough to hear. May well as not have bothered though, because even with the phone to my ear it was hard to hear. Spannah keeps himself between the pair of us, apologetic, but resolute.

"...a sample? Fine, you can have one. I'll bring it over." Wendy's quick frown tells me clear as day the response to that statement. "Then how do I get it to you? Sunup isn't far off, you know?" Pause. Grunt. "Fine. We'll sort it. Stand by. Oh, and have your sister back." He flips the phone over his shoulder and walks off through another door leading deeper into the house.

I fumble to catch the flying device and press it back to my ear. "Pip, what's going on?"

"You need to get me a sample of Wensleydale's blood. What he describes *sounds* like the Q174X, but I can't be sure. I can test it against Scotland results and see what we're dealing with."

"Fine. I'll bring it."

"No." Her voice is a sibilant hiss. "You of all people don't want to get caught up here. You'll never get away. It has to be someone else."

"Like who?"

"Figure it out. You have about an hour before it's too late."

"But—"

The line clicks and the conversation dies. Well, shit.

Rayne moves away from her post by the door. "I could take it?"

"I don't know if that's wise. I think you need to stay away from SPEAR until we get Wendy fixed. Unless you want to stay in for *debrief*."

She looks unhappy but resigned. "Maybe Jadz?"

"Again, werewolf. We don't know if that stuff is still in the air or even if there's more coming. Same for Spannah. We need to keep *edanes* off the streets."

Noel ambles through the same door Wendy just used. He holds a small Tupperware tub half filled with a thick, red looking liquid. "Then me, sí? I'll go."

Rayne's nostrils flare. She turns aside quick enough that she actually bumps into the door frame.

"Did Wendy already give you that blood?"

A shrug from Noel. "He is like you, I think, quick with decisions and impulsive. He explained what your little sister said and I agree. You can't go. So I will."

I smile. Can't help it. "Just can't help but get yourself involved, can you?"

"Bah." He flaps a hand at me. "Why should you have all the fun? Besides I see your eyes. You are tired. When did you last sleep?"

I chance a glance at my watch. "Ugh. Too long ago."

"Then rest now. Spend some time with your Rayne before the sun rises. It won't be long from now, sí?"

"But what about Wendy?"

"You can't help if you are exhausted. Besides, he must wait. While you talked, Jadzia spoke with her pack mates. The drones the colonel spoke of? They still travel the streets and occasionally spray their gas. Werewolves are not safe outside, so regardless, we all must wait. But me?" He taps his chest with fake bravado. "I'm strong."

"You're thick-headed."

"Same difference." He waves the tub at me. "So I will take this and you, Dee-Dee, will stay here in the safe. Sí?"

I'd give a lot to argue with him, but now that he's mentioned sleep I can feel a yawn rising from deep within me. I remember how I should have slept the day before but hadn't been able to because of worry over Rayne. I remember my nap the morning previous; even that was nothing substantial.

Now, at close to four thirty, at last it's beginning to catch up.

With a sigh, I lower myself to the comfy squishiness of Jadz's larger sofa. "Fine. Just don't do anything stupid while you're out there."

"No, no, that is your job."

"Oh, ha-bloody-ha."

He grins and grabs a thick leather jacket from a rail near the door. After feeding himself into it, he tucks the tub of blood into an inside pocket. "See? I'm funny. Now, try to behave while I am gone. I will be as fast as I can."

"You'd better."

Noel places a hand over his heart. "I hear what you truly mean, Dee-Dee, and of course you are welcome. Soon. I will return soon."

And with that he's gone.

I'm alone with Rayne again.

She still stands near the door, a vast distance away within the confines of the living area. She sighs. I sit straight.

It's time we had a conversation.

CHAPTER TWENTY-ONE

Stretched up on her tiptoes, Rayne extends a hand while the other presses flat against the window frame. I pass her a thick strip of masking tape which she uses to further secure the sheet of black-out fabric pressed against the window glass.

"More, please." She smooths the tape in place then holds out her hand for another.

I hold the sticky strip on the tip of my index finger. "Rayne? Can we talk about this? Please? We can't put it off forever."

A loud burst of hammering cuts the air. Even though I know it's Jadz, even though I know she and Spannah are outside boarding up all the windows, I can't help but jump at the sudden interruption.

The bangs continue for a few more seconds, then stop. A flurry of movement...the sound of heavy lifting...then more banging.

Rayne ignores it all. "There's nothing to talk about."

"Clearly there is. But I need you to know, I'm not afraid of you. I know you won't hurt me."

She sighs. "You think it's that simple? That you can say 'I'm not scared' and all will be right again?"

"No, but—"

"You can't possibly understand what this is like, Danika." She stares down at her fingers. "I thought I had control. I thought I understood what I needed in order to be safe, but I hadn't really been tested. I thought I was strong, but..."

"You are strong."

Her shoulders buck, a quick burst of silent laughter. "Not strong enough. "Do you have any idea what you smell like? How rich and sweet the air is?"

"No. But you haven't touched me. You've not done a thing. How can you doubt your control after that?"

At last she turns. Still she doesn't look at me, but at least I can see her face. "Because I haven't touched you yet. Or come close to you. Distance helps, but…what kind of girlfriend can I possibly be if I can't touch you. Don't you remember when I tried?"

"It's not just about touch."

She growls, then begins to pace.

Wow. How can she be so small and dainty and yet such a bundle of power and strength? I can almost feel it pouring off her, the innate strength that comes from her *edane* state of being.

Her bare feet sink into the plush carpet, leaving tiny indentations that fill slowly as she walks by, only to depress again as she retraces her steps.

"Rayne, can't you see, I want to work through this with you. I want to reach a point that we're all comfortable and that you feel safe enough to touch me. That's all I want. Please."

"Well, we can't. Right now there are more important things to worry about. Like light-proofing this room. Tape, please."

I sigh, but what more can I do? I rip another strip off the roll of tape and Rayne returns to the window to further secure the blackout fabric.

Another loud selection of raps indicates another board going into place.

By now, the room should be as light-tight as it's ever going to get.

"Are you sure you don't mind staying here?" Perhaps a change of subject will help. It's clumsy and obvious, but the best I can manage right now.

Rayne shrugs. "I won't make it back to the house now and the Foundation is too far away. Besides, at least this way I can keep an eye on you."

"How? You'll still be asleep."

"I…" She clears her throat. "At least if I'm close I can help you when I wake up. During the day you'll have Jadzia and Spannah to help you out. And Mr. Gordon too."

"Wendy's in no state to help anybody."

She grinds her knuckles into the last of the masking tape strips and stands back to survey her handiwork. "That should do it, I imagine."

"Well, we need to make sure. A mistake with this could be fatal."

Rayne's lips quirk into a strange half-smile. "You carried me out of SPEAR in a body bag. Then you stored me in a cupboard."

The memory still makes me uncomfortable. Though not as much as the thought of what might have happened if I hadn't done so. "Desperate times."

"Mm-hmm. Tell the others to shine the torch. I'll shut off the lights in here."

I can't tell if it's an excuse to get me out of the room or not, but I do as she asks. Out the narrow room, back through the house, and out to the rear garden where Spannah and Jadz stand with hammers in hand.

"Well?" Jadz cocks an eyebrow at me as I approach. "Will it hold?"

I glance up at the sky. No sun yet, but the skyline is paler than it would otherwise be. "I think so."

"You need to do better than that."

"I know, I know. Just shine your torch through it, okay? We'll find out."

Spannah is first to obey. He takes a battery powered torch off the ground and shines it in slow, systematic lines across the mishmash of boards and nails hastily shoved against the windowpane. He doesn't speak, just concentrates with a visible tightness to his jaw and neck. "Seems fine to me."

I open my mouth then, an instant later, think better of it. Instead I smile at him and take the risk of patting him on the shoulder. "It'll be fine. Promise."

He sniffs deeply but says nothing.

Jadz rolls her eyes. "Calm down, pup. It'll all work out. Noel will find out what's wrong with Wensleydale and then we'll get on with it."

"With what, though?"

She grins and, for a moment, a hint of werewolf amber flashes in her eyes. "We find that prick Aleksandar and teach him a lesson he'll never forget."

"He's a Dire Wolf. Aleksandar and his punishment are nothing to do with you."

"Oh? And when he marched his little Dire pups through the streets and picked fights with everybody he came across, that didn't make it something to do with me? And every other wolf in this city? He brought humans down on us like an avenging hammer. Who knows how many of us are hurt or captured or both? Trust me when I say this, kid, if I see him... he's going down. Whether any Dire Wolves are there or not."

Spannah swells like an overripe peach, and I make my getaway before the conversation escalates. Not that I'm worried exactly, but Jadz's devil-may-care attitude is exactly the right thing to wind the loyal and faithful Spannah up the wrong way.

Back inside, Wendy is in the spare room with Rayne, doing his own part to inspect the walls and window. The pair are as far away from each other as the room will allow, but I'm grateful their argument has stilled enough to allow this.

"No light from outside," he mutters. "No air, either. Smells clean."

"Good. Rayne, how long?"

She closes her eyes for a moment. "Ten minutes. Maybe."

"Okay."

Silence.

Wendy gruffs softly at the back of his throat. "I'll...I'll check on the pup." Gone.

Chuckling, Rayne tugs off her shoes and socks. "Not exactly a master of subtlety, is he?"

"He's trying."

"I suppose. Maybe I should just be grateful." Blouse next, which she lays on top of her shoes and places in a corner.

The room has no bed or even a chair. It seems to be a utility room, because there is a washing machine against one wall and a tall drying rack beside it. The shelves on our side are stacked with detergents, fabric softeners, and garden tools, while the wall nearest the window has a bicycle leaned up against it.

Rayne continues to undress, neatly stacking her clothes under the shelves.

I've no idea why she chooses to be naked when sleeping for the day. Not that I mind, the view is wonderful, but somehow watching her strip down in this environment is even stranger than usual. None of the comfort and normalcy associated with our safe, high-tech home.

Moments later, she stands before me in her underwear, soft white cotton with a teasing hint of lace. Nothing fancy, but then it doesn't have to be for Rayne.

She holds up a roll of black bags. "Ready?"

Not really, but what choice do I have? Instead of answering, I take the roll and begin to open up the bags. Each has an eighty-litre capacity, and while not big enough to fit a human standing, a few of them joined with more of the masking tape are enough to secure Rayne.

She helps by climbing into the first like a sleeping bag, tugging it up until the top reaches her ribs. Then two more after that. She smooths down the plastic, as though preparing for some bizarre sack race, then stretches out across the ground.

"Come on, Danika. I can feel it coming."

As if to compound the sentiment, my watch gives a familiar beep. Five minutes to sunrise.

I arrange the next three bags like a hood over Rayne's top half. It's awkward, but I can't help but feel wrong about covering her up this way. Like a kitten some awful person is about to throw in a river.

The bags rustles as she twists and twitches to get comfortable.

"Are you sure about this?"

"Not entirely, but it's a little late now, wouldn't you say?"

She has a point. I stretch the three flaps of plastic out across her face. "Wait."

I pause with the masking tape halfway to my lips to cut with my teeth.

"You won't do anything foolish while I'm asleep, will you?" She bites her bottom lip. "You *will* wait for me before you do anything rash?"

"I—"

She frowns. "Promise me. Please. Don't do anything until I'm awake again. Promise me."

The words catch in my throat. "On my locs and hope to trim."

Rayne smiles. The gesture lights up her entire face and then, the brightness dies. Her eyes flutter closed, breath gusts from her parted lips with a sigh, and her entire body becomes still, floppy, and loose. Dead.

One last beep from my watch and I know the sun is up.

I fight away the last of my unease to finish taping Rayne into the bags, taking especial care not to stick any of the tape to her face and nose. It's not perfect, but it's the best I can do for now, and that's going to have to do.

Back in the living room Jadz sits on the sofa with her legs up and a mug of something steaming resting on her knee. She holds it out of me as I enter the room. "Coffee?"

I want it. Or part of me does, but the rest of me, the part still yawning and struggling knows the caffeine hit won't do me any favours.

As if reading my mind, Jadz turns the mug to point the handle toward me. "Decaf. Just thought you might want something since…y'know."

"Wait, what?"

She shrugs. "Lunar blood always makes me thirsty. I thought maybe you were the same. I'd offer you some chocolate, but I don't have any in the house." Her smile is crooked, the tilt of her head suggestive and playful.

I've no idea what it means, but I accept the mug with a nod of thanks and take the other end of the sofa seats. "Rayne is safe now. It's not great, but the best I can do."

"Mm." Jadz toys with a lock of her hair. "Pretty vampire all tucked away for bedtime. Ready to pull out again when playtime begins in the evening."

"Jadz—"

She raises her hand at me. "Hey, I'm not here to judge. It's none of my business what you get up to. But I am a little curious, if you don't mind me saying."

"About what?"

That smile again. "Why a vampire? There's no shortage of pretty human women, if that's your thing. But a fanger? You? Danika Karson? What happened?"

Now I'm gnawing on my own lip. A nervous tic I've most certainly picked up from Rayne. "Nothing *happened* I just…"

"Wanted to try something new? Exotic? Special?"

She's closer. I'm not sure when she moved, but the space between us is suddenly smaller. That and her knee is brushing against mine.

She's warm and solid against me, a sensation I can't place when I last felt.

"It's not like that. I—she—" The mug wobbles in my grip.

"Oh, I've flustered you."

"No, I just—"

"It's okay. You're cute when you're flustered. The big, bad SPEAR agent all tongue-tied and nervous. Wait until I tell my pack about you. They'll be fascinated."

I sit straighter. "Now, wait a second—"

Jadz's laughter cuts right across me. It's big and bright, just like her, and the gesture rolls through her entire body like a liquid ripple. "I'm joking. Wow, Agent, you *are* a little high-strung. What's wrong?"

"You really have to ask?"

"Look. It will be fine. Noel will be back before you know it and we'll have all the information we need to help your little Dire Wolf friend. Then we can deal with that pus-boil Aleksandar."

I sip the coffee. "I don't think it's going to be that easy."

"Why not? Things are as easy or as difficult as you make them. If you want something, you take it. If you want to be somewhere, you go there. If you have an itch…you scratch it."

Her hand touches my knee.

I find myself swallowing harder than I should need to. "Jadzia, I—you—we can't—"

"Can't what?" The hand becomes a fingertip, swirling light, teasing circles around my kneecap. "I've never had a lady SPEAR agent before. And Noel tells me some delightful things about your body."

"What?"

She laughs at my indignant outburst. "Calm down. I only mean that he tells me about how well you spar and how strong you are. You sound almost like a werewolf. A real queen bitch. I'd love to see for myself sometime."

Queen bitch. Nice. I think. I mean, it must be a compliment coming from a werewolf, right? I'd be flattered, but for some reason my mind is all foggy now. I can't really think. Instead, I take another sip of the coffee and set the mug on the floor.

"I'm going to get some rest. While we're grounded maybe the best thing to do is sleep."

"Good idea. Why don't you come upstairs? You can bunk with me."

"Uh, actually down here is just fine."

Again with the smile. "The bed is far more comfortable, Danika. I can make it comfortable for you. With you."

A gentle warmth rises in my cheeks and neck. Is she actually hitting on me right now? "Uh, I know you and Noel do the poly thing, but I don't—I mean, I'm not—fuck."

"You could try? You never know, you might enjoy it. Have you ever had a werewolf before?"

"No. I wasn't planning it either."

Jadz finally stops running her finger over my knee. The smile wilts and she takes to her feet with a graceful bound. "I'll grab you some blankets."

"Thanks."

"No problem," she says and leaves the room.

CHAPTER TWENTY-TWO

When I wake the room is dim, but not wholly dark. Curtains are drawn across the large bay windows and two light blankets cover my body from ribs to toe.

I'm stretched out on the sofa, as much as its length will allow, head propped on my rolled up coat. For a moment I'm not sure what's woken me until I notice the silhouette of a person standing against the window.

I rub my eyes. Not even sure of when I fell asleep, but from the way the light has changed and the pattern of shadows on the wall, I can guess that it must be getting into late afternoon now. Perhaps even evening. If there's something to be grateful for in the cooler months, it's the shorter days and longer nights.

"Rayne?"

The figure at the window stiffens. Then chuckles.

"Oh. Sorry, Jadz. Is everything okay?"

"Noel isn't back yet." Her voice is flat and emotionless, but not quite enough to fool me.

"What time is it?"

"Late enough that he should be back. What have your people done to him? I tried to call, but he won't answer. And when I went out to look, I could find no trace of him."

I sit up. "I thought we all agreed to stay indoors."

She growls and turns away from the window. A few steps and then the sofa gives as she perches on the other side. "I had to. I had to know."

"And?"

Silence. Long, worrying silence.

"There are no wolves out there. At all. I scented one or two, but they're very well hidden. And like your sister said, there are still drones outside spraying the streets. I had to duck three just to get back. Military everywhere and big tanks closing off the streets. City-wide lockdown."

"But Noel? What did you find out about Noel?"

"Nothing." She growls. "I heard a couple of rumours, but—"

I'm already pushing the sheets off my legs. "I'll call Pippa. Maybe he's still at the Foundation. Or he had to detour to find somewhere safe."

As my eyes grow accustomed to the dim light, I can see more of Jadz in the shadows. She's changed her clothes and brushed out her hair. It doesn't shimmer with the same blue sheen in this light, but that bold cut is hard to miss.

"He would have called me. Sent a message. Something. This isn't right." Her voice cracks, not quite with panic, but as close to fear as I've ever heard Jadz get.

I scoot across the sofa toward her. "Hey, it's okay. He'll be fine."

"Then where is he?"

"I don't know. But if we have to, we'll find him too. Let's give it a little more time. He probably had to lay low until sundown to get more from Pippa before coming back. She's a vampire too after all."

I feel rather than see Jadz turn toward me. "I thought she was your sister."

"She is."

"And a vampire?" A soft exhalation. "Interesting. Now that explains a lot."

"It was an accident. Nobody meant for her to—"

"Oh, I'm sure it was an accident. No one ever means to become a blood sucking parasite." She sniffs. "Sorry, that was mean. I'm just worried." Again, that note of fear in her voice. Before I realize it, I've reached out to put my arm around her shoulders.

She's hot, and that near unnatural warmth in her skin reminds me of her werewolf blood.

"Listen, I'd worry too, but Noel had his guts torn out by a vampire and still sat up the next day cracking jokes about porn. Trust me, he'll be fine."

"Trust you?" She turns to me. Like this, with my arm around her, her face is close enough that her nose brushes briefly against mine. I can see her nostrils flare as she scents me out, picking out the aroma of my words.

"Hmm. I suppose I do trust you. I trust my senses and they seem to believe in you."

"Thanks. I guess?"

"Thank me like this." And then her lips are on mine, pressed hard against my mouth and parting them with a deft flick of her tongue. She tastes hot and vaguely meaty, almost savoury, and her hand slides up to curl into my hair.

Fuck, she's strong. Very strong.

The overhead light flicks on. The bright flare startles and blinds me, jerking me back while I squeeze my eyes shut for several seconds.

By the time I've adjusted to it, I look up in time to see the door to the living room close. The sound of running steps retreats into the distance.

"What the hell, Jadz?" I wipe my mouth with the back of my hand. "How many times do I have to tell you? And who the hell was that? Who put the light on?"

"You can't blame a girl for trying. Besides, I had to taste you at least once." She chuckles and leans back against the sofa. "And thirty seconds after true sunset? Who else could it be but the little fanger?"

Shit. Oh, shit, fuck, shit and shit again.

I scramble off the sofa, half tangled in the blankets still clinging to my legs. I kick them free, then trip again, this time on the mug of unfinished coffee still nestled beside me. Dark brown liquid spills across laminate and into the rug, but I don't care. I chase after her.

"Rayne."

I've already lost the sound of her footsteps so I make my way to the utility room where she spent the day.

"Rayne? Is that you? Will you stop for a second? Please."

There, standing beside the washing machine, forcing her legs into the second half of her jeans.

"Rayne—"

"Don't talk to me."

"But you don't understand—"

"Understand?" She glares at me, the wild light of vampire silver in her eyes. "I understand that I've been wanting you, needing you for weeks now. I understand you're afraid of me. I understand that I'm a dangerous, monstrous beast and that now that there's an easier, safer option, you're happier to go with that instead."

My mouth hangs open. "What? No, it's not like that."

"Then what is it, Danika?"

"I—she—we—"

Rayne snorts and jerks the zips of her jeans up. She shoves her arms into her blouse sleeves, and then fastens that too, all but spitting as her fingers fly over the buttons. "I'm leaving. Clearly you and Jadzia have this all in hand, so I'm going to report to SPEAR. I think it's about time I had my debrief."

She snatches up her socks and shoes, then shoves past me.

I'm chasing after her without thinking, half running, half skipping to keep up with her furious pace. "Wait, you can't do that. They'll just detain you until who even knows when. Come on, Rayne, will you wait for a second?"

"Wait?" She stops dead, sharp enough that I end up running into her back. "Wait? Do you have any sense of how long I've been *waiting?* No, I'm done with waiting. If you trust that werewolf stranger more than me—me!—then I'm not going to wait for the rest of my life. And I know my life is a really long time, but I'd rather not spend it pining over you."

"Rayne, come on."

She's at the main door to the garage now, shoving past a startled Spannah to hit the switch that raises the shuttered door. "I can handle you being scared of me, Danika. You should be. I'm rather afraid of myself at times. But I won't sit around and wait for you to make up your mind while first test-driving each *edane* you come across."

Her words are a punch to the gut. I actually feel my breath catch, forcing me to take a moment to recover. "What? No, it's not like that. This isn't what you think."

"Then what is it?"

"I…uh…"

She growls. "I thought so. Please get out of my way, Danika."

"No."

"Move or I will move you."

"Wait, Rayne, please."

She puts out a hand and gently, but inexorably shoves me to one side. Her next steps take her straight into Noel who appears on the other side of the door with a stack of papers and folders tucked under his arm.

"Ah. Ladies, so good of you to meet me. I have so much news for you."

Rayne snarls, loud and vicious enough that Noel actually leaps back a step. The stack of stationery slips from his grip and fans across the floor.

"Guau, Rayne, what is this?"

"Move aside."

He does so immediately and stares with a bemused frown as Rayne marches up the drive and left along the street.

"Rayne, come back."

She doesn't. Instead she increases her pace. She's not running, but as I follow I'm aware that my pace is well above my usual walking one, even with my longer legs and stride. I trot along at her side, half skipping sideways to keep up. "Rayne, would you just give me a moment to explain? Please? It honestly isn't what you think, and we need to settle this once and for all. You need to understand that—"

Again that sharp stop, only this time, she's far enough ahead that I have space to avoid another collision.

"I understand, Danika. I understand that your prejudices against vampires are never quite going to leave. I understand that you don't trust me. I understand that every other little thing up to this point has been more important than us sitting down to talk about your problems."

"But I didn't kiss her. I didn't want this. This is all a misunderstanding."

She glares at me. "You honestly think this is about something as stupid as a kiss?"

"I...well, I did. Until you said that."

Rayne rubs her temples with her fingertips. "I'm not a fool, Danika. I know full well you don't feel anything for Jadzia. She's been stalking you like deer since we met, but I *know* you're not interested. But do you have any idea how it feels, seeing her, a stranger, get close to you when I can't even hold your hand? You swore a blood oath to her, let her lick blood off your palm, but the last time we shared a kiss, you all but leapt out of my arms. Duo, Solo, Willow, Erkyan, even Shakka, they all get closer to you than I have in the last few weeks, but I'm 'the one you want.' I'm 'the one you trust.'" A tear catches in the corner of her eye. "You say it, but you don't show it. I...I can't believe you anymore."

I think about the past few hours; my hand on Spannah's shoulder, Jadz's tongue against my skin, Shakka's warty hand in mine as he shook it. Even the flimsy flutter of Hawk's wings as he carried me through the night sky.

Oh, fuck, she's right. She's totally right.

"Rayne, I..." Words catch in my throat. "I'm so sorry. I didn't realize. I didn't know. I didn't see that's what I'd done. I'm so, so sorry."

"Perhaps you are." She shakes her head. "But that's not good enough anymore." Rayne turns and continues her walk along the street.

I step to follow, pulled up short at the sound of my name from further behind.

It's Noel. He's running full pelt, followed closely by Jadz with a dejected looking Spannah bringing up the rear.

"Dee-Dee, there is a problem."

"Yes, there is and I need to deal with it first."

"No, no, not jealous spats, my friend, it is the Dire Wolf alpha."

I'm bristling. "This is not a jealous spat, Noel. Rayne and I have to—wait, what?"

"Wensleydale Gordon. He is gone."

Oh. Great.

❖

"What do you mean 'gone'?"

Noel pauses long enough to direct a furious glare at Spannah. "This little one, he tells me the alpha decided to leave during the day. He crept out while you were sleeping."

I drag a hand back through my hair.

Far in the distance, Rayne is becoming a smaller and smaller speck. Soon she'll be wholly out of sight.

"I can't deal with this right now, I—"

"He went to gather his pack." This from Jadz. Her voice is firm and clear, though with a vague hint of what I hope is discomfort. Does she have any idea what she's done to Rayne and me? Maybe, maybe not, but when she looks at me, her gaze flicks down rather than holding true to my own.

Good.

Spannah clears his throat. "I'm sorry. I know what you said, I know what we agreed, but he's my alpha, I have to do what he says."

"I know, I know. Just tell me what happened."

"While you were sleeping Wensleydale decided to retrieve our pack. He said he couldn't wait for more news, and that he had to make sure everyone was all right."

"But his oath...he agreed to stay."

"I don't know about that. But he did say the night was over and that as soon as the sun rose, he could do what he liked. I didn't think to question it at the time."

Aaah. Smart little mongrel.

I'd told him he couldn't leave *tonight*. Sure it was a technical loophole, but it was big enough for him to slip through and keep his word to me under his pledge. The night must have been over by the time he left.

Spannah goes on. "He had me make up a bed to look like he was sleeping and carry one of his coats through the house to settle his scent here."

I sigh. "Then how did we even know he was gone?"

"I asked." Jadz shrugs.

Of course. The Gray Tail ability to scent lies would make it impossible to hide the truth from her. The crazy plan might have worked if Spannah had been able to keep himself out of sight.

I'd applaud the plan, but now isn't the time. Now I need to figure out how to fix it.

Once again, I look over my shoulder. Empty streets. Fuck.

"Um, okay...we need to find him and get him back. Noel, what did you find out?"

He glances back at the house. "Much, but we can talk about it as we drive. None of it is good and we must catch up with the alpha as quickly as possible. He is in terrible danger." He starts walking, pausing only when it becomes plain that I'm not moving. "Dee-Dee, please. He is your friend, yes?"

"Of course he is."

"Then we must stop him."

I find myself staring at the empty street. Rayne hasn't gone far, she can't have. If I follow now, I might be able to track her down. I have to explain all this. She has to know that I never meant to avoid her touch. I have to make her see—

"Dee-Dee." Noel's voice cuts through it all. "Your sister tells me the alpha is weak. The chemical affects blood chemistry. I don't understand it all, but the wolf is not himself. Do you want to save him or not?"

All three of them stand halfway back to the house, watching, waiting.

Noel's words have brought a look of horror and fear to Spannah's face. He is clearly regretting the decision to help his alpha leave, and now his whole demeanour seems to beg for aid.

I have no choice.

I turn aside from the empty street and join the others in a quick sprint back to the house.

CHAPTER TWENTY-THREE

I drum my fingers against the dashboard urging the car to further speed. Despite my urge to bounce up and down in my seat, Noel keeps the car at a relatively safe but wholly illegal forty miles per hour as we make our way back into the city.

As he mentioned, the streets are largely abandoned, sparse pockets of people milling about outside shops. The usual hustle and bustle of the West End is replaced by clean-up crews and obvious SPEAR agents, working together to remove evidence of the werewolf rampage from the night before. Drones still fly overhead, blue and red lights blinking as they patrol the streets. Military trucks and the occasional tank are still obvious, as are the soldiers marching the streets with rifles and shotguns angled over their shoulders.

I adjust my belt and the various tools hanging off it, from my gun to various chains, bolts, magazines, phials, and knick-knacks. Oh, and the additional silver tools Rayne was smart enough to grab when we restocked.

How could this happen so fast? How could things go so wrong?

"Noel, baby, I still don't get it. How can this sedative change the Dire alpha's brain?" Jadz yawns from her space in the back seat. "It's just a drug."

He drums his fingers against the steering wheel. "I don't fully understand myself, but that is what Phillipa said and she is the Foundation's most celebrated researcher. She told me the sedative affects blood chemistry. It makes basic changes to a wolf's mind."

Spannah kicks out behind me, drumming his heels against the back of my chair. "But how? How does this affect Wensleydale?"

"How do men and women become wolves on a whim or at the turn of a lunar cycle?" Noel lifts his hands briefly from the wheel in a gesture of exasperation. "Science? Voodoo? Higher powers? We just don't know, young wolf. But this is the truth I know."

I grit my teeth. "So you're saying as long as this drug is in Wendy's bloodstream, he'll be less than himself?"

Noel fishes into the gap between our seats. There are papers there, the same ones he brought back, and he shuffles through them one-handed before stopping on a slim red folder. "If you know more than me about the biology and the chemistry, then please, read these. I only share the simple version your sister gave."

Even though it's pointless, I skim through the tightly typed pages within the folder. Huge chemical names I can't pronounce and parts of the nervous system I can just about identify by comparing them to my own working knowledge of first aid. But blood chemistry and neurology is well beyond my knowledge when it comes to humans let alone in *edanes*.

"How long does it last?"

Noel guides the car around a corner. "The brain stuff? We don't know. The physical things, perhaps they last for one day. Perhaps four. Maybe two weeks. There is not enough research and results to be sure."

"Well, at least I know now why Pip was so against it. Nobody knows anything."

Again Spannah kicks out at my chair. "Faster. We need to go faster."

The car speeds on.

Despite myself, I find myself scouring the streets for Rayne, hoping, praying to catch sight of her on the way. Of course there's nothing and my heart sinks a little deeper into the toes of my boots.

What have I done? How could I let this happen? Just what the hell is wrong with me anyway? Rayne is unlike any other vampire I've ever met; I knew that right at the start. She wouldn't hurt me or anybody else, so why? Why has it become so hard to let her touch me? It's not like she'd ever hurt me, not like the beast who killed—

Jadz slams her hands into the back of my seat, jarring my neck and cutting off my train of thought. She snarls and leans forward between the front seats to point at two figures standing up ahead. "Not military," she hisses.

Several seconds pass before I figure out what she's talking about.

The two figures standing in the road before us certainly look like military. They have a rifle and a shot gun between them and the same green/black clothing. Their caps are drawn down across their faces to cast thick shadows on their features, but there's nothing about them that says "danger" to me.

And yet…"Noel, stop."

He eyes me warily, but obeys, letting the car idle a few feet back from the matched pair of soldiers.

I open the door and step out onto the road.

❖

The air is still thick with the remnants of the weaponized gas used by the drones. It clearly isn't enough to cause werewolves discomfort because both Jadz and Spannah leave the car with no problems and position themselves to flank me.

The first of the two soldiers steps forward. "You need to turn back, miss. You can't travel this way."

I run my hand across my hip to pick up my ID lanyard. "I'm Agent Danika Karson. Why can't we go through?"

"It's not safe."

"Why? What's out there?"

At my side, Spannah twitches and grasps at my elbow. He doesn't speak, but his grip is crushing, and I fight back a wince of pain.

"Not sure, Agent. We had some reports of a little trouble further up the road, so we're stopping all vehicles traveling through until further help arrives."

Jadz growls. It's all the confirmation I need.

"Who are you really? You're clearly not soldiers. SPEAR? Actually, no, we're smarter than that, and not one of my colleagues would pull what you're trying so give it up and start talking."

One of them levels his rifle at my face. "We don't want any trouble, miss. You just need to stay back here."

Spannah's grip tightens on my elbow. "Listen."

Whatever he's hearing, it's too faint for my human ears to catch, but Jadz certainly hears it. Her growls intensify as she takes a step forward, arms slightly outstretched.

The second of the two fake soldiers looks back over his shoulder. He tilts his head, and for the first time, I can see the wide grin stretching his lips. "It's too late now anyway. There's nothing you can do to stop it. It's over. Only a matter of time."

"What are you talking about?"

Spannah's nails sink through my jacket and hit flesh. "There's fighting, can't you hear it? It's Wensleydale, it has to be. He's fighting. I need to be there. I need to help my alpha."

The rifle swings toward the young wolf. "Don't even think about it, pup. You stay right where you are. That has-been Wensleydale is just about done, and unless you want to join him, you'll stay right here with us."

I raise my hands. "We don't want trouble. But we need to get into Dire Wolf territory. Please."

"But you're already in Dire Wolf territory." The second fake soldier lowers his shotgun to point at me. "Didn't you hear? When Aleksandar laid down his challenge, he extended our reach to encompass all of the West

Side. We're growing, Agent, and it's about time. We're growing and there's nothing you can do about it."

A little whimper from Spannah forces me to pause and remove his hand from my arm. Small shreds of denim dangle from his lengthening, sharpening claws.

"West Side is neutral," Jadz snaps. "Every idiot knows that. Not even a clown like Aleksandar would risk destroying pack truces to extend out here. He's not insane."

"No, he's not. He's a visionary with more ideas and strength to pursue them than some elderly weakling like Wensleydale could ever hope for. He's going to draw us out of the darkness and make our pack strong again. Starting with clearing those Blood Moon freaks."

I lift my hands to shoulder height, palm out and well within view. "Blood Moon? I've never heard of that pack."

The two men steady their grips on their guns. "No? You're slipping, Agent Karson. That's what those new wolves call themselves. The ones with the weird smell and the pack power that makes everybody sick, as if that wasn't bad enough."

"Yeah." The second spits at the ground. "They slither in here all snake-like and sneaky and then, the ultimate disrespect, they name themselves after our biggest and most sacred festival. Vermin. All of them. It's that woman's fault. It has to be. They were the first ones Blood Moon went to."

The first growls low in the back of his throat. "As if any self-respecting pack would allow a woman to lead them."

My head is spinning. After so long trying to learn about this new pack, I finally have some information, something new that I can use.

I risk a step forward, but Jadz is faster. She hooks an arm around my waist and heaves me off the road, shouting back over her shoulder as she goes. "Noel, do it. Move yourself, pup."

I have just time to see the startled looks in the faces of the two wolves before the car guns forward with a roar and squeal of spinning tyres.

The guns fire, the roar of the shotgun followed by the harsh crack of the rifle.

Glass explodes in the front window, but the car keeps coming, bearing down on the two wolves like a huge, metal cannonball. Follow-up shots go wide as the wolves panic, but the car hits them both, sending them high into the air and away. They hit the Tarmac hard and roll several paces.

"Fuck, Noel, what the hell."

He sits up from his slouched position in the front seat and punches out the rest of the shattered windscreen glass. "Jadzia warned me this might happen. We don't have the time."

"But—"

Jadz carries me back to the car with my legs dangling, tucked under her arm like a bag of potatoes. I'd be impressed with the feat if not so wholly pissed off.

"Shut up, Agent. If we want to get to your friend, we need to hurry. It sounds like he needs us."

"But—"

Spannah rushes back to the car and leaps into the rear seat. "She's right. I know you can't hear it, but you have to trust us. Wensleydale is already fighting and I *have* to be there."

I yank free of Jadz's grip and, after one last glare, climb back into the car. Glass litters the seat, and in the headrest, a small, smoking hole shows the entry of a rifle bullet. I shove the worst of the glass into the foot well and sit.

"Fine, I get your worry, Spannah, but what about you? Why do you care what happens to the Dire Wolves?"

Jadz clips her own seat belt into place. For long seconds I wonder if she plans to answer me at all, then at last she lifts her gaze to mine. "I don't. Not really, but I'm not too proud to say that Wensleydale is a strong and just alpha. From what I've heard of this Aleksandar character, I'd say we *all* have something to worry about if he ends up leading a pack with that much of a reputation and prestige. He needs to be stopped."

The car rumbles beneath me, easing off again and rapidly gaining speed.

"You mean that, Jadz?"

"I don't lie."

I believe her.

A breeze whips through the broken window, stinging my eyes, dragging my hair back. As we travel away from West Side and closer to Misona, at last I begin to hear what my companions clearly heard some time ago.

Howls, growls, and shouts. Battle. A dominance battle.

We can't get the car much further once we reach the outskirts of Misona. The crowds are simply too thick.

From the startled looks in the eyes of both Jadz and Spannah, it seems that more than Dire Wolves have turned out to see this fight. I recognize a few faces from other packs, even as, more than once Jadz turns up her nose at others.

When the press is too thick to drive any further, all four of us exit the car and begin the walk.

Most of the sounds I hear now are those from the crowds. There's almost a carnival atmosphere to the streets, though it is clearly a carnival tangled with fear and danger. There is no fighting here, the occasional scuffle perhaps, but nothing serious or dangerous. Most of the sparring taking place on the streets seems to be for a joke, or to emulate what is happening further on.

I hear more than one voice call out Aleksandar's name and others calling Wendy. Money, booze, and cigarettes fly through the crowds like sweets. I can't believe they're betting on this. Don't they understand?

Spannah takes the lead. Whatever sort of connection he has to Wendy it's enough to pull us through the crowds. He moves slowly, but with purpose always with his gaze fully forward. I follow with Noel close behind and Jadz bringing up the rear. It's probably unnecessary, but I feel safer with a werewolf ally at our backs. Noel seems to feel the same way because his hand rests on the hilt of the hunting dagger on his hip. The buckle is fastened, but I know how quickly he can release that pop-stud should the need arise.

We've been walking two minutes before I recognize the burned out husk of my old car. The battered vehicle is blackened and scorched with no glass left in any of the windows. The huge dents from the previous fight have been partially knocked out but clumsily so, leaving uneven surfaces across the roof and bonnet.

A couple writhe together on the back seat, apparently uncaring of the charred exterior. Their embrace is hard and fierce, almost feral, and their happy growls join the surrounding cacophony.

Noel taps my shoulder. "This isn't right."

"You're telling me."

"No fight should take this long. If the younger one was right, then why hasn't this crowd dispersed?"

I shrug. It's all I can do. I mean, I have a couple of thoughts, but each one seems crazier than the previous, and the last thing I want to do is give the universe ideas in how to screw me over.

We're near the children's play area now, the space in which I usually meet Wendy when we have intelligence to share. As ever, the climbing frame is rusted and broken, the swings bare and skeletal. The slide holds a small cluster of wolves who watch as we approach. They turn and whisper among themselves but make no move toward us.

Spannah gives a sudden cry and leaps forward. "Wensleydale." His charge meets a rude stop as three other wolves step across his path, but that doesn't stop him clawing, kicking, and biting at those in his way. "Wensleydale, can you hear me? It's Jim. It's Spannah. Wensleydale?"

So *that's* his real name.

I risk a few more steps forward, then stop of my own accord when it becomes clear that pushing further would do more harm than good. But at least I can see now.

Aleksandar sits on top of a pile of rags, daintily chewing something red and thick from beneath his nails. The crest of his Mohawk is floppy now, hanging over one side of his face like a scarf. It's matted with thick clots of blood and leaves faint smears against his neck and cheek each time he turns his head.

The rest of him appears unharmed but for the ragged remnants of his clothing. Clearly he has been through a partial shift and back again to do such damage to his clothes.

Seven more figures stand around him, most recognizable from the confrontation with Chalks. These must be his soldiers, and bodyguards. Great.

As he spies me, Aleksandar's smile stretches wide and feral across his thin lips. "Agent Karson, welcome at last. Oh, and you brought friends."

Spannah continues to struggle. "Stop it. Get off him. Get off him right now, you bastard."

What the hell is he talking abo—"Oh, shit."

The pile of rags Aleksandar is using as a throne…it isn't rags. Or not *all* rags. Now, at last I can see the arm protruding from beneath them, the rough sole of one battered shoe. And there, at the back, right beneath Aleksandar's rear I finally recognize Wendy's face.

A marrow-freezing chill settles over me.

"Wendy?"

He twitches, but doesn't speak.

"Wendy? For God's sake, get up you mangy dog. You're better than this."

Aleksandar laughs and reaches down to slap Wendy's backside on which his feet rest. "You'd like to think so, wouldn't you? But here is proof of what I've said all along. This dog is weak. He's less fit to lead us than that freak Petra, but at least she put up a fight."

The crowd around us laughs. Noel gives a little moan. Jadz growls low under her breath and settles her weight to the balls of her feet.

Aleksandar ignores it all. He only has eyes for me. "We waited for you, Agent. I said you would come, and like a well-trained little pet, here you are."

"Get off my friend."

"In a moment. After all, I don't want you to miss the show." Aleksandar leans his weight forward a little. He even lowers his foot and grinds his heel into the back of Wendy's hand. "I need you to understand something about the way it's going to be from now on, *Agent*."

Spannah gives a despairing howl. His nails begin to blacken and the hair across his head thickens and spreads down the back of his neck. The three wolves restraining him increase their efforts, eventually forcing him to the ground.

My chest feels ready to explode, such is the pounding of my heart. I can feel it in my head, in my ribs, hell, even in my teeth. The danger here is real enough to smell and taste, but a glance around me makes clear that there's nothing I can do.

Yet.

"You see, *Agent*, now that I'm alpha of the Dire Wolves, I wanted to let you know firsthand. The exceptions made for you at the hands of the previous alpha no longer stand. You are no longer welcome in our territory and certainly no longer considered a pack-friend. As for that blood-sucking rat you call a girlfriend...well, if I ever see her here again, the next time *you* see her it will be in the matchbox I use to return her remains."

I tilt my chin. "You are *not* the alpha of the Dire Wolves. The alpha of his pack is Wendy—Wensleydale Gordan—and you have no authority over me."

I say the words with a strong clear voice, projecting past the wolves in my path.

Inside, my heart continues pounding at my ribs, but a single mantra repeats in my mind over and over: *Get up Wendy. You have to get up. Get up, Wendy. Please get up.*

The cluster of wolves growls and whispers, watching their leader for guidance.

Aleksandar smiles a long slow smile. "Oh, of course. Silly of me, I'm not alpha yet. There's one thing I need to do to cement that. To make clear that I am the strongest, most powerful wolf of this pack. That I am the *only* one able to lead us."

He stands.

Wendy gives a great gushing sigh, sucking in huge gulps of air. He flops to his side, still wheezing and, for the first time, I get a proper look at him. The pool of blood beneath his body is huge. Even with layers and layers of coat to soak it up, still I can see the red fluid dribbling away from his twisted, broken form. One leg is wrenched up behind him, awkward and painful. Clearly broken from the angle. Both arms are beneath him, one with a bruised, battered hand, the other sporting cruelly twisted fingers.

I feel my stomach give a disgusted lurch. "What did you do?"

"Hmm?" Aleksandar looks over his shoulder, for all the world as though he's forgotten the terrible bodily harm he's inflicted. "Oh, that. I got bored waiting for you, Agent. I thought I'd have some fun first. Pity though, I'm not used to my toys breaking so easily."

"You—" Before I can complete the step I hadn't been aware of taking, Noel grabs my arm. He holds me tight against him, one arm actually hooked across my chest to hold me in place.

"Dee-Dee, no. He wants it."

Oh, he wants it. I'm pretty damn sure he wants it, but is he prepared for what he's about to get?

The rage builds in me and I struggle against Noel's grip. "What the fuck is wrong with you? This isn't a game. You're toying with real people and real lives. Wendy is a good man and you've destroyed him."

"Not yet." And with a sly smile, Aleksandar returns to Wendy's fallen form and drags him up by the collar.

I can taste my pulse. Time seems to slow. Somehow I know what's coming, but there's nothing I can do to stop it.

My mouth opens. Words trip off my tongue, but I can barely hear them over the roaring of my own blood thundering in my ears.

Aleksandar hefts Wendy's limp body up to shoulder height and smiles wide and bright. Still watching me, never once breaking eye contact, he shoves the claws of his free hand deep into Wendy's throat, clenches, and pulls.

Blood fountains everywhere. Not as much as it might from a healthy body, but enough to spray out by a good six feet. Raw, panicked choking sounds issue from Wendy's slack mouth while his maimed hands flutter weakly at the gory red mess that was once his throat.

CHAPTER TWENTY-FOUR

There's screaming. Shouting.

No, no, no, no, not again. I know those screams. It's me. It's my voice and I'm yelling, shrieking, cursing, bellowing. My face is wet, tears, blood, or a mix of both. Still I'm pulling, heaving against Noel's grip, but now Jadz is helping him and they're both drawing me backward. Away. Away. Away.

After a few seconds of my struggles, Jadz puts me back under her arm like before. Her muffled exertions give away how much tougher it is this time, but she is still able to pull me away from Aleksandar.

In the time it takes me to writhe free of her grip and back to the ground, Aleksandar has cleaned his claws, sucking blood off each one in turn. I stare as he drops Wendy's dying body to the road. Watch as he lifts one large hand toward me. With a glare of my own, I pull my gun into my hand.

"Kill them," he hisses.

The three wolves pinning Spannah to the ground at last release him. He throws himself down over Wendy's body, sobbing like a child, gathering the body into his arms to rock it back and forth. He doesn't seem to care about the order for his death, doesn't even hear it, simply hugs Wendy's body to his own and wails up at the night sky. Wails that quickly turn to howls of grief and despair.

Noel immediately has his gun in one hand, the knife in his other. He backs up, a sideways shuffle step while turning his head this way and that. "Time to leave, baby."

Jadz tightens her grip on my waist. "Leave where?"

"Just away from here."

But there's nowhere to go. The seven guard wolves plus the other three are closing in around us from every side, forming a solid wall of bodies. They step closer, closer still and show off the tell-tale signs of changes with growing claws and lengthening hair.

The three of us stand back to back.

My gun clicks as I cock it. I can barely see through the tears and my outstretched arm is wobbling enough that I feel the trembles right up to my shoulder. No. This isn't good. I can't shoot like this.

"Don't do it," says Noel. "We are agents of SPEAR. Attacking us is a crime, you know this. We *will* defend ourselves."

Someone leaps at me. Man, woman, I don't even know, but instinct squeezes my finger on the trigger before I can figure it out. The bullet, though effective, goes wide and clips the attacking wolf across the side of the head. They drop to the ground with a spray of blood from their head, howling and kicking back and forth.

"Consider that a warning." Noel's voice ratchets up the urgency. "We won't allow you to harm us. Move aside."

More growls from the crowd.

My hand wobbles again.

A woman partway through her shift works her way forward. Denim and cotton split along the seams as her young body becomes too large for containment. Long, golden hair thickens and darkens to tan which goes still further into a deep brown colour. A growl slides from her lips.

Crack.

The growl turns into a startled howl and the she-wolf drops to one knee, clutching at a wound in her thigh. Hatred burns in her eyes, visible even through the fog of my tears.

"Last warning," says Noel. "Next time I aim for heads."

A shrill yip at our back signals Jadz cutting off an attack. My gaze flicks her direction for the briefest second, but that's all it takes because next thing I know, I'm flat on my back, gun barrel jammed into the mouth of the wolf trying to bite off my face.

With a yelp, I fire and scrunch my eyes shut against the gout of blood that drips from the abruptly slack mouth. The body collapses atop mine and the weight is immense, crushing my chest and stealing my breath.

I can't catch any air. I still can't see, and more gunshots fire into the night as Noel commits himself to a fight.

It's already hopeless. That much is plain to anybody with two brain cells to rub together. Too many wolves, nowhere to run, and a squishy human body to boot. I'm dead. I know I am. As dead as Wendy.

My vision clears as I use a blood-spotted sleeve to wipe my face.

"No. No, I won't let that grumpy old bastard die for nothing."

The pep talk gets me moving. Gets me driving my heels into the ground and thrusting sideways to shove that dead weight off my chest. Air swells my lungs in a rush, but there's no time to enjoy it, just the gleaming amber eyes of two more werewolves in full wolf form, bounding toward me with their tails up.

I don't bother standing, just aim, gun hand cupped with the other for support.

The first wolf drops like a stone, without a sound. The next, dances sideways and takes the rushed second shot along the top of its head. A mangled flap of skin flies away on the breeze, a shredded piece of furry ear.

It keeps coming, jaws hanging wide and angled down to scoop up my flailing feet. I scoot back and aim again, this time to send a bullet powering through face and neck. The wolf drops and skids to a stop beside me, panting and bleeding. Dying.

"Dee-Dee!"

I can't see Noel, only hear the panic in his voice over the rush of blood in my ears and repeated gunshots. Scrambling to my feet scrapes my hands and knees, but it's so much better than being prone.

Perhaps shocked by the follow-through on the threat to shoot, the remaining four wolves of Aleksandar's guard stop advancing. Jadz has shredded her clothing and met her hybrid form, a huge, stooped beast in white and grey. Her tail has a curious little tuft in it, but most interesting is her eyes—bright blue.

Nobody has touched her yet, probably because the look on her furry face is fierce and terrifying. She extends a massive, claw-tipped paw and grabs me by the scruff. "Let's go."

"But—"

"They only want you. The rest of us are incidental collateral. Now move."

I've no idea how she knows this, but I can't fight with a face like that.

Jadz pushes me ahead of her, then reaches back to perform the same scooping motion on Noel.

"Baby—"

"These idiots won't dare attack a Grey Tail, Noel. Not if they want strength left to fight that other pack. Just go."

So we run.

I hate running, especially like this. Sure, I'm fit enough to casually run several miles, but a leisurely hour or two of exercise is worlds apart from sprinting for my life. I can't control my breathing, my legs are unsteady, and every few strides I'm forced to dodge or outright shoot at an advancing enemy.

Far too soon my gun clicks instead of cracks and I'm left with a useless hunk of metal I can't stop long enough to reload.

Noel and I are side by side now, haring back to the car. It isn't far, barely a quarter mile, but it may as well be on the moon for all the good it does us. Jadz still protects our backs, darting back and forth to intercept any of the last four guard wolves.

Around us are the observing crowds, and I catch more bets flying back and forth as they gamble on our fate. But none of them move toward us. Yet. Whatever Aleksandar has arranged here I grudgingly thank it, because we might just manage to escape four werewolves. Might.

We leave one street to take another, rounding a corner marked by a twisted street lamp. Fire burns in my lungs from the breakneck pace, and the first twinges of a stitch starts to tingle beneath my ribs. There's no choice though; keep running, don't look back, even when my locs ruffle on the rush of air from a wolf a little too close.

Only after a few more paces, do I understand why no one seems to be following us. I slow to a bemused walk, while at my side, Noel does the same. He lifts an eyebrow at me and reaches into a pocket low down on his thigh. He fishes out two magazines and tosses one my way. Though I catch it and reload my gun, I really can't see what difference it will make.

Our car is thirty feet away. Thirty impassable feet. Between it and us is a large crowd of at least twenty werewolves, with Aleksandar smiling at us from the centre. He straightens his ruffled clothing and smooths at his hair, but otherwise looks calm and collected.

"They weren't attacking," Noel mutters, holding his own weapon close. "They were herding."

Jadz, still guarding our rear, lets out a rough grunt of agreement. The four wolves she has been keeping off our backs also stop to form a small but undeniable blockage back the way we came.

"I do enjoy a good hunt, Agent. It whets the appetite wonderfully. And I think the best way to reward my loyal pack is to give them some fun. You don't mind, do you?"

The butt of my gun seems to burn in my grip. "Eat shit, Aleksandar."

He tuts at me. "Oh, I intended to, but really, is that any way to talk about yourself? I never knew you had such terrible self-image."

Noel chuckles, deadpan and without mirth. "Oh, he's funny, Dee-Dee. So fucking funny."

"You I have no quarrel with, Human. If you make it out of our territory then you've earned my...not respect...let's say applause. Yeah, *applause* for amusing me. But that's all. Same with you, Grey Tail. Leave us to our fun and you'll not be harmed."

Jadz sniffs the air. "Huh," she gruffs. "At least you *believe* that's true."

"Dire Wolves have always had good relations with Grey Tails. Why should that change now?"

"Because you tortured and murdered the best thing about this pack of slimeballs and alcoholics."

Growls. Snarls of anger. Aleksandar lifts his hand, but several seconds pass before the rumble of disquiet stills.

"I defeated Wensleydale in a fair dominance battle. Anybody here will attest to that."

"Bullshit," I yell. "It can't have been fair." I know I shouldn't, but I can't help myself. "He was drugged. He wasn't himself and you must have known that. Any one of you must have seen that something wasn't right."

Surprise flickers through Aleksandar's eyes. Or at least I think it does. The emotion is so quick that I'm immediately unsure it was there at all. His next words reinforce my doubt.

"*He* challenged *me*, Agent. I had no choice but to fight him after that. I'm sure you know at least that much of our culture."

I do, but it rocks my understanding of Wendy to the very core to hear it.

He had been alpha. Without a direct challenge from a subordinate, that position was safe and secure. For him to issue a challenge to someone lower in the pack was to give up the position of alpha until he regained it. Like a defending boxing champion fighting a contender to maintain their belt.

"He wouldn't do that. He...he could have banished you. He could have stripped you of everything and made you leave. He didn't have to fight. Why?"

"Perhaps he had something to prove? Boredom? Who knows how that fool's mind worked?"

"No. No, you're wrong, you must be. *He* had all the control, *you* were just making trouble. Why would he take that risk? What did you do to him?"

"I? Not a thing. Agent, Wensleydale Gordan was an arrogant fool who clearly thought there *was* no risk. How wrong he was. Now do you see? An impulsive, reckless man like that has no place guiding a pack like this. They need strength, wisdom, and careful thought. They need me."

Noel touches my arm. "The sedative drug. It must have clouded his thinking."

A stray tear slides down my cheek. Why? Why did I let Maury force me into pumping that evil stuff into my friend?

"You took advantage of him."

"Of a situation turned expectedly to my favour?" Aleksandar shrugs. "Yes. Of him? No. He did this to himself."

"But you...you didn't have to kill him. If you won, it was over. Why did you have to kill him?"

He grins. "We're not mundane wolves, agent. While wild packs need the strength of every single body that joins them, we don't. I simply culled the chaff."

My hand is wobbling again. I can only tell because I've lifted it and the gun, to aim right between his smug, smug eyes. "You'll pay for this."

"And who's going to make me? You? Surely not."

"Believe it."

"We'll see." Aleksandar lifts his voice. "Change of plan, friends. Here are the terms of my new game."

"I'm not playing any games with you—"

Jadz snarls and steps up to my side. A strange ripple begins at her head then works down, fluffing out her fur as it writhes through every scrap of skin. It's accompanied by the creak and crack of morphing bone and the wet slicking-sucking sound of sliding muscle. And instant later, she has achieved her fully changed form, a huge grey-white wolf with the same tufted tail and gleaming blue eyes.

Her massive paws are light and soundless, each easily the size of my face. When she drops to her belly, the top of her head still reaches my ribs with space to spare. She nudges me with her muzzle.

Aleksandar chuckles. "Hear me, Dire Wolves. This here is Danika Karson, once declared pack-friend. Know she is no longer and that I... well, I want her heart. Whole, in pieces, I don't much care, but I want it in my hands. Tonight."

Curious murmurs. Shuffles and whispers.

Shit.

"The one to bring me her heart will have my personal thanks and be under serious consideration for the honour of being my second. Consider it an application for the position." Another chuckle, then he steps back with a sweeping "after you" gesture. "Go."

Fuck, fuck, fuck.

I steady my grip on my gun, aiming outward even while my head screams in terror. My mind is racing, plotting escape routes, counting enemies, but none of my calculations have any good news.

Then something hard closes around my forearm. Teeth. Fuck, it's huge wolf teeth.

I twist, ready to fire the gun, but it's just Jadz. She's pulling at me, first gently, then roughly, yanking me down toward her back.

"You're sure?"

I can read the dry look she gives me in return, even through lupine features, so I obey the command and clamber onto her back. Then she's up and the ground disappears beneath my feet. Jadz leaps forward with a flex of her back legs, a bump that rocks me forward into the fur around her neck. I lean low and cling to the thick ruff of fur there.

This is nothing like a horse, or a pony. Jadz may be close to the size of one of those elegant creatures, but her body is built differently. Her sides are thick and powerful, and even through the dense fur, the flex of every muscle is tangible against me.

She dashes straight at Aleksandar, snarling furiously, and though several others clutch and snap at us, the move is too unexpected and downright bizarre. That and only that saves us from immediate death.

"Wait, we can't leave Noel."

Jadz gruffs again and keeps going, a speedy sprint that uses ground, buildings, and parked cars in equal measure. She seems unconcerned and I've no choice but to tell myself that every wolf within a half-mile radius is now more interested in me than a lone SPEAR agent with an accent and an attitude.

I'm riding a werewolf. I'm riding a fucking werewolf. My insides threaten to flop out my mouth, but this is still miles better than flying. All I can do is cling tight and hope I don't fall.

The braying, snarling pack behind us is a fair distance away. Many have paused to shift from human forms to full wolf ones, opting for speed over power. With this head start, we may get away, but others in hybrid form are keeping pace with us in a series of leaps and bounds.

"Do you even have a plan?"

No answer. Of course Jadz can't answer in this form, but I hope she has some sort of idea. Sure, getting out of the Bowl might help, but there's no way of knowing how attractive Aleksandar's prize is. Enough for them to follow us? Maybe, but I'd rather not find out.

The wolves following move exactly as I imagine their natural, mundane counterparts would. They follow, but at a measured distance, some on the flanks actually outpacing us to block off retreat via the sides.

More than once, Jadz dives at a bisecting street, only to skip back and out of reach when her way through is filled with enemy bodies. This happens three more times, each time forcing us to turn rather than continue our route. By the fifth back-tracking two-step that snaps my teeth together, I've no idea if we're running deeper into the Bowl or out of it.

"We can't keep doing this. We need a better plan. Jadz?"

She ignores me, focused on running and avoiding enemies. Beneath my thighs her flanks are heaving and her tongue lolls from the side of her mouth. She may be *edane*, but with my added weight I don't know how much longer she can run.

I check my gun again. Then my sides. I have one magazine of silver bullets left, which is by no means enough. But I also have a couple of little throwing disks made of silver and some—

A misstep in Jadz's stride snatches my attention. She's panting harder than ever and her steps are weakening.

"Jadz? Hey, Jadz, come on. We just need to get out of the Bowl. Then—"

A soft rumbling sound catches my attention. Then a buzz like a small engine.

I look left and right, but there's nothing to see except more wolves, keeping pace with us and herding us where they wish. Nothing behind either and nothing ahead except for a dark, swift-moving streak topped by two bright white points.

What the hell is that?

The streak swishes past me, hard and fast enough to lift my hair and ruffle my clothes. I turn in time to see it strike a wolf sneaking up on our left, hefting it into the air and hurling it several feet. The startled werewolf yips like a puppy and crash-lands into several others, scattering them like bowling pins, but the streak doesn't stop. I lose it, then catch it again, only when it performs the same motion with another wolf, this time punting it across the ground where it skips like a fleshy, furry stone.

Jadz wheezes one last time then slows to a half limping walk, with ears and tail turned down.

I slip off her back and cradle her muzzle in my hands. "Jadz? Can you shift back? Hey, look at me?"

The blue eyes close, then spring back open before she turns her head to my left.

I follow her gaze and catch that streak once more, darting back and forth between the stunned wolves. Everywhere it moves, red splashes up in short, sharp fountains until at last it stops outside an abandoned storefront.

There, fingers dripping, fangs exposed, eyes bright with vampire silver, is Rayne.

My heart leaps hard, a rush of relief and joy rapidly replaced by a sinking sensation when I recognize the glow in her eyes.

It's a brighter, sharper silver, one I've seen hints of only a few times in the months we've known each other. Her fangs are long, extended past their norm to drip a slick mix of blood and saliva against her blouse.

In one hand she holds something soft, red, and dripping, and in the other, the buzzing remnants of what appears to be one of the military drones.

She swings it in an arc before her and a spattering of some thin clear liquid flies through the air. Where the drops hit the confused and bewildered wolves, yips, howls, and snarls of pain spring up.

"Rayne? What are you doing here?"

Her head snaps toward me. "Followed. Help."

"Yes, but—"

"Help. For Danika. Must help." A growl follows on the end of her words, roughening them into something dark and feral. "I won't let them hurt you."

At my side, Jadz gives another low wheeze. She stands but seems to do so with a struggle and nudges her way forward to stand between me and Rayne.

"Wait, wait."

Too late. Rayne has already seen. She parts her lips and screams, a shrill, bone-chilling exhalation of pure rage.

The drone whines in her grip and spits a white gout of pressurized gas. The wolves close by back up at once, but not all of them are quick enough to avoid the fumes so dangerous to their kind.

Some fall, some stumble, all of them toss their heads to and fro and stop any sign of aggression. Many of them begin to whine and paw at their eyes, others loll their tongues and retreat into neighbouring streets.

"It's okay, Rayne. You're here. I'm fine."

Another shriek, and she hurls the remnants of the drone at my head. The machine is small and most definitely broken, but still large enough that I really don't want to be hit by it. I duck with my hands over my head, but Jadz leaps up to snatch it out of the air.

More gas erupts from the mangled piece of a machinery and she gets a mouthful that immediately has her whining, wheezing, and coughing. She spits it to the ground and leaps on it with all four paws, using her impressive weight to pound it into fragments.

Good. Those things are a menace.

"Rayne, you need to listen to me. You need to stay calm, please."

The uninjured wolves, after seeing the drone dispatched, begin to creep around Rayne. They want me, I know they do, but the presence of a vampire on their territory is just too much for them. If not already fired up by Aleksandar's horrific "game" this would have been enough to whip them into a furious rage.

The wolves surround Rayne in a tight circle. They act just like wild packs do, constantly moving, searching for weak points, each taking cues from the other as to when to stand, when to retreat and when to attack. It's a strangely beautiful, if deadly dance…that lasts all of three seconds.

Rayne dives into them like a scythe, using fingernails and teeth in equal measure to tear into the wolves like so much paper.

The first succumbs to a bite to the throat, not enough to tear out flesh and fur, but plenty to send a jet of blood firing into the face of one of the others.

As that one falls, Rayne moves again and drives both hands into the flank of another wolf. Her fingers sink as far as the third knuckle and even from my position, the wet squelch of tearing flesh is sickening.

She lets the beast fall then turns again, now crouched low to sweep beneath the belly of another and punch with all her might.

Bones crack, probably ribs, and the huge wolf yips helplessly as it dangles five full feet off the ground.

"Rayne. Rayne, please, stop. You can't do this."

Jadz is pulling at me again. I've no idea what her growls and rough barks mean, but the terror in her eyes is easy enough to read. She wants me on her back again, and while part of me longs to hop on board and flee, the rest of me knows I can't. Not with Rayne in full-blown mania.

By the time I look back to Rayne, she has three more wolves down, not cutting or biting, just pulling with raw strength. A severed tail twitches on the ground near her foot, while an ear lies nearby in another puddle of blood.

Seconds later, she slams the wolf she holds over her knee, snapping several more ribs and surely the spine as she goes.

"Rayne, snap out of it. Please, I'm okay. I'm honestly okay."

But the wolves won't let her stop. Enraged by the maiming and murder of their pack mates, those remaining continue to attack, with more rushing up every second.

The new arrivals have to choose between capturing their prize and defending territory, and many of them do indeed choose to help their brethren against Rayne. One or two, however, clearly savvier than their companions, spot the distraction as an opportunity to capture me.

I fire the reloaded gun, trying as much as possible to injure rather than kill. But as they inch closer and closer and my ammunition drops ever lower, I know there isn't much choice left.

Again Jadz pulls my sleeve. Her blue eyes are watery and cloudy, long pink tongue dotted with blisters and sores. Yet still she pulls me on.

Fuck.

I know she's right, but I can't leave. Can I? Can I really go knowing Rayne is still fighting in the middle of this madness?

A wolf snaps at my leg. The attempt misses, but my dodge backward takes me right into the claws of yet another paw and agony sings across my left arm.

The pain is unreal, like a flash of fire across my chest. The world swims before me in a dizzying swirl and I'm falling.

Instead of ground I hit something warm and soft. Something furry and solid.

Once more, Jadz lowers herself, this time to shuffle herself beneath me and carry me away. I don't know where she's going, but it's not happening fast, her cautious pace interspersed with a limping hop at every third step.

Blood trickles down my arm. It's not a bad scratch, not deep, but the pain is incredible, like liquid fire scorching across my skin. Is this what it feels like to succumb to the werewolf virus?

I'm still distantly thinking of that when I notice that the yips, growls, and snarls of one-sided battle have ebbed.

I look back.

Rayne is still there, but none of the werewolves are. She stands in the middle of a bloodied, furry pile of death, holding one of the fallen against her lips to suck at one of the numerous wounds littering the body.

"Oh, fuck," I murmur.

Rayne's head snaps up.

My chest constricts.

Surely she couldn't hear me? Not from this distance?

Regardless, Rayne dumps her prize on the ground and starts after us, legs pumping, arms swinging, eyes ablaze with silver.

"Faster, Jadz. She's going to catch us."

There's no "going to" about it. No sooner are the words from my mouth than Rayne's flash of vampire speed has caught up. She snags Jadz by the tail and an instant of confusion follows in which I realize that though Jadz is no longer moving, I certainly am.

My body is flying, sailing through the air like a kicked ball. Then the ground is coming up to meet me, my arms are flailing, legs pedalling, and there's nothing I can do except—

Darkness.

Chapter Twenty-five

I wake in a bed. It's soft, white, warm, and cosy, but not at all where I want to be.

I sit up and cry out when the needles fed into the back of my hand begin to pull and twist.

Great. Hospital? Again?

Yup. Stark white walls, a single window, and long strip lights in the ceiling casting harsh, unnatural light. My clothes are folded on a chair that stands beneath a TV mounted to the wall on an extending arm.

Movement on my right.

I swing toward it, but I'm still hindered, this time by thick sheets tangled around my body.

Close to the bed is a lamp, a low table, and two chairs. In one of the chairs, is Noel.

"It's okay, chica, you're safe. Lie still."

I allow my body to sink back into the mattress. "Oh, thank goodness. Jeez, I thought you might be dead."

He stands and walks to the side of my bed, smiling wide. "Perhaps I would be if you were not such an attractive prize, Dee-Dee. But I am well. Bruised, maybe, battered too, but very well. All things considered."

"What happened? Where's Rayne? Aleksander? What happened to Jadz? Is she okay? Did Rayne hurt her? What happened to the Dire Wolves?"

He scoots around the bed to a low table and pours a cup of water from the jug standing on it. Instead of passing it to me, he drinks heavily, replaces it, then comes back to my side of the bed.

"Ah." He scratches his chin. "So what did happen then?"

I wait.

He groans. "That Aleksandar creep made his game and you ran with Jadz. The best thing you could do I think, because as soon as you did, none of them cared for me." He shrugs. "I missed most of it, but when I caught up there were many dead werewolves. And you, on the ground. Rayne was there too, standing over you. Jadz was…down."

Oh. Oh, hell.

I immediately reach for my neck, my wrists, my hands. Even my thigh, which I can access easily through the medical gown I seem to be wearing right now.

"Wait, did Rayne—"

Noel's eyebrow twitches. "No. She did not. Not you, nor Jadzia. Though I wonder if that was choice or the desire to remain unseen if she wished to do so. The military forces arrived soon after. They tracked a destroyed drone."

I nod again. There's nothing on my neck. Not a scratch. And yet I can't help but feel…violated.

"Rayne had it. She used it to spray at the werewolves."

He frowns. "Then a pity so many are dead. It would have been useful to study them and the effects it has on them. Like your other friend."

Oh, no. Wendy.

The rest of the night comes back to me in a rush and the familiar burn of tears starts behind my eyes.

"Did you see what they did to him? When…when Jadz and I left, did you see what happened to his…body?"

"The other wouldn't leave. The uh, the tool boy?"

"Spannah?"

"Yes, him. The pack moved the alpha's body, but the boy would not leave his side. He said his place is always with his alpha, so he wouldn't leave."

I lower my head to my hands. "What a mess. What a huge, stinking turd. What have I done?"

The bed gives a little as Noel perches on the side of it. "You? Nothing except your job. It's not your fault this happened so stop doing that."

"But Wendy—"

"—is not your fault. He chose to fight. Not a wise choice and perhaps not made with a sound mind, but *he* made the choice. Not you."

I nod, even if my heart doesn't believe it. "How many wolves died?"

"We don't know. The military counts, but mostly they question Rayne."

That sits me bolt up upright. "They have Rayne?"

A soft rumbling sound fills the air, cut by the occasional squeal of a stiff wheel or pulley. A man walks by my open door, dressed in the uniform of the residential Omega agents. He pushes a cart filled with blankets, bandages, and medical robes and gives a start of surprise when he sees me upright.

"How you doing?"

I look him up and down. "Been better. What's going on?"

"You had a fall. Knocked you out."

"How bad?"

He shrugs. "No visible damage or bleeding besides the trauma. If you want, I'll send a senior in so you can get a debrief?"

I think it over, then shake my head. "Thanks, but not yet."

"Up to you." He keeps going, pushing the noisy, squeaky wheeled cart ahead of him.

Back in relative privacy once more, I look to Noel. "Did they take Rayne to Shakka?"

"Don't think so. All debriefed agents are still here."

"Even vampires?"

Another shrug. "They seem to use vampires. Perhaps more than we do. For swimming, for speed, for heights. They seemed very interested in Rayne when she gave her name."

"Can we sneak her out?"

"What? No. No, we cannot, Dee-Dee. Why do you say these things?"

"Because—"

"No. She's fine. They will not harm her, so just relax and be well." His sharp tone softens a fraction. "You did frighten me, chica."

"Aww." I try to shift the mood with a bright smile. "I didn't know you cared."

"Of course I care. I've always cared." Despite my attempts, Noel's tone and expression remain serious. "You are my friend. But not just this." He waves an absent hand toward my bicep and head where, for the first time, I feel the crisp white linen of fresh bandages. "You walk a dangerous line, with vampires and werewolves. Friends and lovers."

"Says you."

He nods. No hint of a smile, just gentle acceptance. "True. I do. But Jadz and I...we have understanding. And when she returns from debrief we'll have more conversations, but we are not too serious. But you and Rayne..."

My body stiffens before I can help it while my mind flashes back to the horrific sight of blood streaming from her open mouth.

I sigh. "Can I tell you something?"

"Always."

I glance at the door. It's empty.

"She scares me, Noel. You weren't there. You didn't see her. I mean, I've seen vampires in blood mania before—hell, I've seen *her* in mania before—but with her it's a whole new level. She...she's dangerous."

"As are all *edanes*."

"Yeah. But I'm only dating *this* one. I…I honestly don't know if I can handle it."

Noel picks at a scab on the back of his hand. "I was curious. Always, though I hated to admit, I knew you would draw the attention of some *edane* one day. So much for us humans, right? And us men."

"What are you saying?"

"You were always close with them, interested in them. Perhaps their strangeness or their power, but humans never caught your eye the same way an *edane* would. Sometimes I wonder if I were a werewolf or a gargoyle… and female." He chuckles. "But never a vampire. Never, ever a vampire and that makes sense. I know what happened to your father."

I grip my sheets with both hands. My knuckles are tight, pale knots. The ceiling lights catch the face of my watch. "I don't want to talk about that."

"And I won't make you. But after that hurt and pain, then for you to fall for a vampire? It confused me. Still does."

"I can't help what my heart wants, Noel."

"But you try. You fight it with your head."

"For good bloody reason. She destroyed ten wolves, maybe more, with *her bare hands*. Just tore them to shreds like paper into confetti. What chance do I have against power like that? And how do I know if…if I'm going to be next?"

Noel stops picking his hand to look me dead in the eye. "She would never hurt you on purpose, Dee-Dee."

"Yeah. *On purpose.*"

A soft knock draws my attention to the door. Both Noel and I turn to face it. He squeaks. I gasp. In the span of a heartbeat, my heart and spirits lift, then crash right down into my toes.

"Hi, Danika."

I swallow back the sudden spiky lump of fear filling the back of my throat. "Hey, Rayne."

Noel vaults from his seat on the edge of my bed. "You two must talk, sí? I'll get out of the way. Now…out of the way." He's still making excuses and muttering as he squeezes through the partially blocked door and darts out of sight.

Fuck.

The room somehow seems fuller without him in it. I can hear the low murmur of a TV or radio in another room. More squeals and rumbles from push trolleys. Even low voices from somewhere down the hall.

Ah, so easy to listen to all of that and take it in, rather than exposing myself to the pain in Rayne's face.

She enters slowly, almost sheepishly, with her head bowed and her hands clasped in front of her. I can see the faint shine of a rubber wristband on her left wrist, thick and black with red stripes. When she sees me looking, she holds the whole hand higher for me to see.

"Identification. It will show the Extra Mundane Control Unit that I've already been through debrief and deemed 'fit for duty.'"

I flinch. "You know that's no better than the chip the Foundation put in your shoulder, right?"

She shrugs. "If I want to keep working, I follow the rules. And I *do* want to keep working."

"So...you heard that, didn't you? Noel and I?"

A nod.

"How much?"

"Enough to know that we need to talk. Right now." She moves deeper into the room and angles herself as if to sit on the bed the same way Noel had. Halfway there, she sighs and instead grabs the chair from beneath the TV. She sits on it facing me, almost six feet away.

I can't remember the last time I felt so apart from her.

"What was debrief about?"

She sighs. "Really? That's what you'd prefer to talk about?"

"I—"

"It was fine," she snaps. "They gave me a psychological test to determine my state of mind and used the score to decide if I were better suited in the field with humans or at a desk in an admin capacity. I passed." She adds with a dry chuckle. "Scored highest they've seen in fact. Made them doubt I'm a vampire at all. I had to tell them to scan my FID for the details."

I'm tangling my hands in the sheets again. My knuckles hurt so, so much. "I...um. Good. That's good."

"I'm not so sure. Most of them didn't want to let me work based on...on what I'd done. There was a discussion over my scores versus my actions. I seem to be on probation."

"I guess that's better than being locked up."

"Perhaps. But others weren't so lucky. Maybe they didn't take the test seriously enough or perhaps they really do think that way, but some agents have been suspended. Indefinitely."

"Who?"

"A couple of Betas. One or two Gammas. Link."

"Link didn't pass?"

Rayne folds her arms and leans back in the chair. "Apparently he told the test invigilator that he couldn't take the test until he had something to eat. Low blood sugar. When they offered him something, he asked if one of the soldiers would flavour it with a few drops of bile or stomach acid."

Can't help but snicker at that. "For real?"

"Mm-hmm. Clearly you find that funny, but they didn't. He's in holding right now."

"What? It was a joke. It must have been a joke."

"Joke or not, it was foolish. He shouldn't have said it. Now he's in a cell along with Shakka and those other agents."

That stops my laughter cold. "Shakka's locked up too?"

"Are you surprised?"

When I stop to think about it, no, not really. But I can't help but wonder why so many of those I'm close to are deemed unfit for SPEAR work. Makes me think I've done well in avoiding their "debrief" so far.

"Now, Danika, are you done avoiding the subject? Or is there something else you want to divert with first?"

Okay, ouch. "Rayne—"

She lifts her hand. "I heard what you said. And you're right. You're impulsive and stubborn and very often you don't think things through, but your instincts rarely lead you wrong. And what I heard is your instinct talking. It's telling you to stay away from me."

I try to swing out of the bed, but again, the bloody needle in my arm stops me. "It's not like that, Rayne. That isn't what I meant."

"Of course it is. And you're right. I don't know if you realize, but a blood mania like that, or one brought on by hunger—they're amnesic." She nods at my sceptical frown. "Mania has different forms and intensities depending on the trigger, but the worst of them often leave the vampire with no memory of what they did, or control while they're doing it."

"I've never heard of different forms before."

"It's…new research."

"But—"

"My point is, that I don't remember what happened a few hours ago. I've been informed, first by Jadzia, then by the soldiers who took me in, and now I have your memory of what you saw. But I have no idea what I did." She sighs.

I wait. Deep inside I know where this is going. I can already feel it and though I hate it, I can't form the words I need to stop it coming. Everything feels shut off and muted, like I'm a sudden observer to my life about to fall in the shitter.

"I have no idea if I hurt you or not. I can't even remember if I *wanted* to. That type of mania doesn't allow me the luxury."

"Rayne, please—"

Again with the hand. "I remember being angry. So, so angry. I left Jadzia's house meaning to walk back to SPEAR, but then I saw the car go by. All of you were in it except Mr. Gordon, so I deduced what had happened. And, as I made my way deeper into the city, the danger was clearer still. I travelled to Misona to find you, but by the time I arrived, word carried fast through every wolf there—the new alpha wanted you dead. He wanted your heart in his hands." Her voice cracks. So does the chair as she grips the flimsy arms.

"I can't describe what went through my mind in that moment, the fear and panic, along with fury. How dare he? How *dare* he threaten *you*? And then…then I was chained and shackled in a van with several unconscious wolves beside me, all of us on the way to the EMCU holding facility." She lifts her hands in an "I don't know" gesture.

"There was blood all over me. I could taste it. From the traces left on my tongue I knew it was *edane* blood, probably werewolf though I couldn't be sure. My nails were choked with gore, guts, and fur. Even my hair was matted with it. I didn't know what I'd done or who I'd harmed. I didn't know anything—they wouldn't tell me.—until after they asked all their psych questions. And now I'm here. I was only permitted a change of clothes ten minutes ago."

My throat is locked up. I can barely move, much less speak.

This account of blood mania is both fascinating and horrifying. What must it be like to lose chunks of memory like that? To simply vanish into your own mind and reappear so much later with no idea of what had happened?

"I don't want to hurt you, Danika. Nor would I forgive anybody who did harm *to* you. But if the person to hurt you is me, then I…" She sniffs. A tear rolls down her cheek, fat and tinged pink. "I won't be the person—no, the *vampire*—to harm you. I couldn't bear it."

"But you won't hurt me. You've said it over and over and I-I believe you."

"No, you don't. With good reason. I don't either." She leaves the chair and finally approaches my bed. She's still well out of reach; I can't touch her without leaving the bed and the needle in my arm won't let me.

"I'm not strong enough, Danika, tonight is proof enough of that. I'm not strong enough to control the monster inside and keep it from doing terrible things. I tried, honest I did, but I'm not Vixen. I might be her bloodline, but that mastery of her darker self is something I don't have and I won't let that weakness put you in danger."

I'm crying now. Through my blurred vision I see Rayne's hand extend and I lean into it. Her fingers brush my cheek oh-so-gently.

"Rayne, please…"

"I'll pack my things tonight. There's plenty of darkness left, so I'll take as much as I need from the house and find somewhere else to stay during the daylight hours. After that, we'll be colleagues. Teammates. Nothing more."

I open my mouth again. Why is nothing coming out? Why can't I say anything?

She smiles gently. "It's better this way. For both of us. Goodbye." She turns away.

No. No, no, no. She's walking toward the door. She's going to leave. She's going to step out of my life. I don't know when I'll see her next if I don't do something. I have to stop her. I have to say something—

"Rayne."

She stops at the door, one foot over the threshold. Waits.

"I...you..." I scrunch my eyes shut. "Don't leave...the house."

"What?"

"I'll leave. I mean, th-the house was modified to be vampire-safe, right? So you have to stay there. It's the best place for you. I...I'll go."

Rayne's shoulders slump. Her fingers tighten briefly on the door frame before slipping away. "Fine. Whatever you like." And she's gone.

Somebody offered me a meal. I've no idea what time it is, but my stomach agrees that it's time for food. I'm still chowing down on greasy chicken, slimy gravy, and gooey potatoes when Maury knocks on my door.

I push the plate and tray aside, wipe left over tears off my face, and beckon him in.

"How you doing?"

I shrug. "Been a hell of a lot better, if I'm honest. I'm sick of seeing the inside of this place."

"No doubt." He eyes the tray of mostly devoured food. "Wow."

"Shut up. I'm hungry. Apparently."

"Good." He pulls a little notepad from his pocket. "That means your lupine immunity shot is working."

"One of them scratched me."

"So we saw. But blood test results are back from Clear Blood, and all of them confirm that you're still human. No werewolf traits at all."

"The shot?"

"Perhaps. Or you're very lucky, who knows? Though given your history I'd be inclined to lean on the latter. How are you feeling?"

I sigh. This is a different question from the first, though they sound very similar. "Well, I can hardly say I'm doing my job properly if someone isn't out to get me, right?"

"You know that's not what I mean."

I glare at the sheets. "Fine. I'm pissed, okay? No, I'm worse than pissed, I'm fucking livid. You *made* me give Wendy that shot when you *knew* it was untested. You *knew* the effects were still being catalogued, and despite all that, you chose to give him the experimental death injection. Now he's gone."

"I'm sorry for your loss, Agent."

"Fuck you."

He sighs. "I'll admit, I acted rashly. Though if I'd known it would have such adverse effects on him I can't say I wouldn't have done it anyway. I'm a SPEAR agent. My job is to protect and serve."

"So is mine."

"Yes, but who are you serving? Who are you protecting?"

"What?"

He gives me a steady look. "We're the Supernatural Prohibition Extermination and Arrest Regiment. Not the *Human* Prohibition Extermination and Arrest Regiment. We arrest and exterminate supernatural creatures. *Edanes.*"

"Wendy didn't do anything wrong. Are you really trying to rationalize this, Maury, because it's bullshit. All of it. You brought an untested drug into holding and used it on an *edane* civilian. Now he's dead."

"Because he fought a dominance battle."

My mouth drops open. "Did you open this conversation with an apology? Because this is a really shitty way to say sorry."

"I'm apologizing for making *you* give him the shot, Agent, not for the act of using it. Like I told you at the time, I was fully authorized to use it. Given that man's strength and attitude at the time, he seemed the perfect candidate for such a strong drug. I only regret that *you* applied the shot, because now, you seem to be blaming yourself for what happened to him, instead of congratulating yourself for a job well done."

"He's dead. My friend is dead because that drug messed with his mind and fucked up his body. If it had been our usual sedation he would have been fine."

"You don't know that." His loud sniff cuts off my attempt to respond. "But that does bring us neatly to the next matter I'd like to discuss with you."

I look left, then right. Grunt. "Not like I'm going anywhere, Maury. Just get it over with."

"You describe Wensleydale Gordan as your friend. Following his passing it stands to reason that you're feeling emotional."

I push back the sheets to launch out of bed. The needle resists for a moment, then gives with a sharp stab of pain as it yanks out of my flesh. "Emotional? Emotional, Maury? What the fuck? I'm not some poor suburban housewife with a dish of burnt casserole—"

"Sit down, Danika."

His use of my name is what stops me cold. I hesitate, but he seems willing to wait me out. So I sit. But on the edge of the bed this time, both hands tucked into my lap to keep the medical gown from flapping.

"Emotional. That's the word used by the *Extra Mundane Control Unit*, so I'll do the same. Given your relationship with the deceased and your recent experiences, you are *emotionally compromised*."

"What the hell does that even mean?"

"It means you and Kappa are no longer handling the werewolves."

Again I stand; once more he waves me down.

"I've no proof your actions led to the Dire Wolf rampage through the streets, but I can categorically say that we're further from answers and resolutions than we were when I gave you the task. So it's no longer yours."

Can this day possibly get any worse? I pound my fist into the mattress but stay seated. I even count slowly to ten in an effort to stop myself saying something rash. It works. Kinda.

"When I *took* the task, I had a healthy, powerful diplomat to help my negotiations between packs. *You* arrested him. Now he's dead and the most powerful pack in Angbec is led by a power-hungry lunatic who wants my heart in a dish."

"Excuse me?"

"There's a bounty on me, Maury."

"Again?" He sighs. "All the more reason for you to stay away from werewolves right now. I'm sure Noel and his team are more than capable of bringing this mess under control."

I risk the tiniest of smiles. So Noel's taking over? Maybe there's a chance this whole mess won't drop still further into a tangled clusterfuck.

"Fine. What about me?"

"You need to bring your team in for debrief. And any other agents who haven't made it back yet. When you're up and dressed I'll have a list ready on your desk."

My smile dies. "You want me on shepherd duty?"

Maury stands. It's sharp enough a gesture that I'm caught off guard, but he steps quickly up to the bed and lowers his voice to a sharp hiss. "It may have escaped your notice, Agent, but things are a little delicate right now. SPEAR is a mess and that Addington prick has full jurisdiction over everything we do. You're lucky to be standing right now, rather than chained to that bed under arrest."

"What are you saying?"

"He knows you slipped that wolf out of holding, along with the other two. He knows you've been avoiding debrief. The only reason he hasn't ordered you grounded is because I told him you could bring in the others."

I stare at him. "*You* told him? Why?"

And just like that, he can no longer meet my gaze. "I'm sorry. Truly I am. I didn't want anybody to die. I've heard some of the agents talking since you came in here. News spreads fast and all anybody talked of was how much safer the Bowl is since you became a pack-friend. No one knows what's going to happen down there now, but they all agree that this Wensleydale fellow was the only thing keeping that pot from boiling over. Now? It's anybody's guess."

"And how does having me round up lost sheep help with any of that?"

He backs up. Smiles. "You're a resourceful agent, Danika. I'm sure you'll figure it out." Back to normal volume, Maury clears his throat and smooths invisible wrinkles out of his jacket. "When you're signed off here, report to HQ for your fresh orders. Understand?"

"Uh. Yeah, I get it."

"Good." And with that, he's gone.

CHAPTER TWENTY-SIX

Someone brought me clothes. No one will confirm, but who else could it be but Rayne?

I test my injured arm by swinging it in a large arc. The bulky bandage shouldn't stop me moving and the pain is manageable for now. Pleased, I pull on a cropped tee and top it with a longer shirt.

My mind races as I button it up.

It shouldn't be too hard to find agents who have eluded debrief, especially if I have their names. What *will* be tricky is convincing them to come in, especially if they happen to be *edane*, and something tells me that's exactly what they are.

For the first time, I consider that maybe Noel was on to something. Could it be that I think more like an *edane* creature than a human? After all, I was quick enough to avoid debrief too. Sure my reasons were different, but does that change the facts?

Jeans next, a snug pair with a high waist and extra pockets on the back and thighs.

Yes, this is definitely Rayne's handiwork.

The thought of her at home, going through my room, picking out things for me to wear, makes me sigh. I put the thought aside, along with several other painful ones, and bend low enough to zip the side of my boots.

Getting back to HQ isn't much of a bother. I'm able to hitch a ride with another team in exchange for answering a string of curious questions without snapping at them. I would say they got the better end of the deal.

They ask about Rayne and the werewolves. They ask my opinion on the new wolf pack and what affect Wendy's death will have on wolf politics. I'm as honest as I can be without giving in to the horrible blend of guilt, anger, and misery stirring quietly through my gut.

Without Wendy, everything is going to be far more difficult. This new pack, named Blood Moon, are dangerous and actively claiming territory while bolstering their numbers. With the recent riot, all of Angbec's established packs have taken hits to their numbers and are in no fit state to fight off a new one. Especially one with such a unique pack power.

By the time we get back to HQ the agents hanging on my every word look as bummed out as I feel. Ah well. At least it's not just me now.

Entry procedure has changed since my last use of it. I still need to use the clean room and be scanned all over, but before reaching that stage is another checkpoint. Two armed soldiers quick-scanning SPEAR ID lanyards. I lift mine from its dangling cord on my hip and hold it up for them to check.

"That belongs on your neck," says one of the pair.

I smile. "Eat me."

The pair share a glance, shrug, then wave me through.

The system takes longer than usual to recognize my credentials. I can't help but wonder if the delay is another EMCU thing, put in place to have more of their soldiers ready to greet me on the other side.

I needn't have worried. When the vacuum seal releases on the door and I finally step through, everything else seems to be business as usual. Oh, except for the huge decrease in visible agents. It's quiet. Eerily so, and though I can't put my finger on it, something inside me pushes back against the oddness of it all.

Most of the desks and workstations are empty. The training room with its glass viewing window is dim and uninhabited. I find myself pining for the blue-skinned grumpy gargoyle who usually gives his lessons there. I've had so many bruises from sparring with that big oaf, but without him, I wouldn't be able to fight as I do. In fact, I'd have been dead long before now.

I find my desk among all the others and take a moment to sit. So strange to be there as though nothing has happened. To remember the last time I sat here before my world became a sad, topsy-turvy mess. As ever the surface is covered in chittarik droppings and my "in" tray is filled to overflowing. I'd attend to some of the items there, but I have work to do first.

Inside a clear plastic folder is a typed list of names, SPEAR IDs, and team numbers as promised by Maury. There must be at least thirty agents on this list, all of them known to be evading military debrief.

It's good to know that I'm not the only one to call bullshit on this debrief fiasco.

I see my own name in there as well as Rayne's, but both have been crossed out with a line of red Biro and a notation next to them reading, "Briefed.'"

Yay. Guess we're off the hook.

I fold the list, pocket it, and prepare to leave, pausing only when I tune fully into the sounds at the edge of my hearing. Footsteps.

I turn. "Pippa?"

❖

My sister grins as she approaches my desk, arms spread wide. I fling myself at her, gathering her smaller frame in for a hug.

Once upon a time, I might have squished her little body with my combat trained body. Now she hugs back effortlessly, even causing me brief discomfort as her vampire strength outstrips mine.

"Are you okay?"

We both speak at the same moment, the exact same question.

She laughs, I laugh, and for a glorious two seconds, we're just two sisters, laughing at each other and the similar way our minds work.

"I'm fine," she says, stepping back to look me over. "The Foundation sent me here to assist with some questions the military had, so I thought I'd drop by up here. It's really quiet."

"I know. Lots of the agents are still out."

"But aren't there normally a bunch of post chittarik roosting here?"

At last I understand why the office is so eerily quiet. Not just the missing agents, but the lack of any fluttering, clicking, chattering, or screeching from the chittarik usually flying to and fro.

Sure enough, as I turn to look, all the roosts are empty with no sign of a small, scaly dragon-pest in sight.

"Guess Addington cleared them all out too. What a dick."

"Well, Norma is at home. She isn't happy about it, but I locked her in. Figured it was best with all those drones flying around."

"Oh, good. Thank you." I am grateful, but suddenly I really could do with a cuddle from my weird little pet.

"So how are you holding up?" She smiles at me, gentle and pitying. "With Wensleydale?"

I flinch. "You heard about that?"

"We all did. Quite a few wolves arrived at the Foundation from the aftermath of that dominance battle. And we've been flooded with werewolves since the drones went active."

"The Quliax killed him."

"I'm so sorry."

"Don't be. It's not your fault."

"Nor yours."

I meet her gaze. "I know."

"Do you? And what's going on between you and Rayne?"

"Nothing."

"Stop that. I know you two have broken up, or something equally crazy. She told me when she came back to grab some of your things. What on earth are you doing?"

"Me?"

"You can't break up with her."

I can hear the angry clack as my teeth snap together. "I'll have you know *she's* the one who dumped *me*. I just tried to be honest about what I was feeling, and she overheard me while I was talking to Noel."

"Well, it's all ridiculous. Do you have any idea what she's been through for you?"

"I know, I know, Quinn and Vixen treated her like shit, but she's still here, putting up with it and being an agent. But like I said this wasn't my idea and—"

"No." Pippa slaps her hand on the desk. "After all that. She's been coming to the Foundation for tests every week. She's trying to figure out how to control the monster."

I don't get it and I know my expression says as much. Pippa, on the other hand, is clearly frustrated over how I can't seem to read her mind.

"Not a literal monster, she's talking about the beast inside. Y'know, that hunger? The urge to kill? All of us vampires have to suffer the animal within, but some control it better than others. She wanted to learn how to control that side of herself and her hungers so she wouldn't hurt anybody."

"What?"

Pippa nods. She leans on the edge of the desk and stares long and hard. "We've been working on it for weeks now, triggering blood mania under controlled conditions to see if a particular thing makes it better or worse."

Wait, so this is where Rayne has been going night after night? This is why I've barely seen her at home recently? Because she was out having tests and experiments?

"What the hell?" This is too much. I have to sit down.

More droppings squish under my butt as I do, but I don't care. How could Rayne have done this? And without me knowing?

"But she has been eating, right? Like, getting her weekly doses from the Foundation blood stores?"

Pippa suddenly looks sheepish. "Yes, of course. I'm not crazy. Starving herself to get the trigger was an idea she had, but I wouldn't let her. It's too dangerous. After that, I made sure she got her share by…uh… making sure she got the good stuff."

"'Good stuff'? There are gourmet blood bags now?"

"Everyone has their preferred blood type. I'm quite partial to O-neg which is great because it's pretty common. Rayne, however, seems to like AB-pos, so in return for her help, I get it for her when I can."

My stomach does a weird little flip-flop.

As if sensing my discomfort, Pippa rushes on. "It's not weird, or creepy. It just means she doesn't have to drink from the big batches the Foundation usually makes to feed the vampire population. Anyway, what

I'm saying is, she's been helping my research into mania, both how and why it happens. She's been having test after test, screening after screening, all in an effort to figure out how to be safe. For you."

"Me?" I feel like an idiot just repeating what she says, but my mind is struggling to keep up.

"Well, why else would she go this far? Since the whole Vixen mess, people are keener than ever to understand vampire blood chemistry and psychology. We have all the samples we could ask for and more, but the funded research is very specific, most into artificial blood synthesis. This is a side project *she asked* me to conduct in an effort to protect you."

Not again. My words are stuck in the back of my throat. I want to speak, but the lump of pride and pleasure is just too big. "I...she..."

"Yes." Pippa actually seems impatient. "She knows she's dangerous, Dani. We *all* do, but she's the only one with a real stake in making sure she's safe to be around. So, she did everything in her power to make it that way. And you *still* dumped her."

"I didn't do the dumping."

"You may as well have." Pippa tangles her hands in her hair. "Okay, look. Just...talk to her, okay? Or something. What you two have, it's special and it's too good to let it end over a misunderstanding."

"Watching her decimate half a pack of werewolves isn't a misunderstanding, Pip."

She leans off the desk. "A pack of werewolves that wanted you dead if I understand all the rumours, Miss Now-I-Have-A-Bounty-On-My-Head. Again. That's *rage* induced mania. It can be triggered by a heightened emotional state, but it needs to be pretty darn heightened. It's actually rare. Mania induced by hunger is the most common and that's easy to treat, just make sure we don't go hungry." She sighs. "But mania in and of itself isn't a bad thing. It's a defence mechanism or a protective instinct."

"Then why is it called 'mania'?"

Another level look. "What would you call it, then? 'Trigger responsive inner strength proliferation'?"

"TRISP? I like it."

Her smile is back, but it's a sad one now. "The more we look into how mania works, the more it becomes obvious that it has different levels in different vampires, and that it can be controlled. Me for instance?" She touches her own chest. "I have a pretty easy, safe, and comfortable job. My chances of succumbing to mania are pretty slim, unless it's hunger induced mania. I don't have battle instincts or people to fight for the way Rayne does. My self-preservation instincts therefore are quite relaxed while hers are off the charts. Probably from such a rough start when she was turned and her life as a police officer before that."

Her expression becomes thoughtful. Even her tone shifts to take on a lecturing air. "But the same way anger management courses can get people out of trouble, there are techniques one can employ to control how much sway mania claims when it takes hold. There's even evidence to suggest that in the right circumstances a vampire can experience all the physical advantages of mania without the amnesic complications."

"Really?"

"Yes. And we wouldn't know any of this without Rayne. So please, please talk to her. Please?"

"I…" Deep breath. "Fine. For the good it will do, but can I handle this first? I kinda have some rampaging werewolves to deal with."

Pippa waves a dismissive hand in my direction and begins to walk away. "Fine. I only came to say hello anyway. Go do…whatever it is you're up to. And don't get killed."

I call after her, knowing she can hear me regardless. "I'll do my best."

And I'm left at my desk with my mind whirling.

If mania truly can be controlled—

My mobile rings.

"Karson, here."

"Hey, there you are, boss. Where have you been?"

"Solo? Are you okay? What happened to Chalks? Where are you? Where have *you* been?"

A chuckle ripples down the line. "Close. It's Duo, but big bro is here if you want him?"

"I—no. No, it's fine. I'm glad to know you're both all right. What happened to you? You went off comms, we couldn't get to you. What happened with the drone strike?"

"Hey, chill, I'll tell you all about it, promise. But I'm fine. We all are. More worried about you to be honest. Rayne told us what happened."

My joy fades a little. "She's with you?"

"Everyone is. Rayne, big bro, Erkyan, Willow, Hawk. We're all waiting for you."

I think back to the list stuffed into my pocket. "You know you're all in trouble, right? The military is looking for you?"

He grins. I can hear it in his voice. "Why else do you think we're waiting for you way out here? You gonna join us or what?"

"Sure. Just tell me where 'out here' is and I'll be right there."

Be right there? If I knew that "right there" was three miles away I may have been less strong in my bravado. But, now that I'm "debriefed,"

I finally have access to SPEAR vehicles once more, so taking one of the vans isn't an issue. No need to do the journey on foot.

And after all that, when I do finally reach my team, I can't deny that I'm pleased to see them.

I catch sight of them before they see me, careful to approach from downwind. They're grouped together outside a cafe, sipping from mugs, quietly chatting.

When I spy Rayne, I find myself hanging back, just for a moment. I want to look at her. I want to see her from a distance and remind myself of what it is I see in her.

Not a difficult task. She's still beautiful, still perfect. Well…almost perfect.

She notices me before anybody else does—not that I'm surprised—and stiffens mid-sentence. When she turns, it's with no hesitation or guesswork, simply angling her body to look right at me. The two wolves spot me next.

Duo grins and slaps his brother around the back of the head. A curious way of getting his attention, but it does the job well enough. Solo then dashes toward me. When he scoops me up off the ground and crushes my body against his I can't help but gasp at the uncharacteristic display of emotion.

When he finally lets my feet drop back to the ground, I step away to get a good look at him. His face is covered in half healed blisters. So too are his hands and neck. Though his eyes are as bright and lively as ever, there is an age there that I'm certain wasn't there before.

"You're okay." He makes it a statement rather than a question.

"So are you. Ish."

He touches one of the scabbed up marks on his cheek. "This? I'll be fine. Most of the damage is already gone at this point. But that gas is no joke."

"What happened when we left?"

He shrugs…and that's all. Apparently that's all the answer I'm going to get.

I join him in walking back to the others.

They all greet me in turn, Hawk and Duo slapping my shoulder, Willow grabbing both my hands in hers and squeezing gently. Even Erkyan has some kind words though she trips over them in her usual clumsy way. Then Rayne. She's the only one who makes no move to touch me. Instead she smiles, a sad half smile, and keeps an even four paces between us.

"You okay?"

Oh boy, that could mean so many things. And there are so many answers. I find myself nodding, carefully avoiding direct eye contact. I have no idea how I'll cope if I have to meet her gaze right now. If I have to look into her eyes and know she's no longer mine. Looking at the tip of her nose, yeah, that should be fine.

My team finish greeting me, telling me how pleased they are to see me, and settle into a more business-like gathering around me.

"So what's next, boss?" Even as he addresses me, Duo stands as close to his brother as he can get without climbing into his arms. He ensures body contact between them too, always putting his arm or his hip against Solo's.

"First, I guess you need to know we're off werewolf control."

The two wolves stand straight. I can almost imagine their tails becoming rigid and their ears sticking up.

"What?"

"Are you serious?"

"What they hell would they do that for?"

The complaints and shocked exclamations come thick and fast. I raise my hands against them.

"I know, I know. I think it's bullshit just as much as the rest of you, but Kappa isn't handling it any more. Apparently I'm *emotionally compromised*."

Willow waves at me, then flutters her hands through a furious tirade of swearing and disbelief. Most of it is so fast that I only catch snatches, but the meaning is pretty clear though.

"Wendy was dear to all of us in one way or another, but Maury singled *me* out. I'm the one 'attached' to the guy, so we're all off. He's given the task to Noel's team."

Rayne recovers quickly from her shock. "That's good. He at least will do everything he can to get to the bottom of it all."

"But his team is entirely human. They'll get squashed." Duo growls under his breath. "What kind of idiot is Maury anyway?"

Solo puts a placating hand on his brother's shoulder. "Fine. We're off that case. So what are we supposed to be doing?"

"Sheep herding." I fish the crumpled note from my pocket. "We're supposed to be tracking down all agents who haven't yet been debriefed. But at least I can say I've found you all."

Hawk thumbs his nose. *"Edane?"*

"Most of them, yes."

"Not surprising." Erkyan tugs on one of her long, warty ears. "I hid. And you did. All of us. They want to capture us."

Rayne shakes her head. "I don't think it's as simple as that. They would rather use us if they're able, under conditions that they set." She lifts her arm to show off the wristband. "So long as one appears useful and compliant, they're deemed fit for duty. They won't phrase it that way, but from the questions they ask, that's what they're looking for."

"*Edane* puppets and guard dogs. Gross." Hawk beats his wings hard. "What do they think we are, anyway?"

"Something to be controlled and used. It's not a new human attitude." Rayne is still staring at me. Her gaze is starting to warm things low and deep inside me, and soon addressing her nose isn't going to be enough to help me.

"Well, it's a shitty attitude and I'm not here to spread it around." I shove the list back into my pocket. "But…if they really want us hunting for renegades, then I suppose we should get on with it."

That silences my team. Every one of them, even Duo who usually has plenty to say, stops and stares at me open-mouthed and wide-eyed.

"What?" I give them a small smile. "You saw for yourself, most of these agents are *edane*, and if you look super close, a lot of them are werewolves. I'd say we have a few packs to visit."

Silence. Then Hawk laughs out loud and slaps his hand against his thigh. "I should have known. I should have known you'd find a way."

"I don't know what you mean," I tell him.

But soon enough we're all laughing, and a rush of warmth and affection flows through me for this merry band of renegade misfits. These guys, these are the people I love and care for. As much as Wendy, in fact.

Once more a curl of sadness worms through my insides. I push it away with a mental grunt.

This isn't the end of Wendy. I'll make sure he didn't die for nothing. Aleksandar and this Blood Moon pack are all going to pay for the damage they've caused.

Willow signs at me again. *"Where do you want to start? I hear the Dire Wolves don't like you much."*

"Agreed, they don't, but we won't get answers there anyway."

Duo lifts his hand. "Did I hear right? Is there a bounty on you?"

"Yup."

He whistles through his teeth. "Well, well. You *have* been busy. We leave you alone for a second and you have a whole pack after you? You're a danger to yourself." His words are firm, but his tone is anything but, and his lips are drawn back into a wide smile. "Maybe we should do this in one big group."

"No time. We have to split up, take a pack each."

"Fair enough. Big bro and I will speak with the Fire Fang. Makes the most sense."

"Good call." I unlock the van and point out the groupings. "Fine. You two speak with Fire Fang. We need to know anything they've heard about Blood Moon—who they are, where they came from, what they're doing here, all of it."

Duo arches an eyebrow. "And look for any of the agents on the list?"

"Of course."

Another chuckle. "Fine. Hey, bro, wanna tell the little ones we're coming home?"

Solo nods his agreement and closes his eyes, that strange posture he takes on when looking into himself. At least I understand it now. I had thought that the link between him and Duo was a result of their being twins. But if they really are part of Fire Fang, then it's not just each other they can speak to. The telepathy of that pack links them all with a curious bond like to a hive mind that can stretch across hundreds of miles.

Can't imagine what it must be like to be forever aware of someone else, multiple someones in fact, and to sometimes hear their thoughts without a filter.

The thought sends my gaze skipping over to Rayne who, as usual, is watching me.

I sigh.

"Okay, you two do that. Hawk, you take Erkyan and Willow to see the Long Tooths."

Erkyan sighs. "I must have to?"

"Unless you'd prefer to visit the Loup Garou?"

She shudders. "No, no. We see the long teeth ones. Hope no eating this time."

I offer her as comforting a smile as I can muster and bend low to whisper in her ear. "You'll be fine. They were just messing with us last time. They wouldn't dare eat you." I say it in Goblin, or as close as I can get with my rusty skills in that arena. "Besides, that's why Willow and Hawk are going with you."

She grunts, but nods her agreement, also replying in her first language. "Fine, but if they come near me, I'll slice their ears off."

"That's the spirit." I switch back to English, clap her on the shoulder, and then turn my attention to Rayne.

I hadn't intended to leave myself paired with her, but given that the team is always split this way, I should have guessed. Habit more than anything has left me paired up with my ex.

Wow. Ex. Just thinking of her that way twists my stomach into painful knots.

She tilts her head at me. "So Loup Garou for us?"

"Yeah. And…uh…we'll take the van. I wanted to talk to you anyway."

One delicate eyebrow arches toward her hairline. "Really? Very well, Danika. Let's go."

She opens the passenger door to the van without another word, and starts to adjust the seat to suit her small frame.

My companions offer me wide-eyed, questioning stares.

Willow forms more symbols with her fingers. *"Are you well? You both seem distant and upset."*

I open my mouth to speak then switch to sign instead. *"We're fine. Just need to talk about some pigs."*

Erkyan snorts.

Willow frowns. *"Pigs?"*

"Things." I mutter out loud. "Give me a break, okay, I'm still learning. Talking about *things*. Things, things."

She giggles but doesn't tease any further. Instead she gestures to Hawk who just grins. He seems more than ready to take to the skies again and the meagre weight of both Willow and Erkyan will be no hindrance to him. With a smile and a wave, he is airborne within seconds, carrying the pair of them southwest to where the Long Tooth wolves have made their base.

Solo and Duo share a look, then set off together. They don't shift, simply fall into a gentle running pace, heading south toward the edge of the city where the Fire Fangs are based in the countryside.

Then, it's just the two of us. Rayne and I, looking at each other with that gulf of four paces still loitering between us.

"I—"

She lifts a hand. "We have work to do. If you really want to skirt around the edge of Agent Cruush's orders, then fine. I'll follow you like I always have. But be prepared for the backlash."

"From who?"

"Agent Cruush. Colonel Addington. Noel. Pick one."

"Noel will understand. He's my friend."

Rayne nods. "Mm-hmm." And with that cryptic response, she climbs into the now adjusted passenger seat.

I follow, sliding into the driver's side and slamming the door. My heart is pounding, my mouth dry, and yet I've no idea what to say.

Pippa's voice rings in my mind, over and over, telling me to smooth things out, talk it over, make it work. But Rayne sits as far away from me as she possibly can, leaning against the window glass to widen the space between us.

It abruptly feels cold and lonely in this narrow metal box.

With a sigh, I put the van in gear and start us moving. How do I stand any chance of fixing the mess I've made when Rayne won't even engage?

The thought fills my head as I drive northeast.

CHAPTER TWENTY-SEVEN

We drive north and through Angbec.
    In each direction we turn there are signs that things aren't as calm and peaceful as they once were. The military presence is less strong away from the centre of town and areas like the West End, but there are still soldiers on the streets.

But at least out here there are civilians too. The rampaging wolves clearly never made it this far, and human locals go about their daily business. So strange to think that a bare five miles away, the streets and stores are on lockdown.

I spy one or two drones as we progress. These are smaller ones and don't seem to have the same offensive capability as those used close to Misona. Instead they are light and nippy, flying around at street level rather than across roofs.

"It's like a whole new country." Rayne's voice is soft, barely there, but I know she intends me to hear her.

I nod but keep my eyes on the road. "This is what all of Angbec should be like."

"Upper-class, stuck up, and cut off to *edanes*?"

"You know that's not what I meant."

She twirls an invisible pattern across the dashboard with the tip of her finger. "Part of the reason it's so quiet here is because this is a wealthy area. Most *edanes* can't afford to live here unless they're old. And if they are that old they have better things to do than cause trouble. Do you have any sense of how many vampires live out here?"

"Some."

"A lot," she mutters. "And you would never know. Not old enough to walk by day like Vixen occasionally did, but old enough to know how to live inconspicuously."

I drum my fingers against the steering wheel and pull the van around a right turn. "Is this really what you want to talk about?"

"Touché."

"Oh, come on, Rayne. Please. Are we really going to let it end this way?"

"It has already ended."

"No. No, it hasn't. It doesn't have to. Please, can we talk about this?"

"And say what?"

Her monosyllabic answers are starting to grate on me. I grit my teeth against the urge to cut back with something sharp and inhale for a slow count of ten.

"You're getting better at that."

"Screw you, Rayne. Don't patronize me right now."

"I'm not. I'm encouraging you."

"Fuck's sake." I wrench the wheel to the left, mounting the curb with the two near tyres. A stab at the big, triangular button on the wheel sets my hazard lights blinking, and I swivel in my seat. "Look at me, Rayne."

She does, at once, and oh, holy hell, it cuts right through me.

I swallow past the sudden spiky lump of emotion at the back of my throat. "I fucked up. I know I did. But you have to let me fix it. Please give me a chance to prove myself."

"But there's nothing to prove. I. Am. Dangerous. That's a simple fact and every instinct that makes you an excellent SPEAR agent is telling you that. It's wrong to fight it."

"Pip told me what you've been doing."

There. At last, a flicker of emotion in those warm, brown eyes. It doesn't last long, but the sight of it is enough to give me hope.

I press on. "She told me about the tests. About the different levels of blood mania. She told me that you're fighting to make yourself safe."

"And so?"

Part of me wants to punch her in the nose. The rest would be happy with a simple hug. "Damn it, stop being so difficult. So I know you're doing your best. That you're trying to be safe."

"And yet you're still afraid of me."

That stops me dead.

My mouth is still open, but nothing is coming out of it. I look at Rayne, stare into the deep, consuming pool of that stunning autumnal brown in her eyes…and realize that she's right.

I want to deny it. I want, with everything in me, to tell her it's not true, but…

My shoulders slump. I lean back in my seat.

Rayne stares ahead through the windscreen. "Tell me."

"What?"

"Tell me why it's so impossible for you to believe that I could be different."

"It's not impossible, I just—"

"Tell me about your father."

My body seizes up, every muscle, every limb. I watch my fingers flex once, twice, three times on the steering wheel. I can't tell if I want to curl up in a ball or lash out with my fists. Both seem fantastic options.

Instead I lower my hands to rest them in my lap.

"Danika?"

"How do you know anything about him? Who have you been speaking to?"

"Is that really important?"

"Who?" I yell.

She doesn't even flinch. "Phillipa told me. Not outright, but she said his passing has had a large effect on you. It influences your decisions and feelings, whether you want it to or not. But she insisted I speak with you myself."

"Why? It's her dad too."

"You know why."

Fuck.

For the first time, I notice that my fingers are shaking. No, both hands are trembling visibly, a tremor that extends up my arms. The backs of my eyelids begin to burn.

"Dad was murdered. By a vampire. Some youngling turned him and…and he had to be exterminated. A SPEAR agent," my voice cracks. "He attacked a rookie SPEAR agent and they killed him."

Rayne nods, but doesn't speak.

The burn behind my eyelids intensifies. "My dad was the sweetest, kindest, gentlest man in the world. He was built like a rugby player, but he never would have hurt anybody. He used to rescue bees off the ground so they wouldn't get stepped on. He'd volunteer in animal shelters and local soup kitchens. He was amazing."

I squeeze my eyes shut, but it doesn't help the tears gathering there.

"He gave everything to look after me and Pip and Mum and then, in one night, in one horrible moment, he became a monster. He-he hurt people. Attacked them. It was blood mania."

Still Rayne remains silent, but now her shoulders are scooped downward and her eyes are closed. Though subtle, I can see the tension in her arms and back, spot the tiny point of one fang cutting through her bottom lip as she bites down.

"The one that turned him was too young and didn't have any control. They passed on the madness. He never stood a chance. But if someone that good, that kind and peaceful and noble—if someone like my dad could murder people then—then…"

"Then how could I possibly be any different?" At last Rayne speaks. Her voice is the softest of whispers directed at the ground. She refuses to look at me, instead visibly taking care over each word she speaks.

"Rayne..."

"I suspected, but I didn't know. Phillipa refused to say more than that he died via an *edane* attack. It didn't take much to figure out what type of *edane*. Noel seemed to know more, but he insisted I speak with you. But I couldn't. I didn't want to see that look in your eye. The one you're wearing right now."

I can barely see her. My gathering tears have started to blur my vision. I dash them away with the heel of my palm and sit straighter in my seat.

"It's nothing to do with you."

"You're right, of course it isn't. But the fact remains, you, for all your bravado, sass, and smarts, are afraid of what vampires can do. A werewolf is still the same person after being bitten. Sprites, gnomes, gargoyles, and goblins are all born exactly as they appear. Some are good, some are bad. But vampires? We—no, *I*—am fundamentally different from the person I was before. I drink blood, or I die. I have urges to kill, kept in check only by my own will and the social niceties of the city I live in. I *am* a monster."

Rayne straightens her back and settles her hands in her lap. Without saying the words, she makes clear this part of the conversation is now over. "Thank you for being honest with me. I'm glad you could, but now, we have work to do."

"But—"

"Let's get moving."

Silence.

In the end, I break the deadlock of wills by turning off the hazard lights and pulling back onto the road.

We continue the rest of the way without speaking, each of us trapped in our own thoughts. I've no idea what Rayne might be thinking of, but my own mind is a whirlwind of painful memories, cruel truths, and guilt. Guilt that despite everything, I still haven't told Rayne the entire story.

On the borders before the inner city becomes the suburbs, there are checkpoints, military tanks lining the road to form blockades, manned by soldiers with guns and walkie-talkies. When we stop, two soldiers flank each side of the van with guns drawn while a fifth gestures for me to wind down the window.

He takes his time looking in, assessing ID lanyards, and peering into the back. "Where are you heading?"

I smile, the lie all prepared on my lips. "Maurice Cruush assigned my team and I to round up any straggler agents. Intel suggests a couple of them have tried to leave the city. Do you need to see the list?"

He takes the ragged paper from me and gives that a good once-over too. Boredom and fatigue stain his features. "But there's nothing out here."

"Exactly. If you were trying to hide, wouldn't you go somewhere quiet and abandoned?"

"Fair enough." He hands the list and my lanyard back through the window. "Just be careful. We have more drones watching the countryside, and while they aren't weaponized like the city ones, they can fire tranqs if we find any trouble."

"We'll be good."

"Sure. Whatever. Head on through."

At his command, the makeshift blockage parts to let us through.

Beside me, Rayne coughs into her hand. "When was the last time you came out here?"

I turn the van onto a small lane leading off the primary A-road we've taken out of the city. "Four months, maybe six. I check in on them every now and then, but for the most part they look after themselves. Besides, a SPEAR coming out here too often would defeat the point of the ruse, y'know?"

"I suppose. And you think they'll welcome us now?"

"Probably not, but we have to ask. You know what they're like. Maybe they learned something."

"All the way out here?"

"You'd be surprised. Besides, some of the Dire Wolves mentioned a pack run by 'that woman.' They had to be talking about these guys. I want to know what they were talking about."

The van rumbles along the Tarmac which gradually morphs into stones, then packed earth, mud, and finally dirt. Another mile on and any signs of light from the larger road is gone. Even the road noise has faded, leaving us in the silence of the countryside. With the headlamps on full beam, I can see that even the dirt of the "road" is gone, replaced with grass that clearly hasn't been disturbed in weeks.

Though there's no obvious sign or marker, after another few feet I stop the van and let the engine idle. "Ready?"

Rayne nods. "They're expecting us?"

"No, but they know we're here. Don't doubt that for a second."

She climbs out of the van. I follow, putting aside the brief thought of leaving the engine running. Part of me wants to take the time to turn the van to face back the way we've come, but if we have to leave so quickly as to need that, it won't make a difference which direction we're facing.

Together we walk across the grass, following a trail too narrow to be called a footpath. It winds through a pair of low hills and across a large stream, crossed via a series of stepping stones. Beyond it and in the middle of a small valley is an old, rundown church. The moon and stars don't offer much light, but I remember well enough what the place looks like. Dilapidated stones, broken windows, and fractured doors make up the exterior while the roof is puckered with holes from missing tiles. In the bell tower, a large rusted hook shows were the bell once was, though now the structure is empty.

Rayne sniffs the air and angles herself to the right. I press my back to hers and wait.

Doesn't take long.

Within a minute, I watch the first woman approach from across the grass. There's nothing behind her but open plains of long, gently waving grass; she may well have sprung up from the earth itself. She wears something long and billowing in dark colours that blend into the gloom. The only reason I can see her at all is because of the faint glow in her eyes.

"Been a long time, Agent." Her voice carries on the breeze. "To what do we owe the pleasure?

I keep my hands to my sides. "It's business I'm afraid. We need information."

"We?" This voice comes from behind me and to the left. Again soft and gentle, almost matronly. Can't see the source though. "You brought a friend."

"You know Rayne."

"I know *of* Rayne, but we've not met before. So you are her? So short and dainty. To think this sweet little thing came from the likes of that deluded revolutionary Vixen."

Rayne growls softly.

I take a step forward. "Stop mucking around. Can we talk or not?"

"We're talking now, aren't we? Apparently you can."

I roll my eyes. I know it's dark, but our mysterious friend in the dark can no doubt see it anyway. "Tell me what you know about the Blood Moon pack."

Silence. The breeze whips across the grass with a rustling whisper like pixies in the dark. Maybe there are pixies out here; it's quiet and remote enough.

"Ah. This really is business. Perhaps you'd better come inside."

Finally. "Thank you. Come on, Rayne."

"But—"

I shake my head. "You lot may be fine in the dark, but I'd rather be able to see, thank you very much. Plus it's cold out here."

"Fine." Rayne starts walking toward the broken-down church, and though her steps are firm and confident I can tell she's less than happy at the idea of joining these women inside.

Inside the church, lights are bright and warm. Almost welcoming. Rather like stepping through a portal or magic mirror, the inside is nothing like one would expect from the outside.

Clean, modern, and well-equipped, the interior has been converted into a living space for multiple people.

The aisles and nave are an open space filled with comfy chairs, bookcases, TVs, and small nooks made private with elaborately decorated folding screens. Up in the chancel there's more of the same, though more entertainment oddments are there too including a pool table, more books, and boxes of board games.

It can easily be mistaken for the hall of a large student house if not for the wall in the apse which is lined top to bottom with weapons. Nowhere near as large as the stores that SPEAR has, but the display is impressive nonetheless.

Each of the windows have been blacked out from this side to prevent light leaking into the darkness. Over the huge screens, instead of the stations of the cross like one might expect from a church, there are pictures of women, in varied styles of clothing from the 1700s through to more contemporary times. Each picture is a painting, created with incredible care and skill, showing the women in repose or positioned for battle, but no matter the clothing, style, or pose, each woman boasts long sharp fangs and huge black claws.

The nave is full of women, some reading, others chatting quietly, more of them gathered together on squishy chairs and beanbags.

I manage to count fifteen bodies before I realize it's pointless. For every one I see, there are likely two more hidden somewhere else.

Rayne eyes the scene slowly, giving each area her undivided attention while she maps it out. I understand what she's doing, because I do it too, but to see her scan and assess only reminds me that no matter how normal this scene might appear, it's anything but.

Behind us, the two women from outside join us on the threshold. Now, with light to help me, I see their features clearly, including the long black tunics they wear and the white wimples to match. Just like every other woman in the place.

The first of the pair links her hands before her waist and smiles. Her face is plain without a lick of make-up. From beneath the wimple, the smallest curl of fine blond hair is visible. "Good evening, Danika."

"Sister Opal."

She laughs. "Come on, there aren't any tourists here. No need for that."

"I figured since you were all dressed up—"

"There's been trouble in the city. I assume that's why you're here. I told the girls to dress *appropriately* in case we had any...visitors."

"Riiiiight. Well, yeah, that's why we're here. Got anywhere we can talk?"

Opal looks me up and down twice. Her gentle smile gives way to a more serious expression. "We can go downstairs. Gina?" she addresses the other woman. "Keep the girls up here and make sure no one goes outside until the agents leave. I want to know what we're up against."

Though she stares hard at Rayne, eventually Gina nods her agreement and walks around us to settle herself with the cluster of women sitting on beanbags and cushions. As she joins them, the rest swivel to face us, and I see more than one set of bright white teeth showing between parted lips.

Rayne moves closer to my side, her body stiff with tension.

"Easy. Come on, follow Opal."

"I've never seen a pack like this before."

"There has never been a pack like this before. Come on, just go. Move it. We'll talk more in private."

True to her word, Opal leads us through the open living area and down a short set of steps to what might normally be the area behind the nave. More steps on the right take us deep beneath the church to old burial plots no longer in use.

She walks easily through the dim space, seeming not to mind the lack of true light. But for a bare bulb at uneven intervals there isn't much to see by, forcing me to keep a close eye on where and how she steps.

At last, she pushes another door that opens onto a short corridor with thick oak doors on either side. Right at the end is another door with a small black plate nailed to the surface. There's no name there, just a curly symbol like a *squiggle, squiggle, line, squiggle.*

Opal pushes the door open and gestures us through.

CHAPTER TWENTY-EIGHT

It's an office. A minimalistic computer sits on one end of the narrow desk while on the other lies a stack of folders. The short walls are filled with shelves stacked with books, loose sheets of paper, and the odd piece of what looks like bone. Beyond that, I spy a clock, a long rope attached to a pulley that vanishes into the ceiling, a locking cabinet, and a wire paper bin, empty but for a single ball of scrunched up copy paper.

"Sorry it's a little cramped, but for true privacy this is as good as it gets."

Rayne shows no subtlety in her decision to stand by the door. She folds her arms across her chest and waits, taking on that eerie stillness only vampires seem capable of.

Opal offers me the only chair, but I shake my head and lean against the edge of the desk instead.

"Blood Moon," I mutter.

"Trouble," says Opal, at once. "New, aggressive, and dangerous. Their desire to bolster their numbers is strong enough that the alpha came here, offering us a place within the pack."

Can't help but snort at that. "They don't know Loup Garou very well, do they?"

"They don't know us at all. I'd almost forgive them, but he came with spells and tried to trick us to their side. That kind of deceit is less easy to forget."

"Spells? Come on."

With a sigh, Opal pushes her wimple back off her head. A vast cascade of blond hair spills out, thick and curly with slashes of pink highlights running through it. Without the wimple, it's now possible to see the six little rings piercing the upper cartilage of her right ear. "I know what you're thinking, but it's not that kind of spell. More a covert hypnosis or something like that. If I didn't already have my guard up...let's just say they made quite a compelling argument."

"What else do you know about them?"

"The pack alpha is a man named Flint. He's from a city further south of here and brought the remnants of his pack with him when he moved."

"Remnants?"

"There was a coup. He fled with what remained of his followers and took the name with him." Opal wrinkles her nose a little. "That alone told me how cocky and arrogant the man is. The gall—to name his pack of reprobates and bullies 'Blood Moon.'"

Rayne sniffs. "Can it not be considered a sign of respect to name your pack for the ancient festival?"

"No. It's sacrilege." Opal pounds her fist on the table. The computer bounces once, then recovers. "Anyway, he wanted the Loup Garou to join with Blood Moon because—let me make sure I get this right—because 'such strong wolf factions are destined to form a mating pair and produce the most powerful of werewolf offspring.'"

A small shudder ripples through me. "Gross."

"Exactly. As if any of us would associate with a disgraced pack like that. Anyway, after that they didn't stay long."

"You chased them off?"

"Yes and no." For the first time, Opal looks uncomfortable instead of angry or disgusted. "I've never felt anything like this, Danika. First, the creature who came to us wasn't a wolf. Or it didn't feel like one."

"It?"

Opal gives an apologetic shrug. "I don't know how else to describe him. It wasn't a wolf or a human or a vampire, even though it appeared like one on the outside. It was more a shadow of a living creature or a parody of one."

"You're not making sense."

"I'm aware of that, but I'm doing the best I can." Opal yanks a piece of paper off her trays and begins to sketch. "It's hard to bring the face to mind even now, but I'd guess it was trying to appear male. Like this."

The sketch she swings round to show me is a gruff, masculine looking figure with hair in cornrows to the shoulders and a scar across his face from right to left.

"Looks normal enough to me."

Opal adds a few more lines and erases a couple of others. "This is Flint Liddell, alpha of the Blood Moon. This is what he looked like and yet, if I stared at him too long I felt as though there was a shadow on him. Darkness." She shudders. "You know I don't scare easily, but honestly, I couldn't get that thing away from here any faster. It frightened me if I'm honest."

For the first time, Rayne ventures away from the door. She studies the sketch from multiple angles before looking directly at Opal. "What frightened you about it?"

"I don't know. So hard to explain. It was just a feeling I had, like dread and powerlessness. It was weak, but the longer he stayed here, the more intense it became. There was an aura about it, like fear and filth. I could barely stand it. In fact, I had to have a shower after he left, but even that didn't help."

"Was anyone else affected?"

A slight smile touches Opal's lips. She looks at me. "Your Rayne has the same instincts you do, Danika. No wonder you're such a famous team."

Rayne looks at the ground.

I stare at my hands. "Um, yeah."

"Oh." Opal pulls back the paper. "Apologies, I had no idea there were struggles. I mean only that Rayne has touched on something it took me several hours to notice. When Flint was here, the countryside went quiet. As if every small creature had run away to hide. Even the chickens and pigs we keep in the back retreated from the building as if in fear. That thing, whatever it is, carries menace around it. And it happens each time he comes."

"Each time?"

"Oh, yes. Flint has been here every other night since Blood Moon first arrived. In fact, the very reason I was outside tonight was because I hoped to head him off before he reached the building."

"But what does he want?"

"The same as the first time. As the only pure-female pack, it seems we are of especial interest to Flint and the rest of his pack. He seems to think we wait only for a strong man to take us over and believes that he is the man strong enough to do so. Mating isn't the only thing he has in mind. He wants to control us."

I laugh despite myself. "Well, he's in for a rude awakening. The only reason you guys aren't classed as the strongest pack is because you're way out here, keeping to yourselves."

"We don't want to be disturbed. Especially by men."

"Ain't that the truth. But if we don't do something about this pack, then I don't think you'll have much choice in the matter."

Opal nods. "Fine. I've been putting it off, but I don't think I can afford to do that any more. I'll call a moot."

My eyes widen. "Never heard of it. What's a moot?"

"Hardly surprising. They don't happen very often. Certainly we've not held one since the introduction of the Supernatural Creatures Act. Before that, the last was easily fifty years ago." Opal stands and crosses to the long rope hanging in the corner. She pulls it twice, and though there is no sound down here, a set of bells rings loudly somewhere above us.

I glance at Rayne. She shrugs.

Opal goes on. "A moot is a gathering of werewolf packs. Usually such meetings are reserved for"—she growls—"a blood moon or a cross-pack celebration, but they also take place in urgent and dire circumstances. All wolf packs in an area must follow a certain set of rules. Nothing is written, but there are traditions and expectations to be upheld. The Blood Moon pack is ignoring all of them and I'd considered this after our visitor left. Now however, it's clear we need to gather."

My skin seems to tingle with the energy put off from Opal's words. This is something new and important, and the SPEAR in me is already working on the best way to learn about it and put the knowledge to good use. The rest of me is excited and fired up. This is going to be awesome.

I rub my hands together. "So when do we go?"

"We? No, no." Opal opens the door to the small study and walks through it. A silent but obvious command to follow. I do, with Rayne close behind, and walk back along the corridor and out through the burial area as Opal continues to speak.

"There is no *we*, Danika. Humans aren't welcome at a moot. This is werewolf business. I will call upon each of the pack alphas and they will come. They along with their second in command. Once all five packs—ugh, sorry, six packs—are in one place, we'll discuss what to do."

I stop dead in my tracks. "You're inviting the Blood Moon alpha too?"

"Of course. He may stomp on tradition, but I refuse to. In truth, he should have been the one to request a moot in the first place. Any new pack entering an established order must put themselves before the existing packs in order that territory may be set. I'm beginning to understand better than ever why this Flint may have lost his previous pack."

Back to the stairs now and the bright lights of the living area begin to break through the gloom.

I increase my pace, almost running to keep up with the business-like march Opal now employs.

At the top of the second set of steps a small cluster of habit-clad women wait for us. None of them are smiling now; none of them are calm. I see bristling fur and long nails among the crowd waiting for us and a visible sag of relief as Opal steps into view.

She spends a brief moment scanning the crowd, seemingly counting. "Bethany? Ingrid? Katherine?"

Gina lifts her hand. "They're coming."

No sooner has she said it than the main doors to the church open. Through it hurry three wolves in hybrid forms, bounding awkwardly along on hands and toes. They skid to a stop at the rear of the gathering and ripple back into their human forms. They're naked and sweaty, but clearly ready for any sort of action, two of the three still holding on to their sharp claws.

"Thank you for coming so quickly, girls. Given SPEAR's update on the outburst of aggressive werewolf activity last night and persistent visits from the Blood Moon alpha, we can no longer afford to be passive and aloof. Girls, we must vote, as discussed earlier."

Mumbles and whispers shoot through the crowd.

I watch the collection of women, trying to read the mood. The emotion I notice most among those gathered is nervousness. Not fear, but certainly agitation and caution. None of them appear happy at the prospect of a vote.

Opal lifts both hands. "We vote now. One, do we finally agree to meet with this Flint and learn the truth of what he wants from us? Two, do we do as Gina suggests and seek protection or at least assistance from other packs? Three, do we continue to turn away the Blood Moon on our own with our own strength? Or, a new option, do we call a moot and settle the issue of this new pack once and for all?"

Many of the woman can no longer contain themselves. At this new option, the murmurs and whispers become a full-on conversation with no pretence at subtlety. I hear varied thoughts and options, but mostly excitement.

Most, if not all of these werewolves, are young. They are troubled females booted from their old packs or left to fend for themselves before finding this one. While all packs have a strong sense of loyalty and family, the Loup Garou are well known for taking this to an extreme, more so even than Long Tooth wolves who are in fact related by blood. To see a pack led by democracy is fascinating, even if Opal does hold the ceremonial title of alpha.

After a minute or two, Opal lifts her hands again to still the crowd. "Vote now, with a show of hands. The first option of meeting with Flint to open negotiations on joining our packs?"

Not a single hand raised. Not surprising, but still warming to see.

"Second, allying ourselves with other packs."

Gina and two others lift their hands. They do so boldly and without shame, but their raised fists are lonely in a sea of lowered ones.

"Third, do we put off the advances of this new pack ourselves, depending only on our own strengths?"

Many hands shoot into the air this time. In fact, so many that I begin to count, because at a glance it looks like more than half.

Rayne twitches beside me. "This is close."

She's not kidding.

Opal seems to realize it too. I can see her lips moving as she counts the raised fists. "Very well. And the newest option, do we call a moot and discuss the next steps with every Angbec pack?"

More hands raised.

I count, but Opal is quicker, and she sighs when done. "An even split. To those of you who chose not to vote, are you certain? You have the power to swing the decision one way or another, but of course you're not obligated to vote."

Two women, older in appearance than the rest, share a weary glance before shaking their heads. The first murmurs, "We're too old and tired to fight. Each option you put to us will end in some sort of battle."

The second nods her agreement. "We'll follow you, Opal, as we've always done. But we won't choose to endanger our pack."

"Your pack is already in danger." I shouldn't, I know that, but I just can't help myself. "Hiding your heads in the sand isn't going to make things better."

For the first time, Opal directs anger at me. "Silence. This is no place for you to speak."

"But—"

"This isn't your place. My pack mates may vote however they feel comfortable with no fear of shame or retaliation. A decision to abstain is as valid and will be respected."

"You don't understand—"

Rayne grabs my arm. "Danika."

Up on the platform, Opal takes a single step forward. It's small and by no means aggressive, but in that moment, I can feel her *edane* presence licking against my exposed skin like heat off an open fire. "Whatever the decision we make tonight you and your companion will be escorted off the premises. Loup Garou take care of our own. We always have and will continue to do so. We've no need of SPEAR assistance."

Great. She's hit full-on alpha mode.

I raise a hand, palm out in defeat, and snap my lips closed. If she wants to play it that way, fine, but there's no way I'm leaving this place if a moot is about to happen.

"Now then, if you two are certain you won't vote then the final decision in the place of a tie falls on me. Do you all agree? Now is the time to switch your vote if you wish to."

Nobody moves.

I hold my breath.

Opal curls a lock of her hair around her finger, winding it tighter and tighter until it springs free and spirals like a corkscrew. "A moot it is. Ladies...prepare for company. Bethany, Ingrid, Katherine, you are back outside on guard. Ursula, you will invite the Dire Wolves, Yvonne, you will contact the Grey Tails. Charlotte, you visit the Fire Fangs, and try to behave while you do. Zoe, you see the Long Tooths, and I will visit the Blood Moon myself."

Uproar.

For those who voted for the moot there is excited chatter and movement, from everybody else, reactions vary from anger, to fear, to concern, to bemusement.

Shouts come from all over the crowd.

"We can't invite them here."

"There hasn't been a moot for years."

"We aren't prepared."

"There aren't enough weapons here."

"But they don't respect us, you know they won't come."

"You can't go to the Blood Moon pack alone."

And so on. Aside from the few frantic cries I can decipher the rest is a cacophony of objections, agreements, and worries.

Rayne, still with her hand on my elbow, sighs deeply. "I don't know about this."

Neither do I, but of all the options this pack seemingly had on offer, it's the best one as far as I can tell.

"Ladies, ladies." Opal waves her hands again. "I'm sure I don't have to remind you that a moot requires plenty of preparation. There's a lot to do before the others arrive, so there is no time for argument. The decision has been made. Let's follow through."

The women named by Opal's role call peel off from the gathering at the base of the nave. They strip down quickly, leaving tunics, wimples, and undergarments draped over chairs or folded in corners. They shift with barely any effort, bypassing their hybrid forms to go for the larger, faster wolf forms.

They nose the door open and vanish into the night with a swish-flick of their large tails. Those that remain also erupt into a flurry of activity, moving furniture, collecting up games and books, stripping off their clothing.

Rayne and I stand in the middle of it all, while Gina approaches her alpha.

I try not to listen…but not very hard.

"Opal, are you sure about this?"

"Not at all. But of all the choices we discussed earlier, this is the most proactive. You know the girls appreciate action."

"But action for the sake of action is foolish."

"And what would you do in my place?"

"I…" Gina lowers her head.

"My love." Opal catches Gina's chin with her hand. "Thank you, but I need you to be strong now. Consistent. While I put the invitation at the foot of the Blood Moon alpha, I need you to be here and watch our girls. Can you do that? For me?"

Gina turns her face into Opal's hand, pressing her lips against her fingers.

I turn my back on them, offering what small illusion of privacy I can. Despite that, I can hear their heavy breathing and the desperation in the sudden kiss they share.

My cheeks grow warm and, despite myself, I sneak a glance at Rayne.

My heart stutters. She's looking at me.

Our shared gaze grows hotter, more intense with every passing second. My fingertips start to tingle, my chest grows tight. Low down in my body, my muscles remember the happy clench and flex of when she touches me.

"Rayne—"

She turns away and walks toward the door.

CHAPTER TWENTY-NINE

By the time I reach the outside the Loup Garou wolves have scattered to go about their separate jobs. As my eyes adjust to the night vision, I spy Rayne stalking across the grass.

"Rayne." I have to run to catch up with her, and though I know she can hear me, she doesn't turn or slow.

"For goodness sake, will you wait? Please."

She vaults across the stream without using the stepping stones, putting even more distance between us as she stalks back to the van.

By the time I do reach her side, I can see the darker smudge of black against the night sky that marks where I parked the vehicle.

"Where are you going?"

"Away from here. We did what you wanted. We've got information and it looks like the Angbec packs are going to sort this mess out for themselves. We don't need to be involved any more."

"But—"

"But nothing. Why 'but'? Why always do you have a 'but'?"

I slap my rear. "Just shaking what my mama gave me."

Rayne gives a rippling snarl. "Stop that. Be serious, for once in your life."

My smile fades. "I…I'm sorry. I didn't mean to—"

"You never do, but please, just this once, can you accept that your job is done? We shouldn't even be here, but I followed you like I said I would. You've mobilized the Loup Garou, they'll call the moot or whatever it is, and we can get out of the way. We don't belong in this fight."

The word "but" dies on my lips. Instead I walk slowly around Rayne's body, forcing her to turn with me until the light of the moon shines on her face.

"What's wrong?"

"Nothing," she snaps.

"Bullshit. What has you so…so…riled up?"

She puts her back to me and the moonlight. Instead of her face, now I can see the rim of silver light across her back and shoulders, marking out the tense set of every muscle and limb. "Do you trust me?" she whispers.

My gut knots. "I—"

"Not with blood, not with blood mania. We both know how you feel about that. But do you trust my instincts as a SPEAR? Or even as the police officer I used to be."

"Yes. You're an excellent agent."

Her shoulders hunch briefly toward her ears then settle again. "Then trust me now. Stay away from this moot. Something awful is going to happen, I can just feel it."

"Like what? To me? To Opal? To the other packs? What?"

"I don't know." Frustration adds a growl to her voice. "But I can feel it. Don't you? Your instincts are usually better than mine. Why can't you see this is a bad set-up?"

"Because it's not. You're right. The wolf packs are going to look after themselves, but at the very least shouldn't SPEAR have a presence so we know what's going on?"

She hesitates. "Then let Noel do it. This is his case now, anyway."

I run my fingertips back and forth over the pockets on my utility belt. Maybe he could take my place out here. Maybe he *should*. But he'd likely never make it in time and, quite obviously, this is so much more than who has jurisdiction over the werewolf case.

"Rayne?" I follow as she turns aside from me again. "Rayne. Talk to me. What's bothering you?"

"I'm frightened, okay?" Her words are a harsh bellow in the darkness, echoing over the empty grass. "I'm so, so afraid and I can't believe that you aren't too. The way Opal described this Flint Liddell…I can't remember when I last heard a werewolf admit to fear. Doesn't that bother you?"

"A little. But not knowing bothers me more. It's dangerous."

"So let's leave."

"I mean dangerous for others. We need to see who this guy is. More than ever, this moot gives us reason to stick around."

Rayne tangles her hands in her hair. "And if something goes wrong? Because it will. What then? I don't know anything about this Flint, and if even the Loup Garou are afraid of him, this one man—I'm not sure I can protect you."

My eyes narrow. "I don't need protection, Rayne."

"Of *course* you don't. But I still want to. I need to. I need—" She gives another low growl.

"What? What do you need?"

A setting of her jaw. "*We* need to leave. Right now. Get in the van."

"No."

"Get in the van."

"I'm not leaving."

Rayne gives me the full weight of her glare. I stare right back. There's no way I'm leaving. Not now, not least because of the moot but because Rayne clearly has more to say, and driving away from here gives her the perfect way to escape it.

I open my mouth to press the matter, but Rayne, as ever, is so much faster. She grabs me, actually scooping me up over her shoulder into a fireman's hold. She walks me over to the van while I'm still recovering from the shock of such a bold move, and then she's shoving me into the passenger side.

"Rayne—"

"You'll thank me later. We need to go." She slams the door on me and walks around to the driver's side.

I grit my teeth. No. No freaking way. I have the keys out of the ignition before she opens the door and then I'm scrambling back out onto the path. I pull back my arm, but damn it, she's too fucking fast, and catches my wrist before I can throw.

"Don't you dare," she warns me.

I let the keys fall from my grip toward where I scoot my free hand round to catch. Hers moves to intercept. Rayne's vampire speed wraps her fingers around the keys before I even get close so I turn into her body and shove back with my shoulder. The hard bone strikes her in the nose and again the keys fall. I continue turning, swinging my right leg round and catching the bunch with the side of my foot, punting the whole set of keys far into the darkness.

They sail away in a bright arc and land *somewhere* in the grass far away.

Rayne, with one hand cupped around her nose, the other still on my wrist, stares at me in bewilderment. "What are you doing?"

I glare right back. "I'm. Not. Leaving."

"Did you forget that Opal is the one who told us to go? She doesn't want us here."

"She doesn't have to know."

A wordless grunt of anger leaves Rayne's lips. "This is *their* land. You really think we can stay here and they won't know? Are you insane?"

I pull my wrist away. It takes effort, but shock has loosened Rayne's grip which is the only reason I'm able to do so. "I'm pissed off," I shoot back. "Wendy is dead, Rayne. Aleksandar killed him and he did it so he could take the Dire Wolves to attack the Blood Moon. Them coming here and flouting all the unwritten wolf laws is what did this, and I *have* to follow through. I told Wendy I would look after his pack and instead I just helped deliver it into the hands of that madman. Now I have the chance to be part of the force that stops all the infighting and brings a little peace back to Angbec. It's my job."

"It's personal."

"Of course it is. But so is everything else. I saw you in there, Rayne. I know you. You saw Gina and Opal sucking faces and I saw the way you looked at me. Don't you dare tell me this isn't personal. Would you make this much fuss over any other member of Kappa?"

Rayne looks down at the ground. "Please stop…"

"No. We're going to talk about this. You can't just dump me then talk about protection and shit like that, as if you still have some claim to—"

"Shut up, Danika."

It's the panic in her voice, not the words, that make me pause.

Before I've thought it through, my gun is in my hands, held facing out into the dark.

"What? What is it?"

She darts up to me and snags my wrist. Again. "We need to move. Right now."

I pull against her, but the grip is firm, even against me twisting. "Come on, Rayne—"

"There's someone coming. They're coming from behind and they're not friendly. We need to move."

I turn toward the van, but Rayne's grip pulls me in the other direction. Back toward the seemingly abandoned church.

"Wait, we can't go back there."

She glares in the direction the keys fell, then back to me. "You'd rather stay out here in a van we can't even lock, let alone drive?"

Touché.

And with that, we're running. I know she's pacing herself, carefully measuring her steps so as not to move too fast, but this speed is a flat-out sprint I know I can't keep up for long.

We leap and bound across the grass, darting around rabbit holes and fox dens as we approach the stream. At the edge, Rayne springs across it, half dragging, half carrying me to make the distance in two long strides. Then onward, where the huge bulk of the church grows larger and larger before us.

Then from ahead comes a loud, quivering howl. It's joined by two others, and then three wolves in hybrid form spring out of the grass and past us in the direction we've come. I can only assume it's the trio Opal picked out to be guards, because they continue to howl and gruff their intent to each other while stretching out behind us.

Clearly we're not a threat to them compared to whatever is coming.

The unexpected sprint is getting to me now. My breath is rasping in my throat, my legs sore from the abrupt burst of motion without proper stretching. Having one arm trapped and unable to provide balance also makes my gait clumsy and awkward.

"R-Rayne."

She releases my wrist then chivvies me on ahead, now guarding my back as we get closer to the church.

The doors are open, perhaps the howls have alerted those within, and now a large rectangle of orange light falls out of the gap to illume the space below. I aim for that, now more comfortable with something to see.

Just as we reach the doors, more howls spring up, along with the rough bark of angry wolves calling out a warning.

I stop, unable to run anymore, and turn, despite Rayne's protests, to see what is happening.

Wolves. At least twenty of them, loping slowly over the grass toward the church in one long line. They move at a casual pace, clearly unconcerned with cover or being seen. They seem to form a wide V-shape and, at the point, is a single figure carrying a torch. The stranger appears to be in human form, walking calmly on two legs.

Rayne nudges at my back, trying to get me through the door, though her attempts become a little half-hearted when she notices the approaching force. "What is that?" She shudders.

"I think that would be Flint Liddell."

Gina looks out through the open door. She sees the approaching wolves, then us. Surprise, then irritation flit across her gaze. "You were supposed to leave."

"Change of plans."

"You annoying little…human."

I shrug. "You're not the first person to say that."

She rolls her eyes and throws the door open still wider. "Get inside and stay out of sight." She shucks her clothes as she speaks, leaving them pooled on the ground as she steps around us to meet the approaching force.

I surprise even myself by choosing not to argue. Instead, I push on through and back into the living area where the other werewolf women wait in varied states. Some still in human forms, others fully shifted, though most favour the larger, heavier hybrid forms best suited for fighting.

Most ignore us as Rayne and I walk through, instead focused on the door. So I step up onto the raised platform before the apse and hunker down beneath the wall of weapons.

Rayne points to the steps. "She said get out of sight."

I spread my hands. "You really think they don't know we're here? A single human and a vampire among a huge pack of wolves? They'd know exactly where we are regardless of where we hid. At least this way we can see what's going on."

"I can't convince you to move?"

"You know better than that by now."

"Hmm." She sighs and drops to a crouch beside me, with her hands dangling between her knees. "You're a royal pain in the arse, you know that?"

I gape at her. "A pain in the arse clearly rubbing off on you."

She smiles. "Yes, well. You have that effect on people."

A sudden silence sweeps through the church. It raises the hairs on the back of my neck and sets my fingers tingling around the butt of my gun, but there's nothing to see. Not for me, anyway.

Every single werewolf is now tensed and facing the door, teeth bared, fangs at the ready. Rayne shifts from a crouch to one knee and plants her fingertips on the ground, like an Olympic sprinter.

"What's happening?"

Her smile dies. "They're coming in."

❖

Gina backs into the church with her hands slightly raised. As she moves, fur begins to bristle across the back of her neck and down her spine, while her red hair deepens to a rich auburn colour. With each step, she grows taller and broader, until she's moving on her toes with her tail swishing back and forth behind her for added balance.

Her hybrid form is taller than her human one but not by more than a foot. What she lacks in height she makes up for in pure breadth, blocking most of the entrance way with her wide stance and thick limbs. "My name is Gina Byron," she calls in a loud, gruff voice, "second of the Loup Garou and ambassador for Opal Smith. You enter our territory en masse, in aggressive numbers without warrant or invitation. You have ten seconds to explain why we shouldn't kill you where you stand."

Bold words, but she keeps backing up, giving ground to whatever is approaching from the other side.

And then I see him. A man with skin so dark it appears almost purple and hair caught up in neat cornrows to his shoulders. His eyes are hidden beneath narrow, stylish sunglasses, but they don't wholly cover the scar. It cuts across his whole face from his hairline on the right, across his eye, nose, and cheek before stopping on the left beneath his ear.

Rayne twitches beside me. "He's evil. Pure dread and evil."

Part of me wants to shrug off the comments, but even I feel the sudden shift in the air. As though all the oxygen has been sucked out and replaced with a poor substitute, watered down and thinned with fear, despair, and misery.

Gina spreads her arms and though she stands firm, her voice trembles. "Answer me immediately."

The man steps forward with his arms spread. "I said I would come again, and so here I am."

"Alpha Opal already gave you our response."

"Not so. She insisted that she would 'confer with her girls' and return to us with a decision. But what better way to speed things up than to collect the final answer in person?" His voice is strange, like a mix of gravel and grinding metal plates. It's also familiar, though I can't for all my efforts place where I might have come across this man before.

The cluster of female werewolves move forward, forming a solid semicircle in back of Gina. None move closer than about six feet, a wary distance that speaks of caution and fear rather than anything tactical.

What's wrong with them?

Gina's long pink tongue flicks out across her lips. Such a human gesture of nervousness looks odd on a creature so large and powerful. "You have no right to enter our territory without invitation." Her voice cracks, but she presses on. "Leave."

"But we have been invited, little girl. There's a moot."

Rumbles and whispers of surprise. Even Rayne looks my way with a raised eyebrow.

Gina swallowed audibly. "What have you done with Opal?"

"Me?" Flint presses his fingers against his chest. "Not a thing. Are you always so suspicious?"

"When I have cause to be. She left here to invite you to meet with us and now you're here but she's not? I'd say that's suspicious. Especially since you've clearly received her message."

"What are you accusing me of, little bitch? You should take care in how you speak to your new alpha."

Nerves and fear give way beneath a flash of anger. "You're not my alpha."

"Not yet, perhaps. But soon enough when that dainty doll, Opal, sees sense." The man lifts his hands. "My name is Flint Liddell, alpha of the Blood Moon pack. Here is your so-called alpha." He clicks his fingers and two of the hybrid figures at his back drag Opal's wolf form into view.

She's big, like most werewolves and a simple grey in colour. Her ears are large and tufted and the faint streak of darker fur forms a ridge down her belly. Small details I can plot easily now because she doesn't appear to be moving.

Rayne hisses softly.

Gina shrieks. "What have you done with her? Opal? Opal."

Flint grins. "Me? Not a thing. In fact all I've done is bring her home to you like the gentleman I am. Why don't you come take her, little girl."

The Loup Garou wolves tense visibly, all of them now looking to Gina. The desire for an order is strong and obvious.

Gina looks about ready to erupt. "You'll pay for any harm done to my alpha, Flint Liddell. Hear me and know my words to be true."

"Oh?" He sweeps off his sunglasses with a flourish. "Will I now?"

Gina jerks back with a cry.

The wolves around her cower and I see several tails lower to swing soft and timid between trembling legs.

I gasp. Can't help it. Flint's eyes are yellow. Not amber yellow or the golden hue of a werewolf about to shift, but bright sunshine yellow. Almost cartoony, crayon yellow.

Rayne jabs me in the ribs, but it's too late. Apparently my exclamation is loud enough to draw attention our way and Flint angles his head toward the apse. A strange warmth washes across my chest and the moisture in my mouth vanishes as though burned away.

"Oh, more friends. Mmm, a human and a blood sucker, how sweet. For us? You shouldn't have."

"No...no please." Gina's voice is barely audible. "They aren't for you."

"Such poor hospitality." Flint sighs in mock-hardship. "I thought the hosts of a moot were to provide food and sport. Why else would I bring my people but to enjoy a hunt with the rest of the packs?"

Rayne gives me a savage glare that says well enough what I know she must be thinking.

I lift my hands in defeat.

Fine. Maybe we *should* have left. But we can't now, so there's no point crying about it, is there?

Chapter Thirty

I stand from my crouch, walk down the chancel, and off the single step leading down. My steps are dragging, feeling heavy and weak, but I force myself to keep going. I won't be bullied by this creep. No way.

The semicircle of Loup Garou part to let me through and snap shut behind Rayne who stands right at my side. The pair of us take places to either side of Gina and stare at the arrogant newcomer.

"I'm Danika Karson."

Flint's creepy eyes grow wide. This close his pupils are visible as long black slits rather than the circles one might expect. His nostrils flare as he scents the air. "The SPEAR? Yes, yes, even I've heard of you. Seems you have quite the reputation. Can't think why."

"I'm good at my job."

"Is that so? And I thought it might be just because you're rather... striking. Not beautiful, I think that descriptions belongs more with your miniature companion here, but you have quite the presence about you."

A quick glance at Rayne shows me the fangs between her lips. "My name is Rayne. Spawn of Vixen."

This time all subtly is lost. Flint looks at Rayne from top to bottom. Then bottom to top. "Interesting."

"Shut up," Rayne snaps. "I want to know what you are."

Flint growls. "Whatever do you mean, pretty girl?"

"What. Are. You? You're not human, nor vampire. You're certainly not a wolf."

He cocks his head. "Do I not look like a werewolf? Maybe this will help." He lifts his arms and tilts his head back. His shift seems to begin in reverse, from his feet rather than the top of his head. It licks up his body like a weird backward waterfall, bringing fur out on to his exposed skin. The scarred ruin of his face stretches and elongates to produce a muzzle and nose with the same odd slash mark from right to left.

"Is this better, pretty girl?"

I fight the urge to cringe. "He looks like a wolf to me."

"But he doesn't smell like one. He smells wrong. Like rot and evil and hate."

"You slander me, pretty one—"

"Don't call me that." Silver springs into her eyes. "You're not welcome here. Did Miss Gina not just say you need to leave? Remove yourself before I put you out."

I raise a hand. "Hey, hey, calm down. We're not here to fight, remember. You said it yourself. We shouldn't even be here."

Flint grins and talks right over me. "I'd like to see you try, blood sucker. Maybe I'll enjoy some sport after all."

"Try me," Rayne snarls.

"Woah, there, now." I step across her with my arms raised. "What's the matter with you? Calm down."

But she doesn't hear me. That or she ignores me. Her right hand lashes out, shoving me aside and into Gina so she can reach Flint. Her expression is a mask of uncharacteristic rage as she launches at him.

Her tackle slams into his front and the pair hit the ground hard enough to send tremors racing up my legs. Rayne aims a bite at his throat, but Flint is slippery-quick, bringing an arm across to block her mouth. As she chomps down on his forearm, he brings the free hand around to grab at her ID lanyard.

"No, damn it, Rayne."

Their angle is awkward, causing his claws to scrape across her throat as he moves, but Flint does catch the cord. Two quick turns of his wrist tightens the long length into a makeshift noose and he yanks hard, jerking her head away.

Panic fills Rayne's eyes. I see her hands scrabble for the throttling around her neck and the wheezing breaths as she struggles to breathe around it. Blood drips from her fangs and teeth and both eyes roll in her head as she kicks against the ground.

The Blood Moon wolves point and laugh, some of them slapping high-fives and whistling encouragement to their alpha. Their voices are loud and raised in pleasure, encouraging their leader against the "blood-sucking parasite."

I try to step in, but Gina has my arm, holding me back and away. She has the presence of mind to keep her claws from digging in, but even I can see she's terrified. Several of the other Loup Garou have scattered toward the back of the church, others simply lowering themselves to the floor to curl into tight, frightened balls.

What the hell is happening to everyone?

On the ground, Rayne is still struggling. A small trickle of blood runs down her throat, but most startling is the persistent wheezing and gasping of a woman struggling to breathe.

What the hell is she doing? Vampires don't need air.

I jerk free of Gina's grip and move in closer, gun raised to eye height. My injured arm gives a twinge of protest, but I hold the weapon steady. "Get off her."

Flint ignores me. Instead he bends close to Rayne's ear, speaking in low whispers. I can't hear it all, but I do catch the words *pain, suffering,* and *forgiveness*, as well as my own name, before my patience gives way.

"Rayne, get a grip. What are you doing? Just waste this meat head so we can get out of here."

"Oh, she can't hear you, Agent." Flint's voice rattles through his thin, canine lips. "She's gone now. Far, far away. And you can't help her. No one can."

"What are you talking about?"

Again that smile. Or an approximation of it. He drops Rayne's twitching body and turns on me with slow, deliberate steps.

I point the gun at his face. "Don't move."

"But why? You've made this all so easy for me, little SPEAR." He's still coming closer. "I thought I would have to hunt you down after handling these werewolf packs. But no, you're right here. It's so easy I could cry."

"Last warning, Flint. Stay back."

He stops, but only long enough to ripple back into his human form. Those awful, awful yellow eyes consider me steadily, the vertical black pupil widening slightly. He brushes aside the tattered shreds of some of his clothing. "I wonder what you'll taste like. What memories you hide deep under all that pretty hair."

He steps forward again.

I fire.

My bullet slams into his shoulder, drilling a deep hole before powering through the other side. I expect the velocity and power of it to spin him around, or at least make him pause, but Flint keeps moving, his gaze now fixed hot on mine.

"First blood," he murmurs. "Boys? Get them."

Shit.

❖

The Blood Moon wolves behind Flint, mostly quiet up to this point, move as one solid mass. They rush forward in a wave of claws, fur, and teeth and crash hard against the line of Loup Garou. I turn, wanting to help, but there's not much I can do with my puny human body against the sudden explosion of fighting behind me.

Instead, I look back at Flint.

He's still there. Staring. Smiling.

The creeping sense of dread intensifies. Even traditional bullets should hurt a werewolf, especially at this range.

I back up step. "What are you?"

"You don't remember? I'm hurt."

"We've never met."

"Not in this body perhaps. But there's nothing about me that looks familiar? Feels familiar?" He blinks again.

Those eyes. Those creepy, almost reptilian eyes.

A trickle of bright yellow ooze dribbles from the bullet wound in Flint's shoulder. It's thin and bile-like, similar to nothing I've ever seen before. Except...

My tongue suddenly feels thick in my mouth, heavy and awkward.

Except for that tall, thin, spindly creature hiding with the vampires, trolls, and giants in Vixen's underground hideaway. Didn't that thing have the same rattling voice, the same terrible yellow eyes?

But Flint is a werewolf; he can't be anything like that strange creature, can he?

My gun hand begins to tremble.

The yips, growls, and howls behind me grow louder.

Flint smiles. "Is that a twitch in your eyebrows, Agent? A flicker of recognition in your gaze? Do you know me?"

"Vixen..."

The smile broadens to a full-on grin. "So you *do* remember. Good. I'd hate to think I'd made all this effort for someone who didn't remember me. The height of narcissism perhaps, but I hoped I had made an impression."

"But you're not the same creature. That thing was—we still don't know what it was. But you're a werewolf. You can't be the same."

"Trust your instincts, little SPEAR. You should know that by now."

And then he's in front of me. I have no idea when he moved, but the distance between us is gone in a heartbeat and Flint has his fingers wrapped around my wrist, forcing my gun up and away from his face. The other hand grasps the back of my head, drawing my face closer and closer until our noses almost touch.

For one horrifying moment I wonder if he intends to kiss me, but instead, he brings his hand around, stroking gently at my head, my ear, my cheek. My lip. His long fingers close around my jaw, holding my head in place.

By the time my brain catches up, I'm already trapped against him, my head pinned by his iron-like grip. Fear spikes through me, like a red-hot stab to the gut.

"Rayne."

"She can't hear you. Don't you believe me? Look."

He turns my head. I have no choice but to look.

Rayne is on the ground, no longer wheezing, but not struggling either. Her eyes are wide and glassy, her hands limp on the ground at her sides. Even with her body right there on the ground before me, I know she's not really here.

"What did you do?" My voice doesn't even sound like mine. It's small and weak, pitiful and young, and I hate it. I hate it but there's nothing I can do.

"She's on a little trip down memory lane. Such wonderful stops on the way. I wonder what you'll find when you go?"

I kick out at his shins, his ankle, his knees. My free hand I use to chop down against his grip on my chin. But I may well be punching at a wall for all the difference it makes. He doesn't move. If anything, his grip intensifies.

My wrist begins to ache from the crushing effect while my jaw creaks beneath him.

The sense of dread and fear upgrades to full-on terror.

"Gina? Rayne? Fuck, please. Somebody...h-help."

"Help?" Flint cocks his head at me. "Interesting. So that's where you go first? A feeling of helplessness and weakness? I suppose I should have known. Those humans with the biggest mouths are always those with the smallest reserves to back up their bravado."

He lifts.

My feet are dangling. Between his hand on my wrist and the other on my jaw, there's nothing more I can do than kick. But that feeling of terror begins to spread and soon even the thought of doing that is too much. I can't even feel the gun in my hands anymore. My fingers are too numb. The other hand, curled impotently around his grip, does nothing to free my jaw.

Nothing I do does anything.

"Somebody...help..."

Fresh pain spikes through my arm, and from the corner of my eye I spy a thin stream of blood trickle down my forearm. He's cut me, punctured the inside of my wrist with his claws.

It's not deep but the pain that comes from it is like nothing I've ever known. Like a prickling heat, cut through with thousands of needle-sharp stabs.

Something inside me screams and my impotent kicks intensify.

Flint laughs. "Singing already? Beautiful, little SPEAR, beautiful. Sing for me, little bird."

The room begins to blur.

"Sing a sweet, sweet song of pain and misery for me."

My vision grows cloudy.

"There you go, little bird."

The light begins to dim.

"There you go."

CHAPTER THIRTY-ONE

I slip through the door at the rear of the large building and let it close softly behind me. Yeah, sure, I could use the front like everybody else, but I'd rather not deal with the crowds.

This staff entrance to the shopping centre is small and inconspicuous and leads to a long corridor that winds down the width of the building before opening to stairs that lead to upper staff levels.

I secure my fresh new lanyard more firmly around my neck, hitch the rucksack a little higher on my shoulder, and keep walking. Oh, and pull my jacket forward to cover my gun.

So strange that I get to walk the streets with a gun. Most police officers don't do that—in fact none of them do—but I get to wear one?

Can't help but touch it as I walk, tracing my fingers over the cool plastic of the handgrip that sticks out over the top of the pop-stud.

This is it. This is how I know I've made it.

My heart gives a curious flutter that I know is both nerves and glee.

Stairs.

I take them two at a time, now almost beside myself in my excitement. At the top I turn back to exit through the door that leads onto the outer areas of the shopping centre.

The two floors below are teeming with shoppers. Up here on a mezzanine style set-up, I can look down on them from thirty feet above and watch them mill about like ants.

Men, women, and children, all scooting back and forth about their daily business. Everyone laden with bags and boxes while obnoxious but thankfully low music pumps from multiple speakers. In among the civilians, I catch the black and red of the centre security team, further marked by their peaked caps, shoulder radios, and high-vis stripes on both legs and arms.

One man stands out from the others, one, because I'm looking for him, but also because his hair, a fine ash grey, spills out from beneath his ill-fitting hat and cascades down his back in thick, chunky locs.

I can't help but smile. He's always so easy to spot.

With half an eye on his location, I make my way down the two escalators and three sets of half-steps required to reach his post, some boutique fashion store with trendy headless mannequins in the window.

He sees me before I can sneak up on him and smiles bright and wide. "Bean." A quick glance at his watch. "What are you doing here? I don't finish for another half hour."

"I know, sorry, sorry, but I just couldn't wait." I throw myself at him, not caring that he's in uniform, not caring about appearances, just keen to share. "I had to see you, I had to tell you—"

He grips me by the shoulders. "Wait, did you do it? Did you pass?"

I scoop up my lanyard to wave it back and forth in front of his eyes. "Gamma, Grade Three!"

"Yes. Yes, yes, yes. Oh, Bean, I'm so proud of you."

"Ah, ah, you can't call me that anymore, Dad. As of right now I'm Agent Karson."

"But of course." He treats me to a mock salute and plucks the ID badge from my grip for a closer look. "Danika L. Karson, certified member of the Supernatural Prohibition Extermination and Arrest Regiment. Field agent, Grade Three. Team, Gamma. Wow. Just wow. You did it. I always knew you would. You're incredible."

"Don't get mushy now."

"I'm not." He lets the ID fall and returns his hands to my shoulders. He looks down at me and though the height difference is only an inch or two, I suddenly feel so small and childlike under the fatherly expression in his eyes. "I'm just…just so proud of you."

"Really?"

"Of course I am. Despite everything stacked against you, despite every roadblock the Lord put in your way—"

"You mean that Mum put in my way."

The smile droops a little. "Don't be hard on your mother, Bean. She's scared for you, that's all. But never doubt she's as proud of you as I am. If not more."

"You know she couldn't even wish me 'good luck' this morning. Just some obscure reference to a bible verse I've never heard of."

"Was it one from Ezekiel?"

"No, Haggai I think."

Dad puts his hands on his hips and tosses his head back. His laughter is enough to draw eyes from all directions, but he doesn't seem to care. Then again, neither do I.

"That is *an obscure one. You know she only wants the best for you, right?"*

I sigh. *"Yeah."*

"Look, I want you to tell me all about the exam, okay? I want to know who tested you, what the physical was like, what the sparring was like. Do you really get to use a sword?"

This time I'm grinning, wide enough that my cheeks start to hurt. *"It's probably the coolest thing I've ever done. And I got to fight a gargoyle."*

"Seriously?"

"Yeah. He's practically nine feet tall, blue, and his wings are the hugest thing I've ever seen. From his shoulder blades rather than webbing under his arms. Oh, he's grumpy, but I guess a lot of extra mundanes are like that."

"Maybe you bring it out in him?"

"Daaad."

My playful admonishment trails off as a loud shriek cuts through the air. I turn in time to see a body falling from the mezzanine. It plummets like a stone, slamming into the ground thirty feet down and throwing out a gory pattern of red in a near perfect ring.

Deadly silence, then another scream. And another, and another.

I'm turning round and round, trying to catch where they're coming from, but there are too many people running.

Dad's shoulder radio crackles to life, some disembodied voice demanding immediate evacuation of the shoppers. Something about a "Code E41."

All the colour drains from Dad's face. He flings his hat from his head and catches his hair, winding it into a thick, bumpy braid down his back. "Bean, you need to get out of here."

"Why? What's happening?"

"Emergency evacuation. Extra mundane."

"What?" My insides seize up. I can't breathe. Panic rushes through me in a cold, crippling flood, and I can barely keep my feet as the sudden surge in the crowd nearby sweeps toward the door.

Dad snags my hand and drags me against him. He turns his back and shields me with his bulk, wading through the madness to reach one of the pillars that supports the upper levels. He uses the wideness as a blockage to stop the crowd from taking us and holds me tight against his chest.

"They didn't give me details, just called the code. I need to get these people out. That means you too."

"But—"

"No buts, Bean. I've got a job to do, okay? Join these people and get outside."

"What about you?"

He touches my cheek. "Don't you worry about me. I'll be fine. I always am. This is part of the job, y'know?"

Job. Of course. Yes, of course.

I curl my fingers around the laminated plastic of my shiny, new ID card.

"I can help."

"No, Bean—"

I shove the ID in his face. "I'm an agent now. I can help you. Please, let me help. It's my job too."

He hesitates. I can see the war in his eyes. The uncertainty. The fear.

"Hey." I touch his arm. "I've trained for this. I know what to do. Let me help."

"I—" He inhales sharply and lifts his shoulders. "Yes. You're a big girl now. No, not even girl—woman. Not my little bean anymore."

I pop the stud on my hip clasp and draw my gun into my hands. "I'll always be your Bean, Dad. No matter how old and tough I get."

"Steady now. Any tougher than you already are and you won't be a bean anymore so much as an old pebble."

"Watch it, old man. I'm a martial arts master."

"I don't doubt it. Okay," With one hand on my shoulder, he steers me in a half circle and points to the rushing crowd beneath the first escalator. "There's an emergency exit down there that leads to the west side of the centre. It looks like people have missed it or they're too panicked to see, so you need to get those people, using that door. We'll empty the place much quicker if we use every exit. You got that?"

"Sure. Trust me."

"Oh, I do, Bean. Of course I do. Just stay away from the vampires if you can."

I gesture to the belt of phials, packets, and tubes hanging off my hip. "No way. I know what to do, I promise."

Dad sighs. "I won't say I'm not scared, but you've wanted this for long enough. Just…remember those things aren't people anymore. No matter what the law or the mayor says. They're not what they once were. Don't hesitate."

"Never."

"That's my girl." He chucks me under the chin, the lightest of touches…

❖

…that sends me reeling onto my back.

There are screams all around me, but I can't find the source.

From above me, Flint peers into my face, blinking slowly over those terrifying, soulless eyes.

"You're smiling a lot, little SPEAR. Did I send you to a happy memory? That won't do. That won't do at all. Even your vampire friend is trapped in the nightmare of her own past. Let's see if we can't send you down a similar path."

I try to flip to my side, but my body doesn't want to move. My arms are leaden, both legs weak and jelly-like. Several feet away, I see Rayne clawing at her face. She's thrashing from side to side on the ground, shrieking over and over. Her petrified calls are haunting, all the more so because in them I catch the sound of my own name.

"Danika...please no, no. Not Danika. Not Danika."

Flint straddles my hips and whispers into my ear. "Go back, little SPEAR. Find an unhappy place."

I flail at him, striking with all my might, but my hands strike nothing but air...

She's too quick. How can she be so fast? I was sure that punch would have hit.

I run up to the wall and put my back against it, using the shadows of the tall building to cloak me. No doubt the creature can see me regardless, but at least it can't sneak up from behind this way.

My fingers are sweaty around the butt of my handgun, making the grip slip and slide. One by one, I wipe the residue against my jeans and resettle my grip. Better.

Though it takes several seconds, I force my mind to focus. To collect the facts I already know and form them into some form of coherent picture.

Vampires. Two or three, but spilling into the shopping centre through multiple doors is enough to make people panic. Hardly surprising when it's weird enough that we even acknowledge vampires as real things. Sure it's been a few years, but not everybody has accepted the truth as easily as—

My thoughts scatter as a heavy fist slams into my stomach. Air gushes out of me, leaving me gasping, wheezing, choking.

I can't breathe, fuck, I can't breathe. Am I going to die? Already?

Colours swim before my eyes as I sink to my knees on the dirty paving slabs.

Think. I have to think. I have to figure out a way to—

She has me again. By the throat this time, hefting me into the air with my back to the wall. She forces me against the brick, and my legs are dangling, lifeless and helpless.

Kicking does nothing, punching does nothing.

Oh, God, no, no, no, she's looking at me. Bright silver eyes and long fangs dripping with saliva tinged pink with blood. Other people's blood.

This thing has already been feeding and now she wants me.

My heart is racing so hard, part of me fears it might slam straight through my chest. I can hear it thudding in my ears, in my skull, in my brain.

"One more for the hold," she says. "You're strong too. A good catch."

I've no idea what that means, but at least it means she doesn't intend to eat me right now. But she does bite.

Pain races through my shoulder as she bites there, grinding her teeth together like a pit bull. She shakes back and forth, seemingly intent on causing as much pain as she possibly can while I scream and cry out.

I remember the gun just as my vision starts to cloud.

From this angle, I can't possibly get a kill shot, but maybe I can injure her?

I fire, barely aiming, just trying to squeeze off at least one bullet before I pass out from pain and oxygen deprivation.

The gunshot is thunderous in my ears and the gun kicks back against my grip. The sensation is such a shock that I end up dropping it. No way was the recoil so strong when I fired one of these at the training facility. Was it?

Doesn't matter. The vampire snarls and rips her fangs from my shoulder, peering down at the mess my shot has made of the front of her chest. Oh, good. I hit her, maybe I'll be okay, maybe I'll—

White light. Stars. Ringing.

It takes me several precious seconds to realize she's punched me, and the taste of pennies floods my tongue. I'm sliding down the wall now, sucking in air, but throbbing from so many different areas, that I barely know which way is up.

My vision is blurred out completely, with tears, sweat, or both. Both hands shake as I retrieve the gun, trying to find my target in the darkness.

Is she there? Or to my right? Above?

It's definitely tears blinding me now, and my lower lip trembles to match my hands.

Never in my entire life have I felt pain like this. Not when the girls at school used to bully me and pull my hair. Not when I got into fights to protect my sweet little sister. Not even when training with the big blue gargoyle who liked to perform elbow strikes with the spikes on the end of his forearm.

No, this is something new, this is something—

It's back. The vampire grabs me with both hands on my shoulders, drawing me close. I can see the white flash of fangs in the darkness and lift the gun, jamming it right against those twin lines of white before I fire.

Again, the retort blinds and deafens me, but that's nothing to the shriek of agony from the thing in front of me. A moist red mist sprays into my face and the vampire falls back away from me, clutching her face with both hands.

She's gurgling, trying to speak, but my bullet has wrecked her vocal cords.

"Why won't you just die?" I scream at her, levelling my gun again and firing one more shot. And another. And another. And another.

The third seems to do the trick, because the shrieking woman abruptly falls silent and presses both hands to her chest. She glares at me with hate burning in the silver of her eyes, then spits up a huge glob of thick, black ooze.

The first gobbet is followed by a second, then a third, then a stream of the stuff, thick and stinking, spilling down her neck and chest.

I've read a lot of books on vampires and other supernatural creatures, but nothing so far has ever described the smell. It's like spoiled meat, tarnished pennies, and bodily wastes all piled into one stinking wave.

I gag, then heave, then vomit.

The vampire melts and oozes away into that same sticky black matter, spilling out of her clothes as each limb gives in to the decay. By the time I'm finished emptying my stomach, she's gone, leaving nothing but her clothes.

Slowly, relieved, I sink to my knees. The stuff is probably all over me, but I don't care, I'm alive. I'm alive. I did it. I survived. I killed it.

Several minutes pass before I manage to find my feet again. Another two before I can walk.

Then, at last, I'm able to limp away from the wall and toward the front of the shopping centre where the emergency services have gathered along with all the staff.

I can tell Dad all about it. He'll be so proud.

The thought dries a few of the tears from my eyes as I slowly inch my way around the building...

...Only to drop to my knees again. My body just won't cooperate, wracked by painful memories. I don't want to remember, I just don't. I can't. I can't go back to that awful, awful night.

Right behind me, Flint follows with the widest of smiles on his face. "You look much more distressed now, Danika, that's much better. Are you there yet? Have you reached your worst memory? Or perhaps there's a little further?"

He crouches beside me, resting his elbows on his knees and continuing with such a conversational tone that we might have been discussing recipes or TV shows.

"This is how I picked my pack you know. Especially this one here." He gestures to his own body. "He thought himself so strong, but gave up soon enough when I showed him just the sort of person he is. What sort of person are you, little agent?"

"Fuck…you…"

"This one abandoned his family. Did you know that? He became a wolf and left his wife and child. The same night he took his things from their home, a pack at odds with his own attacked and murdered his family. Can you imagine?"

Through bleary eyes I can see just how little progress I've made. I'm trying to get to Rayne, but my legs still won't take me there.

She's stopped thrashing now, no longer screaming, but her eyes are glassy with tears, her jaw slack and lifeless. Again and again she whispers my name, but she clearly can't see me.

What the hell type of memory is she living? How can I get her out of it?

More scenes from the past flash before my eyes.

I fight to push them aside, but they grow brighter and brighter before me the more I fight them.

The gathered emergency response units outside the shopping centre in what used to be the old West Side. The milling bodies rushing to and fro. The uniformed security teams blocking the doors and holding back the crowd. The distinct lack of one, grey, long-haired head.

"Dad…"

My voice cracks. Tears gather in my eyes.

"I'm so sorry. Dad…Dad…"

"Dad. Come on, where are you? Say something."

Dozens of people around me call my father's name, staff from the security team, police officers, members of SPEAR. Some of them are people I trained with, others are older and more serious in the face. It's easy to tell the difference between new recruits and the veterans and not just by age. It seems those who trained with me, those new to SPEAR, still have hope in their eyes. The others, mostly older men littered with crucifixes and shotguns, seem less optimistic.

One of them even pumps his shotgun and slows to a walk, saying, "We'll hear the critter better if we're quiet. Keep your eyes peeled."

My arm hurts. My legs hurt. Hell, my eyes hurt; everything hurts. There are Omega units outside who fought against my desire to return to this place, but they don't understand, and I didn't have time to explain.

All the other security guards are outside, but not my dad. And when questioned about their colleague, none of them seemed to know where he was or what happened. One or two mentioned seeing him herding civilians, but after that, nothing.

I seem to be carrying my heart in my mouth, but I can't help it. Horrible, terrifying thoughts fill my head, most of them involving blood, fangs, and screams. Screams from my father.

My stomach forms tight little knots of fear that nothing but action seems to affect.

He has to be all right. He has to be all right.

I tell myself over and over.

He's fine. He has to be. Probably stuck helping a few more civilians. He's always been that way. Maybe I'll find him up in the security staff room, grabbing his things so we can head out for the drink we had planned. Surely he's fine. He has to be fine. He has to be.

I keep up the mantra all the way to the lifts that lead to the staffing areas.

Now that we've spread out, there are two other agents with me. One is a little older than me with thin, angry lips and a permanent frown slashed across her forehead. The other is a lot older with scars all over his hands and wrists. Oh, and down the side of his neck. Makes me shudder just to look at him.

As we step from the lift, he points out the three different routes for us to take. "I'll go left toward the car park entrance. Francine, you go along the centre to the other part of the mezzanine. Rookie, you take the left and into the staff rooms.

Francine nods her grumpy little head and sets off at once. I'm sure she's a Beta because she didn't train with me, yet she moves with more assured confidence than I could ever dream of.

When I hesitate, the older man claps me on the shoulder. I think his name is Zachariah. "First field mission, Rookie?"

I nod. My mouth is too dry to manage speaking.

"You'll be fine. You wouldn't have that badge if you didn't train for this. And we wouldn't let you have it if we didn't think you could handle it."

With much effort I swallow past the dryness enough to work a little moisture into my mouth. "It's my dad. He's the one that's missing."

His eyebrows lift ever so slightly. "You gonna be okay?"

"I...yes. I'm fine."

The gun in his hands creaks ominously as he tightens his grip. "Whatever happens, don't hesitate. You can't afford to. You got that? Don't. Hesitate."

"Wait, what do you mean?"

But he's already gone, jogging across the walkway toward the door that leads to the car park.

I'm alone.

My own gun, now replenished with wood-tipped bullets, feels almost too heavy to hold. My bitten shoulder sings with pain, and part of me regrets not letting the Omega agents take a look at it before coming up here.

I make my way across the walkway and through the open door marked "Staff." Good thing emergency evacuations unlock all doors.

It's so quiet in here. Eerily so, with one of the lights overhead flickering like a bad horror film.

The first three doors lead to bathrooms: male, female, and mixed. To check them, I have to enter each one and knock back the door on each stall. Every time I do, the fear curling around my heart grips a little tighter.

What if I can't find him? What if something has happened to him? What if one of the vampires got him and he's bleeding out somewhere?

By the time I finish checking the mixed bathroom, my stomach is so tense that I feel I might vomit again.

"Dad? Are you here? It's your little bean, Dad? Hello?"

My voice echoes in the empty stillness of the corridor and I try the next door. Coffee room, where all the staff can sit for their breaks if they so wish.

The scent of coffee still hangs in the air, along with the faint sound of a radio playing. Soft, squishy chairs and a few tables lined with plastic chairs stand opposite a work surface holding a microwave, coffee maker, empty mug tree, and dented biscuit tin.

Next door.

This one is marked "Management" and isn't open like all the others. In fact, it's hanging on its hinges, tilted hard toward the frame as though pulled. Oh, and there are scratch marks on the wood.

"Dad…"

Once more I have to pause to wipe the sweat from my hands. Then I open the door.

Devastation. The room has been turned over, flipped and turned again, with broken office furniture littering the space. Drawers have been ripped out of the cabinet lying on its side, and three potted plants spill their earthy guts across the carpet. Blood liberally paints the remains of the desk and the computer sparking and spluttering in the far corner.

But all that…it's nothing to what I see lying on the floor. A tall, dark-skinned man, with long, grey locs and a security uniform.

"Dad?" I drop the gun. "Dad." Rush to his side. "Dad, please." Drop to my knees beside him.

He turns when I touch him, slow and weak. I catch traces of the raw, chewed up mess on the side of his throat before I see his face. Both eyes closed. Red stained lips slightly parted. Breathing shallow, but present.

"Dad, please. Open your eyes." I drag him into my arms and cradle his head against my chest. "It's me, it's Bean. Dad? Dad, please?"

One eye opens. Painfully. Slowly.

"Bean?"

I drop him. Can't help it.

His eye is silver.

"Dad?"

He opens the other eye with the same, slow, careful deliberation and fixes me with a hot, hungry gaze. "My little bean," he whispers. Each word struggles around the needle-sharp fangs bristling at the front of his mouth. "I was looking for you. Where have you been?"

"Dad? Oh, God, Dad, what happened?"

The thoughts seem to move slowly in his mind. For a brief moment his gaze becomes distant, then he returns his focus to me with a palpable snap. "You smell...amazing. Why—what—you..." He sniffs hard, then clutches at my arms to pull himself forward, dragging himself up my body. Toward my shoulder.

His tongue flicks out and revulsion powers through me as he laps at the blood staining my clothing.

"That's nice. I like that. More of that, please." His mouth opens wide.

"No, no, no." I'm back-pedalling on my hands and arse, but the cabinet is in the way. I try to scoot left, but suddenly he's there and now I can't get to the door. He's right there, blocking my path, taking his feet to loom above me with every inch of his impressive height.

Dad grins, showing off fangs. "Just a taste, little one?"

He lunges and only the protruding leg of the shattered table saves me. He trips on it, giving me precious seconds to throw myself to the side, again deeper into the room.

"Dad? Please, don't. Don't you know me? It's Danika. Your Bean. Please."

He hefts the table out of the way with one careless swipe of his hand. It slams into the wall and several more pieces break away from the main surface.

I scream, a mix of fear and panic seizing my body into a useless lump of immobile flesh. I can't move. Why can't I move? Why can't I do anything?

Dad doesn't reach for me like the other vampire did, instead he gets down to my level. He crawls across the ground like some sinister panther and pushes right up into my face. His breath, his tongue, his lips are rough against my throat as he scents me like a fine, gourmet meal.

His mouth opens. I still can't move.

"Dad, please."

With a sudden shriek, he reels back from my body, clutching his head with both hands. His moans are the pitiful cries of a wounded animal, filled with pain and terror.

"Can't..." The words struggle through his bristling mouth. "Have... help me...please..."

I stand, make a move toward him. "It's okay, Dad, I can help you. Let me help, I—"

"Don't touch me." It's a frantic bellow of panic, paired with shaking hands. "Don't. Don't come closer. I can't control it. Don't. Stay there, Bean, stay. Stay." The silver in his eyes winks in and out. Each time it fades I can see his eyes, my father's eyes, and the life and love that lives behind them. But when the silver returns, the man I know is gone, replaced by a monster gaining more and more control.

I have no idea what to do. Nothing in my training has prepared me for this and every inch of me wants to curl up and hide. But from my dad?

This can't be happening. This just can't be happening to my father.

The silver is back. He's grinning. Both arms are spread wide as he paces toward me, blocking off escape with his bulk. Long lines of drool slide from his mouth, shiny and slick in the half light. I scramble to my feet, but he's too quick, fisting his hand in my jacket to drag me close.

"Dad?" My voice is the lowest of childlike whispers.

But it's not him. Not anymore. There is no recognition in his eyes, no love or care, just hunger, blind and savage. He aims a bite at my throat, catching a mouthful of fabric as I twist in his grip. Another attempt, this time caught on my elbow as I aim a strike at his face.

"Dad. Please, stop, please, please, please."

I tuck my arms and slither out of the jacket, landing hard on my arse. A quick scramble puts me on my hands and knees, crawling for the meagre remains of the table. Shelter. Protection. A blockade.

Two hands close over my ankle, pulling me back. I flail. Kick. Scream. Keep scrambling.

Table. I'm under it as far as I can go, tucking my legs in and hugging myself with both arms. Blood pumps from the agitated wound on my shoulder, and even I can smell it.

Dad's eyes are wild, his expression feral. He pounds on the table with his fists, apparently too far gone to realize that all he need do is lift it.

I brace myself beneath each shuddering impact of the table remains, trying to think, struggling to formulate a plan. What do I do? What the hell can I do?

I'm mentally racing through every book I've ever read, recalling every single lecture, practical and theoretical, on these strange entities known as vampires. But the only thing my mind settles on is the thirst for blood, the strength, the insanity. Because they are crazy, we know that. And when hungry, nothing can break through to them.

Zachariah's face swims across my mind's eye, his grim expression and deadpan order to not hesitate. Did he know it would come to this?

The small piece of table forming my shield cracks down the centre from repeated blows. It won't stand up to much more punishment. Already my legs are sticking out from beneath, naked and vulnerable.

I feel across the ground for some sort of weapon. I can't even see my gun, but there has to be something here I can—wait, wood. There's heaps of it, all over the floor. I grab the nearest shard, a thick, chunky piece with a jagged end that was probably once one of the legs.

With the hefty piece held like a club, I swing up, batting the table remains away and catching Dad's face on the follow-through. The heavy wood connects with a thud that jars my arm from wrist to shoulder, but it stops him for just a second.

"Dad, snap out of it. You have to. Don't you know me? Don't you recognize my voice?"

More snarling, more snapping and raging. He dives at me again, hands outstretched, and I...I can't. I freeze, hands still wrapped about the table leg, my eyes scrunched closed.

Thud.

The impact drives me back into the wall, knocking two framed photos off their hooks. They slam to the ground and shatter, strident snaps in the sudden still.

No more snarling. No growling. No moving.

I crack my eyes open.

He's staring at me. Yes, him, it's actually him. The silver is gone from his eyes leaving his own soft brown, shiny with tears. He opens his mouth and blood pours out, staining his long fangs red.

"Bean?"

"Dad? Dad, are you okay? Are you back?"

He looks down. "I..."

The hope dies in my heart as I follow his gaze to the table leg sticking out of his chest.

"Dad, no."

He nods sadly. "Yes, Bean. It's okay. You're going to be okay, I promise."

"I'm so sorry. I didn't mean—but you were—and then I—we just—maybe I can—"

"Don't..." He coughs hard enough to splatter hot blood droplets against my cheeks and forehead. *"Don't..."*

"It's okay. I can fix this, let me fix this. I'll pull it out and we can go downstairs and—" Even as I speak, even as I pull on the table leg, the brown melts away one last time, replaced by wild, feral silver.

"Bean...don't—."

Dad clutches for me, fingers hooked like claws, and I scream, slamming my palms, one after the other into the butt of the wooden chair leg. Something cracks. He stops dead...and black ooze begins to seep out around the jagged edge.

He falls back from me, landing hard on his side while that foul-smelling black stuff begins to trickle from his ears and nose.

I slide down the wall with my hands pressed to my mouth, fighting and abruptly failing to hold back my horrified screams.

Chapter Thirty-two

Fuck. Oh, shit, fucking fuck, fuck, balls.

 I claw free from the nightmare of my own memory, screaming and thrashing, calling out for my father in a voice so plaintive and pitiful I barely recognize it as my own.

Flint is still crouched beside me, grinning from ear to ear, only now he has his hand on the back of my neck.

"That's it, little SPEAR." His voice rattles against my senses. "Yes, yes, that's what we want. That's the fear we need. The pain. The horror of it all. Did you enjoy your trip to the past? Hmm? Was it every bit as awful and heart-rending as you remember?"

"G-get away from me." I swing out with my fist, but he's nowhere near. He doesn't even try to dodge. In fact he leans closer and speaks directly into the shell of my ear.

"I think you'll be a much better vessel going forward. This wolf is good, but imagine the chaos I could cause from within SPEAR. I couldn't hope for a better chance to make my mark."

I continue to flail at him, but I can barely see where he is, let alone aim. Though I'm mostly free of the memory, my vision is blurred with mingled images of the past and present. My father's broken, bleeding body. Flint's wild yellow eyes. My own trembling hands. Rayne still lying on the floor. Francine Quinn rushing into the office with her gun aimed. The white teeth of Flint's mocking smile.

"Don't touch me.

Flint merely smiles and grabs at the back of my clothing. Three quick slashes of his claws opens up my jacket and the shirt beneath, laying my back utterly bare but for my bra straps. He doesn't unfasten them, simply pulls until they snap and then starts carving.

The passage of his claws leaves lines of acidic fire across my skin. I know he's tracing some form of pattern or sigil, but the fiery burn of his werewolf claws on my human skin soon spreads enough to encompass everything. The whole of my back is aflame with agony and I can't move. One hand on the back of my neck, his legs straddling my backside, makes sure of that.

I lie flat beneath him, pain-wracked and impotent, still sobbing at the forced reliving of my father's last moments.

I'm clawing at the floor, at the air, at anything I can reach, but nothing stops him from etching his marks into the flesh of my back.

The acrid scent of burning flesh fills the air, hot in my nostrils.

No, no, no, what the fuck is he doing? Why is he doing this to me? Why can't I do anything? Why will no one help me?

A dark blur streaks across the ground in front of me and the weight on my butt is suddenly gone. I hear bodily thuds and grunts of exertion and find Rayne grappling hand to hand with Flint.

The vacant look in her eyes is gone; in fact the look of *anything* is vanished from her eyes, replaced by that cold, feral silver glow. Her entire face is contorted with rage, her fangs long and sharp, just like back in Misona. Just like when carving up all the Dire Wolves.

Fuck, no. As if we need her in mania to make this night any worse.

She spins him round, pounding her fist into his face again and again. He struggles to be free, but her grip on the front of his shirt won't let him escape. When he tries to simply tear the fabric, she switches her grip to his throat and continues to pound on his face.

"Rayne."

She pauses, mid punch and whips her head round to stare at me.

Fuck, those eyes. The silver is bright enough to glow, haunting and ghostly in her dainty face.

"What is it, Danika?"

I gape at her. That isn't the "what" of a violent, mindless beast. That's Rayne's own voice, her inflection, her tone. If anything she sounds *worried*.

"I—"

"Are you okay?" She still has her fist raised, still has a black-eyed and bleeding Flint dangling from her grip. "Can you see me? Can you hear?"

"I...I'm fine, but you—"

Flint gives an angry little growl.

"Just a moment." Rayne returns her attention to the werewolf and finally lands that punch. It sends him to the ground and she follows him down, diving onto his body and wrapping her arms around in him an impressive and effective choke-hold. "Are you all right?"

"Y-yes, but you..." My words break up as my back flares with pain and I have to grit my teeth against it for several seconds.

Rayne uses the time to press harder on Flint. She pulls handcuffs off the holder on the back of her belt and flicks them open. But her eyes are still silver, her fangs overlong. Her entire body has that prickling, battle-ready aura about it, the one I've come to learn is inexorably linked to mania.

How is she doing this?

Flint struggles back against the cuffs, fighting to escape the hold to the point that he begins to choke himself on her forearm. If anything, he is far more frantic and mindless than she is right now.

He opens his mouth and lets loose a scream, something high, shrill, and cutting to the senses. "You can't hold me," he rages. "I have what I need now, you'll see. I don't need *this* body anymore. I have a new one to inhabit."

While I'm busy trying to figure out what on earth that means, black smoke begins to pour from Flint's mouth. Slow and heavy, it billows out across the ground in one thin tendril that seems to thicken as it goes. In fact it *does* thicken, it even takes on a shape, coalescing into a spindly arm with long, clawed fingers at the end of the skinny hand. More smoke follows, and as it comes, the stuff continues to form more and more limbs. Bicep, shoulder, neck, head.

Rayne gives a little screech and rolls across the ground, but the thing crawling out of Flint's mouth continues to come with more and more of the black smoke.

Her eyes blaze as she shifts her grip, now trying to force Flint's mouth shut. But even as she succeeds there, smoke pours instead from his ears and nose, forming inky clouds that join to the rest. Soon, another shoulder joins the arm and head protruding from his mouth. The rest of the arm. A second clawed hand.

Like a genie spilling from the spout of a lamp, the weird black thing continues to force its way out from Flint's body...and crawl toward me.

Rayne's voice shudders with panic. "What is this? I've never seen anything like it before. What do I do? Danika?"

But I don't have any answers, only little whimpers of pain. Whatever marks Flint drew on my back, they're pulsing now, throbbing rhythmically like a heartbeat that has nothing to do with me.

The partial body crawling out of Flint turns toward me. "Little bird," it says.

That voice, those eyes. Just like it had back at Vixen's little hideaway, the creature blinks slowly at me with harsh, yellow eyes. The two strange slits beneath the eyes flare wide, the way nostrils might, and the long gash beneath those seems to act as a mouth.

"Wait there for me, I'm coming, little bird."

A terrifying snarl ripples from Rayne's mouth. "Touch her and you die."

But more of the thing is crawling free, the smoke moving faster now in bigger clouds. Despite Rayne's hold, a chest and trunk follows the rest, then one long leg. And another. It moves like a spider, unfurling itself from the smoke like a creature of old nightmares.

When it finally pulls free of Flint's body, it stands tall and attenuated, with elongated arms and legs and a head far too large for such a slender body.

It seems weaker than last time, or at least less tangible as if still formed of smoke. Through the long limbs I can still see Rayne as she drops Flint's now lifeless body and leaps to her feet.

"Danika." Her words tremble with fear. "Don't let it touch you."

Oh, she doesn't need to tell me that. The last thing on earth I want right now is for that thing to come anywhere near me, but I still can't move more than a pitiful shuffle in any direction.

I roll over and immediately regret it when my bare back scrapes against the hard, cold floor. I cage a scream behind my teeth and pat down my sides searching for something, anything at all that can help. More magazines for my gun, little phials of holy water, chains in silver, lead, and steal, darts tipped with the greasy residue of old sprite blood, throwing knives, but nothing to help against this thing. Whatever the fuck it is.

I fight to my knees. And it *is* a fight, with every muscle of my body screaming for mercy. "Don't come near me—"

It's right in front of me. Did I lose time? Did it move that fast? I've no idea, but the thing is standing in front of me, peering down again with that creepy yellow gaze.

"Hold still," it whispers. "It will all be over soon." More smoke. This time from its mouth, reaching out to me like thin, ethereal claws.

"No." Rayne dives at me, actually *through* the strange creature, scattering its increasingly wispy form as she passes into and then out of it.

It hisses, loud and sibilant like a thousand angry snakes, and begins to break apart.

"You'll not escape me again, little bird. I know you now. I can find you wherever you go. When you sleep, I'll be there. When you wake, I'll be there. Every day of your miserable life henceforth I'll be there at your side, in your mind, in your memory."

The two silver points of Rayne's eyes are a beacon in that cloud of that close, choking blackness. She reaches through it and pulls me close, wrapping her body around mine like a shield.

"Whatever you are, you can't have her, hear me? While I live, while I drink blood and walk this earth, I'll make sure you never touch her again."

The marks on my back flare with fresh pain, almost in concert with the furious shrieks of dismay from the tall creature. And then, it breaks apart, one limb at a time, falling away into soft black motes of a soot-like substance that carry the scent of rot and sulphur.

Seconds later, it's gone, the last few shreds of darkness drifting up toward the ceiling and drifting away on an invisible breeze.

❖

I stare at the high ceiling, barely daring to hope the thing is gone. Still latched to my body, limpet-like, Rayne buries her head against my neck.

I put my arms around her, slowly, tentatively, no longer sure of who or what I'm holding.

When she looks up at me, the silver in her eyes is still there, the wild, animal glow of her manic self. And yet…she's smiling. She's smiling and crying.

"Are you okay?" she murmurs.

I open my mouth to answer, but sudden shouts from behind cut me off.

I turn in time to see every Blood Moon wolf drop to the ground. Each of them convulses and twists as though pumped full of volts, then from the mouth of each curls a small, but familiar wisp of black smoke.

The Loup Garou women leap back from their fighting, some of them ducking out of range, others of them swiping at the black motes with large, clawed hands. But the smoky stuff simply dissipates without a trace, leaving behind a pile of semi-conscious Blood Moon wolves.

I can't take much more of this.

My knees give out, but my landing is soft as Rayne guides me gently to the floor. Then, instead of letting me lie, she pulls my body across her lap and cups my face in one tender hand.

"How are you doing this?" I can't help myself. There are so many other questions to ask right now, but I can't compute this. "This is mania, isn't it? This is TRISP?"

She cocks an eyebrow. "What's a trisp?"

"Never mind. Just tell me. Are you in mania right now?"

Rayne looks first at me, then her hands. She turns them back and forth, then scan-assesses the rest of her body. At last, she presses her hands to her face. "It seems I am."

"Then how? How are you holding me, right now? I…I'm covered in blood, I'm hurt, I'm weak. Why aren't you trying to rip my head off?"

A smile. "Because I'd never do anything to hurt you, Danika. Not now, not ever."

I can't speak. What am I going to say? What *can* I say? This flies in the face of everything I've ever known. This is a bizarre and unheard of phenomenon that—fuck it.

I reach for the back of her neck and yank her down for a kiss, fangs and all. There's blood there, and sharpness, but I don't care. I want to pour myself into her and feel her receive me, I want to tell her how sorry I am, how much I love her, but none of the words are there.

So I kiss her instead.

And Rayne responds. Her control of the kiss spikes as she wraps her arms around me and as the embrace deepens, her fangs recede and the silver finally fades from her eyes.

Puffy lipped and breathless, I pull back. "Ah, there you are."

Brown. Brown in the varied shades of autumn visible in her gentle, tender gaze. Such a beautiful colour. A beautiful expression. A beautiful woman.

I kiss her again and again, I can't help it. I feel like an eon has passed since the last time I did and my fingers tangle in her hair, gripping it, pulling her closer and closer.

Someone behind us clears their throat.

I wave my hand, a vague "go away" gesture, but they do it again. Then again.

Grunting now, I pull back from Rayne's lips and turn. "What?"

It's Gina. Her shifts through various forms have shredded her clothing, so she stands before me naked now. Her eyes are downcast, not embarrassment—I think—but confusion and fear.

Oh, yeah. There's a lot happening right now.

"Are you okay?"

I've no idea how to answer that. Without the distraction of hot, passionate kisses, my back once more throbs with pain. Less, but still very much there and the accompanying stiffness makes movement difficult.

I settle for a gruff, "I'll live," and pull myself from Rayne's grip into a sitting position. Fuck, that really hurts. "What about you?"

She looks over her shoulder at her pack mates and the fallen Blood Moon. "I think we're okay. What the hell was that thing? Did it actually *come out* of Flint?"

"It would appear so." Rayne scoots to her feet then bends to help me do the same. She supports my weight with an arm low around my waist, the other gently holding my opposite hand. "I've no idea what it is, but its powers are dangerous and…" She clears her throat. "Frightening."

"What about those guys?" I point to the Blood Moon.

Gina flaps her hands in a half-hearted "I don't know" gesture. "They attacked, so we met them. They weren't trying to subdue us or even really hurt us. They just seemed to want to draw blood."

Rayne nods.

I wait.

"Whatever power they had was passed by blood, didn't you see? Just like Flint, they all have some sort of old scar. Probably where the virus was passed on."

"You've lost me now, what virus?"

Patient as ever, Rayne continues to support me, though now she walks us over to Flint's body as we move. "Have you ever heard of a werewolf that can drop a person back into their memories? No, this... power...whatever it is, comes from the creature inhabiting Flint's body. He was likely ground zero for the spread of it all, but it had to do so by infecting blood. It cut me, remember, around my throat? And you..." She lifts my injured wrist. "It had to infect your blood to affect you, so likely they were all doing the same."

Her voice is low and soft, gaze focused everywhere but on me. I long to ask her what she saw in those moments, when the thing forced her to relive the most awful moments of her life. But given what I saw under the same, I'm too afraid to ask.

Instead I take a moment to realize that she's holding my bloodied wrist and shows no signs at all of being interested in the blood there. I gape at her. "Rayne..."

In front of the church doors, the large grey wolf with the dark streak begins to stir. An instant later, she's on her feet and searching.

Gina gives a little cry of relief. "Opal."

A second later, the wolf ripples effortlessly back into Opal and runs headlong at Gina who grabs her into a huge hug.

The pair embrace fiercely, whispering to each other, stroking each other's hair, checking each other for injuries. The other Loup Garou manage to stay back for a full thirty seconds before they can no longer help themselves, dashing in to touch and check on their leader. A mix of wolves, hybrid, and human forms gather around the relieved couple as the large cluster reassures themselves of the others' safety.

Beyond Opal the doors open and in march a selection of wolves I don't recognize. After assessing the scene before them, they shift back into human forms revealing a handful of faces. Alphas of all the other packs— Fire Fang, Long Tooth, Grey Tail. Even Aleksandar is there, though his growls on spotting me are tempered by the raised guns and weapons of my team who have walked in behind them.

"Guys."

Solo, Duo, Hawk, Willow, and Erkyan, all of them form a barrier between Aleksandar and me that moves as he does.

They smile when they see me, though expressions of shock and worry quickly take over when they see the state I'm in.

Funny, I'd normally feel nervous and exposed to be so partially dressed among all these people, but being naked is nothing to a werewolf. The other alphas, back in human forms, are also nude and one could almost argue that everybody else is overdressed.

For the first time since the night began, I find myself relaxing. Just a tiny bit.

Hawk speaks first. "When you didn't check in, we came to look for you."

Duo nods. "Good thing too, you crazy bitch. What were you thinking?"

I raise my hands as far as the stiffness in my back will allow. "I didn't do anything."

A grunt from Solo. "When the Loup Garou emissaries arrived about the moot we figured we should all meet you here. Seems we missed something rather dramatic."

Willow waves her hands through a series of complicated signs. "*Your aura is clouded and you look weak. Are you well, friend?*"

I can't manage anything more complicated than a simple thumbs up, so that will have to do. "I'm glad you're here."

Hawk shrugs. "It's not just us. There's a bunch more agents en route."

I stiffen. Glance at Rayne. She shrugs. I sigh.

"Well, what did you want us to do? We had no idea what was happening, you weren't on comms, and your van was just out there on the grass. We had to get backup. They'll be here soon."

A familiar beeping catches my ears.

My watch. Looking at it is even more painful than usual. My blood dots the face which is cracked from repeated impacts, but I can still just about see the time through it. Sunrise is on the way.

Rayne catches me looking. "I'll be fine," she murmurs. "Get yourself checked out by Omega."

"Not a damn chance." I wave off her look of surprise. "I'm not leaving your side until you wake up again this evening. We…have a lot to talk about. Besides, if I do leave you, those military lunatics may just drag you outside to get you back to HQ."

"They aren't stupid."

"Don't care. No risks." I take her chin in my hand. "No. Risks. Okay?"

She stares into my eyes. God, there are so many questions, there, all of them brimming in her beautiful eyes. "Very well. That means you too, deal?"

"On my locs and hope to trim." My words stutter a little over my usual little vow. For the first time in a long while, I'm forced to remember *why* I refuse to cut my hair, having always wanted it to be as long as my father's.

I keep the little internal voice to myself and wait with Rayne, occasionally wincing as my back gives another twinge. Each of my team comes to embrace me in turn, with their own opinion about the marks. Solo describes them as a sigil, Duo as a sunburst. Hawk assesses the marks while hovering upside down and tells me they resemble tribal tattoos he's seen humans wearing in summer. Erkyan and Willow confer together and decide as one that though they've never seen such marks before, they resemble a brand or burn.

Frankly, none of it is comforting, but at least there isn't any black smoke or yellow pus flowing from the wounds. Rayne performs her own little study as we retreat to the relative safety and privacy of the chancel, but says nothing other than she has some references to check in the evening.

Then my watch beeps again and she passes out in my arms, limp and lifeless against me like a doll.

I pull her to me and wait for Omega to arrive while the wolves all talk about what should follow. I'm sure they'll still have their moot, but the Loup Garou and Blood Moon seem to have particular issue with Aleksandar. I can't hear all of it, but I hear my name come up more than once, along with the phrase "pack-friend."

I don't care. All of that can wait.

What I want now, more than anything, is to settle down in a soft warm bed—preferably on my front—and sleep for a week.

Of course, as I suspected, Omega agents try to coax me with them out of the old church and back to SPEAR facilities. I refuse, making clear that in the middle of the day, it's my responsibility to protect my colleague and that I won't be leaving her side.

Many of the Omega agents already know about the relationship between Rayne and me, but the military certainly doesn't. It takes several heated conversations and threats of setting my wolf friends on them to get my way. Foolish, perhaps, but I'm not leaving her. No freaking way.

Only after all this do I realize, in all the commotion, that Flint hasn't moved from where he fell.

With my team on guard around attempts to move Rayne outside and into the sunlight, I limp over to check him out.

Dead. Without doubt.

His eyes, nose, and ears are singed black as though burned from the inside out. The skin around his mouth is stained the same sooty black and stretched wide enough to break skin. His entire body seems flatter than it should, as though emptied of vital organs. And when I take the chance to touch his curled, twisted hand, his skin is icy cold and stiff.

I wish I could ask him what happened. He's likely the only one with reliable intel on what the hell that black creature really is, but now he's gone.

Though with this being the second time Rayne and I have seen the thing, we can no longer brush it off as an unknown entity. We need to figure out what the hell it is before it causes any more damage.

Yep, because things are always that easy.

I leave Flint's body on the ground and return to my team, joining the conversation on how to get Rayne safely back to HQ.

Chapter Thirty-three

It's kinda nice not to be the one waking up in one of those medi-bay rooms. Weird, but nice. I sit on the stiff plastic chair beside Rayne's bed, watching her lifeless body beneath the sheets. In a situation like this I would usually have clues like soft breathing or eyelash flutters, but there's none of that from Rayne.

If a stranger were to walk in on me right now, they might assume I was mourning a dead body.

Perhaps I am. But at least this body is going to wake up in a few minutes.

Outside the room, the rest of my team forms an unofficial guard. I know there are a couple of soldiers out there too, but Hawk is large and broad enough keep any of them from entering. I'd laugh if it wasn't verging on ridiculous.

My back aches beneath the light dressing Omega finally decided to put there. Not pain like before, but certainly uncomfortable. It itches too, as if the lightest contact of any fabric irritates the strange marks. After more bullying—no, *negotiating*—with my alpha colleagues, I've been able to study the quick photos they snapped of the wounds.

Hawk is right, the marks are almost tribal, but there's something strangely even and symmetrical about the signs. They're certainly not something I've ever seen before and no wracking my brain through the course of the day has brought to mind any memory of something similar.

It has brought up other things though. Recollections that leave me first angry, then scared, then desolate, one after the other.

It's been so very long since I allowed myself to think of Dad. Even with Mum acting the way she is right now, it's easier to leave such painful memories in the past. But now they're as fresh and raw as the day after, and my insides ache with the pain of it.

I can almost feel that chair leg in my hands, the hot splash of coughed up blood against my face.

"Oh, Dad, I'm so sorry. I'm sorry. I never wanted to do that to you, I never, ever did."

"He knows, Danika."

My head snaps up.

Rayne is awake. She hasn't moved, but her gaze is fixed on mine, her smile soft and kind. "You really stayed with me all day?"

"Damn right I did. I even told Maury that—"

She presses her index finger against my lips. "When the creature forced me back into my memories, I saw one of my foster siblings dying. He had leukaemia and spent the last three months of his life in hospital going through procedure after surgery after test. He was so miserable in the end, I think he was glad when it ended. He was only twelve."

"Rayne…"

She grips my hand. "But beyond that my life has been pretty clean and happy. I'm very lucky. So instead my mind gave me the worst-case scenarios of every last one of my nightmares." She frowns. "I saw you die, over and over, in every conceivable way. But always at my hand. I did it, every single time. Because…I lost control."

I tighten my fingers on hers. I've no idea what to say, but part of me knows that I'm not really supposed to say anything.

"I killed you, Danika, over and over, with my hands, with my fangs, with weapons. I let my monster take control of my senses and lost you because I was weak. Then, when that thing finally let me out, I saw you on the ground. You were crying, screaming for your father, and I knew I would lose you for real if I couldn't save you. If I couldn't control that monster living inside me."

"And that's how you learned to control your mania?"

She nods. "I don't know how. I don't even know if I could do it again. But I do know, in that moment, nothing on earth could have stopped me helping you. Not even my own beast."

"I—"

Again she touches my lips. "You don't have to tell me anything. I just want you to know that it's over now. That whatever happened you're not the same person and that you're stronger now than you've ever been. Your father would be proud of you."

My tears are instant. There's nothing I can do. They spill forth without warning and stain my cheeks, running off my chin, into my mouth. "I killed him, Rayne. I did it. I was the one."

There's a gasp from somewhere behind me, but I don't care.

"The records all say 'vampire attack,' but by the time I reached him he'd already changed. I had to. He attacked me and I had to. I *had* to."

Rayne shoves herself off the bed and pulls me to her. I don't even care about the twinge of pain from my back, I just let her hold me, clinging to her soft, cool body while tears wrack my own from top to bottom.

She doesn't say anything the entire time. I feel her there, her hands around me, her chin against the top of my head, but not one word.

And I cry. I cry like I had that day in the manager's office. I cry the same way I had when Quinn found me, covered in black ooze and numb from shock. I cry the same way I did when telling Mum and Pippa what happened. Or a *portion* of what happened.

"I had to keep it secret." I whisper the words against Rayne's neck. "Mum would never have forgiven me, and Pip...I couldn't lose Pip. She couldn't know what Dad had become. And now there's you and her, and I can't help but think or wonder, what if? What if I'd been able to save him? What if there was some other way? If you and Pip can be so good and normal, then what about him?"

Rayne's arms tighten around me. "What happened? Tell me. As much as you can."

"But—"

"Indulge me." She rubs her cheek against the top of my head. "You're a good person, Danika. Headstrong, sure. Stubborn, totally, but you're still a good person, and I refuse to believe that's happened in the last eight years. You were *always* good, and I can guarantee you've been carrying this guilt for far too long. Let me help you."

So I tell her.

I open myself up and reveal the truth in a way I've never done before. I tell her about the vampire in the alley and the very first bite against my shoulder. I explain how afraid I was, how clueless and lost. I share the fear as it gripped my heart, watching my dad turn and open his eyes to reveal bright, cold silver. I recall the frenzied fight in that lonely, cramped space, and the way he begged me so desperately not to kill him.

Rayne's hand stops stroking down my hair. "Don't hesitate," she murmurs.

I stiffen against her.

"Danika, you've got this wrong. The man you've told me about, the one you loved, he would never have begged for his life like that."

I clutch at her, shaking my head. "But he did, you didn't hear me, he said—"

"He said 'don't,' right?"

I freeze. "Y-yes."

"And the other older agent you mentioned, did he not say to you 'don't hesitate'?"

"Yes, but—"

"Shh." She pulls away long enough to see my face and gently wipe the tears off my cheeks with the pad of her thumb. "It's the first and single most important rule us SPEARs follow. You know that. *Trust your gut. Don't hesitate.* What if your father was trying to tell you the same thing?"

"What?"

Rayne pulls me up onto the bed and cradles my head and shoulders against her. Despite her smaller size, I feel safe and protected with her arms around me like this. Like she's the bigger one and I'm the dainty doll wrapped close in her grasp.

"He must have known what was happening to him. And you've seen what mania is like. Perhaps not back then, but you have now. You've seen me. When caught in mania like that, we don't have control or conscious thought. We can't make decisions like rational creatures. But you described him pulling back again and again, doing everything in his power not to hurt you. He fought it, Danika, right to the end until he couldn't fight any more. And when he understood he had no choice, he begged you, his daughter, someone he loved, to do what he knew only you could, 'Don't hesitate.'"

I'm numb. I can't think, can't see, can't even feel.

Rayne is still talking, something about the people I might have saved, the agents I may have spared by acting so decisively, but all I can think about is Pippa and Mum. Could it be that I saved them by murdering Dad? Did I save him too? From himself?

I can't process it, can't fathom it. My mind is looping the thoughts until nothing makes sense and all words become a blur.

Don't hesitate.

Could that really be what he meant to say? Was I wrong after so many years of self-hatred, blame, and fixation on widespread vengeance?

Though it hurts, though my back twinges with the pain of it all, I voluntarily take myself back to the night so many years ago. I put myself back in that room, against that wall with my heart thudding in my ears and my sweaty, bloodied hands wrapped around the shaft of that broken table leg.

"Don't," Dad says. And for the first time, I recognize the resolve in his eyes. I see the peace and acceptance in his expression before the wicked flash of silver takes over once more and swallows the man I knew and loved.

"Oh, fuck."

Rayne stops speaking and peers down at me, still cradled in her arms. "What? What is it?"

I bite my bottom lip. "I did the right thing?" It's not a question, but I voice it as one, for the first time in eight years, allowing myself the hope of redemption and forgiveness. "I didn't murder him?"

"You ended his life at his request and with his blessing, Danika. It can't possibly be any other way." She hugs me. "And I'm sorry. I'm sorry it's taken eight years for someone to tell you this, but it wasn't your fault. There was nothing you could do except exactly what you'd trained for as a SPEAR. *Protect and serve. Learn and understand.*" Once more she wipes hot tears off my face. "*Hunt and exterminate.* Your father would have been proud of everything you've accomplished. You're everything he could have wished for, and more."

Something seems to flood out of me. I can't name it or even describe it beyond a sense that some long-held tension or weight has been lifted. It washes out of me like a river and vanishes into the air, leaving behind a peace I can't remember ever feeling.

Acceptance. Understanding. Calm.

I gaze into Rayne's eyes and search for the truth behind her words. I have to know she believes it. I have to know that she isn't just saying this to make me feel better.

The honesty of the slow, sensual kiss she presses to my lips says everything I need to know. She curls into me, gripping tight, and I return the embrace pouring every ounce of myself through my lips into hers.

And then I'm crying again. But these aren't painful tears or distressed ones. These are the tears of true relief, an emotion I haven't truly felt in a long, long time.

CHAPTER THIRTY-FOUR

After a further night and day in observation the Omega team Grade Sevens allow me to leave. None of them are happy about it, but as far as anyone can tell, the marks on my back are healing like any other injury, maybe better, and seem to have no lasting effects.

They do insist that I return for regular check-ins and the Grade Six who passes on the message looks more than a little irritated when I firmly but politely decline.

I've no intention of returning to medi-bay unless I need to be there. Not when plenty of other agents likely need the space I'm occupying.

I know the woman wants to argue, but Rayne is quick to point out that both she and I have a meeting with Colonel Addington and that we can't keep him waiting.

Seems the little white lie we told back at holding has spread further than we anticipated. The colonel has rapidly garnered a reputation for loud, angry outbursts and a virulent hate of tardiness which makes me both laugh and twitch with nerves.

As we leave the lower floors of HQ and travel upward to our more usual levels, Rayne holds my hand and gently squeezes my fingers.

"You okay?"

"Yeah." I smile with more confidence than I feel. "Can't get too much worse than everything else we've been through, right?"

"Indeed."

The lift reaches the ground floor and stops long enough to let on another cluster of people. Among them are my teammates, Duo, Solo, Erkyan, Willow, and Hawk. The others are Delta desk agents, simultaneously alarmed and amused to find so many field agents in their midst.

They escape quickly on the first floor and leave me inside the traveling metal box with my team.

Nobody speaks. Or rather, they do, but not with words. I see plenty of raised shoulders, lowered gazes, and shuffling fingers. A low, inward curved tail and bowed heads also send a pretty clear message.

I clear my throat. "We're going to be okay, guys."

"Suspended is not okay." Erkyan frowns up at me. "What will I do with no job? Before, I did work in cake store, but now I am SPEAR. I have training. I want to help. Can I still?"

The honest answer is I don't know and I tell her as much. "As far as anybody else knows, we were investigating the missing agents when the weird Loup Garou-Blood Moon stuff happened. "I don't really know what this is about, but all we can do is see. Anyway, I'm the team leader here, so *you* don't need to worry. Any disciplinary or punishment they've got lined up is all mine."

Duo yawns, flashing his rear-most teeth. "It all sounds like red tape and HR pandering if you ask me. But don't worry. We're behind you whatever happens."

"But of course." Hawk gives his wings a ruffling shake. "We'll stand by you like we always have. You won't be taking the blame alone."

Nods of agreement from all those gathered. "No. They're used to me pulling silly stunts by now, it goes with my rep. There's no need for you to get dragged in too."

Rayne touches my shoulder. "Dragged into what? Like he said, we're all with you. Always."

Stunned, I look round at my team, the misfits and rejects of the wider SPEAR population. Agents unafraid to break a few rules to get to the bottom of a problem. Agents who think up, down, and left and right instead of in straight, immovable lines. Agents who ask questions and require answers. Agents like me.

I find myself grinning. "You guys sure about this?"

"Hell yeah and we're going to make damn sure that—"

Solo cuts off his brother's gleeful response with a smart smack around the back of his head. "Very sure. Know that whatever happens, Danika, we will back you. No matter what."

Those warm, encouraging words still ring in my ears when we open the door to the conference room.

It's a small area with one large table with three chairs down each of the long sides. Can't help but notice there isn't enough space for all of us to sit.

Erkyan and Willow take one look at the table and immediately head for the corner on the left. They sit on the floor with their hands in their laps, looking all the world like attentive school children. Duo and Solo share a glance, then position themselves in front of the door, guarding it from outside entry. Hawk gives a jaunty little wave and hops onto the right end of the table where he sits cross-legged and occasionally digs into a bowl of wrapped sweets with the end of his tail.

All this before I see who is in the room.

I clear my throat. "Um, hi."

Addington, Jack, and Maury all sit on the far side of the table wearing mixed expressions of anger, surprise, and amusement respectively.

Maury merely shakes his head and gestures to the two chairs on our side of the desk.

We sit.

Addington stands. "This is a private meeting between Agents Karson and Rayne. The rest of you degenerates will wait outside."

Duo picks his teeth with his index fingernail.

Willow signs something quick and rude that I'm certain I'm the only one to see.

Hawk stops digging at the sweets and sweeps a collection of empty wrappers onto the table.

Solo yawns and leans more heavily against the near wall.

Erkyan shoves a finger in her ear and twists until something grimy and slightly crusty comes out on the end of her finger.

Not one of them makes a move to leave.

Rage visibly fills Addington's features. "Did you hear me? Get out of here right now. Now, or I'll see you all suspended from duty."

Rayne coughs gently. "Forgive me, Colonel, but my understanding of these disciplinary hearings is that all members of an affected team must be present to give evidence and character references. My teammates simply wish to follow said rule."

Maury nods approvingly.

Jack sinks low into his seat, clearly wishing to be anywhere else.

"Evidence?" Addington's voice jumps several octaves. "What evidence is there to be had? You two are the sole cause of this entire werewolf debacle, and your actions have endangered hundreds if not thousands of lives. You should be dismissed where you stand."

Willow leaps to her feet and walks over to the table. As ever, her steps are light and dainty, and as she moves, a faint scent of willow bark fills the air. She stops between our two chairs to face Addington directly and begins to speak in sign.

After a few seconds, the blustering colonel looks ready to erupt. "What is this tomfoolery, what is she doing?"

"It's Sprite Sign, Colonel." Jack finally speaks, narrowing his eyes at Willow's busy hands. "I don't know it, but I recognize some of the gestures. She's speaking to you."

"Well, how the hell am I supposed to know what she's saying?"

Jack sits a little straighter. I might be making it up, but I'm half certain he gives me the faintest of winks before speaking. "Perhaps a little additional training is in order? You can hardly do your best job aiding us in the protection of the citizens of Angbec if there are those you can't converse with."

Willow keeps signing, faster now, and I have to fight hard to stifle my laughter. She's furious, telling Addington what she plans to do to him if he dares to take any of the team off duty. There are also plenty of rather rude names tossed in there which, truth be told, it's probably better Addington can't translate.

"Willow? Wait, what are you even saying—"

Maury clears his throat, hard and loud. "Okay, Agent Willow, calm down, no need to get so distressed. Perhaps I should translate?"

Willow immediately stops signing. She looks a little worried, but Maury gestures for her to continue as he keeps speaking.

"I will be more than happy to tell the colonel exactly what he needs to hear, Agent. Feel free to keep signing."

Addington's face grows redder and redder. Any moment now I fear he might explode all over the conference table and splatter all of us with his impotent rage.

Meanwhile I can't help but gape at Maury. "*You* know Sprite Sign? Since when?"

"I have a number of skills you know nothing about, Agent Karson, most important of those is when to keep my mouth shut." He pauses, gaze boring into mine. "Do you understand me?"

"I understand you're as much of a pain in my arse as you always were. Why can't you just—"

"The first part of Agent Willow's impassioned speech," Maury cuts across me, "was an account of what happened a couple of days ago. But if Agent Willow would be kind enough to keep signing I'd be happy to translate the rest for you, Colonel."

I freeze in my seat. Even Rayne has become still, that statue-like lifelessness that only vampires can achieve.

"Fine." Addington returns to his seat, quieter but not at all calmer. "Not that it makes much difference, but I'd be pleased to hear it."

"Go on then, Willow. Just as you were before." Maury's voice is low and heavy, with curious stress on each syllable.

Willow eyes him for a few moments more, then returns to signing, this time fast enough that I have no hope of catching it with my meagre knowledge. Maury, by comparison, speaks quickly and elegantly, his gaze fixed on the motions of Willow's hands.

"*While it may be that my companions were involved with the rampage of the wolves earlier this week, it was not in an instigating sense. They sought only to smooth inter- and intra-pack relations and, if you wish, I have several witnesses who will attest to this. They will also confirm that without the calm, rational decision-making, and quick-witted action of these two agents, the resultant damage would have been far worse.*"

The still in the room is palpable. Not quite as intense as Rayne's but obvious just the same.

Willow gives Maury another of those odd looks.

"It's okay, Agent. Keep going." Maury gives a comforting smile. "I take it you have more to say?"

She nods and signs again.

Maury translates. "*It's also true that the recent restructure of werewolf packs has left something of a power vacuum. It's likely that without proper SPEAR intervention, more battles for dominance will break out in the coming days. Despite the unfortunate passing of the Dire Wolf alpha, it remains clear that all the packs of Angbec trust Agents Karson and Rayne above any and all others. If SPEAR wishes to be involved with werewolf packs on good terms going forward, I believe it imperative that they be allowed to continue service.*"

My mouth is hanging open. I know it is. I can't help it. Rayne gives me a savage jab in the ribs, and as subtly as I can, I smack my lips shut.

Maury stops speaking. Willow stops signing. "Is that everything you wanted to add, Agent Willow?"

She hesitates for the barest second, then nods. With the same dainty steps, she returns to her seat on the floor next to Erkyan who stares at Maury as though he's grown a second head.

"Well, then." Maury rubs his hands together. "As I and several others have been telling you, Colonel Addington, these two agents are among the best we have. To remove them from duty now would be to make all our jobs that much more difficult."

The colonel blusters and slaps his hand on the desk. "But you saw the reports, Maurice. That one in particular," he points at me, "could be a vehicle for all manner of evil. We have no idea what those signs on her back mean and what kind of problems they could cause down the road."

Jack clears his throat. "Yes, about that. I meant to bring this to the table earlier, but I got distracted. The Clear Blood Foundation has come into some funding which I intend to funnel into new research. With SPEAR's assistance of course. We would be more than happy to put our research team in charge of discovering anything and everything we can about this strange black creature and the mark it put on Agent Karson. Phillipa is one of most talented and trusted researchers. I'm sure she'd be more than happy to head the team."

I can't help but sit straighter at that. Pip is going to look into my back?

I open my mouth, but Jack continues right over me, louder and faster than before. "She has already shown promising results with investigation into blood mania and synthetic blood substitutes, all things I'm sure you'll agree are incredibly important to our continued understanding of *edanes* here and in the wider world."

"That's as may be, but you seem to forget about Project Revival. While the emergency protocols are in place, I have full operational control over all aspects of SPEAR, including assessing the field-worthiness of all agents."

Again I try to speak, but this time Rayne grabs my hand. It's under the table and subtle, but savage enough a squeeze to choke the words at the back of my throat. I try to catch her eye, but she's still looking at the three men on the other side of the table, her expression fixed into one of polite interest.

Seems I have no choice but to watch these men discuss my future, but damn it, I'm not happy about it.

Jack nods slowly. "Indeed you do, but the crisis for which I initiated the protocol is now over."

"What?" Addington seems to lose steam.

"Well, yes. I required aid for the corralling and control of werewolves on a rampage, but as you've clearly seen over the last day and heard from—Agent Willow, is it?—the werewolves are now on a path of peace and self-policing, just as they always have been. All thanks to Agents Rayne and Karson."

"But—"

"Quite right, Mr. Mayor, you're quite right." Maury widens his eyes as though shocked. "To think, Colonel, I've kept you here all this time when your help was no longer required. I'm so sorry. I hope you'll forgive me."

"But—"

"It's quite all right, Colonel. You've no need to worry. I'll issue the orders right now. Operations here at SPEAR are to return to normal with immediate effect, while you and your soldiers are free to return to your base. Thank you for your time, Mayor Cobé. I'm sorry to bring you here unnecessarily."

Jack grins widely and holds out his hand for a shake. "Don't worry about it. Things can be difficult to keep track when one is so busy protecting the people. I'm sure I understand."

"Right. In that case, I'll start the cessation procedures." And Maury is suddenly up on his feet and scooting round the table. He offers Hawk a genial pat on the shoulder as he goes and a quick handshake for Solo who is red-faced and sweaty. At the door, Duo holds it open and gestures our commander through with a quick sweep of his arm.

Addington bolts from his chair so hard the whole thing tips. He follows Maury's path around the table, straight past Hawk and the two wolves just in time to chase my supervisor as he strides out the door and out of sight. I can hear him calling as he hurries down the corridor, frantic to regain Maury's attention.

❖

With a long, slow smile, Duo wraps his hand around the handle and pulls the door shut. "So that went well," he murmurs.

Solo bursts out laughing. It's such a loud, free, and genuine sound that I'm startled to hear it from his ordinarily serious mouth. But he's not the only one. Duo joins him, Hawk too, and the three of them gather together at the end of the table slapping each other on the shoulders and roaring with mirth.

On the floor, Erkyan and Willow grasp hands and hug each other, bouncing up and down from their seated positions.

And Jack? Jack slumps back in his chair and rubs a hand across his forehead, exhaling hard and sharp through his nose. "Damn it, Danika," he snaps, "you might be the best agent we have, but did you hit your head or something?"

I gape at him. "Okay, what?" I cry. My voice is higher than I might like it to be, but I don't care. "What just happened in here?"

Rayne rubs a comforting hand over my knee. "I think our mayor and good Agent Cruush just saved us all from further bullying at the hands of Colonel Addington and his men."

"You nearly blew it when you interrupted Willow. Good thing she caught on and kept going."

"What?"

"Come now. You know as well as I do that Maurice can't speak Sprite Sign." Jack rolls his eyes. "Good thing he and your teammates are pretty quick off the mark. Oh, and that the colonel is a narrow-minded idiot."

I gaze around the room. Duo, Hawk, and Solo are still laughing, but they're walking over now, joining Rayne and me on our side of the table. Even Erkyan and Willow approach until they too are close by, all seven of us facing Jack over the conference table.

Jack sighs again. "Maurice and I probably could have done it alone, but you stepping in was a brilliant touch, Willow. Thank you. Couldn't have done better if we planned it."

She looks a little startled but accepts the praise with a blush and faint wave of a green tinged hand.

Maybe I did hit my head. Maybe I have been off my game after Flint's attack, but I still have no idea what's going on. I look helplessly at Rayne.

She cups my cheek. "We were going to be suspended, Danika. Anybody could see the colonel was ready to lock us up and toss the keys from the moment we entered the room. By having independent agents—who have already passed their tests, by the way—give such glowing accounts of our work with the werewolves, Agent Cruush was then able to pass credit for soothing them onto us. And after that moot, all the werewolf packs are in a current state of truce, so it's easy to say that Colonel Addington and his soldiers are no longer needed."

"What, and that's it?"

"Not at all." Jack strokes gently at his designer stubble. "But our priority was to get him out of here before he could pass a judgment on you two. Which we've done. Details we can smooth out later, though we'll probably end up with a few operational changes. I swear, Mikkleson has a lot to answer for in putting Revival on the books the way it is. I suppose he never thought he'd have to use it, but I can't believe how much control it simply hands away to the military." A sigh. "But it's over now. You two are safe. Maurice and I will handle the colonel."

Jack moves around the table and stops behind my chair. I stand to greet him, meeting his gaze with what I hope is a grateful expression.

He hugs me. I'm not ready for it at all, and I instinctively stiffen in his arms, but he refuses to let go. Then, the others all pile in, wrapping their arms around me until we stand in the middle of the conference room in a huge tangle of limbs.

"Um, guys?"

Slowly, they peel away, one by one. As the first to go on, Jack is last to step back, and he plants both hands on his hips when he does. "I knew I was right to insist you took this case. You've never let me down. Not once."

"Give me time, Jack."

"Stop it. You're an excellent agent and friend. I was worried about you."

"Why?"

He rolls his eyes. "You definitely hit your head. Look I didn't want to give out all the details in front of Addington, but Clear Blood is arranging for a special unit to investigate the creature that possessed Flint Liddell. So far, all we know is that it's a thus far unidentified *edane* entity and has the ability to vanish."

Rayne frowns. "That's not much."

"About as much as we knew when you saw it at Vixen's, actually. But that leads to something else we can speculate: this creature, whatever it is, may be answerable to someone else. First it tried infiltrating vampires, though we're not entirely sure why. Then it moved on to werewolves and had a more direct hand in affecting them by possessing a werewolf body."

"Steady, Jack." I can't help but smile. "'Possession?' You almost make it sound like some sort of demon."

"Well." Duo looks me dead in the eye. "Who says it isn't?"

Silence.

I look round at my companions. "Come on, guys, what?" Everybody is just so serious, I can't help but chuckle. "N-no. No way. A demon? Like biblical, fallen angels and Satan?"

"No, nothing religious. I mean dacmons or daimons. Brush up on your Ancient Greek."

"And how do you know so much about it?"

Duo shares a look with his brother. The pair shrug. In unison.

Creepy.

"Our family before the bite was…weird."

What? Oh, no, no, no. I want to press for more, but before I can, the two wolves are moving, opening the door, and stepping through.

"We're taking the rest of the night off, by the way. Since Cruush is telling everyone there's a truce we'd better go arrange it." They leave on that note, out of sight within seconds.

I glare at Jack. "So that was a lie too?"

"Hey, don't look at me. Maurice took a bunch of Alphas out while you were in medi-bay and visited the packs one by one. That awful Dire Wolf alpha has lifted his bounty—you're welcome, by the way—as a means of meeting my terms."

"Terms?"

Jack stands a little straighter and adjusts the collar of his suit jacket. He even smiles, that old, toothpaste ad smile, and I half expect to hear the tinkling of a bright, white sparkle from his teeth. "You might forget it regularly, but I'm still mayor. I told all the packs that if they want to stay here, they need to actively participate in repairing what they destroyed."

Rayne nods thoughtfully. "But most of these packs don't have money. They're everyday civilians."

"Money is far less important than public image. Remember, Angbec is the 'home of the *edane* movement' and my entire campaign was built on the promise of unity and trust between humans and supernatural beings. I intend to fulfil those promises to the letter, but I can't do that unless everyone is on board. So," the smile broadens, "the werewolves will be spearheading our new community service drive."

I let my mind play with that image, calling up a mental picture of Aleksandar picking up litter or cleaning graffiti. Doesn't seem very likely, but I'll take it. "Seems you were busy while I was out."

"Extremely." Jack once more messes with his collar. "And now if you'll excuse me, I have to go and…be even busier. This city won't run itself. Just try to stay out of trouble, won't you?"

"Always."

He cocks an eyebrow. "Mm-hmm. And check-in with your sister as soon as you can. She'll give you the research timetable so we can get started on your back. Maurice has already given blanket approval for any time off you need so try not to keep us waiting. Okay?"

"Yeah, yeah, yeah."

Jack walks to the door, but changes his mind without going far. He puts one hand on my shoulder. "Please, take it easy, okay? I know that's probably impossible for you, but at least try?"

I'm ready to brush it off, to say something quick and flippant like I usually do, but the expression in his eyes stops me. Instead, I grip his fingers and give them the tiniest of squeezes. "I'll be good. Promise. And I'm sure Rayne will set me straight if I do anything daft."

"Count on me, Mr. Mayor."

Jack nods, though he doesn't seem convinced. Instead, he looks to Erkyan and Willow. "And you two, how would you feel about teaching me a little of that sign language you both use? I think it would be pretty useful for private conversations if you take my meaning." He gestures ahead of him, and my teammates, with a pleased little smile, head through the door.

I can hear Erkyan chattering excitedly as they head down the hallway, a sound that gradually fades to nothing.

Silence.

No, not quite silence. My own breathing, the rustle of my clothing and the soft sigh from Rayne as she extends a hand to brush my cheek.

"How are you feeling?"

I resist the urge to twitch my shoulder blades against the itchy sensation running up and down my back. "I don't know. I mean, I'm glad everyone is okay and that Jack has everything under control, but I feel…strange."

"Your back?"

"Yes. And no. Call it an instinct."

Rayne's hand drops away from my face. Her lips turn down at the corners. "I see."

"Hey, hey, no, don't do that." I catch her chin and turn her head toward mine. "Not us. We are fine, I promise you that. I just…I'm worried this isn't over, you know?"

"It isn't. It never is. There will always be bad guys to face and problems to solve. That's why SPEAR exists."

I nod, but I don't think she gets it. Or maybe she does and she'd rather avoid it. Whichever it is, I'm happy to put the discomfort to one side for now.

I let my hand drift down her neck and shoulder, along the length of her arm until I can tangle my fingers with hers. "Should we go home?"

"I think that's a great idea. There's still plenty of time before sunup. Perhaps we can tidy that mess you call a room."

I squeeze her fingers. "Actually, I was thinking that we could mess it up a little more. If you get my drift."

"Excellent idea." She grins, and for the briefest moment a little rim of silver lights up her eyes. "If you think you can handle it?"

Suddenly eager, I tug her toward the door. "We're going to have fun finding out, regardless. Come on, let's get out of here."

She makes no complaint, simply follows after me, her small, dainty fingers tucked snugly into my larger, longer ones.

About the Author

Ileandra Young is one face of Da Shared Brain, who also writes erotica and romance as Raven ShadowHawk. This face writes urban and traditional fantasy, has a real obsession with vampires, and would pick a sword over a gun any day.

When not writing, Ileandra can be found LARPing, crocheting, or playing Minecraft with her twin sons.

Visit her website at www.ileandrayoung.co.uk.

Books Available from Bold Strokes Books

A Love that Leads to Home by Ronica Black. For Carla Sims and Janice Carpenter, home isn't about location, it's where your heart is. (978-1-63555-675-9)

Blades of Bluegrass by D. Jackson Leigh. A US Army occupational therapist must rehab a bitter veteran who is a ticking political time bomb the military is desperate to disarm. (978-1-63555-637-7)

Guarding Hearts by Jaycie Morrison. As treachery and temptation threaten the women of the Women's Army Corps, who will risk it all for love? (978-1-63555-806-7)

Hopeless Romantic by Georgia Beers. Can a jaded wedding planner and an optimistic divorce attorney possibly find a future together? (978-1-63555-650-6)

Hopes and Dreams by PJ Trebelhorn. Movie theater manager Riley Warren is forced to face her high school crush and tormentor, wealthy socialite Victoria Thayer, at their twentieth reunion. (978-1-63555-670-4)

In the Cards by Kimberly Cooper Griffin. Daria and Phaedra are about to discover that love finds a way, especially when powers outside their control are at play. (978-1-63555-717-6)

Moon Fever by Ileandra Young. SPEAR agent Danika Karson must clear her werewolf friend of multiple false charges while teaching her vampire girlfriend to resist the blood mania brought on by a full moon. (978-1-63555-603-2)

Quake City by St John Karp. Can Andre find his best friend Amy before the night devolves into a nightmare of broken hearts, malevolent drag queens, and spontaneous human combustion? Or has it always happened this way, every night, at Aunty Bob's Quake City Club? (978-1-63555-723-7)

Serenity by Jesse J. Thoma. For Kit Marsden, there are many things in life she cannot change. Serenity is in the acceptance. (978-1-63555-713-8)

Sylver and Gold by Michelle Larkin. Working feverishly to find a killer before he strikes again, Boston Homicide Detective Reid Sylver and rookie cop London Gold are blindsided by their chemistry and developing attraction. (978-1-63555-611-7)

Trade Secrets by Kathleen Knowles. In Silicon Valley, love and business are a volatile mix for clinical lab scientist Tony Leung and venture capitalist Sheila Garrison. (978-1-63555-642-1)

Death Overdue by David S. Pederson. Did Heath turn to murder in an alcohol induced haze to solve the problem of his blackmailer, or was it someone else who brought about a death overdue? (978-1-63555-711-4)

Entangled by Melissa Brayden. Becca Crawford is the perfect person to head up the Jade Hotel, if only the captivating owner of the local vineyard would get on board with her plan and stop badmouthing the hotel to everyone in town. (978-1-63555-709-1)

First Do No Harm by Emily Smith. Pierce and Cassidy are about to discover that when it comes to love, sometimes you have to risk it all to have it all. (978-1-63555-699-5)

Kiss Me Every Day by Dena Blake. For Wynn Evans, wishing for a do-over with Carly Jamison was a long shot, actually getting one was a game changer. (978-1-63555-551-6)

Olivia by Genevieve McCluer. In this lesbian Shakespeare adaption with vampires, Olivia is a centuries old vampire who must fight a strange figure from her past if she wants a chance at happiness. (978-1-63555-701-5)

One Woman's Treasure by Jean Copeland. Daphne's search for discarded antiques and treasures leads to an embarrassing misunderstanding, and ultimately, the opportunity for the romance of a lifetime with Nina. (978-1-63555-652-0)

Silver Ravens by Jane Fletcher. Lori has lost her girlfriend, her home, and her job. Things don't improve when she's kidnapped and taken to fairyland. (978-1-63555-631-5)

Still Not Over You by Jenny Frame, Carsen Taite, Ali Vali. Old flames die hard in these tales of a second chance at love with the ex you're still not over. Stories by award winning authors Jenny Frame, Carsen Taite, and Ali Vali. (978-1-63555-516-5)

Storm Lines by Jessica L. Webb. Devon is a psychologist who likes rules. Marley is a cop who doesn't. They don't always agree, but both fight to protect a girl immersed in a street drug ring. (978-1-63555-626-1)

The Politics of Love by Jen Jensen. Is it possible to love across the political divide in a hostile world? Conservative Shelley Whitmore and liberal Rand Thomas are about to find out. (978-1-63555-693-3)

All the Paths to You by Morgan Lee Miller. High school sweethearts Quinn Hughes and Kennedy Reed reconnect five years after they break up and realize that their chemistry is all but over. (978-1-63555-662-9)

Arrested Pleasures by Nanisi Barrett D'Arnuck. When charged with a crime she didn't commit Katherine Lowe faces the question: Which is harder, going to prison or falling in love? (978-1-63555-684-1)

Bonded Love by Renee Roman. Carpenter Blaze Carter suffers an injury that shatters her dreams, and ER nurse Trinity Greene hopes to show her that sometimes love is worth fighting for. (978-1-63555-530-1)

Convergence by Jane C. Esther. With life as they know it on the line, can Aerin McLeary and Olivia Ando's love survive an otherworldly threat to humankind? (978-1-63555-488-5)

Coyote Blues by Karen F. Williams. Riley Dawson, psychotherapist and shape-shifter, has her world turned upside down when Fiona Bell, her one true love, returns. (978-1-63555-558-5)

Drawn by Carsen Taite. Will the clues lead Detective Claire Hanlon to the killer terrorizing Dallas, or will she merely lose her heart to person of interest, urban artist Riley Flynn? (978-1-63555-644-5)

Every Summer Day by Lee Patton. Meant to celebrate every summer day, Luke's journal instead chronicles a love affair as fast-moving and possibly as fatal as his brother's brain tumor. (978-1-63555-706-0)

Lucky by Kris Bryant. Was Serena Evans's luck really about winning the lottery, or is she about to get even luckier in love? (978-1-63555-510-3)

The Last Days of Autumn by Donna K. Ford. Autumn and Caroline question the fairness of life, the cruelty of loss, and what it means to love as they navigate the complicated minefield of relationships, grief, and life-altering illness. (978-1-63555-672-8)

Three Alarm Response by Erin Dutton. In the midst of tragedy, can these first responders find love and healing? Three stories of courage, bravery, and passion. (978-1-63555-592-9)

Veterinary Partner by Nancy Wheelton. Callie and Lauren are determined to keep their hearts safe but find that taking a chance on love is the safest option of all. (978-1-63555-666-7)

Everyday People by Louis Barr. When film star Diana Danning hires private eye Clint Steele to find her son, Clint turns to his former West Point barracks mate, and ex-buddy with benefits, Mars Hauser to lend his cyber espionage and digital black ops skills to the case. (978-1-63555-698-8)

Forging a Desire Line by Mary P. Burns. When Charley's ex-wife, Tricia, is diagnosed with inoperable cancer, the private duty nurse Tricia hires turns out to be the handsome and aloof Joanna, who ignites something inside Charley she isn't ready to face. (978-1-63555-665-0)

Love on the Night Shift by Radclyffe. Between ruling the night shift in the ER at the Rivers and raising her teenage daughter, Blaise Richilieu has all the drama she needs in her life, until a dashing young attending appears on the scene and relentlessly pursues her. (978-1-63555-668-1)

Olivia's Awakening by Ronica Black. When the daring and dangerously gorgeous Eve Monroe is hired to get Olivia Savage into shape, a fierce passion ignites, causing both to question everything they've ever known about love. (978-1-63555-613-1)

The Duchess and the Dreamer by Jenny Frame. Clementine Fitzroy has lost her faith and love of life. Can dreamer Evan Fox make her believe in life and dream again? (978-1-63555-601-8)

The Road Home by Erin Zak. Hollywood actress Gwendolyn Carter is about to discover that losing someone you love sometimes means gaining someone to fall for. (978-1-63555-633-9)

Waiting for You by Elle Spencer. When passionate past-life lovers meet again in the present day, one remembers it vividly and the other isn't so sure. (978-1-63555-635-3)

While My Heart Beats by Erin McKenzie. Can a love born amidst the horrors of the Great War survive? (978-1-63555-589-9)

Face the Music by Ali Vali. Sweet music is the last thing that happens when Nashville music producer Mason Liner, and daughter of country royalty Victoria Roddy are thrown together in an effort to save country star Sophie Roddy's career. (978-1-63555-532-5)

Flavor of the Month by Georgia Beers. What happens when baker Charlie and chef Emma realize their differing paths have led them right back to each other? (978-1-63555-616-2)

Mending Fences by Angie Williams. Rancher Bobbie Del Rey and veterinarian Grace Hammond are about to discover if heartbreaks of the past can ever truly be mended. (978-1-63555-708-4)

Silk and Leather: Lesbian Erotica with an Edge edited by Victoria Villasenor. This collection of stories by award winning authors offers fantasies as soft as silk and tough as leather. The only question is: How far will you go to make your deepest desires come true? (978-1-63555-587-5)

The Last Place You Look by Aurora Rey. Dumped by her wife and looking for anything but love, Julia Pierce retreats to her hometown, only to rediscover high school friend Taylor Winslow, who's secretly crushed on her for years. (978-1-63555-574-5)

The Mortician's Daughter by Nan Higgins. A singer on the verge of stardom discovers she must give up her dreams to live a life in service to ghosts. (978-1-63555-594-3)

The Real Thing by Laney Webber. When passion flares between actress Virginia Green and masseuse Allison McDonald, can they be sure it's the real thing? (978-1-63555-478-6)

What the Heart Remembers Most by M. Ullrich. For college sweethearts Jax Levine and Gretchen Mills, could an accident be the second chance neither knew they wanted? (978-1-63555-401-4)

White Horse Point by Andrews & Austin. Mystery writer Taylor James finds herself falling for the mysterious woman on White Horse Point who lives alone, protecting a secret she can't share about a murderer who walks among them. (978-1-63555-695-7)